Penguin Books
The Search

C. P. Snow was born in Leicester in 1905 and educated at a secondary school. He started his career as a professional scientist, though writing was always his ultimate aim. He won a research scholarship to Cambridge, worked on molecular physics, and became a Fellow of his college in 1930. He continued his academic life in Cambridge until the beginning of the war, by which time he had already begun the 'Lewis Eliot' sequence of novels, which, on completion, is to be known by the title of the first volume, *Strangers and Brothers,* published in 1940. The other books in the sequence are *The Light and the Dark* (1947), *Time of Hope* (1949), *The Masters* (1951), *The New Men* (1954), *Homecomings* (1958), *The Conscience of the Rich* (1958), *The Affair* (1960), *Corridors of Power* (1964), *Variety of Men* (1967), *The Sleep of Reason* (1968), and *Last Things* (1970), the final volume in the novel sequence.

In the war C. P. Snow became a civil servant, and because of his human and scientific knowledge was engaged in selecting scientific personnel. He has had further experience of these problems since the war, both in industry and as a Civil Service commissioner, for which work he received a knighthood in 1957. His Rede Lecture on *The Two Cultures and the Scientific Revolution* (1950), his Godkin Lectures on *Science and Government* (1960), his address to the A.A.A.S., *The Moral Un-Neutrality of Science,* and his Fulton Lecture, *The State of Siege* (1968), have been widely discussed. He received a barony in 1964, and was made Parliamentary Secretary to the Ministry of Technology.

In 1950 he married Pamela Hansford Johnson.

C. P. Snow

THE SEARCH

Penguin Books

Penguin Books Ltd, Harmondsworth,
Middlesex, England
Penguin Books Australia Ltd, Ringwood,
Victoria, Australia

First published by Gollancz, 1934
This edition published by Macmillan 1958
Published in Penguin Books 1965
Reprinted 1971

Made and printed in The Netherlands by
Van Boekhoven-Bosch N.V. Utrecht
Set in Intertype Baskerville

Note

The Search was originally published in August 1934. It attracted some attention, enough to give me a taste of success. But in fact I did not feel that. Although it was praised by people whom I should not have expected to like it, although incidentally it nearly made me rich (it missed by the odd vote being the Book-of-the-Month Club choice in the U.S.A., so I was told later) I knew that for me it was a false start. It was a false start because of the things it did well as well as the things it did badly. I wanted to say something about people first and foremost, and then people-in-society, in quite a different way, and at quite a different level, from anything in this book. So I had to put it on one side, and find my way to a form which would give me a chance of saying what I wanted to say. It took me some time: the fact that *The Search* had been partially successful made it not easier, but a good deal harder.

When at last I felt that in the *Strangers and Brothers* sequence I was doing something of what I set out to do, I found that *The Search* had an interest for me. I hope that it may now have some interest for others. Perhaps it is reasonable to add an autobiographical comment. Arthur Miles is not much like me: he is much less a preliminary sketch for Lewis Eliot than Sheriff is for Jack Cotery or Professor Desmond for Herbert Getliffe. I was educated as a scientist, as Miles was: but I never had his single-minded passion, and in fact knew my own ultimate vocation from the time I was about eighteen.

Miles's intellectual attitudes are simpler than mine were; I deliberately made him four or five years older than myself, so that he could represent the pure idealist in science, less involved in either politics or applied science than

5

would have been possible for my exact contemporaries or for me.

But he is like me in one respect. What Hunt says of Miles in Part 4, Chapter 3, is, I think, true of me. I have a knack, sometimes inconvenient, of getting immersed in what I am doing, more or less irrespective of what it is. So, becoming almost by accident a professional scientist as a young man, I got immersed in the scientific life. The account of scientific experience in *The Search* is first-hand. A good many of my scientific friends, including some of the most creative, among them Rutherford, have told me that this account is in essence true. Whether they are right or not, I am now too far away to judge. But I hope they are, and I think the chance is just good enough to make the book worth re-issuing.

I ought to say that I have cut the original version quite considerably. It was in places more discursive than I can now bear. I have added nothing.

C.P.S.

10 February 1958

Contents

The Private Moments

The stars

1

When I was a child of about eleven, a new excitement suddenly flared up in my life.

It must have been a Sunday night, for my father and I were walking after church. I had not been to the service myself; my father would never have thought of taking me. But occasionally on Sunday evenings he would look embarrassed and tell me: 'I shall be in Wentworth Street at eight o'clock, if you'd like to come along.' Wentworth Street was round the corner from our parish church, but we were not supposed to know where he was going. He would set off, as though he and the church-bell had nothing in common.

This particular Sunday night was warm and twilit, and I fancy summer was nearly over. As we came to the end of the town, the sun had just gone down behind the river, and – I remember it as though it were yesterday – in the yellow sunset sky there was a sickle of new moon, and high over our heads a sprinkling of stars just coming dimly out. We stopped and looked.

My father said:

'I wonder if they're what we think they are? Stars! Stars like this!' He waved vaguely. 'People think we know about them. I wonder if we do.'

I gazed up at him.

'I wonder if we *can*,' he added.

I didn't know what he was thinking. All of a sudden I felt that all the things around me were toys to handle and control, that I had the power in a tiny, easy world.

'I wonder if they are what we think they are,' my father

11

was saying again.

'Let's find out,' I said. And then: 'I'm going to find out.'

My father looked puzzled. 'Well,' he said.

The night had taken hold of me. I wanted to do something with those stars. I did not quite know what, but I was elated. Their beauty stirred me, but it was not only that. If I had been older, I should have said I wanted to know, to understand, to alter. I wanted to rush out and have them for my own. I laughed:

'I'm going to find out all about them.'

I remember my father's face as he stared at me. His eyes were kindly and bewildered, he was chewing one end of his moustache, there was a sort of baffled amusement round his mouth.

'Perhaps you will,' he reflected. We began to walk home.

'A lot of people have tried, you know,' he said doubtfully. 'Sir Isaac Newton – and Sir Robert Ball – and Sir William Herschel – and Sir Oliver Lodge –' My father's reading was odd, I discovered later, and he always found it an effort to shorten a title. He must have called his friends 'Mr –' when he was alone with them. 'Sir Oliver Lodge,' he repeated: 'Very great men. They've all tried.'

'I don't care,' I said defiantly.

My father had lost himself in some more speculations. 'They may be wrong after all,' he was saying to himself. 'All these stars. Bigger than the world. Bigger than the sun. It seems strange if they're put there just for nothing. It doesn't seem right.'

But I was full of schemes by now. As soon as we got home I rushed to the book-case and took out all the eight volumes of the *Children's Encyclopædia* and began to turn the new shiny-smelling pages in search of pictures I hazily remembered. I didn't know anything of indexes then; and, despite my father's gentle wishes, I had scarcely glanced through the Encyclopædia, which he had bought for me a year or so before. While I dashed over the pages, my mother kept calling me in to supper. At last I found what I was looking for. My mother was placated as soon as I began to eat some of the trifle or fruit or blancmange – it must have been one of the three which we had for supper that night. Soon I broke out:

'Father!' I only used the word very rarely, when I wanted all his attention.

'Father! I want you to help me make a telescope.'

'Why?' he said.

'To look at the stars.' We smiled at each other.

'I used to think I'd like a telescope,' my father said. 'But somehow I never got one –'

'It's ever so easy to make one,' I hurried on. 'It'll only take us an hour or two. The Encyclopædia tells you all about it. You only want a cardboard tube and two magnifying glasses and some sticking stuff – and you can see mountains on the moon! And moons round some of the stars! We must make one!'

'We'll see after supper,' he said.

I leant out of my bedroom window that night, and the stars seemed like friends.

The next evening, when he came home, my father laid a parcel on the table. Usually he started tea as soon as he came in, but now he watched while I untied the string and found a cardboard tube, some extra cardboard, two lenses and oddments in the way of wax and seccotine and string.

'Oh fine!' I shouted. 'Let's make it now.'

'My tea,' he murmured, but I said:

'Come on, it won't take long,' and we began. We fixed one lens into the tube and it looked so much like the Encyclopædia picture that we laughed with delight. But then the difficulties began. For the other lens we had to make a thinner tube out of cardboard; it sounded simple and I cut out and my father glued, and everything seemed straightforward. In a minute or two, though, my father was chewing his moustache a little puzzledly.

'It's not a very straight tube,' he said.

'It's not far off,' I said.

It was, in fact, a queer-looking sort of cone.

'We'll have to try again,' he said dubiously.

We cut and glued time and time again, but the best we could do was a poor irregular thing beside our fine bought tube.

'Perhaps it'll do.' My father held it in his hand and closed one eye and stared along it. 'After all, we're just starting, aren't we?'

I was worried and anxious, but I tried to smile.

'I'm sure it will do,' I said.

Then, very gingerly, he began to put the small lens into the tube we had made. I remember seeing him stand there, his fingers a little tentative and uncertain, his forehead puckered, his bluish friendly eyes undecided: his hand slipped, and the lens lodged in at an angle.

'Oh confound it!' he said. 'I never could do anything with my hands.'

I felt like crying, but he looked so wretched that I knew I mustn't.

'Let's try it like that. It may be all right.'

'Shall we?' He held the thing in his hands. 'It may not – it may not be so bad after all.'

'We'll go and look at the moon.' I turned my face away from him. I was afraid everything had gone wrong: I was hoping that we should manage to see something. Anxiously we went upstairs and rested our contraption on the window-sill; the moon had just risen, a crescent over the bank of clouds on the sky-line. With a catch at my heart, I looked at it through our lenses. I saw a faint distorted shape.

'I can see it,' I said. 'Much better than I can without the telescope. Ever so much better.'

My father gazed down the tube himself.

'I can see something,' he said, after a pause. 'I wonder if it *is* better.'

'Of course it is,' I replied. He mustn't be disappointed, I knew in some half-conscious way. 'Wait till it's a full moon. We'll see the mountains.' Privately, I vowed I would make the telescope myself by that time.

My father still looked worried. 'It would be better if I'd got the lens in straight,' he said, and went disconsolately off to tea.

For a day or two I was busy with tubes and lenses, petulant at times, but going on with a rush of hope. In a way, my father's failure had made me more certain that it was left for me to know about the stars: he couldn't do it, no one could do it – but I knew I could myself, and I read the Encyclopædia and an old handbook of astronomy my father had picked up somewhere, and made tubes more or less cylindrical, while my mother grumbled that I was leaving meals half-finished, going to bed late, and littering rooms with scraps of paper. Proudly I told her: 'I'm doing astronomy.'

When I had the telescope about half ready, and was mastering the gumming of tubes and fixing of lenses, my father came in one evening and watched me begin on the eye-piece. I noticed he was smiling.

'Don't bother about that,' he said.

'It'll soon be finished,' I replied.

'No, it won't. Look here.' His hand came from behind his back with a new telescope a foot long, all shining in gold and bronze, so bright that I could see my face in the barrel as he handed it to me. 'This is for you.'

I felt a choke in my throat. I knew that gift was far too expensive for him, but his eyes were bright with enjoyment.

'It's better to buy things than make them,' he was saying, 'if they've got to be exact. These things must be exact. Exactness is important, you know. Exact scientific instruments . . .' he trailed off, smiling.

Perhaps I had a twinge that my own telescope, made by my own hands, was dishonoured for ever. The cardboard looked shabby, hopelessly – hopelessly futile, by the side of the metallic perfection of this newcomer. But the resentment flickered and passed; here was a better thing ready to use, a real way to find out about the stars.

'Oh thanks,' I shouted, and, looking back, I think my father must have felt repaid.

That night I saw two of the moons of Jupiter. There were no clouds those nights, I remember, and there comes back to me the sight of silvery circles floating on the glowing luminous black-purple of the sky. The black-purple into which, beyond which, I longed to go: often I would lie awake thinking of how I could see into the dark space which lay beyond the stars.

I kept a record of my watchings. There were drawings of Saturn's rings, sometimes like a thin straight line, sometimes like a tilted saucer: of Mars, and I was sure there were rivers and canals and tracks: of all the stars invisible to my eyes that the telescope enabled me to see.

Evening after evening at sunset, I would watch for a sight of Mercury flashing across the west; and many dawns I got up, unknown to my mother, until I had assured myself that the morning star was really Venus reappearing. Once, I followed a comet that would not come again for forty years.

All the time my mind was investing what I saw. Before long I was peopling the planets and devising expeditions to the stars.

2

The walk with my father marked the beginning of a theme that was to take a great part in my life. Of course, it really went further back than a chance starlit evening. Yet that evening was a symbol, and I have never forgotten it.

The astronomical phase lasted irregularly for several years, gradually declining until I found, rather to my surprise, that it had gone altogether. In its first violence it stayed until I went to the secondary school in the town. I had looked forward avidly to my first science lessons; and when they came I was puzzled and disappointed. The chief science master, Luard, was a figure in the school, I had heard of him before he took us for our first chemistry lesson, of his bitter tongue and fits of anger. Everyone feared him, it seemed – and yet 'he's interesting some-times,' said a boy who had been a year or two at school.

When I saw him come into the class-room, I was not sure whether it could be he. Even to a boy, eager to be impressed, he was not an impressive man. He was thin, with a yellowish sallowness, and wore pince-nez. Although he could not have been more than forty, he was going bald and his voice sounded flat and tired. He taught us in an indifferent, uninterested way; during that lesson, and the rest of the term, we did nothing but stand in the labora-tory and heat little pieces of wood and similar things, and tiny portions of powders from bottles on the benches, in tubes which Luard called 'combustion-tubes'. He told us to notice what happened. Zealously I looked and wrote down: 'The Black powder did not appear to change. The white powder did not appear to change. The specimen of wood went first brown, then gave off fumes, then went black.' I studied the tubes very carefully. For the first few months I still thought I must be missing something. This business couldn't be as pointless as it seemed. But no one explained what I was doing. It became just a drill, like any other drill, one of those inexplicable pieces of school routine, a good deal less interesting than the French verbs that I was beginning to learn in the lesson before we went to the laboratory. School 'science', I decided, was something quite different from my own exciting private science, my world of space and stars.

Then one day, just before we broke up for Christmas, Luard came into the class-room almost brightly.

'We're not going into the laboratory this morning,' he said. 'I'm going to talk to you, my friends.' He used to say 'my friends' whenever he was lashing us with his tongue, but now it sounded half in earnest. 'Forget everything you know, will you? That is, if you know anything at all.' He sat on the desk swinging his legs.

'Now, what do you think all the stuff in the world is made of? Every bit of us, you and me, the chairs in this room, the air, everything. No one knows? Well, perhaps that's not surprising, even for nincompoops like you. Because no one *did* know a year or two ago. But now we're beginning to think we *do*. That's what I want to tell you. You won't understand, of course. But it'll amuse me to tell you, and it won't hurt you, I suppose – and anyway I'm going to.'

Someone dropped a ruler just then, and afterwards the room was very quiet. Luard took no notice and went on: 'Well, if you took a piece of lead, and halved it, and halved the half, and went on like that, where do you think you'd come to in the end? Do you think it would be lead for ever? Do you think you could go down right to the infinitely small and still have tiny pieces of lead? It doesn't matter what you think. My friends, you couldn't. If you went on long enough, you'd come to an atom of lead, an atom, do you hear, an atom, and if you split that up, you wouldn't have lead any more. What do you think you would have? The answer to that is one of the oddest things you'll ever hear in your life. If you split up an atom of lead, you'd get – pieces of positive and negative electricity. Just that. Just positive and negative electricity. That's all matter is. That's all you are. Just positive and negative electricity – and, of course, an immortal soul.' At the time I was too busy attending to his story to observe anything else; but in the picture I have formed later of Luard, I give him here the twitch of a smile. 'And whether you started with lead or anything else it wouldn't matter. That's all you'd come to in the end. Positive and negative electricity. How do things differ then? Well, the atoms are all positive and negative electricity and they're all made on the same pattern, but they vary among themselves, do you see? Every atom has a bit of positive electricity in the middle of it – the nucleus, they call it – and every atom has bits of negative electricity going round the nucleus – like planets round the sun. But the nucleus is bigger in some atoms than others, bigger in lead than it is in carbon, and there are more bits of negative electricity in some atoms than others. It's as though you had different solar systems, made from the same sort of materials, some with bigger suns than others, some with a lot more planets. That's all the difference. That's where a diamond's different from a bit of lead. That's at the bottom of the whole of this world of ours.' He stopped and cleaned his pince-nez, and talked as he swung them:

'There you are, that's the way things are going. Two people have found out about the atoms: one's an Englishman, Rutherford, and the other's a Dane called Bohr. And I tell you, my friends, they're great men. Greater even than Mr. Miles' – I flushed. I had come top of the form and this was his way of congratulating me – 'incredible as that may seem. Great men, my friends, and perhaps, when you're older, by the side of them your painted heroes, your Cæsars and Napoleons, will seem like cocks crowing on a dungheap.'

I went home and read everything I could discover about atoms. Popular exposition was comparatively slow at that time, however, and Rutherford's nucleus, let alone Bohr's atom, which could only have been published a few months before Luard's lesson, had not yet got into my Encyclopædia. I learned something of electrons and got some idea of size; I was fascinated by the tininess of the electron and the immensity of the great stars: I became caught up in light-years, made time-tables of a journey to the nearest star (in the Encyclopædia there was an enthralling picture of an express train going off into space at the speed of light, taking years to get to the stars). Scale began to impress me, the infinitesimal electronic distances and the vastness of Aldebaran began to dance round in my head; and the time of an electronic journey round the nucleus compared itself with the time it takes for light to travel across the Milky Way. Distance and time, the infinitely great and the infinitely small, electron and star, went reeling round my mind.

It must have been soon after this that I let myself seep in the fantasies that come to many imaginative children nowadays. Why should not the electron contain worlds smaller than itself, carrying perhaps inconceivably minute replicas of ourselves? 'They wouldn't know they're small. They wouldn't know of us,' I thought, and felt serious and profound. And why should not our world be just a part of an electron in some cosmic atom, itself a part of some gargantuan world? The speculations gave me a pleasant sense of philosophic agoraphobia until I was about sixteen and then I had had enough of them.

Luard, who had set me alight by half an hour's talk, did not repeat himself. Chemistry lessons relapsed once more into exercises meaningless to me, definitions of acids and bases which I learned resentfully, and, as we got further up the school, descriptions of the properties of gases, which always began 'colourless, transparent, non-poisonous.' Luard, who had once burst into enthusiasm, droned out the definitions or left us to a text-book while he sat by himself at the end of the laboratory. Once or twice there would be a moment of fire; he told us about phlogiston – 'that should be a lesson to you, my friends, to remember that you can always fall back on tradition if only you're dishonest enough' and Faraday – 'there never will be a better scientist than he was; and Davy tried to keep him out of the Royal Society because he had been a laboratory assistant. Davy was the type of all the jumped-up second-raters of all time.' Those moments, though, came too rarely and I gave up anticipating chemistry lessons as anything but dull.

It was a long time before I understood Luard. I had to go to two Universities, to listen to the educational theorists, to examine in University scholarships myself, before I fully realised why he had lost heart and made his lessons so conventionally arid. Indignantly I discovered the mixture of vested interests, muddled thinking and memory of their own past that had made men adhere to the 'logical' method of teaching science. 'If you want to interest your pupils,' I remember someone telling me as I was pleading for a gleam of something to catch boys' imaginations, 'you can put them in the position of the original discoverer.' Put them in the position of the original discoverer! The pedagogic nonsense of it all! When you think of the chances and stumbling, the flashes of insight and the sheer mistakes, that have gone to every discovery since science began! And then to expect to teach in that way. 'The real method of teaching science apart from the frills,' the man went on, 'is to go from the observations to the conclusions. Start with simple experiments, note your deductions from them, and don't worry them with the new-fangled stuff. It's the way of experience, Miles, it's the logical way, and you can't do better than that.' The logical way. They might as well teach French by starting with an agglutinative language like Eskimo and follow the logical changes in language through the Basque down to the European tongues. They might as well teach Biblical history by making the boys spend forty years in Sinai.

And this pedantry goes on when there is every chance of rousing a child's enjoyment, from stars to motor-cars, from atoms to the lives of birds. When I think of the conspiracy of dullness in which these exciting years are wrapped, I no longer wonder at the drab routine the Middle Ages made of Aristotle: I wonder instead that they kept him so fresh and clear.

Chapter 2

Background of childhood

I

Mine was a very happy childhood. The interests I have been describing merely added glow and savour to what must without them have been a pleasant time. The emotional isolations, the preoccupation with God and themselves, the struggles for freedom, which seem to have possessed many of my friends at the same age, I knew almost nothing of. For one thing, with a father like mine one could no more struggle for freedom, than with a well-disposed St. Bernard, and I had begun to be independent early, quite effortlessly because there was no one to be dependent on.

His habit of turning religion into an amiable eccentricity prevented my being worried by another traditional authority. Probably I should not have been in any case: I fancy my 'religious' urges had gone into my desire to understand, at a very early age; but, with my father about, there was none of the residue I might otherwise have had. So long as I could remember, he had concealed his church-going in the way I have already mentioned: and, as a rule, after he had been to church he would drink a pint of beer, which he hated, as a sort of atonement. This went on until I was fourteen or fifteen, and then I was no longer asked to meet him in Wentworth Street at eight o'clock. He used still to go off mysteriously on Sunday nights, but neither my mother nor I knew where. It was some time before I had any inkling at all, and a good deal of what I am writing now as though I knew it as a boy came, of course, with later knowledge.

He started a voyage of religious exploration. It was done

in a spirit of vague hopeful curiosity, I think. He had grown interested in comparative religion; and though a provincial town does not offer much in that way, he contrived to get a little amusement, a little comfort. I suspect the scepticism and the hope were always rather mixed. His was not a mind of sharp edges. So far as I could gather, the Catholic Church attracted him for a time; but he was more given to vague doubt than to concrete faith, and so he moved on to the Spiritualists. They were both too practical and not convincing enough, and he tried the Wesleyans and the Baptists. He was beginning to feel a little impatient at being limited to Christianity; but apart from the synagogue, which did not attract him, he could find nothing in the town more non-Christian than the Unitarians.

This was when I was about sixteen, and one night he asked me to meet him out of their church. It was the first time he had said bluntly that he was going to a service, and I felt there must be some special reason. When I met him at the church in a remote suburb, his eyes were more distant than usual, and his face more amiably vague. As we walked down the street, he pointed a thumb behind towards the church.

'Their God doesn't seem like mine,' he said, and looked at me. I was a little the taller, now. 'He doesn't seem like mine – or like anyone else's, I should have thought. I can't help thinking they have got Him wrong. We all may have got Him wrong. Somehow, Arthur, if He were what these people say – why, it would be better if there weren't any God at all. It would be better, I think.' His voice was gentle; but I had never heard him so emphatic. He was enquiring rather than sad, I thought. 'Have you ever thought about these things?' he asked.

'I don't believe in God, you know,' I said.

'I thought you didn't. I wonder if you're right. But then there are ourselves. We live and die. What happens when we die? Do we just go out into – into that?' He waved a hand to the sky. 'It doesn't seem right to me, Arthur. It may be, mind you, it may be. But somehow there seems to me something in myself that's more important than – than a finger-nail. Something that's going to last longer than a piece of nail that's thrown aside. I can't quite believe that there's nothing after all this. If so, is it all as – as useless as it seems?'

I didn't answer. We walked on, silently.

'It's a funny business,' my father said at last. 'I don't seem to get any further with it all. I wonder if we've taken the wrong track – I wonder if everyone's always been wrong?'

My father's puzzled sceptical hopes represented religion for me when I was young. If I had had a God, it would have been a puzzled and rather nebulous God as uncertain of His functions as the gentle little man who created Him.

2

My father's wanderings on Sunday nights were the chief eccentricity in our tranquil family life. On the surface, my mother took a small place in my interests when I was a boy. I was sometimes hurt, sometimes irritated when she was angry; and always I was deeply upset and anxious in the illnesses which came upon her fairly often. Later on I realised that the ties went deeper than I had thought, and that perhaps I had defended myself against my own need of her. But, even so, between us there was certainly nothing of the compelling, cramping affection I have seen between other mothers and their only sons. My chief memory of her is the sharply humorous resignation with which she bore my father's vagueness: and I remember, too late to make any amends for it, that she was more oppressed by our poverty than my father or myself. My father's only indulgence was in philosophical speculation, and fortunately that was inexpensive; and in some mysterious way he contrived to bring me the things I wanted, even when, as with the telescope, they were quite outside our income. We were actually very poor. My father was the Secretary of a small Trade Association, and I think he never earned more than two hundred pounds a year. At the time I noticed the absence of money very little, but it has left its traces since. More than once in the conflicts and indecisions that are coming into this story, I acted with the fear of poverty at the back of my mind: the poverty which I knew in its precariousness and obscurity and helplessness. The last in particular I could not forget.

As a boy, though, I should have been annoyed if you had sympathised with me. I had my own hours and days of zest with scientific things. I read everything about stars and matter and atoms that my father could get for me. I searched the shelves of our public library. Soon I began to read widely outside science, and, although most weeks there would be a new scientific book in the house, I ran through boys' books and, dissatisfied by them, into novels which got hold of my imagination.

I remember the pace at which I read *The War of the Worlds* when I was about fourteen. My father had given it me as an Easter present on a hot afternoon. I read until tea-time, swallowed a cup of tea and went back to this world which seemed so much more real than the one I was living in. When I finished, our little garden was growing dark and I caught myself shivering. 'But has this happened?' I asked. 'Has it *happened?* When did the Martians come?' That night I dug about in old *Daily Mail Year Books* and the like to see if I could put a date to the invasion. At last, half-relieved, half-disappointed, I concluded that it was all an invention. But I read the book again next day.

Since then I must have gone through a good deal of the imaginative literature of the world, and only twice have I felt that complete reality sweep over me again. Once was at a performance of *The Cherry Orchard*, when suddenly all the barriers fell and I was living in a feckless charming country house and my hostess, poor dear, was too badgered to have a word to spare for us. The other was when I read *Swann in Love*; I, also, smelt the cattleyas at Odette's breast and saw her smile, and afterwards I walked that dull street in despair and wondered why there was a light in her window. I have admired books and plays and poetry more than these, but, as a fact, they were the only ones which captured me utterly.

Often I would argue at school about the books I was reading. At that period they were more common property than my scientific pleasures. Several of my acquaintances at school read as widely as I did; I have wondered sometimes whether there is not a difference now, but to me at fourteen, and my friends, the cinema was an event and most other amusements unknown; so, if books were anywhere about, we read them. Most of us read in an eclectic way. For a few months, at the cataloguing age, I kept a diary of the books I was reading, and in one week, when I was between fourteen and fifteen, I put down – *The Invisible Man, The Boys Own Paper, Sexton Blake (4d. Library), King Henry IV Pt. I, Penny Popular, Anne of Geierstein* (three-quarters finished), chapter on 'Comets' in Robert Ball's *Story of the Heavens*. From the talks we had, my friends at school read much the same.

School was a jovial place. At that time it was the kind of secondary school which did not ape the minor public schools. We had a hearty, hard-drinking, bottom-whacking headmaster, with no sense of his own dignity or anyone else's. He used occasionally to come in and interrupt the lesson by giving us a genial eulogy on the master who was taking it. They could do nothing but stand by and blush: I can still see the embarrassment on the French master's face when Smithson ambled in and told us: 'You know, we've all got used to Mr. Girraud. It's almost as though he was an Englishman.'

I enjoyed almost all of my time at school. Often I wished to take my own way in learning: the impatience which has since developed was beginning to show itself. But there was a rough affability and life about the place. Smithson and most of the masters liked me. I was more competent at school subjects than my contemporaries, and I seem to have been – it is difficult to imagine myself – a bright and cheerful boy. I was not unpopular with other boys.

3

Before any man can make a comparison with his own experience, though, there is one other side of my boyhood which everyone will see through different eyes. If you take the picture I have given and imagine me at fifteen, becoming tallish, brown-haired, playing cricket with my friends, avidly eager for all sorts of knowledge, tearing my way through books and devoted to science, you are right so far as it goes, but you are leaving out a good deal. And then if you add to the portrait a taste for Kiplingesque pranks and a liking for innocent fun, you are still leaving out a good deal and you are not even right as far as you go, for both I and many of my friends would have been affronted by the suggestion that we could possibly want to go in for childish practical jokes.

The truth hurts and is a little awkward to those brought up in a different convention from mine. And also I am afraid that by not distorting the truth to myself, I shall have some people distort it more than if I had been as discreet as Mrs. Humphry Ward. If I mention that I was sexually interested and conscious as a boy, I may be classed as sexually obsessed all my life: which is so far from the truth that I am going to take the risk.

The sexual theme has not been decisively important to me as a man. My successes and failures and changes were not due very largely to the two women I have loved. But the theme has been there all the time; and I have gained great happiness and great sorrow from it; and it has immeasurably enriched my life.

Well, this sexual theme began when I was a boy, between fourteen and fifteen, so far as I remember. I cannot recall anything of the guilt or secret difficulties that the sexual educators talk about: indeed sometimes I fancy that the sexual educators took up their profession in order to educate themselves. Sex to me, at first, was a trifling and amusing thing: it was only much later, when I fell in love, that I felt its urgency.

This beginning is, I think, not uncommon. So far as I can gather, it is true of several of my friends. There are, of course, peculiar difficulties in finding out the truth about sexual lives. First of all, the tradition of concealment gets in the way; and then, nearly as difficult an obstacle is the counter-tradition of frankness. It is a pity that honesty about one's sexual life should so often mean the painful confession of things that never happened. Perhaps in the future someone with patience, experience and a habit of sympathetic disbelief, will make a study of the sexual lives of a number of 'normal' men and women. It would be a service to all the young who are at this moment thinking 'But is it possible that I am really not like everyone else?'

Despite the hedges of self-protection and self-revelation, I am inclined to think that a fair proportion of men go through my own introduction. With girls, almost inevitably, the beginnings are more diffuse. But actually I can only speak for myself: from the age of fourteen or so I had these preoccupations coming in it at the edge of my life, so to speak, and taking up the odd hours; I knew a little of the practical meaning of sex before I was fifteen; I had romantic friendships with boys which were uncomfortably chaste, although I was conscious of their erotic flavour; and at seventeen or thereabouts, I began to be interested in girls, excited when I walked along the streets at night and saw for a moment their faces lit under the lamps, fascinated by a film-star who represented love to come.

4

There is one curious feature of my childhood. I look back to it as an excitingly peaceful time, when I discovered my enthusiasms, had hours of leisure, worked and played and sometimes delightfully dreamed. In my memory there is an air of tranquillity about it, and I have cast back occasionally for that lost peace. Yet the four years of the War fell right across it. I was nearly thirteen when the War began and just seventeen when it ended. Yet all that happened in the world outside during those years seems remote to me now. It cannot ever have been close. A year or two ago I was driving through the north-east of France on my way to the Rhine, through the flat countryside the names of whose towns I remembered in the newspapers of my boyhood – Amiens, Cambrai, St. Quentin. There the War seemed as distant as Waterloo. Twice in two hundred miles a ruin stuck out by the wayside, almost as if it had been left there on purpose. My memory of the War, it occurred to me, was very much like that. Most of it had gone, the newspapers I read, the speeches I'd heard: and there remained one or two relics of a curious irrelevance. The news of Tannenberg I shall always remember, why I don't know: and the death of Kitchener, which at the time sounded to me like the loss of the War: and the summer battles in 1918. That is all – and yet I could reproduce most of the history of the War from the accounts I have read since.

The contrast between a boy's indifference to those years and their effect upon my older acquaintances first forced itself on me just after the War, in my last talk with Luard.

5

Luard was the only man whom, as a boy, I saw become old before my eyes. From the day when he had broken out on us with the news of the atom, he had grown thinner, older each year, and the yellow sallowness was more pronounced. He was less than forty in 1914 – I remember in my most ardent Wellsian phase discovering that Luard had been at the Royal College of Science just after Wells left – but he was already worn out long before the War ended. His teaching was now only a tired pretence: he always sat down, even in the laboratory. Towards the end of my time at school, he was often away. He died the year I went to the University. Some time later, when I heard of the protein cure for pernicious anaemia, I suddenly realised what had killed him.

One morning, in my last term, he sent for me. It was one of his worse periods, and I had not seen him for some time. He was sitting down in front of a class of small boys; he looked wretchedly thin, and his voice sounded duller. I felt awkwardly conscious of my own health.

'They tell me you're going to the University,' he said. 'Is it true?'

'Yes, sir.'

'You needn't bother to say "sir".' He smiled. 'A man who shortly expects to hear St. Peter say "Sir" at the gate doesn't want to hear it from his young friends.'

I half-smiled in reply.

'Why are you going to the University?'

'I want to get my science straight,' I answered. 'Learn it thoroughly. Fill in all the gaps I've left, and then go on to the serious stuff.'

'What'll you take your degree in, physics or chemistry?'

'Physics.'

'Why?'

'There's more clear thinking.'

'And after your degree?' he asked.

I hesitated a moment. 'I want to do research,' I said.

'Oh,' he said.

'I've wanted to do research ever since I heard you talk about the atom,' I burst out. 'Six years ago, it must be now. Before that, even, science was exciting me, but you settled it.'

'Did I?' He paused. 'Perhaps I ought to ask you to forgive me.'

'No –'

'My friend.' His voice sounded more like years ago. 'How old are you?'

'Nearly eighteen.'

'That isn't very old, you know. Lots of things are going to come into your life which you don't know much about yet. How are you going to live when you're doing this research of yours?'

'I ought to get scholarships.'

'You will. You'll be good at it. But think how old you'll be. Twenty-two before you begin. Twenty-five or six before you've got anywhere. What'll happen if you want to marry?'

'I just shan't be able to.' I was a little resentful.

'Doesn't that disturb you? Or are you so very young after all? And what do you look forward to at the end of it?'

'There are jobs – in a University, I hope –'

'A few hundred a year in some academic niche. Is that your idea, my friend? In God's name, why?' He was speaking loudly enough for the boys in front to grin.

I smiled, defensively. 'I want to do research.'

'Let me tell you why. You've got some ideal that's going to drive you on and put you at the mercy of every twopenny ha'penny little man with an eye to the main chance. I know, I was like it at your age – and when I was a lot older. I haven't got over it yet. I wanted to do research, too – but it wasn't so easy in my day and anyway I wasn't good enough. But I wasn't a fool, I was abler than the majority of men who have got on: and I went in for school teaching. I thought it was a good thing to do. God! If it hadn't been for my nice respectable ideal I'd have made money, I should have been someone in the world. I shouldn't have been sitting here in front of a crowd of silly little brats with nothing left to hope for, as weak as a – as weak as a kitten, and getting weaker.' He stopped. I looked away down the room.

'I tell you, you'll go that way, my friend.' His words seemed to be forcing themselves out. 'You and I, Miles, we're just too proud – that's it, too proud of our nice little ideals – to start playing beggar-my-neighbour. Has this war taught you nothing at all? Hasn't it got rid of just a bit of the lip-service we used to pay to the unselfishly true? Going in search of the unselfishly true – it's like throwing ping-pong balls into a furnace. Before the war I'd have wished you luck; now I'd hold you by force – if I had any force.' His laugh was shaky.

I only vaguely understood.

'Perhaps I oughtn't to be talking to you like this.' He was speaking quietly. 'It won't make any difference to you – except make you rather uneasy at times, just when you ought to be sure of yourself. But I had to tell you, somehow.'

'Are you happy about this?' he said, after a pause.

'Very happy,' I said at once.

'Won't you just think it over before you decide definitely? You could do most things, you know. You could be a success.'

'I'm sorry.' I looked at him, embarrassed. 'I'm afraid I've decided already. I'm grateful to you for speaking – you know that? But, you see, I know what I want to do more than anything in the world; and I'm going to do it.'

Chapter 3

The first friends

I

It was in that mood I went to the University. No one at school had any clear idea of open scholarships to Oxford and Cambridge: it was a little before the time when all secondary schools began to compete in these as a matter of course, and ours, under Smithson, was more casual than most. But we had a few leaving scholarships, descended from the eighteenth century, which were awarded at the discretion of the Headmaster on condition that the candidate could recite the Nicene Creed, a relic of some benefactor with a distaste for heresy. I remember rattling through it in front of Smithson, who occasionally looked up from the letter he was writing and broke into a loud guffaw. At the end he slapped me on the back and promised me fifty pounds a year; and with another forty pounds from the town Education Committee and twenty that my father incredibly produced, I went up to King's College, London.

I found a bed-sitting room in Highbury near the park, and I had my first tea there early in October looking through the plane-leaves opposite the window into the mist that was collecting like a shining haze. I felt lonely, with a catch at the throat – and sad and eager and exultant, all together. For I was by myself now, with all I wanted ahead, going the way I wished to go.

I went into the Strand that night, and drank a glass of beer at Romano's, after walking possessively along the pavement in front of King's. I had been in London before; I had drunk in London before: but it had never been quite like this. Every light in the soft blue dusk, every face that came near me as I drank, was friendly. I was half-wistful, half-exhilarated; and the exhilaration grew. As I paid for my drink, even, I felt a glow. For I had never had money to give away, throw away, pay away, as I had now: though I was wretchedly poor, yet I had some money by me, more money than I had ever had before. I went through all the luxuries of extravagance and asceticism, in those first days in London. I bought myself a dressing-gown I couldn't afford, and paid for it with an air. I did without lunch six days out of seven, and to myself it seemed like an ascetic's whim.

The excitement of settling into my lodgings, and making arrangements for the course, took up several days: and then there came an hour I had awaited for months, ever since I arranged to go to King's. I remember reading the University Calendar, learning the names of the professors, looking them up in Who's Who and in the indexes of the modern textbooks. The Professor of Physics, Austin, had caught my imagination; I was planning to do my research under him; he was down to lecture on the Friday of my first week.

It was my first sight of someone who had actually done famous things. I remember watching him, while he was writing on the board – and wondering whether he had written the notes of his great experiments in that same neat little hand and whether he had announced the results in this same round emphatic voice. He was a plump man with something of a presence; most of his lecture was read from notes, but at times he looked up and spoke to us with a slightly pompous affableness. 'We're beginning to think –' he said once, and told us the modern development of an idea, and I had the thrill of being intimately in touch with the hub of the world. He mentioned the nucleus and said, 'Rutherford has suggested a constitution for it, but I'm not sure that he's right.' Before that, I had never imagined that these new concepts were anything but unanimous; I had heard of controversies in the past, but the science I was studying had seemed without people or contradictions. I began to feel the warmth of being let into a family secret: so arguments happened and were kept quiet – and then the truth came out.

That lecture – it was like letting a young artist see Titian mix his colours. Or letting a young writer dine the night that Tolstoi and Turgeniev were reconciled. A stoutish man was talking about his job: and every word he said was romance to me.

A few days later I had a different pleasure. One of the junior lecturers told us of the explanation of the Periodic Table of the elements by means of the electronic structure of the specific atoms. The subject was not very advanced, it was long before the Stoner sub-groups, but even at the time it went straight to the mind as being true. For the first time I saw a medley of haphazard facts fall into line and order. All the jumbles and recipes and hotchpotch of the inorganic chemistry of my boyhood seemed to fit themselves into the scheme before my eyes – as though one were standing beside a jungle and it suddenly transformed itself into a Dutch garden. 'But it's true,' I said to myself. 'It's very beautiful. And it's true.'

2

I worked very hard all through my first term. I soon discovered that, though I knew more of modern science than anyone in my year, I had a number of gaps left by the happy go-lucky régime at school. Several industrious young Jews from the North London schools could beat me easily at systematic physics. Night after night I used to sit in my room, lonely, grudging the shillings which the gas fire devoured, working at routine stuff I should have been taught at fifteen. 'It's got to be done,' I encouraged myself. 'I'll have caught up after this term, but it's got to be done.' I would rest from the mechanics, and look forward to days when I could get on to some advanced work, and have the time as well to amuse myself at the College. As yet I only had a few laboratory acquaintances there, but often, as I left after tea for Highbury, knots of young men arguing made me eager to join in, and the sound of dance-music disturbed me as I passed the common-room.

Then I met Sheriff. I could not very well have helped it. One afternoon near the end of term, I was finishing off an analysis in the chemical laboratory. It was a dark, cold day, and I was a little jaded. I looked up from my tube, and saw a man walk by the bench and turn. I had noticed him in the class before, but we had never spoken. He had very wide shoulders, and black hair which shone. He was walking three steps backwards and three steps forwards along the gangway which connected the benches. Three quick steps and turn and three quick steps and turn, with his eyes on the ceiling. The mannerism made me smile.

He saw me watching him, and smiled back.

'I've finished my calculation. I like to do my thinking on my feet. Do you? Look here, we've done enough for honour and accuracy. Let's go and have some tea.' The words were quick and easy in a light, pleasant voice. As soon as he spoke, I knew I wanted to talk to him.

We went on drinking tea and talking until the refectory girl dodged round us to take away the plates. I told him of school, the boisterous inefficiency there, Luard, my own patches of ignorance, the books I'd read, the plans I was making: he told me – and he talked most of the time – of the public school where he had been taught science comically badly, the troubles which had sent him to London instead of Cambridge, the personalities at King's, the diversions he had already found, theatres he had been to, the glimpse of the inside of a night-club – and how he had set himself to do science all his life.

'I'm glad you've told me you're infatuated, too,' he said. 'Or else we'd have had to chat about something respectable – like College football.'

'Or rags –'

'Yes, clever little plans for getting Phineas from Gower Street –'

'And painting him to look like Gregory Foster –'

'Or like an Academy nude. Oh God, what tedious, solid, follow-my-leader bores most people are. With their clean, honest fun and no nonsense about thinking. It might lead to introspection. And you know where that will take you.'

Over and above his words, his face kept lighting up, changing, mimicking, quickly serious and then laughing with every muscle. He was the most mobile person I had ever met. 'Let's go out,' he said, when we had to move. 'I don't think you're tired of talking – and I never have been, of course.'

Although it was a cold night with rain in the wind, we strolled down to Westminster Bridge and stood staring into the water. The lights were blurred along the Embankment; trams rattled past, with long streaks across their windows; over the water, the coloured patterns leaped into the dark low sky, and died away again; the black gloss of the river kept breaking, as rain slanted down. In the distance, the light of a barge shone indistinctly, and flickered and lost itself.

'This is good to look at, somehow,' said Sheriff.

'Yes,' I said.

'I can't understand,' he went on, 'why people can't like all sorts of weathers and all sorts of scenes. A fine day in the hills is beautiful – but so is a dirty cold night in London. This' – he stretched his arm over the balustrade – 'this is beautiful. It goes to your heart.' He laughed. 'We ought to be panaesthetes and pan-zoophiles and pan-anthropophiles and pan-meteorophiles.'

I had noticed before how he laughed at his own speeches and climbed down, as it were, into a joke.

'It's a bit too charitable to be easy.' I smiled. 'But this is a good night,' I added.

Neither of us spoke for a while.

'We're lucky to be alive just now,' he said. 'Coming into things like this. Coming into science at this time of all times. It's the Renaissance of science, it's the Elizabethan age – and we're born right in the middle of it.' He smiled. 'Lord! We shall have lots of fun.'

3

At the beginning of the next term we met like old friends. We came to have tea each day at the same table in the refectory. We went for walks at week-ends, and once to the theatre where we sat in the pit to see *Bill of Divorcement*. In the bar at the interval we nodded to a group of men we knew slightly at College; I felt a touch of pride, as though I were a regular theatre-goer, and Sheriff behaved like one.

Among the King's men in the bar we noticed a lanky figure with a pale thin face, standing slightly apart from the rest; as we looked, someone spoke to him and his face broke into a smile which made me start. It was alive, mockingly intelligent and singularly charming. Then it disappeared, and he was once more pale, almost dull-looking.

'We ought to know that man,' I said.

A couple of days later he was sitting with Sheriff at our table when I came down to tea.

'Hunt, let me introduce Miles,' Sheriff broke off a conversation in which the other man had been patiently listening. 'He's doing the same course as I am. He's going to be a scientist, like me.'

Hunt smiled.

'There seems to be a difference between you in spite of that.' I liked him at once. We sat while Sheriff entertained us, and sometimes I would break in, and once or twice Hunt's smile transfigured his face and he made a quiet gibe.

There was no explanation of how Sheriff had found him, but he seemed at ease with us, and soon he was inviting us to his rooms. He lived over a shop in Euston Road, and though there was a musty smell in his sitting-room and a thud and jar of noise from outside, it was spacious compared to Sheriff's room or mine. I could not understand why he kept apologising for it; and why his composure became mixed with a tinge of fussiness, as soon as we had got inside.

'Can't I get you a drink – or fetch some beer, there's a pub down below – or make you some tea – or something?' he went on, until I felt awkward myself and was grateful when Sheriff asked:

'Is this your first year, Hunt?'

'Yes.'

'Why is it your first year, then?' Sheriff said. 'I mean when I was being sent to bed tired at my school, and Miles was doing the reverse at his – you must have been busy. You're older than we are, of course.'

'I'm twenty-two,' said Hunt.

'We're neither of us twenty,' Sheriff said. 'Which seems remarkably odd. But what have you been doing with the spare years?'

'I've been working in an office,' Hunt said deliberately. I could see he was uncomfortable, and tried to turn the conversation, but he kept on. He seemed to insist on aggravating his discomfort, as though he were rubbing a sore place. 'A very sordid and unpleasant sort of office. I went there when I was fifteen. It was certain I should go to some place like that, do you see? I was an hereditary office boy. An office boy by right of birth.' He paused. 'Well, I stood it for six years. I tried to make believe it didn't matter. I read. I tried to learn. But it wasn't good enough. So I threw in. I'd saved a little. I'm borrowing the rest. And here I am at a University. It doesn't seem – quite real.'

I do not know how much I gathered at the time of Hunt's revulsion from his past; I was perhaps too near, as well as too far away, to understand with full sympathy. For I too was of a class where a University seemed a remote preserve of other people: and yet it had not affected me like this: now I was there, I took it as my right. It was only as I got older that I could feel the differences and reconstruct Hunt as he was; on the spot, I sympathised without knowing why. And when his manner altered, as on this night, and he became diffident and faltering instead of pleasantly contained, I always felt I was near to understanding but not quite there.

As soon as his 'quite real' had ceased echoing, a little sadly, in our silence, Hunt became himself again. He gave us beer, made us at home, listened while Sheriff talked, and slid in some of the remarks that I was beginning to hope for. He was reading economics, and Sheriff held forth:

'Economics happened just because science and art got too fond of one another. And when it came they hated it so much they wouldn't give it any blood. Thin little men in pince-nez making worlds of their own out of the real world. You can't do it, Hunt. It's like a skeleton. It's like a skeleton when you're asking for flesh and blood.'

'But I've never asked for flesh and blood,' said Hunt.

'These Economic Men of yours, gutless, heartless, adjusting their demands of bowler hats very neatly to the supply. There never were such men outside a text-book and yet you talk about them —'

'They tide over gaps in the conversation,' said Hunt.

So it went on, with all three of us throwing in ideas, Sheriff laughing at Hunt's probes and his own eloquence, but sometimes bringing out a speculation which would defy Hunt's chase.

'I *know* it's wrong,' Hunt said once or twice, 'but I can't prove it.' Then I suggested a way out, and we started over again.

That night was the beginning of our triple friendship. I have never had again — what shall I say? — the excitement of the time when my two friends and I were discovering our world. Excitement — that is something if not all the quality in those first friendships as a young man. Excitement at the world, at the new freedom, the new things to see and talk about: and beneath the pretence that it is all emotionless and detached, excitement at the discovery of friendship itself. For one's boyish friendships have been commonplace or else romantic; and if romantic, they had the distrusts of love; one has to be a little older before friendship can endure. And suddenly one feels the glow of meeting at the same place and time and half by accident, as though it were all offhand, the first friends to whom one has opened the heart and felt secure.

Our friendship had become an accepted thing before the middle of that second term. We were intimate until we took our degrees, over two years later. Two or three nights a week we drank together; often we were slightly drunk, sometimes drunk enough, when we could afford it, to make us repent for a few days. Hunt was our guide through stretches of lower class London Sheriff and I knew nothing of; we had favourite public-houses in Pimlico and Fulham. We sat in the cheapest seats of the most advanced theatres. When our money gave out, as it did often, we went to museums or picture-galleries, or walked in the parks. There was always something to interest us. There were not many sides of life in a large town that we missed. And the odd thing is, we gained a fresh appetite for work from it all. I can remember afternoons in Highbury getting through the fascinating new ideas on magnetism; evenings at music-halls with a meal of fish and chips and beer afterwards in Pimlico, and back to my room at Highbury for another two hours' work.

The world was an exciting and restless place just then, and we should have been worthless if it had not stirred us. The Peace Conference had done its job, and the paint was already cracking. We used to argue violently over the new racially determined nations: somehow we reconciled our internationalism and liberal-socialism and democracy with the more ridiculous effervescences of nationalism, in a way I could never afterwards understand. I had conceived a romantic fondness for the Jugo-Slavs and Hunt used to point out the solid virtues of the Czecho-Slovaks; Sheriff was all for the Irish Republic and, of course, the three of us were savage about the Black and Tans. We wanted India free at once – and I have a memory of standing rather uncertainly in some Putney public-house and making a vigorous case for Celtic independence. Ireland, Wales, the Highlands – Brittany, of course – I was a little doubtful over Cornwall. But it is too facile to laugh at oneself when young, in order to flatter one's present wisdom. I ought to confess that some of the thinking I did then was as clear and definite as anything I have ever done: and I settled a good many questions in a way that I should still maintain.

We were all interested in Russia. We drank to the defeat of the Allied Expedition, and we celebrated Trotsky's victory over the Poles. Sheriff announced one Sunday when we had gone out of London and were walking over the Downs:

'Compared with Lenin, Napoleon looks just tawdry.' But we were all too early to be captured by Communism.

Of the three of us, only Hunt was conscientious enough to join a party: soon after we met, he joined the I.L.P. and made occasional speeches at municipal elections. I can still see him, pale, hesitating a little, persistent, shadowy in the gaslight of a schoolroom in some obscure suburb, being clear on elementary economics before a handful of an audience which did not understand a word. Sheriff and I were diverted, interested, often vehemently angry at the political spectacle, but for us it was just one of many facets in the world we were discovering, on a plane with the books over which we argued and talked so eagerly.

Among all our talks, we returned continually to an argument about science.

4

Hunt could not believe in it.

When Sheriff or I assumed, as we so often did, that science was inevitably going to change the future, and that we were optimistic because of it, Hunt protested:

'I can't understand the way you two *believe*.'

'Don't you see,' Sheriff would break out, 'that science has got the future in its hands? It will make people live longer, give them leisure, give them power – why, we shall soon have Nature at our mercy. Isn't that enough for you?'

There was a pause. Hunt was always a little slow at finding his reply. And then:

'It's not. We shall have a fine healthy population, maybe – and give it some wholesome exercise now and then by making it run away from poison gas.

'But I'll grant you everything will get more hygienic every year. We shall pull off a gigantic piece of plumbing. Do you think that's enough for me? Do you want me to have a mystical belief in a super-plumbing organisation?'

Sheriff got nettled.

'One can make anything ridiculous by reducing it to its lowest terms.'

'And anything romantic by raising it to its highest.'

'Romantic be damned!' Sheriff cried. 'We're getting the power, and that's making our civilisation the first stable one there's been. It's because it's the first civilisation that has got hold of science – not enough yet, but enough to give it power. Call it plumbing if you like, but it's making us unique. And as well as that, we've got scientists: the first collection of people in the world who've been trained to be honest and detached about the things they see. They've vowed honesty and detachment, and that's something staggeringly new. And a good deal more useful than vowing chastity and obedience' – he laughed – 'though perhaps not quite so difficult to carry out.'

There was another pause.

'You're a scientist, or are going to be. I never have been.' Hunt turned from Sheriff. 'I ask you, Arthur,' he said, 'who is the more detached, Charles or me?'

I laughed. The contrast was too much like a caricature. Hunt, restrained, sceptical, never taking a point on trust – and Sheriff, with his love for the flamboyant, so easy to arouse until his eyes shone with enthusiasm as they were doing now, the most volatile of creatures.

'What about these scientists of yours?' Hunt asked.

He kept coming back to the subject frequently during our last year. He was a pertinacious man, and I suspect he must have been worried by our settled faith that we were just going to start on the best job in the world. One night I took him to an evening symposium on the new crystallography; the physics staff and the research students and a few of the keener third year men were there, and I had promised to show him a group of scientists in action. Sheriff, for some reason I have forgotten now, did not go with us that night. We were a little late, and Austin was beginning his introduction when we arrived. I remember climbing on tip-toe up to the back of the gallery, and seeing, dim in the half-light, Hunt's chin supported in his hands as he stared at the first lantern slide.

Then I forgot all about Hunt. For by this time, a few months before my degree, I had nearly decided to do my research on crystallography. I had narrowed it down to that or nuclear physics, and on the whole crystallography was attracting me the more. Crystals, their shapes and colour and growth, had fascinated me since I first saw needles of cinnamic acid glinting at the bottom of a test-tube while the light shone through them and was reflected glitteringly at each line-sharp edge. At the University I seized hold of Bragg's work; it fed my interest to learn how in every crystal there is one regular simple pattern of atoms, which repeats itself indefinitely until we get the crystal we can see and touch; there was something beautifully satisfying about this crystal architecture, and often I longed to trace the atomic patterns for myself. Walking home on the nights when I left Sheriff and Hunt too late to catch the tube, I devised atoms in patterns of my own: tried to find connections between the arrangements of atoms inside the crystals, and the shape of the crystals themselves: saw extensions of this new method into the older, more conservative sciences of chemistry and metallurgy.

So this discussion was absorbing, and every word had to be criticised, and either rejected or fitted into the lines of work I could see ahead. I ventured a suggestion myself, based on a paper of Bragg's I had read a month or two previously. Austin bumbled. I realised with delight that no one was able to contradict me. Towards the end of the meeting, with men shuffling down the gangway now and then, and the lights over the blackboard still unlit, forgotten after the last slide, I knew for certain what my research was going to be. With a feeling of something settled, of confidence, almost of complacency, I walked by Hunt's side away from the College.

Suddenly he said:

'So that's what your scientists are like.'

It came as a jolt.

'Why, yes,' I said, 'that's what they're like.' I smiled. I was happy.

'Austin's a great scientist, isn't he?' Hunt asked.

'Yes,' I said.

'He's also very stupid. Very stupid indeed,' said Hunt. 'And jealous of some of his bright young men,' he added.

I was stung.

'How do you know?' I said. 'Damn it, how do you know?'

He stopped. His smile changed his face.

'Don't you agree with me?' he asked.

I resented his words. His mind moved much more slowly than mine, I knew; yet he was so quick and certain on some personal things. For myself, I could not see Austin very clearly. I was not able to forget the elation of that first lecture. There was admiration at the back of my mind, whether I admitted it or not. But I recalled things I had been told and also noticed for myself: conflicts with his subordinates: the pompous egotism of some of his lectures: some views he had once pontificated on the union between Christianity, Conservatism and Science.

'You're going too far, but there may be something in it,' I said grudgingly.

'And the something isn't very nice,' he said.

We turned down a side-street and ate sandwiches at a stall.

'Look here,' he said, 'this science of yours is getting beyond a joke. All this talk of Sheriff's. You're getting the power, that's obvious. It's a good thing, on the whole, I suppose, though I don't see why anyone should be so excited about it. But when I see the people who're giving us the power –'

He munched reflectively. 'Like to-night –'

'They may not be typical,' I protested.

He went on: 'The people who have the power in their hands. Look at them. They're not like you, Arthur. They're not wider than the average. They're infinitely narrower. Like this Austin of yours. Like clever children with an aptitude for mechanical toys.'

'That's unfair,' I said.

'It's fairer than your picture of bright clear minds – and everyone else in darkness.'

I thought for a moment.

'Even if you are right,' I began, 'which you're not, I don't see that it would make any difference. I mean, the important things to me aren't the latest sort of artificial silk or the speed at which we can fly an aeroplane. I'm passionately bored by the marvels of science, as you ought to know. Charles may like them, but I just don't care. And I don't really care if Austin reads nothing but detective stories and beats his wife, which, if she's as silly as she looks, might be a good thing. All that doesn't matter, do you see? What does matter is – oh! you know how hard it is to explain – that there's something in science itself that pulls one on. Something bigger than its twopenny tricks and the people who do it. It's – it's – it sounds like Charles at his Sheriffest, but it's something like the idea of discovering the truth.'

'But those are all words,' he said, 'you haven't got a monopoly of the truth.'

'In a way, I think we have.'

Hunt smiled, a little annoyed. 'God, you're as arrogant as the rest. How?'

I spoke quickly; I had thought this out:

'We make experiments and we get results and we infer that there are such things as atoms. Then we work out that if our atoms are right we ought to do some more experiments and get certain definite results. We try it: and our atoms fit the facts.'

Hunt paused. 'Your atoms are just a guess that works. They're not the truth.'

'Because the guess works, it is the truth.'

He stroked his cheek, impatiently.

'We're just making patterns with words at one another. What good is that? But I can't believe you ought to be making a passion of science.'

'Suggest something better,' I smiled.

'I've got to get things clear myself first,' he said. 'But, Arthur, you've got imagination; you're even sensitive to people, when this science doesn't get in your way – however can you throw yourself body and soul into anything so – so preposterously unreal?'

'Unreal! Do you think stars and atoms are unreal to me? Can't you understand,' I said, 'that the atoms in a crystal are more real to me than the gas-flare flickering on that stall or that woman smiling under the lamp-post over there or all this smell and noise of life? Can't you understand that the atoms in a crystal are more real than anything else I know?'

5

He came back to the argument on an odd occasion.

We had all three of us been to a College Dance, and

Sheriff had persuaded two girls to come to Hunt's rooms afterwards for an after-midnight cup of tea. We were a little self-conscious and Hunt was more than usually uncomfortable as host. I watched Sheriff talking softly, with his self-mocking smile, to the girl who was sitting by him on the sofa. She was called Mona, I don't think I knew her surname until later. Hunt had danced with her early in the evening as though he were fond of her; but towards the end Sheriff had been at her side all the time. I had seen Hunt go into the supper-room, when she and Sheriff were sitting out: stand in front of them for a second: and then go out and dance with someone else picked up at random. Mona had a delicate-skinned face, and she was looking at Sheriff with large, intent eyes. I could not understand how either of them could be attracted by her.

We had talked a good deal about sex, the three of us. We were of our generation and these matters seemed very simple, too simple sometimes even for us. We assumed we should have women, quite a series of them, and that it would all be very sensual and sensible, and we should part when tired without tears and with no harm done. It was to be cleanly sensual (a phrase of ours) on both sides and our women were to have the same liberty and the same amorous succession as ourselves.

About the present we were discreetly vague. Occasionally Sheriff emitted dark-sounding hints. They made me very curious. At twenty I was more interested in the concrete facts about people than in the people themselves; whether Sheriff was really carrying out an affair seemed much more significant than the man himself. So I tried to fit together his absences and innuendoes and the times I had seen him with women. I was also inquisitive about the nights when, without a word either before or after, Hunt did not join the other two of us.

I watched them now, Sheriff charming Mona on the sofa, Hunt diffidently giving her tea, and wondered how she would affect them. Then the other girl broke in.

'Do you know,' she said, 'I think everyone would be very shocked if they knew we'd seen the dawn in a man's rooms.'

I looked out of the window and through a gap in the houses opposite where the sky was lighting up, coldly yellow; then I smiled at Audrey, whom I had had to entertain while the others were competing for her friend. She was only just nineteen, and there was a careless, youthful awkwardness about the way she walked and the wave of her red hair. When she spoke, she sounded sure of herself and youthfully eager at the same time.

'If they'd ever seen it, they wouldn't be so shocked,' I said. 'Look!' For the morning was cold, and we were all, even Sheriff and Mona, a self-conscious day-time distance apart.

'But it's different, anyway,' Audrey said.

'Different! Is that the best you can say?' Sheriff turned on her, laughing. 'You people who are afraid to admit that you're excited! Why, you're no better than the creatures you want to shock! We ought to be excited at everything we do' – he chuckled – 'and laugh at ourselves for being excited.'

'You get excited, do you?' Mona asked, smiling. I was still more amazed that they could like her.

'Of course I do,' he said.

'At some things more than others?' said Mona.

Hunt broke in:

'The thing which excites these men more than anything else in the world is science.'

Mona said to Sheriff: 'You can't be, really?'

Hunt faltered, and went on: 'They won't believe you if you tell them that human beings should come first.'

Sheriff said quickly: 'This is all rather misleading for four o'clock in the morning. When we say that science ought to come first, it doesn't mean we want to do nothing else but science. It's simply that we think science is going to be the most amusing way to spend our lives.' He turned to Mona. 'Let's go on with our talk,' he said, and she smiled.

Audrey said to me:

'Do you agree with what he said?'

'Yes,' I said, 'I think I do.'

'It sounds strange.' She screwed up her mouth. 'But – but I fancy I can understand.'

I took her to her lodgings and Sheriff saw Mona home, and then I went back to Hunt's rooms, and he walked with me towards Highbury, through a cold, windy dawn, with streaks of cloud across the orange eastern sky. We did not speak for a time.

'I'm rather ashamed of myself,' he said at last.

'Childishly jealous,' he added. His face was very pale.

'Trying to get back on Sheriff by going for your science. God, how childishly, childishly futile!' he burst out.

'She wouldn't notice,' I suggested.

'Then she's too stupid to live,' he said.

We walked on; I did not try to console him again. The wind was driving into our faces and it freshened my eyelids after the sleepless night. The morning star was dimming now. I remembered how in my childhood I had got up to see it, day after day. It was still a familiar, friendly sight.

'At least,' Hunt said suddenly, 'I know why I do these things. Mean as they are.'

A lorry clattered past us towards the town.

'I know why I spoke like that,' he muttered. 'I know how I was jealous of Sheriff.

'I know *why* I was jealous of Sheriff,' he added, and his voice had got fuller. He began talking to me instead of to himself. 'Perhaps that's as much as we can hope for. Perhaps that's what we ought to do.'

'What?' I asked, puzzled.

'Look here, Arthur. I'm getting things straighter at last. Do you think Sheriff knew why he was taking that girl away from me? He doesn't care a damn for her, of course. Do you think he knows why?'

'I suppose not,' I said.

'Well, we've got to know why,' he said. 'We've got to understand the things we do – even if we can't control them. If Sheriff and I can do this sort of thing to one another – he takes my woman, I sneer at him like a guttersnipe – there's not much hope for social living, do you see? Sheriff and I are friends. And we go and invent for ourselves all sorts of fine reasons for our own actions, all sorts of mean ones for the other's. Sheriff's doing that now. I only stopped because I caught myself in time. We've all got to catch ourselves in time. We've got to understand the real reasons for the things we do. The reasons right below anything we say.'

I was tired out and not very interested. I made some sort of reply, because he was unhappy and I wanted to soothe him.

'It's more important than your science,' he was saying. His face was lit up with a queer light that seemed mixed with pain. 'It may not be hopeful for the world. Even if we try to become conscious in this way I want, we may never be good enough at it. Unless we do try, though, I'm certain there's no hope for us or the world at all.'

He paused. I wanted to get off and sleep.

'Oh, I've not put it very well,' he said. 'But when I said you ought to put human beings first, that didn't mean anything at all. The *how* of human beings – every village gossip has been doing that since talking started. Now I know what I ought to have said. It's the *why* of human beings you've got to understand, Arthur. Or else you'll be giving all your science to a mob of children. Whatever they do with it, they won't know why. We can never trust them. Unless they know the *why* about themselves, then everything in the world is like giving a child some poison and telling it to go and play in the kitchen.'

6

This argument with Hunt has taken a larger place in my account than it did in fact; at the time, indeed, I fancy it was overshadowed by many talks which I have long forgotten. Later, I was forced to remember the way in which Hunt expounded his doubt, I my faith.

However, the arguments and rivalry ceased in our last month together. I heard no reference to Mona, Hunt talked no more of science, and, meeting more rarely with the examinations ahead, we were peaceful in our friendship. The future was straining our nerves a little. If by any chance we did not get our Firsts, Sheriff and I would have to give up research as a dream, and Hunt would go to some dull job, to pay back the money he had gambled on himself. We told one another that anything but Firsts were inconceivable; but each of us was often afraid. I remember lying awake at dawn, and all the bleakest possibilities pressing on me, until I had to get up and work in order to shut them out. And at other times I would feel the wildest confidence.

With the future disturbing to look at, we turned to each other for support during those last weeks. The past began to assume a flavour of its own, the comfortable, adventurous, speculative past. We went back to our old habitual places, and retraced the days we had spent, the talk we had gone through, the hopes and accidents of three years ago. Under a cover of laughter, we were all sentimental, and it gave us ease of mind.

One hot afternoon we had tea at a café in Hampstead which once we had used frequently and then, for no reason, left for months, and sat on into the warm evening. We watched the lights of the town springing into the dusk: lamps covered by a soft haze, trams winding down the hill, cars gleaming through vague trees. Hunt was lying back in his chair, his face content, smoke from his pipe rising into the tranquil air. Sheriff leaned forward with the self-mocking smile I had seen so often, and said: 'It's been a good time, you know.'

He waved to the town which seemed so peculiarly our own, our own by right of association, by right of every drink and talk and passing fancy, by every happiness and unhappiness and interest, that we had had in London since we met three years before.

'A very good time,' I said.

'In some ways we shan't find a better,' Hunt said slowly.

'In some ways we shan't,' Sheriff agreed. Then his mood changed. 'And in some ways we shall. Infinitely better. In twenty years' – he smiled at us – 'what shall we three have done in twenty years, anyway?'

It struck a Dumas note of a year or two before, when secretly I had once cast us as the musketeers, a little ashamed of myself for the fancy. I wonder if the other two did the same? I expect so; it is too easy a temptation for three young men. I wonder what their casting was? Mine was Hunt as Athos, of course: Charles Sheriff as D'Artagnan, and myself as a rather unfitting Aramis.

None of us was stupid enough for Porthos, I thought. And what would happen to us twenty years after? I jerked myself from the fantasy, and said:

'Hunt will be an economic pundit, of course. He'll be advising at the Peace Conference after the next war – at least he'll begin to advise and then he'll resign.'

Hunt was pleased, and smiled. 'And Charles,' he said, 'will be a respectable, scientific figure, perhaps a Professor or something like that.'

'Oh,' said Sheriff disappointed.

'What about you, Arthur?' Hunt asked.

Sheriff recovered. 'He'll be a great scientist by then. A real large-sized one. He'll give interviews every Sunday, and we'll never be able to forget having known him. I'll guarantee he's going to come through.'

'What do you think about it, Arthur?' Hunt asked again.

I felt a moment of heart-deep confidence. The road was stretching before me: I knew what I longed to do, and everyone was helping me towards it.

'Unless something happens to me on the way,' I said, 'I think maybe I shall.'

Chapter 4

The beginning

I

Sheriff and I got Firsts, and Hunt a Second. As I read the announcement, my own name leaped out and I had a surge of delight; Sheriff's was in the same list; then I searched for Hunt's, and found it, incredulously. I sent a wire to Sheriff, who was away with his family. I walked up and down the road between the post office and the Imperial College. Details of the future kept running through my mind – whether I could begin reserarch before October, whether I should go to the Royal Institution, what scholarships I could get – and in my heart I was trying to find an excuse not to see Hunt.

At last I forced myself to it. He was sitting in his rooms when I arrived.

'Hallo,' he said. I noticed the skin twitching underneath his left eye.

'You know the result?' I muttered.

'No.'

'I'm sorry – I can't believe it –'

'What is it?'

'A Second.'

'Oh.' He paused. 'You got a First?'

'Yes.'

'I'm glad. And Charles?'

'Yes.'

We sat silently.

'God, Arthur,' he said at last, 'it's a little hard. One jolt like this – and there's nothing left for me. And I gambled on getting free. And I've lost.'

'Oh well,' he added, 'this doesn't help.' His voice sounded

flat. 'You're fixed now, that's something. Where are you going to work? What are you going do?'

'No,' I said, 'what are *you* going to do?'

He paused.

'Get an unimportant sort of job – and have an unimportant sort of life.'

'Something can be done.'

He smiled.

'What? As far as I'm made for anything, I'm made for academic work. And that's out of the question now.'

'Let's go out,' I said, 'and try to make some plans.'

He hesitated.

'No. We wouldn't fit to-day.'

'Nonsense,' I protested.

'I'm going out by myself,' he said.

I am ashamed to write that I searched out a casual acquaintance who had also got a First, and passed the night with him, enjoying our success, matching our elation.

2

I began research at the end of September. I had accumulated nearly two hundred and twenty pounds a year in scholarships, which seemed like luxury, and my bed-sitting room became two rooms in the same house. I was too busy to change my lodgings altogether. For three weeks I almost lived at the Royal Institution, learning the latest crystallographic methods. The staff there were very good to me, an unknown young man not yet started research, and spent hours instructing me in the new instruments, giving me the most recent publications and criticising my own projects. It was my first glimpse of scientific unselfishness; I was impressed and wished I had gone there to work. But Austin had introduced difficulties about finding money, if I left King's; so I gave in, and he put me under the supervision of Tremlin, a lecturer whom I had scarcely seen, and who was, in the fluidity of those post-war years, a biochemist with an interest in crystallography.

They gave me a room to myself: and the first morning I went into it, I have always thought of as the beginning of my research. I looked round at the couple of benches, polished and undusty, carrying a few of the pieces of apparatus out of which I was to make my first X-ray spectroscope. Over in the corner was a tiny desk. It was a fine morning, and through the window came a beam of September sun, in which the motes were dancing. I felt gigantically proud: this was a day. I can even trace the date, for that same morning I had bought a thick note-book with red covers, and now, at my little desk, I sat down and printed on the outside, with a pen that seemed to give a quiet throb, the word – RESEARCH. Then I turned to the first page, drew a line down the middle of it, and wrote:

Experiments.	Inferences.
1922 Sept. 28. Began assembling parts for X-ray spectroscope. Window for ionisation chamber not yet in place. X-ray tube running well. Must get standard crystal of KBr at once, to avoid delay when machine is ready.	

I have the book in front of me now. There is something oddly touching about it as it lies there: too much a reminder of myself when young, confident, exuberant, a little wistful, a little absurd.

I rushed into the work at once. I don't think I ever actually enjoyed the process of making things with my own hands. I never liked craftsmanship for its own sake, as many scientists do, as Sheriff, for instance, had done all his life. But with an end in view I settled down to it cheerfully enough, and probably worked harder because I sometimes resented the mechanical routine. For weeks I was in my room eight or nine hours a day, fitting up apparatus, testing it, taking it down, full of impatience to get the instrument finished and turn it on to some of my own ideas. Yet I gained pleasure out of it. On the evenings I went to my rooms tired and irritated, I used to read the latest

53

papers on crystal structure, and think to myself: 'Soon I shall be getting amongst it.'

Although I was too busy to be much oppressed, I was more lonely during this period than at any time since my first term in London. Hunt was teaching in a school in Manchester; Sheriff, just as he had made all his arrangements to start research in organic chemistry, had been operated on for appendicitis and was still convalescent at home. Most of my acquaintances had gone down, and for the few minutes I spent each day in conversation I was driven on to the people in the laboratory.

Apart from Austin, these were all strangers to me when I began work; and, as my only meetings with Austin were on his daily round of the laboratory, when he would come into my room, ask pontifically, 'Things going well?' and not listen to my answer, I heard comparatively few friendly sounds.

I saw little of my supervisor, Tremlin; there was obviously nothing much he could do to help, and he had no reason to talk to me; but I think we should have made an excuse for meeting if there had not been a strange constraint between us. It was not dislike on either side; we simply felt uncomfortable with each other, more uncomfortable than with people whom we liked far less. He was a precisely thin man, only seven or eight years my senior. On arriving in the laboratory he put on a beautifully white overall; his eyes were always exactly in the centre of his spectacles; he was the most *accurate* looking man I had ever seen. I could not imagine coming into touch with him. By an odd irony he was to enter, through no will of his own, into the most critical days of my life. When that happened, years later, I was angry because he gave me no pretext for resentment.

I remember the first remarks outside my immediate work that he said to me: curiously enough, they were about another man I was afterwards to know well. I had mentioned Desmond of Oxford. He stared at me quizzically.

'I know that distinguished investigator,' he said. He made a habit of whimsically affected polysyllables. 'I suspect next year he will be elected with acclamation into the

Royal Society. As a result of idea-appropriation on the largest scale imaginable.'

I looked surprised.

'You know all these papers of his,' he went on, 'Desmond and Smith, Desmond and Collins, all the rest of them. Collins is working at Leeds now, he's still trying to remember what share Desmond had in those papers – except inscribe his name very legibly at the top of them.'

I protested: 'How does he manage it, though? If that were true, they could always throw him off.'

'The economic factor is a powerful motive in human affairs,' said Tremlin. 'Amicable relations with Desmond seem mysteriously to be an aid to a young man's career.' He smiled slightly. 'But we must remember the truth you've no doubt heard already, Miles: it doesn't matter who gets the credit, so long as the work gets done.'

As I walked to the laboratory after lunch, I wondered for a while how much there was in his account of Desmond. He was obviously not impartial. I was not very practised at detecting undercurrents of feeling, but that academic cynicism was the worst disguise of all. And yet – and yet there was probably something in it. I was young and devoted, but I was not a fool; and it was clear that one must expect an occasional rogue. It was not quite so clear why a rogue could get away with it as easily as Desmond seemed to do. I puzzled over this for a few minutes. Ah well! I thought, if one keeps clear of the Desmonds, it does not matter much. I went and did an afternoon's work.

3

By the end of November my instrument was almost ready for work. There was one provoking week when nothing would make the ionisation chamber show any sensitivity whatever. One morning, after tampering with it quite uselessly for five long days, I wanted badly to throw it on the floor and put my heel on it.

'Damn you!' I said. 'Oh, damn you!'

Abashed, I went to my desk, picked up my notebook and

wrote down – 'Possible Causes of Insensitivity of ionisation chamber (a) ...'

It did not help, but it eased my mind; and late the following night I found the trouble. I went across to Romano's and stood myself a drink. It was a long time, I realised suddenly, since I had tasted beer. The evenings of last term seemed very far away. But I was tiredly happy, a month of straightforward work, and I could hope for my first results. After Christmas I should be thinking with my head and not my hands. I should have got through to the jumping-off point of my plans.

The next week Sheriff came back, paler than I had seen him, but mercurial and optimistic, talking of a love-affair in hospital and full of the research he was beginning. His first night in London, we went to Hammersmith and drank and talked; but, in the effort to make up for the two months he had lost, he was working even harder than I was, and for the rest of the term stayed in his laboratory until late. I visited him there one night, when I was held up myself because a standard crystal had not yet arrived. I laughed as I saw him disconsolate behind a mesh of glass tubing which had collapsed just before I came in. But when I saw him set to work to mend it, his mobile face comically distended as he blew T-pieces in the glass, I was envious. I knew I should never have that delicate sureness of hand, that tactile imagination. If he had been taking up my subject, the instrument would have been ready a month ago, I thought. But when it was ready, he would not have been full of ideas on how to use it. He would probably have chosen some quite trivial problem. So I thought, with an envy that I have always had in front of dexterous men.

The last Sunday before we went home for Christmas, Sheriff took me to his Professor's for tea. Hulme had an At-Home each Sunday, and though it was organised by a harsh-looking housekeeper and one munched thin biscuits and had to drink weak tea, it was thronged by his students and their friends. Everyone was charmed by him. To a great many, I think, he was the hero of their scientific dreams, the wish-fulfilment of their own pictures of themselves. I was fascinated myself as Sheriff introduced me and I saw his subtle ascetic face, with its deep lines carved into the skin. He smiled at us, and talked, with a frank delight, it seemed, as though to equals, of the differences between beginning science in our day and his. He had all the impish pleasure of the unworldly in being worldly-wise; I remember our laughing as he said: 'My chief sorrow is that no industrial people have ever thought it worth while to buy me. I've never had any scope for dishonesty all my life: and I'm sure I should have been good at it.'

As soon as we had left his house, in a dark and shabby street in Chelsea, Sheriff broke out:

'That's the nearest approach to a saint we shall meet in our time, Arthur. When you think of his career – to be as simple as that! To keep his interest in the way things are going! To be as simple and sincere and clever as that – he's a saint, a scientific saint!'

More than once during the fortnight at Christmas which I spent at home, as I took long solitary walks through the sodden countryside, my thoughts came back to Hulme. To me, anxious, quivering on the edge of my first attempt at discovery, he represented all the peace of a consummated search. There was a calm about him such as I imagined must have come to Faraday quite early in his life. There can have been no lives as satisfactory as theirs, I thought; I tried to imagine myself coming through to something of their serenity, but they were too high to reach. I could not picture Hulme as I was, fretting with discontent after three months' work, uncertain how soon, how completely it was to be requited.

I got back to the laboratory as soon as it was open; and things went smoothly from the first day. At last I could see the instrument taking its final shape under my hands. Every detail came off a little better than it might; I had extraordinarily good luck with breakages and accidents. By the middle of February the apparatus was working. The trial runs with crystal of sodium bromide (ordered, in my exuberance, five months before) went perfectly. I stood back and looked at this instrument of mine: the shining X-ray tube with the discharge that purred and glowed,

hedged in by a wire guard, on which I had put a placard
'DANGEROUS – 2,000 VOLTS'; the tangle of glass and metal,
orderly under its shield; the square dark ionisation chamber; the lighted spot of the galvanometer steady on its scale,
a gleaming circle against which one could see the black
upright measuring line.

I did not want to give up looking at it.

4

I had explored the possibilities of crystallography very
carefully during the past months: by the time my apparatus was ready, I was quite certain of the line I was going to
take. There was an element of expediency in the first
steps, for it was patent that I could not expect the authorities to take me as a rising scientist on trust. I had to prove
myself according to their lights. After that I was going
my own way, and I knew what that way was going to
be.

To begin with, I was going to start on a safe problem. It
was not exciting, but almost certain to give me some results. So I decided to work immediately on the structure
of some of the manganates; the arrangement of the atoms
seemed to me almost certain to fall into one of the simpler
symmetries, and yet, for some reason, they were still unknown. If I could bring this off, it would give me a little
reputation.

I weighed it up as dispassionately as I could. I wanted
to get at a big problem soon. I had my schemes for tackling
one of the simpler families of organic compounds, where
no one had dared to guess at the structure. I could foresee
the method of analysis, with sidelines of analogy and dis-
similarity, which later I actually employed: I was ambitious
enough to look further ahead, to the proteins and others
of the vital substances, whose chemical formulæ were uncertain – I was sure that with courage and luck crystallography could carry me even there. But I had to wait my
time. To suggest my real plans now would be idiocy: it
would sound like the talk of a boy who ought to be com-
mended but discouraged, like a young member at his

maiden speech making an intricate proposal for the abolition of the slums.

I knew perfectly well how wild it sounded; and so, the day the instrument was finished, I set to work on the structure of manganates. Tremlin approved: 'A scholarly choice,' he said (I have always had an aversion from the word 'scholarly'). Austin came in and asked his daily question, 'Getting on all right?'

'The machine's ready, Professor,' I said. 'I'm just going to try to get the structure of the manganates.'

'Ah,' he said. He went out of the door, and came back again, playing with his watch-chain. 'This modern crystal work,' he announced, 'is complicated.' Then he departed.

I was willing to contain my wider projects while I puzzled out the manganates: but it was asking too much of my patience for me not to try to settle this first problem as soon as it could conceivably be done. I had to be thorough, but I was in a hurry, and I worked longer hours than ever before in my life. I ached to get the answer to the manganates and put them behind me. Sometimes, though I disciplined them, my thoughts would wander to the broader fields ahead.

For three months, until the middle of the summer, I was in my room by half-past eight in the morning; the lighted circle of the galvanometer slid smoothly over its scale and stopped, I wrote down the reading, repeat, change angle of chamber, again I watched the lighted spot begin to glide. Every day this went on till Sheriff came to take me away to lunch. We used to go to a sandwich-bar close by and I stood against the counter: I got tired of sitting on stools after a morning of it.

Then in the afternoon I sat in the laboratory's library surrounded by graph paper, plotting out the morning's results. For a long while they were meaningless, but soon I could look at them and think: 'That rules out the second idea,' or 'It looks as though it's coming like the others.' From tea to dinner I did another three hours' observations; and then after dinner I came back until it was time to take the last tube to Highbury.

I can still remember those nights in my room. I was often

tired. There was, however, a romantic flavour, I suspect, even in the tiredness. Blinking to shake off the self-hypnotism that came after watching the moving spot for hours, I could enjoy like a spectator the hum and drone of the apparatus, the order and neatness of this room before me. Under the galvanometer lamp my notes were a pleasant sight with the rows of neat little figures. Often, in order to struggle against the tiredness, I would take a few minutes off in the middle of the sitting in order to walk round the laboratory; as I left my room and stepped into the dark corridor, I looked back and drew satisfaction from it all.

The corridors seemed long and unfamiliar when I went down them at night, cutting my steps short in the thick darkness. Once or twice in the maze I would come to a door where a chink of light shone through; in time I made acquaintances of most of those who were in the laboratories at night. It broke my vigil to chat to a zoologist about the fish he was dissecting; or to have a cigarette with a pathologist busy among a culture of virus; or to call on Harvey, who was trying to disintegrate the fluorine nucleus, and watch his – particles scintillating against the screen.

One night I crossed the zoological laboratory and saw the door of the feeding-rooms open, and a small man in a cloth cap gazing sorrowfully at a pair of ferrets. I knew him by sight: he was Jepp, the assistant who looked after the animals.

'Good evening, sir,' he said gloomily. His nose was turned up a little; he had bird-like brown eyes.

'What's happening?' I asked.

'We're seeing the effect of different foods on the breeding time of ferrets, sir.' I thought quickly, and decided that 'we' must be Jepp and the Professor of Zoology. 'We've found something that seems to bring them on heat right in the middle of the off-season, as you might say.'

'That's rather exciting.'

'If it's true.' Jepp sounded mournful. 'We've fed four of them on it. And three of them have been bucking round like – like film stars on the quiet, sir. But the other doesn't look as if it ever wanted to do anything but sit and eat. It won't even look at the males.'

'Perhaps there's some special reason,' I murmured.

'I'm hoping so.' He brightened up a little. 'I've got an idea it might be a virgin. They're always harder to start. You know, it's the same with human beings, sir. '

When I got back to my room, I had to take the first reading four times before I could vanquish my picture of Jepp's reproachful look.

5

By the end of the spring I was fairly confident that I had reached the structure of the manganates. As I had thought, it was a straightforward piece of analysis; I had had the luck to keep off the one false trail. But there was a couple of months' work ahead going over my data, examining one or two remote possibilities, making the whole thing so firm that, criticising as minutely as I could, I should still be able to convince myself.

Although I resented the delay, I was happy in those weeks of filling in the details and applying checks and counterchecks. It was good to see each fact fitting in its right place; each night's work went to show that the structure I had built up was the only one these crystals could possibly have. I began to be sure that I was right. I used to stand and look at my charts, rubbing the back of one leg with the instep of the other, a childish trick that came back when I was gratified, and say:

'It must be right. There's no escape from it. I've got it right.'

At last I had done so much that one night's work would put my structure beyond the shadow of doubt. Either a curiously fantastic hypothesis must be true, or else my own structure, the one I had suspected all along and almost confirmed two months before, was definitely established. I was a little nervous, as I began that last night's work.

Soon the readings told me that everything was going according to my plan, and my heart steadied. In an hour I was certain. In two hours every scrap of doubt had gone.

My first research was over. I stood up, content.

I felt a sweet and selfish pleasure. There was nothing in it of the high ecstasy I was to know later and of which I had had the foretastes in my youth. This was a contentment of security, and the satisfaction of being right. There was not much imagination in it, and not much outside myself. It was like pleasures I knew little of, as yet: like hearing oneself praised and given a reward: like waking in the night, beside a woman with whom one is secure, and seeing her smile as she sleeps.

Chapter 5

Disturbance

I

My first piece of work did all that I wanted of it. I wrote it up in three weeks, and after a long and stately process of submission to referees it appeared months later in the *Proceedings of the Royal Society*. The title stood out on the glossy paper, and I didn't want to read any further: 'The Structure of Crystals of the Manganates,' by A. R. Miles, Physics Laboratory, King's College, London (communicated by N. E. Austin, F.R.S.). I remember, too, the fondness with which I handled the green-covered offprints and the inscriptions I wrote on them as I gave them to my friends.

The work gained me more esteem than I hoped. Tremlin, who by etiquette had some sort of claim to be part-author, was generous in facetious polysyllables and went out of his way to see that the paper was read before publication by the crystallographic authorities. One of these took the trouble to write me a letter of congratulation. I showed it to Austin, who began to realise that he himself had considered the work important all along.

He offered me a studentship of two hundred and fifty a year. Although I wanted to go to Cambridge soon, I knew my big research ought to be begun at King's, for there I had everything ready, while at Cambridge I should have to build another instrument. I had no choice but to stay.

People were beginning to talk of me as a bright young man. I was elected to the senior scientific club in the College, and University College asked me to give a talk to their society. Several lecturers took me out to meals. For the first time I was invited to lunch with the Austins and, rather unwillingly, I went. It was just after I had completely finished my paper, at the end of June. I was feeling more tired now than when I was working ten and eleven hours a day. One morning, when I shaved, I was annoyed to see suddenly how pale I was. And so I was taking a rest in my own private method, by leaving everything and watching cricket for a fortnight. Mrs. Austin's invitation broke into the first day of the match between my county and Middlesex at Lord's.

I went out to Kensington in an irritable mood. Mrs. Austin had a high-pitched voice which seemed to go on continuously even in the gaps between words: her drawing-room was full of pictures of Austin as a Nobel prize-winner, bound volumes of his publications, complete sets of Mrs. Gaskell, Hall Caine, Galsworthy and Eden Phillpotts: everything was opulently depressing. The other guests were a middle-aged lecturer and his wife, to whom Austin was laying down the law, and an emaciated young man who was chatting nervously to Austin's daughter. I had seen her before at a tea-party in the laboratory; her teeth projected and she was interested in travel.

Through the window I saw the sunlight glittering on chestnut leaves. I exchanged words with Mrs. Austin on the desirability of newspaper-rooms in Colleges. She was occupied, it seemed, with the problem of journals of extreme views, which might be read by young students.

Then another guest was announced, and I saw Audrey for the first time for months. As she came from the door to Mrs. Austin, I noticed she had lost the youthful gawkiness I remembered; she walked gracefully now, with long full steps.

We sat opposite each other at lunch, and we caught each other's glance and smiled. She had the slightest of casts, which gave an odd depth and sparkle to her eyes. It surprised me that I had not seen it before. I was amused to watch her, in a neat hat which concealed all but a glimpse of her red hair, listening quietly to an account by Austin of the progress of women's education. An account which seemed both heavy and inaccurate, so far as I could gather when Mrs. Austin gave me a hearing space. I pictured the last time I had seen this girl at a party: Sheriff and the provokingly coy Mona, Hunt pale and jealous, she and I, all of us talking in a yellow dawn. I wanted to remind her of it. In a moment of quiet, I asked:

'How is your friend – Mona, I forget her other name?'

'Much the same as when you met her,' Audrey said. I felt the same incongruity had struck her. I smiled with pleasure.

Mrs. Austin started again, refreshed, and I listened to the hardships of life as a professor's wife in Melbourne.

'Australians simply don't understand the way we look at social pleasures, Mr. Miles. They're hospitable people, very hospitable, if you know what to expect. But do you know in Melbourne I left cards on a great many people' – she paused – 'and they simply didn't know what to do.'

'How amazing,' I said. I was trying to understand why Audrey had been invited to this lunch. The overawed lecturer was explicable enough, and I assumed that the nervous young man was designed for Miss Austin: but Audrey was in her second year, and quite obscure, so far as I knew. Later I found out that she was the niece of a friend of theirs.

Austin was enunciating:

'The Universities will get more and more specialised in this generation. We shall concentrate on original work, you'll find, in a few centres; men will go to Rutherford at Cambridge or come to me here, and the minor universities will cease to exist as research institutions. Our friend Miles here, for instance, when he started his research, either had to go to Cambridge or stay with me. He had no alternative whatever.'

I saw Audrey's eyes sparkle before she looked down at her plate.

After lunch Austin united his mumble to his wife's high note, and together they were in favour of Mussolini (it was not long since the march on Rome), English universities, public schools, Lord Birkenhead, the English family, and Thomas Hardy; and against Lenin, co-education, Mr. Ramsay MacDonald, and modern literature. They did not argue, but Mrs. Austin sometimes said 'of course.'

'Of course,' she said, 'one can't read Huxley.' (*Antic Hay* was just becoming well known.)

Just after this I saw my chance, thanked Mrs. Austin hurriedly, and went. I was standing outside the house, trying to remember the quickest way to Lord's, when Audrey came out.

'I hoped I should catch you,' she said.

I was startled by her directness.

'Where are you going?' I asked.

'I should like to talk a bit. Can you? What are you doing?'

'I was going to Lord's. To watch cricket,' I said. She was so natural that it did not occur to me to be polite. 'But –'

'I'll come to Lord's,' she smiled. 'If I shan't be in the way.'

'No, you won't. But are you sure you want to watch cricket?'

'I should hate it,' she said. 'You can watch and talk at the same time, though?'

'We can get tea, anyway,' I replied.

'I'm sorry to break up your amusements,' she laughed at me. 'But, you see, it's a long time since we met.'

2

When we arrived at Lord's I glanced at the cricket for a few minutes. But with Audrey at my side it was not easy to watch two Middlesex batsmen playing back correctly to two medium-paced bowlers, although she sat very considerately still; and so it was my move and not hers when we went in for tea. It was early, and we had the tea-room to ourselves.

'Ah!' she sighed.

'Tell me,' she said, 'what do you think of your professor?'

'He's done some very distinguished scientific work.' I smiled.

She laughed. 'I'm glad it wasn't my fault. It's the first time I'd met him – and I wondered if I'd suddenly gone mad.'

'In justice to my sex,' I said, 'I might point out that Mrs. Austin hasn't the excuse of doing some very distinguished scientific work.'

Audrey poured out some tea and looked across at me.

'You've done some distinguished work yourself, apparently,' she said. Her conversation away from her own lips takes on a brusquenesss, I fancy, which I, who heard it, can never imagine there. She had a trick of dispensing with some of the smoother phrases; it may originally have been due to a sort of nervousness, but when I knew her nervousness, or its complementary aggression, were the last qualities one would give her. She was naturally at ease herself, and she induced the same state in me. The way she spoke seemed as natural as everything about her. With anyone else I should have been amused or annoyed at being made to talk in the tea-room at Lord's, of all absurd places; with Audrey it passed unquestioned, and, indeed, we had not said very much before I had ceased to notice the room round us, the people straggling in to tea.

'I've made an adequate start,' I said. I had been used to congratulations for the last few weeks. Then I was impelled to tell her the real state of affairs. 'But anyone competent could have done it,' I went on. 'It didn't take the imagination of a newt. I just picked on a safe sound bit of work to make a niche for myself. Now I'm starting something new: that really ought to be exciting.'

She paused.

'I've often thought about the reasons Sheriff gave for doing science,' she said. 'You remember – that night after the dance?'

'Yes.'

'Do you still believe in them?'

'On the whole, yes.' I smiled. 'Though I shouldn't put them quite as he did. I'm not a Charles Sheriff, you know.'

'I was reading *Arrowsmith* the other day,' she said. 'It made me think of you two. That's easier to understand than *your* science, of course. Practical science, medical science, saving people's lives, wiping out diseases – all that *Arrowsmith* science would fascinate anybody. I wanted to go and do it myself as soon as I'd read the book. Why didn't you go in for the – *Arrowsmith* kind?'

I thought for a moment.

'First, I'm not so passionately concerned with practical benefits to the human race. They don't seem to me the most important things. Second, if I were, I shouldn't do science at all: I should have a shot at the jobs which are really urgent. If anyone wants to help the human race just now, he'll be more useful doing politics or economics than science – there's not much use saving us from consumption if we're going to starve because our system breaks down, or get killed in a war because politics have gone wrong again.'

'Oh,' she said, and drank some tea. She looked dissatisfied. 'You want to keep your science pure?'

'Yes.'

'It's all very – abstract. And you're not an abstract sort of person.'

I was unaccountably pleased.

'You don't think so?'

'Not a bit.'

'Look here,' I said. 'We're spending all our time talking of my work and my opinions and my temperament. What about yours? What are you doing with yourself?'

'I'm supposed to be reading history,' she said.

With a queer vehemence she added:

'And it ought to live! And it doesn't! And I'm tired to death of it. I want something to do.'

'Does it matter?'

I could feel her anger, in a sudden gust, almost before she spoke. Her eyes glinted. 'Of course it matters. Are you as stupid as everyone else? Do you think a girl my age wants to live all the time below the neck? I'm not mentally deficient.'

'I'm sorry.' I was apologetic and annoyed with myself. 'I ought to have known.'

'I too,' she laughed suddenly. 'But you prodded me where it hurts. You see, you said it doesn't matter: and I expect most women of my sort are always half-afraid that it doesn't, after all. I know *I'm* afraid. And when I see you quite certain that you are doing the right thing, I just wonder if there *is* anything for me. I haven't any roots. I wonder if there are any I ever can have. Except getting married. I wonder if there's anything I can do.'

'This is all very gloomy,' I said. 'Of course there is.'

'I haven't found it yet.'

'You will.'

'I don't know,' she smiled. 'But anyway I've enjoyed letting this off to you.'

'I've enjoyed it more.'

'I don't think so,' she said. 'We'll test it: shall we go out and watch your match – or shall we stay here, and talk some more?'

'We'll stay here,' I said.

We left at last. Sunlight was falling softly across the ground between long shadows, and two of my county's batsmen were playing out the last quarter of an hour.

3

For a week I did not go near Audrey. I could have telephoned her, and I knew she would have met me. I wanted to see her very much. I could have contrived to meet her by accident. Yet I renounced my holidays, went to the laboratory all day, too tired to work, often thinking of her against my will.

I had fallen in love with her, and I resented it.

Never before in my life had anyone seemed more real than myself, as she did now. My parents when I was a child, my friends when I was a youth, had always been a little way off the main track of my life: I began to see this now, for the first time. They were close enough to affect me very much, but they never got as far as the heart which Audrey had reached. I could not help facing the truth, as I stayed in my laboratory and – the only word is *sulked*.

'I must be a very selfish man,' I thought. 'No human being has really mattered up to now. That's just the fact. The only thing outside myself has been my work. Is this girl going to upset *that*?'

I managed to argue myself into a state of righteous self-pity. I told myself I was keeping away from her because she would get between me and my vocation. I was dedicated to my work, I told myself, I was travelling alone and light, and now she had to come and stand in the way. I was priggish and humourless and self-dramatising. I remember a time, three or four days after our meeting, when I walked for hours through a pale-blue dusk and on into a warm luminous London summer night, asking myself 'Can I get out of it? Am I too weak to stay away?'

I do not know how many of my pretences deceived me at the time. Perhaps I was only half-deluded. For, of course, the postures and speeches were only an excuse for the fright which comes to any of us when we know we may soon be abjectly at the mercy of another; and added to that fear was a boy's nervousness of the time coming when he must prove himself a man.

No woman had yet been more to me than a stranger to dance with or a shape under the lamp light or a glitter on the stage. I had always drawn back from the explorations which Sheriff had talked about, almost from the beginning of our friendship: I still did not understand how this part of his life was shaping itself, nor did I know for several years the truth that lay among Hunt's silences. Sometimes, when I walked along and heard dance music throbbing in the distance, I would be possessed by a faint ache, an ache for something I did not know; and the sight of lovers with their arms around each other and their faces tranquil had occasionally stabbed into my calm. But my life was a hard and busy one, and I grew up late. I was still a boy when I met Audrey.

Very soon the conflict was settled. Perhaps I made an attempt at a conflict where none could be. I began to think of nothing but her ease, the way she moved and laughed, the lack of all sham. I grumbled in advance at all the complications into which I was heading, and persuaded myself that my work would suffer: but nevertheless my thoughts wound themselves about her, I wondered how fond she was of me and made fantasies of the shape we could make of our lives. I dreamed of her at nights, though never as a mistress; it was not until long afterwards that she played that part when I was asleep.

A week after our meeting I gave in. Still grumbling, still a little resentful, but full of an exultation I could not disguise from myself, I decided to ask her to meet me. As I went to the telephone I could feel my heart beat. I was almost wishing that she would be out. I waited for her voice, and my hand tapped the receiver against my ear in time to the beats of my heart. At last she came.

'Could you meet me this afternoon?' I asked.

'I've been waiting for you to ask me,' she said.

4

She came to my rooms for tea. I think it shows how she brought ease to me even then, when I remember that I was not upset because my landlady could only give us a shop fruit-cake and some thick toast. With any other young woman, I should have been embarrassed: with Audrey, it did not seem to count.

'I'm glad you came,' I said.

'I'm glad to come,' said Audrey.

She looked round my dingy room. Opposite the window there was an oleograph of highland cattle; and under it my landlady's old piano, which I could not play, took up all the wall. My books were piled in heaps by the better of the armchairs.

'So this is where you live!' she smiled. 'I've often wondered what it would be like.'

'It's not very good,' I said.

'It's not very good – but somehow it fits,' she said. She took off her hat, and her hair shook loose.

'If it were superb you'd accept it just the same. Wouldn't you?'

'I suppose I should.'

She laughed. 'It comes of having a purpose in life, you know. If you hadn't, you'd be like me, and spend all the morning designing wallpapers.'

'You must be bored, Audrey,' I said. The name took a delightfully long time to say.

'To tears. Beyond tears,' she replied, and the corners of her mouth lifted in a smile. 'I've got my wretched history. At which I'm quite good, by the way: they've just given me a prize. But, Arthur, it's all stupid: real people made into dummies by silly little historians who've never seen a real person in their lives.'

'Do it better,' I suggested. 'Get your degree, do some research. Show them how it ought to be done.'

'You're a strenuous young man,' she said. 'I don't think I should have the energy: I'm a very lazy creature. And how do you know that I could? Do you realise that I'm only twenty-one?'

I knew her age, but it meant nothing to me. Sometimes she seemed much younger, sometimes much older than I was.

'You've got the ability. And you're independent enough. You don't take your opinions on trust,' I said. 'But if you won't do history, there are plenty of other things.'

'I told you the other afternoon I couldn't find any. I'll rely on you to produce them.'

'I've been thinking –' I began, and stopped. My thoughts upon her future had only concerned myself.

'What?'

As she spoke and looked at me, her eyes intent, all our talk seemed to drop away like a pretence: as though we had been talking in tones which did not belong to us, while below there was a shout which we were trying not to hear. Reluctance and nervousness went: I could not, for the moment, find any words, but they mattered as little as the shoelace which was undone, I saw detachedly, as I walked across the room and sat on the sofa by her side. She watched me come: and as I sat by her without speaking, she made the slightest movement towards me, which let me feel that now everything was a delight.

I broke the silence:

'Oh, my dear,' I said, and the voice sounded more staccato than my own. 'I've been loving you since I saw you –'

We had our first kiss.

She smiled drowsily, through lids which concealed the sparkle of her eyes.

'Arthur, if you hadn't made love to me –'

'Yes.'

'I'm afraid I should have made love to you.'

I kissed her mouth, where a tooth showed white against her lips.

'Am I shameless?' she asked.

'No.'

'I think I am.'

'I don't deserve you,' I said. 'Do you know that I cursed you for days after we last met?'

'Why?'

'Because I knew I was in love with you and I thought you might keep me away –'

'Shall I?'

'No,' I said. 'And if you did – I don't want to see further than your arms.'

She stroked the hair at the back of my neck.

'You don't mean that,' she said.

'Perhaps I don't, I said. 'But you know what I mean.'

'I think I must have loved you,' she said, 'since we looked at the dawn in your friend's rooms, months ago.'

'I shall love you,' I said, 'until we've seen the dawn in all sorts of places for years and years.'

'We'll see everything there is to see,' she said. 'Dawns thrown in.'

'I should never quite believe this could happen to me,' I said, 'unless I had you too near –'

'There is no doubt, my love. I'm yours.'

'Not so much as I am yours.'

'More.'

'You couldn't be.'

There was nothing but ourselves, and soon we were both lost. There was nothing but a surge of noise in the ears, a blinding darkness on the eyes, from which at last, beyond our wills, we came. As we lay side by side in quietness, she turned her face towards mine and smiled for me. I saw it, I was satisfied through desire, and I wanted her still.

We proposed all manner of ways to spend the evening. Audrey was equally enthusiastic about going to the docks, the Forty-Three, and Madame Tussaud's; and in the end we sat in Hyde Park and listened to the band. Absurdly, it seemed to fit the triumphant march inside me; the soft warm wind, carrying a sprinkle of rain, made me want to sigh with happiness. Audrey's arm was touching mine, and we were discovering oddities about each other that made us laugh in love. She was amused by my necktie, she extricated my passion for cricket (though she would have found it more difficult if it had not been for the afternoon at Lord's), she smiled at my political indignations. Then I mocked her undergraduate pride at having a taste for cocktails, the conscientious care with which she dressed carelessly, the interest she took in every pair who walked by our seat.

'Who do you think they are?' she would say. 'Someone from Barnes who's picked up a shop-girl? Or are they both from Fulham, and in love?'

'In love, they must be,' I said.

'I think so,' she said, and we smiled.

'We mustn't get too anthropomorphic or erotomorphic or whatever the wretched word would be,' I said. 'The nuisance we shall make of ourselves, if we go round insisting that every pair is in love.'

I laughed: it was impossible that anyone would be as much in love as I with Audrey, sitting by me as the lights sprang up outside the park and the warm wind blew.

I was jealous of all her past: I wanted to construct her childhood, her awakening youth, her first thoughts of men: I wanted to know her family, to follow what she was doing when she left me, to be able to see and think every minute of her day.

Never before had I been engrossed like this in another: but the drive came spontaneously, as though love had released something already waiting in my mind. I did not connect it with Hunt's vision of understanding, that was drawn out by his pain the night he lost Mona to Sheriff, the night Audrey and I first met. Yet the attempt to understand Audrey, which I could not escape, began to give new dimensions to other people: I did not realise it at the time, but by adding one other life to my own, I could not help being touched by many more.

Slowly I learned about her. There was pain as well as pleasure in the intimacy. There had been a lover before me. She had not been very fond of him. It was a couple of years ago: but I could picture too well the restlessness, the careless seeking with which she had started to make love. I knew the man slightly. He was one of those anomalous figures who stay at the London colleges for years, with very little money, taking Union politics very seriously. Provoked, I said: 'How useless he must be.' Audrey smiled.

'You mustn't be jealous,' she said. 'But – it was a good job it happened. Otherwise it mightn't have been so pleasant with you and me. If neither of us had known anything about it.'

I was hurt and a little shocked; she was amused at some of my relics of youthful pride and stiffness. 'What *use* is it?' she would say. I could only laugh, rather abashed, and search into her past to see how her realism had grown.

6

We were together almost every day for the rest of that summer. I had neither the money nor the time for a long holiday: and, though we contrived some week-ends at the sea, we were in London each week from July to the beginning of the October term. Audrey's family lived just outside, in Surrey, and she invented excuses for spending her days at the College. The hours when I was working must have been tedious for her, but she enjoyed the self-sacrifice. I won't let you interrupt the work for me,' she said. 'I'd never forgive myself,' she smiled. 'And what matters more, you'd never forgive me.'

I worked hard and well during those months. My hours were not so long, for every evening now I shared with Audrey; but my time at work seemed to take all of myself even more than it had done before. Sometimes now after tea I would hurry to get away: sometimes an uncompleted thought would worry me whilst I was with her and might be lost before I had the time to work at it alone; but on the whole I had never worked so thoroughly or with so much drive. My new problem gripped my mind as the first had never done: it was original, I was taking a risk, and the risk was going my way. I could see a little way into the structure of the organic group before the middle of August: dimly I could prophesy the birth of one province in crystallographic organic chemistry.

I would have liked to share the excitement with Audrey, to give her a glimpse of the discoveries distantly in sight. It would have added to the zest if I could tell her: 'I can't say for certain, but if it is! Don't you see the scheme all those facts will fall into? – and look at this connection here. Why, we're making sense of all this jumble!'

It was impossible, though. Several times she had asked me to explain my work, but, quick and intelligent as she was, she never got far at understanding it. I was uncomfortable when I saw her eyes, usually so alert, look distant and uncomprehending. She said, worriedly: 'I'm sorry, my dear. But still I don't quite get it.'

I could only tell her that my ideas looked promising, and that I was optimistic, that I might be on to something big; and she did her best to show her enthusiasm over something she did not understand. Even so, it pleased me to tell her fragments of news like that, and I was warmed by her echo of excitement.

My concrete ambitions she caught at, eagerly. There was one which was growing as I became more confident. I wanted to direct a big laboratory along my own lines.

'You see,' I explained, 'in a few years there'll be all sorts of physical methods to attack organic problems. And biological problems, too. And they all *must* be done together. Ten men working together would be more use than a hundred on their own. They could finish great stretches of chemistry and biology in a few years. And I mean to make them do it.'

'You'll sit at a roll-topped desk and telephone all over the lab, will you?' She smiled. 'And they'll all call you professor, and you'll get some money.'

'I suppose so,' I said. 'I shan't mind giving up working with my own hands. It's a waste of time when I can get people to do it better. But – I want to run the work. That's the important thing.'

She frowned: 'You'll like the power?'

'I think I shall,' I said. I burst out: 'Of course I shall. But it's not all.'

'Yes,' she said slowly, and then laughed. 'It'll be splendid. And you'll do it superbly. Getting impatient and working yourself to death and making speeches. You'll enjoy all that side. And the work will go like mad. How long before you get the chance?'

'I must get it before I am forty,' I said. 'Sooner with any luck. Perhaps ten years.'

I was tremendously happy, but the days went by too quickly for me to stop and realise it.

Sometimes, towards the end of the summer, I had a touch of anxiety that Audrey was not sharing all my active happiness. If she missed seeing me for a day, there was a note of strain in her voice when next we came together. She was, I knew, dissatisfied at having nothing to occupy her aspirations as science did for me. Yet I was worried when I saw a line which sometimes seemed etched into her forehead, upright between the eyes. Then she would think of some new scheme for spending the night, and, as her face lit up in its excited smile, my concern was allayed and passed away. She was ingenious in devising entertainments. For weeks, of course, we were content to sit in cafés and enjoy our talk, but the time came when we wanted to do things which would gain an added flavour from the other's presence. We were both restless people. We went to the Fabian Society and the Holborn Labour Party. Audrey made me see the artistic possibilities of the cinema long before they had been developed, and we visited all manner of films in most of the picture-houses in London. We listened to the last debates of the Coalition Government, and at the election we amused ourselves travelling between meetings in Westminster and Poplar. She taught me to dance well and we helped to introduce the Charleston at several of the suburban Palais de Danse. She had a short passion for competitive sports of the more obscure kinds, and I remember going unwillingly to an international ping-pong match and the next week sitting near the water and watching some very large Hungarians playing a very rough game at water-polo.

Our amusements were often bizarre and sometimes absurd; but they were very cheap, as they had to be; with two hundred and fifty a year, I could not have entertained her if she had wanted a respectable dinner and theatre and dance; her own allowance was too minute (her father was a rather unsuccessful accountant) to pay her share of the conventional evening out. And we gained an enormous pleasure from the more ridiculous of our expeditions. Comfortably tired after a day in the laboratory, I even enjoyed the water-polo match, hearing Audrey's comments, having her laugh at my side, with the certainty that in an hour she would be in my arms. Through all these evenings, there was the same note of going together towards the new things, not caring what they were, because we returned always to the starting-point of love.

One evening I recall which captures something of our quality in those days. Or perhaps it was Audrey's quality rather than mine, for more and more she controlled our leisure. She was forcing herself to be cheerful on this evening, for I had been doing a long run of experiments, and she insisted that I should have a rest; but once, when I caught her unawares, her face was strained.

'You're too tired to go out to-night,' she said.

'Nonsense,' I replied.

'You're a bit fine-drawn.'

'I'm extremely well.' Which was true. I hadn't been out in the daylight for three months, and so was pale; but otherwise I was completely healthy.

'You'll stay in and I'll give you some hot milk.'

I got up. She wanted to go out, I knew. 'I'm going,' I said. 'But you stay here, my dear. I'll be back about twelve.'

She laughed: 'I've a good mind not to give in. Because I want to.'

'Where shall we go?'

Here she paused. Suddenly she smiled. 'I know,' she said. 'It'll do you good to drive down to the sea. I'll get the car from home and we'll go – we'll go and see Sheriff and his lass.'

'We don't know how much she's his,' I smiled. I had just had a letter from Sheriff, who was staying on the south coast near Chichester. He had made references to a conquest of his down there, and Audrey and I had amused ourselves with speculations. I had heard much of his love affairs; but neither Audrey nor I had ever watched one at close quarters.

'If she's really his, it'll be funny,' said Audrey.

'If she's not, it'll be much funnier,' I said.

It was a warm misty dusk when we drove out of London. The sky was faintly starlit, but there was no moon. As we passed over the river, I saw long reflections of light on the still water.

'Oh,' said Audrey. 'What a breath-taking sort of night.' She was driving fast, as she always did: I glanced at her intent face.

'Don't you feel like that?' she added. 'It takes my breath – calm and lovely and sad. And exciting. Like love.'

She took a corner very fast. Our headlights swept round the palings opposite, pulling them one by one out of the dusk, and then spread on to the road again. Audrey's face was contented now; and her voice, as she talked, was as I loved to hear it, full and low.

'We've got all those things in our love,' I said. 'And more.' I thought a moment. 'And the sadness just because it comes into anything a little. One can't help it: and it makes the other things seem finer.'

We rushed down a straight road, between high trees.

'I think you're right,' she said. 'It makes the good things seem better, the things we do and talk and laugh about.' She smiled. 'And I'll take the sadness, if it's got to come – for the sake of being here like this.'

'For that, I'll take more than sadness,' I said. 'If it's got to come.'

We saw a cyclist's lights bobbing dimly a long way in front. It seemed a moment only before we swept past him. The night was dark now.

'I wish I could drive you for miles. Across Europe,' she said, her eyes leaving the road for a moment. 'Following the sun.'

'We'll go soon.' I was becoming unpleasantly conscious of how poor I was. I ought to be able to give her these things she wants, I thought.

She caught my mood.

'Oh, I know we can't. And we mustn't. Your time's precious, my dear.' She was gay. 'And to-night we've got –'

I broke out: 'I'm grateful for every minute.'

'To-night we've got,' Audrey laughed. 'And we'll surprise Sheriff and have our private joke. I wonder how that diverting young man will take it.'

'He's more than that,' I protested.

'Oh, a lot more,' she smiled. 'He's got a funny face and rather good eyes.'

Here our headlights shone full on to a hedge; she pulled us round right and then left in a winding Sussex road.

'And everyone likes him,' she said. 'And he's good at science and he makes the roundest phrases I've ever heard.'

'You're being unfair.'

'Of course I am. I'm jealous of your friends. They knew you before I did, you know.' She tapped my hand. 'He's a very charming man, really. He's oddly different from you, isn't he?'

'How?'

She overtook another car, and said:

'Whatever happens to you, if you become a good solid comfortable professor – I can't imagine you – I don't think you'd ever be conventional at heart. And Sheriff, if he racketed about all his life, would never be anything else.'

'I'm not quite sure what you mean,' I said, 'but it sounds very flattering.'

Sheriff took our visit very well. It was nearly ten o'clock before we rushed through hedges, sweet-smelling and so high that they shut us into the darkness, out to a road at whose end we saw the mist-touched sea. We smiled at each other, and went to Sheriff's hotel. He came, laughed helplessly for a moment, and then was warmly polite to Audrey. He took us in, ordered some drinks at once and supper in twenty minutes, and then went away to get us a room for the night.

'The lass?' Audrey asked me.

I drank some beer contentedly, and laughed.

We heard a firm step outside, and the door opened. We looked up together, avoiding each other's eyes. For Sheriff was ushering a tweed-skirted, pink-faced, strapping girl into the room. He introduced her, smiling at her and then at us as though he was letting us into different secrets. The name was Stanton-Browne. I was amused by a curious mixture of a giggle and a snort with which she expressed interest. She used it in asking Audrey what make the car was: and learning it was a Morris-Oxford, she used it again. She interposed it again in a conversation on cars and roads, in which we kept up a polite end. Then she looked at her watch, remarked that she had promised to play half-an-hour's bridge with her father, snortled once more, and said good night. Sheriff went out with her and returned just in time to interrupt our first remarks about her.

'Her family are very nice people,' he said. His manner was unusually defensive. 'Her father retired from the Army not long ago.'

'That must add a lot,' I smiled.

Sheriff looked a little baited; but he never would resist other people's laughter, and he joined in with that volatile laugh that seemed to spread all over his face.

We began supper, and as Audrey and I ate cold meat hungrily, Sheriff sipped a glass of beer and talked.

'I've enjoyed my holiday more than any I've had,' he said. 'I've discovered people I've never really met before: natural simple people. People who've had enough money to live comfortably, and who've made a decent shape out of their lives. And I'm coming to think they get their values straighter than people like us ever will have. Oh, I know we can talk more ingeniously, and we can out-argue them every time; and we can read books written by people like ourselves and make-believe that what we think of life, and what our writers think of life, is all life is.'

Audrey gave a flicker of a smile.

'Well,' Sheriff went on, 'that's all intellectual impertinence on the grandest scale. It strikes me that the people who know what life is will never have thought of it all.' He laughed in the way that had disarmed me so often. 'I know this sounds like noble savages and old Uncle Tolstoi, but I don't mean it quite like that. I really mean that healthy natural simple people won't ever think of what's happened in their lives: but only what they can do with them. It's the same thing as physical health. We don't try to analyse our bodies, when they're healthy. We just think of what they can do, play, swim, dance, run. The natural simple people are like that in their lives: they're interested in what they can do; and that's why they're realler people than us and our probings. The only people who can possibly know what life is,' he was speaking emphatically, 'are those who have never heard of the question.'

'The only people who really know what love is,' he added softly, 'are also those who have never heard of the question.'

We argued with him gently, half-humorously, for a few minutes. When we got to our room, I walked to the window and looked out over the sea. The mist had lessened now; and by the light from a lamp nearby, I could see tiny waves lapping on the beach. Audrey was sitting on the bed.

'How much,' she asked abruptly, 'does Sheriff believe of that nonsense?'

'A good deal, when he's saying it,' I smiled. 'And almost nothing when there's something else he wants to say.'

'Is he in love with that girl?'

I said, 'In the same way as he believes in his theories.'

Audrey laughed. 'It'd be funny if all his adventures were like this. All the Celias and Pamelas and Vanessas he tells you about. Are they all respectable young English misses travelling with respectable families at obscure little watering-places? And do Sheriff's conquests consist entirely of being introduced to the family?'

'Very likely,' I said. Belatedly I added: 'Most women seem fond of him, though.'

'Oh,' said Audrey. 'Well, we've seen one of them close. Was it worth while, my dear? To come a hundred miles for it? Breaking up your work, bringing you down here, just because I must be always on the move? Just to see Sheriff's Natural Simple Girl?'

I sat down beside her, and ran my fingers through her hair.

'Worth it?' I said. 'I enjoyed seeing the lass. Good prophetic word of yours, by the way. But – what wouldn't be worth it?'

Her face had an intentness from which all the strain had gone. It gave me a lover's pleasure to see her like that, as no one else had ever seen her, in sight of peace, relaxed in love.

'Come a hundred miles?' I burst out. 'The day I won't come as far as you can go, you'd better leave me. Leave me sitting in a nice pair of slippers by the fire. I shouldn't deserve to think of love again.'

'That sounds true,' she murmured, and nestled in my arms, as though they shut out the world.

'Arthur,' she said, after a moment. 'Can men fall in love with girls like that Stanton-Browne creature? Promise, whoever you desert me for, she'll not be quite as stupid as that.'

'I suppose they can fall in love with anyone. If I hadn't had the incredible luck to have loved you, I should find someone as stupid as that myself, I expect.' I smiled. 'But mine would have been better to look at.'

She laughed, and pulled down my head. I whispered:

'But what's the use your asking me how men can fall in love with other women? When I can't believe they're not all in love with you?'

Chapter 6

The moment

I

I published a paper at the end of the year, and another in the spring. The first was an extension of my work on the manganates and contained a scheme for the prediction of structures of bromates and iodates. The other was a discreet preliminary account of the experiments on the organic group; my ideas were still too tentative for me to put forward the interpretation which was engrossing my mind. Neither of these papers was in any way exceptional, but they were sound and competent enough to add to my reputation as an able young man. I was quite often greeted at scientific meetings, and figures in the scientific world sometimes recognised my name when I was introduced to them at Hulme's or Austin's.

My life went on much as in the summer. Audrey was close all the time, disturbing me by the depression which sometimes wrapped round her, always delighting me in our love. She was in the last year of her course, and the work for her examination, although she despised it, made her less discontentedly idle than in the summer. Together, we were very happy: I cannot remember a quarrel, scarcely a bicker, during all those months.

At Christmas, Hunt came to London for a week-end, and he went out with us several times. He was pale, still not resigned to teaching, and his dissatisfaction would flash out in a harshness foreign to the Hunt of two years before: but I thought I could feel a change in him which puzzled me. He and Audrey talked eagerly together; each of them was impressed with the other. As I saw Hunt off at St. Pancras on his way back to Manchester and the dull school, he smiled wryly: 'You're too lucky, Arthur.' And when I got back to my rooms, Audrey said: 'That's the most intelligent man you've shown me.'

I thought. 'In some ways, perhaps. But –'

'Oh,' she said, 'he's not quick. He's rather slow, in fact. He's not got a nice shining metallic sort of brain like lots of your men. He wouldn't be good at cross-word puzzles. But at any serious thinking, he'd be worth ten of your Tremlins and your Sheriffs.'

'Sheriff's very clever,' I said.

'Yes.' She smiled. 'I retract a bit: if he cared to think about serious things, he'd be good at them. Hunt, though, thinks about them naturally.'

I had a letter from Hunt soon after his visit, and Audrey occasionally mentioned him in conversation; but we went on into the press and hurry of the spring term, and though we sometimes talked of driving up to Manchester we had little time except for each other, and Hunt had to pass into the background again.

Then, in March, I had an invitation to go to Cambridge and it was inevitable that Audrey's life and mine should change.

The offer came casually during a tea-party at Hulme's, where I went often at this time. Hulme was fond of me and approved of my work, and I was eager to listen to the old man with his subtle, fertile mind. Of the scientific celebrities I had been able to meet, he appealed to me far the most. And at his house I had met a variety of interesting men. On this afternoon in March, he introduced me to Macdonald of Cambridge: Macdonald was square-headed and sturdy, with waving fair hair and unexpectedly dark eyes.

'So you're the young crystallographer, are you?' he said. I had heard of him as one of the few Englishmen who had an interest in the philosophy of science; I was surprised to find what a matter-of-fact person he seemed. He was smoking a very strong tobacco, and wore a golfing suit.

'I've done a little,' I said.

'I'm told its rather good,' he said.

Hulme put in quietly: 'He'll have some better work coming out in a year or so.'

'Will you let him come to Cambridge?'

'He's Austin's pupil, you know.' Then Hulme added, surprisingly, smiling: 'But it would be very good for him. He's been in London a long time.'

I wondered whether he thought I was living too hard: he saw a surprising amount in his naïve-worldly way. Macdonald turned to me sharply:

'Will you come?'

'What for? Oh, and I've no money except a scholarship here.'

'As for money: I can guarantee you £300 a year. As for your work: you can have a completely free hand. You can do anything you like in crystallography. They call me Professor of Geology, you know: I'm a physicist, they wanted to give me a chair, and I interpret geology to mean any subject that interests me. I want some crystallography. You can do it. Will you come?' He blew out a whirling cloud of smoke.

'I'm grateful,' I said. 'But I must think.'

'Will two days be long enough?' Macdonald asked.

'Yes,' I said.

I talked it over at night with Audrey.

'One can't have a scientific career without going to Cambridge,' I told her. 'It's the best place for one thing; and also everyone goes there, and I couldn't afford to go against the fashion. And it's the best place because everyone goes there because it's the fashion, and it goes round in a circle. So I've got to go sometime. But I don't want to go now.'

'Of course you must,' said Audrey.

'We shouldn't be able to meet much. Except week-ends,' I said.

'God knows what I shall do.' The line had come upon her forehead. 'But you've got to go.'

My research would go faster in Cambridge, I knew. I had almost finished a long series of experiments, so that I could build another instrument while I was analysing these results. And the analysis would be easier in Cambridge; I should get more help and more criticism there. Yet if I could think of an excuse for not going –

'My dear,' she said: 'There'll be week-ends and holidays. And answer this: what would you do, if I weren't here?'

I thought for a moment. 'I should go,' I said.

'That settles it, don't you see?' Her mouth was working. 'Even if I want to take you away — you've got to pretend I don't. Haven't you?'

2

It was in that mood, mixed of pleasure at being able to thrust into my work and distress at altering my life with Audrey, that I arrived in Cambridge one cold wet April afternoon.

I was driven by discontent more completely into science than I had been since my first term of research. In the first month I discovered that I had never had such opportunities for work before. Research in Cambridge was on a different scale from anything I had seen. There were more great figures than junior lecturers in London. And some of the figures were among the greatest. By now I was used to men who had made their contributions to the structure of modern science; the day when I had been excited at hearing Austin lecture was very far away. But I recaptured some of that old thrill when I saw Rutherford walking underneath the arch of the Cavendish. As I watched him, I remembered the first time I heard his name, when Luard broke out and inspired me with the news of the nuclear atom, when I was in the lowest form at school, twelve years before; it was strange to see a man whose name had become part of my mind.

Before I had been a term in Cambridge, I heard him announce another of the great Cavendish discoveries; the rumour had been running round the laboratories for days, and now I sat in the crowded lecture-room and heard the first authoritative news. In a week it would be told to the Royal Society and published for the world in a month or two: but it made the blood go faster to be told, as though in private, something which had never been heard before and which would alter a great part of our conception of the atom. We were all asking ourselves: how soon are we going to be able to disintegrate atoms as we wish?

I shall not easily forget those Wednesday meetings in the Cavendish. For me they were the essence of all the *personal* excitement in science; they were romantic, if you like, and not on the plane of the highest experience I was soon to know; but week after week I went away through the raw nights, with east winds howling from the fens down the old streets, full of a glow that I had seen and heard and been close to the leaders of the greatest movement in the world. The lecture-room, packed from the top gallery to the floor, from the bottom row where professors sat to the ceiling where the degree-students took notes feverishly: the lantern, which, as seemed ironically appropriate in the most famous centre of experimental science, was always giving out: the queer high stretch of excitement that bound us all at times, so that we laughed for relief at every shadow of a joke: the great men. It is all so vivid that even now I can hear the words and feel the same response. There was Rutherford himself; Niels Bohr, the Socrates of atomic science, who talked to us amiably one night in his Danish-English for something like two and a half hours; Dirac, of whom I heard it prophesied very early that he would be another Newton: Kapitza, with a bizarre accent and an unreproducible genius; Eddington, who made some of his Carroll-like jokes; and all the rest, English, Americans, Germans, Russians, who were in atomic physics at the time when the search was hottest.

At those meetings I made some of the friends who were to be important to me later; Constantine and Lüthy I remember meeting on the same night, when W. L. Bragg had given the talk and we three had stayed behind to ask him questions. I had seen Constantine's tawny mane of hair often in the streets, and I heard reports of his eccentric ability. I liked him at sight, but somehow or other I did not see much of him till afterwards. Lüthy was a polite young Bavarian of about my own age, in Cambridge for a couple of terms. He was very useful to me from the start. Looking back, I think I was abler than he, even at the time: I was certainly more original, had more ideas and wider scope; but he had a capacity for detailed scientific criticism and a formal background of physics that I altogether lacked. I suppose he was much the better trained.

Urged on in the atmosphere of science, helped and criticised by Lüthy and some others, and spurred by the success of their researches, I made great roads into my own work. By Christmas I had done more in eight months than in nearly two years in London. The clue to the structure of the organic group still eluded me; I felt, irritatedly, that the generalisation was almost in my hands, and yet I kept missing it. Lüthy's quick destructive mind wrecked my tentative ideas as soon as I built them up. So, after a few weeks in Cambridge, I left the bigger problem on one side and started on a side-line; and this went so well, and opened up so many speculations worth testing, that I was busy on it for the best part of a year. In that time I published two substantial papers, and had another more ambitious one in hand. I was now getting the name, quite widely, of a very promising young man: in my own subjects there were not many English rivals; I was asked to contribute to all the conferences on crystallography; my personal future was near to being comfortably determined for the next four or five years. My College was one of the few in Cambridge which elect Fellows as the result of an open competition; I was eligible to send in a thesis as soon as I took my doctorate, and my tutor Merton and Macdonald both told me there was no room for doubt.

'I shall be one referee and the other is an admirer of yours,' said Macdonald. 'They can't get out of taking you.' More urbanely, Merton said the same thing: 'A good many factors come into Fellowship elections as a rule, you know. But in competitive fellowships ability is peculiarly difficult to ignore except by the rather irregular process of altering the referees' reports. And even with someone more deplorably disreputable than yourself, my dear Miles, a majority would disapprove of such an action.'

It was comforting to know that I should be secure for a while. Although I had schooled myself to wait until the end of two years at Cambridge before I thought seriously of position or money, for some time it had not been easy to put these things aside. Myself apart, I was worried by the thought of Audrey. Also, my parents were getting old, and I might have to help keep them. With the future temporarily assured, I turned eagerly once more to the problem which had enticed me for so long.

Now, however, I was in a very different mood to tackle it. I had done enough for place and reputation, and I could afford to gamble on what might be a barren chase. The structure of the organic group was not going to come out easily, I knew; I might very well be wasting a year or more, from the point of view of my career; but my career had been sound enough, and now I was working on something which I could allow to envelop me completely, simply for its own sake, in a way I had not yet known. So strong was this feeling that when I was beginning the work I often kept away from the laboratory for a day, as though my research were a pleasure of which I could, if I pleased, deprive myself. Working on my other problems – my bread-and-butter problems, as it were – I could not waste a day without a twist of uneasiness. Now I was on a piece of work I supremely wanted to do, it was natural to leave it when I was tired, to come back to it when I wished, until I was swept on beyond prudence and ambition and made to think and work and discover until the passion was drained out of me.

There was another reason which gave me far more hope of seeing my way into these molecules at last. I had gained a good deal of experience and technique in research; I had sharpened my mind on Lüthy and the rest, and broadened it on Macdonald's metaphysical schemes; and, perhaps more important, I was full of confidence. If I had an idea, it would stand a chance; even if it seemed improbable, it would be looked into; for I had learned by now that more than one of my less likely ideas had worked. This confidence would have been a dangerous state of mind to begin some routine work: I might easily have been careless, simply because my luck had kept coming off. But for work which no one had dared to touch, I had to start with something like an exaggerated belief in myself. I have often thought I was quite unpardonably confident at the time – but perhaps tackling a difficult job was the least objectionable way of showing it.

3

Almost as soon as I took up the problem again, it struck me in a new light. All my other attempts have been absurd, I thought: if I turn them down and make another guess, then what? The guess didn't seem probable; but none of the others was any good at all. According to my guess, the structure was very different from anything one would have imagined; but that must be true, since the obvious structure didn't fit any of my facts. Soon I was designing structures with little knobs of plasticine for atoms and steel wires to hold them together; I made up the old ones, for comparison's sake, and then I built my new one, which looked very odd, very different from any structure I had ever seen. Yet I was excited – 'I think it works,' I said, 'I think it works.'

For I had brought back to mind some calculations of the scattering curves, assuming various models. None of the values had been anything like the truth. I saw at once that the new structure ought to give something much nearer. Hurriedly I calculated: it was a long and tiresome and complicated piece of arithmetic, but I rushed through it, making mistakes through impatience and having to go over it again. I was startled when I got the answer: the new model did not give perfect agreement, but it was far closer than any of the others. So far as I remember, the real value at one point was 1.32, my previous three models gave 1.1, 1.65 and 1.7, and the new one just under 1.4. 'I'm on it, at last,' I thought. 'It's a long shot, but I'm on it at last.'

For a fortnight I sifted all the evidence from the experiments since I first attacked the problem. There were a great many tables of figures, and a pile of X-ray photographs (for in my new instrument in Cambridge I was using a photographic detector); and I had been through most of them so often that I knew them almost by heart. But I went through them again, more carefully than ever, trying to interpret them in the light of the new structure. 'If it's right,' I was thinking, 'then these figures ought to run up to a maximum and then run down quickly.' And they did, though the maximum was less sharp than it should have been. And so on through experiments which represented the work of over a year; they all fitted the structure, with an allowance for a value a shade too big here, a trifle too small there. There were obviously approximations to make, I should have to modify the structure a little, but that it was on the right lines I was certain. I walked to my rooms to lunch one morning, overflowing with pleasure; I wanted to tell someone the news; I waved violently to a man whom I scarcely knew, riding by on a bicycle: I thought of sending a wire to Audrey, but decided to go and see her on the following day instead: King's Parade seemed a particularly admirable street, and young men shouting across it were all admirable young men. I had a quick lunch; I wanted to bask in satisfaction, but instead I hurried back to the laboratory so that I could have it all finished with no loose ends left, and then rest for a while. I was feeling the after-taste of effort.

There were four photographs left to inspect. They had been taken earlier in the week and I had looked over them once. Now they had to be definitely measured and entered, and the work was complete. I ran over the first, it was everything I expected. The structure was fitting even better than in the early experiments. And the second: I lit a cigarette. Then the third: I gazed over the black dots. All was well – and then, with a thud of the heart that shook me, I saw behind each distinct black dot another fainter speck. The bottom had fallen out of everything: I was wrong, utterly wrong. I hunted round for another explanation: the film might be a false one, it might be a fluke experiment; but the look of it mocked me: far from being false, it was the only experiment where I had arrived at precisely the right conditions. Could it be explained any other way? I stared down at the figures, the sheets of results which I had forced into my scheme. My cheeks flushing dry, I tried to work this new photograph into my idea. An improbable assumption, another improbable assumption, a possibility of experimental error – I went on, fantastically, any sort of criticism forgotten. Still it would not fit. I was wrong, irrevocably wrong. I should have to begin again.

Then I began to think: If I had not taken this photo-graph, what would have happened? Very easily I might not have taken it. I should have been satisfied with my idea: everyone else would have been. The evidence is over-whelming, except for this. I should have pulled off a big thing. I should be made. Sooner or later, of course, someone would do this experiment, and I should be shown to be wrong: but it would be a long time ahead, and mine would have been an honourable sort of mistake. On my evidence I should have been right. That is the way everyone would have looked at it.

I suppose, for a moment, I wanted to destroy the photo-graph. It was all beyond my conscious mind. And I was swung back, also beyond my conscious mind, by all the forms of – shall I call it 'conscience' – and perhaps more than that, by the desire which had thrown me into the search. For I had to get to what I myself thought was the truth. Honour, comfort and ambition were bound to move me, but I think my own desire went deepest. Without any posturing to myself, without any sort of conscious thought, I laughed at the temptation to destroy the photograph. Rather shakily I laughed. And I wrote in my note-book:

Mar. 30: Photograph 3 alone has secondary dots, concentric with major dots. This removes all possibility of the hypothesis of structure B. The interpretation from Mar. 4–30 must accordingly be dis-regarded.

From that day I understood, as I never had before, the frauds that creep into science every now and then. Some-times they must be quite unconscious: the not-seeing of facts because they are inconvenient, the delusions of one's own senses. As though in my case I had not seen, because my unconscious self chose not to see, the secondary ring of dots. Sometimes, more rarely, the fraud must be nearer to consciousness; that is, the fraud must be realised, even though the man cannot control it. That was the point of my temptation. It could only be committed by a man in whom the scientific passion was weaker for the time than the ordinary desires for place or money. Sometimes it would be done, impulsively, by men in whom no faith was strong; and they could forget it cheerfully themselves and go on to do good and honest work. Sometimes it would be done by a man who reproached himself all his life. I think I could pick out most kinds of fraud from among the mistakes I have seen; after that afternoon I could not help being tolerant towards them.

For myself, there was nothing left to do but start again. I looked over the entry in my note-book; the ink was still shining, and yet it seemed to have stood, final, leaving me no hope, for a long time. Because I had nothing better to do, I made a list of the structures I had invented and, in the end, discarded. There were four of them now. Slowly, I devised another. I felt sterile. I distrusted it; and when I tried to test it, to think out its properties, I had to force my mind to work. I sat until six o'clock, working profitlessly; and when I walked out, and all through the night, the question was gnawing at me: 'What is this structure? Shall I ever get it? Where am I going wrong?'

I had never had two sleepless nights together before that week. Fulfilment deferred had hit me; I had to keep from reproaching myself that I had already wasted months over this problem, and now, just as I could consolidate my work, I was on the way to wasting another year. I went to bed late and heard the Cambridge clocks, one after another, chime out the small hours; I would have ideas with the uneasy clarity of night, switch on my light, scribble in my note-book, look at my watch, and try to sleep again; I would rest a little and wake up with a start, hoping that it was morning, to find that I had slept for twenty minutes: until I lay awake in a grey dawn, with all my doubts pressing in on me as I tried with tired eyes to look into the future. 'What is the structure? What line must I take?' And then, as an under-theme, 'Am I going to fail at my first big job? Am I always going to be a competent worker doing little problems?' And another, 'I shall be twenty-six in the winter: I ought to be established. But shall I be getting anywhere?' My ideas, that seemed hopeful when I got out of bed to write them, were ridiculous when I saw them in this cold light.

This went on for three nights, until my work in the day-time was only a pretence. Then there came a lull, when I forgot my worry for a night and slept until mid-day. But, though I woke refreshed, the questions began to whirl round again in my mind. For days it went on, and I could find no way out. I walked twenty miles one day, along the muddy fen-roads between the town and Ely, in order to clear my head; but it only made me very tired, and I drank myself to sleep. Another night I went to a play, but I was listening not to the actors' words, but to others that formed themselves inside me and were giving me no rest.

4

While my nerves were still throbbing with work that was getting nowhere, Audrey came up for the week-end. As soon as she met me on the platform, she said:

'You're very worried. And pale. What's gone wrong?'

'Nothing,' I said.

'Can't I leave you for a fortnight without seeing you look like death?' she said.

We tried to meet each week-end, but she was living at home now, and her father often expected her to entertain his guests.

'I'm quite well,' I replied.

We walked towards the gate. She said nothing. I talked on: 'But what's the news? I'm rather out of touch. Anything happened in the world? Have you read anything since I saw you?'

I went on until we got into a taxi; then she said:

'Stop that.'

I murmured; she took my hand.

'I'm not altogether a fool,' she said. 'And you've never been able to control your face. And there are lines here – and here –' She traced them, on my forehead and round my mouth – 'Why, you're ten years older than when I saw you first.'

'It's nearly four years,' I said.

'Don't put me off.' Her eyes were shining. 'What's the matter?'

Although I half-resented it, I was grateful that she was taking me in hand.

'The work's not going too well,' I said, and put my arm round her for comfort. 'I found there was a hole in my idea.'

'A fortnight ago you thought it was almost perfect.'

'That was a fortnight ago.' I could not help my voice going dulled.

'It's all wrong, now?'

'Quite wrong,' I said. 'As wrong as anything can be. And I can't see how I can put it right,' I added.

She did not try to sympathise in words, but in the way she leaned against my shoulder and glanced up at me I gained more ease than I had had for many days.

'You'll do it, of course,' she said at last.

'I'm not so certain,' I said. 'I might go on for years like this. Just fooling and not seeing any sort of way. It's not easy —'

The line had crept between her eyes.

'I wish I knew this stuff of yours,' she burst out. 'Then you could talk to me. And it might help a bit.'

She was anxious, now. I said:

'Oh, never mind. Let's talk of other things. That'll take me away from it.'

But even exchanging private thoughts with Audrey, hearing her say words that had become currency after long use, I still had moments when her voice and mine in reply sounded like noises in the outside world. Disturbing noises which I would get away from if I could. We sat in my rooms and she made me eat lunch and told me of Sheriff's latest affair, and how he had asked her to dinner and introduced his girl – 'a little better than Miss Stanton-Browne, but they might be cousins,' Audrey said. And she had had a letter from Hunt, who rarely wrote to either of us. He was still at his school, but seemed to be a little less disconsolate. 'Why, I don't know,' she said. And all the time those names ... Sheriff ... Hunt ... would get mixed in structures that were dancing in my mind. I shook myself free for a while, and I was myself, talking to Audrey. Then she mentioned the Labour Party and my mind leapt to the association Labour Party – MacDonald – Macdonald, my professor – and so to my problem, and I was preoccupied once more.

In the middle of the afternoon Audrey said, suddenly: 'It'll be good for you to get out of here for a bit. We'll go somewhere.' Rather unwillingly I borrowed a car, and Audrey drove along the London road. I tried to talk, but I was glad when she said something which required no answer. There was a cold wind, but once as we stopped for a moment I caught a smell of spring: it gave me an empty nostalgia, for what I did not know, except some end to this.

We had tea at a village whose name I have forgotten: it must have been Baldock or Stevenage, I think. But I remember the room as sharply as the café where I read my newspaper this morning. It was a stiff, austerely clean little parlour, with hard chairs and round wooden tables; and pale sunshine fell across it on to a grate, where a few lumps of coal lay half burnt. Audrey's hair was the only warm colour in the room. We ate hard little home-made cakes, and Audrey bit at hers firmly, in order to punctuate her views on her women friends.

'What can you do with most of them? Whatever are they for? Except have their children and keep their houses, and make their men feel important because they've got a silly woman who believes what they say.' She stopped.

'Most of these women haven't the intelligence of a penguin – and they're not as good to look at.'

'Really beautiful women are quite as rare,' I heard my own voice saying, 'as really intelligent ones.'

'I don't believe it,' she said, 'but I'd give anything to meet either after a morning with these – these incubators.' She thought a moment.

'I suppose it's inevitable,' she added. 'I suppose women are meant to be incubators first and foremost. But it's a little strange they should glory in it so.'

'Yes,' I said, absently.

'I'm ashamed of it when it comes up in myself. And it

97

does come up, you know. Sometimes I'm afraid I'm a real incubator at heart,' she laughed. 'My dear, when you're all upset like this, and paying no notice to anything I say, I ought to get up and go out, if I had a decent independent spirit – but instead I can't help staying to look after you.'

I started. My thoughts had stopped going back upon themselves. As I had been watching Audrey's eyes, an idea had flashed through the mist, quite unreasonably, illogically. It had no bearing at all on any of the hopeless attempts I had been making; I had explored every way, I thought, but this was new; and, too agitated to say even to myself that I believed it, I took out some paper and tried to work it out. Audrey was staring with intent eyes. I could not get very far. I wanted my results and tables. But everything I could put down rang true.

'An idea's just come to me,' I explained, pretending to be calm. 'I don't think there's anything in it. But there might be a little. But anyway I ought to try it out. And I haven't my books. Do you mind if we go back pretty soon?' I fancy I was getting up from the table, for Audrey smiled.

'I'm glad you had some excuse for not listening,' she said.

She drove back very fast, not speaking. I made my plans for the work. It couldn't take less than a week, I thought. I sat hunched up, telling myself that it might all be wrong again; but the structure was taking shape, and a part of me was beginning to laugh at my caution. Once I turned and saw Audrey's profile against the fields; but after a moment I was back in the idea.

When I got out at the Cavendish gateway, she stayed in the car. 'You'd better be alone,' she said.

'And you?'

'I'll sit in Green Street.' She stayed there regularly on her week-end visits.

I hesitated. 'It's –'

She smiled. 'I'll expect you to-night. About ten o'clock,' she said.

5

I saw very little of Audrey that week-end. When I went to her, my mind was active, my body tired, and despite myself it was more comfort than love I asked of her. I remember her smiling, a little wryly, and saying: 'When this is over, we'll go away. Right away.' I buried my head against her knees, and she stroked my hair. When she left me on the Monday morning, we clung to each other for a long time.

For three weeks I was thrusting the idea into the mass of facts. I could do nothing but calculate, read up new facts, satisfy myself that I had made no mistakes in measuring up the plates: I developed an uncontrollable trick of not being sure whether I had made a particular measurement correctly: repeating it: and then, after a day, the uncertainty returned, and to ease my mind I had to repeat it once more. I could scarcely read a newspaper or write a letter. Whatever I was doing, I was not at rest unless it was taking me towards the problem; and even then it was an unsettled rest, like lying in a fever half-way to sleep.

And yet, for all the obsessions, I was gradually being taken over by a calm which was new to me, I was beginning to feel an exultation, but it was peaceful, as different from wild triumph as it was from the ache in my throbbing nerves. For I was beginning to feel in my heart that I was near the truth. Beyond surmise, beyond doubt, I felt that I was nearly right; even as I lay awake in the dawn, or worked irritably with flushed cheeks, I was approaching a serenity which made the discomforts as trivial as those of someone else's body.

It was after Easter now and Cambridge was almost empty. I was glad; I felt free as I walked the deserted streets. One night, when I left the laboratory, after an evening when the new facts were falling into line and making the structure seem more than ever true, it was good to pass under the Cavendish! Good to be in the midst of the great days of science! Good to be adding to the record of those great days! And good to walk down King's Parade and see the Chapel standing against a dark sky without any stars!

The mingling of strain and certainty, of personal worry and deeper peace, was something I had never known before.

Even at the time, I knew I was living in a strange happiness. Or, rather, I knew that when it was over I should covet its memory.

And so for weeks I was alone in the laboratory, taking photographs, gazing under the red lamp at films which still dripped water, carrying them into the light and studying them until I knew every grey speck on them, from the points which were testing my structures down to flaws and scratches on the surface. Then, when my eyes tired, I put down my lens and turned to the sheets of figures that contained the results, the details of the structure and the predictions I was able to make. Often I would say – if this structure is right, then this crystal here will have its oxygen atom 1.2 a.u. from the nearest carbon; and the crystal will break along this axis, and not along that; and it will be harder than the last crystal I measured, but not so hard as the one before, and so on. For days my predictions were not only vaguely right, but right as closely as I could measure.

I still possess those lists of figures, and I have stopped writing to look over them again. It is ten years and more since I first saw them and yet as I read:

Predicted	Observed
1.435	1.44
2.603	2.603

and so on for long columns, I am warmed with something of that first glow.

At last it was almost finished. I had done everything I could; and to make an end of it I thought out one prediction whose answer was irrefutable. There was one more substance in the organic group which I could not get in England, which had only been made in Munich; if my general structure was right, the atoms in its lattice could only have one pattern. For any other structure the pattern would be utterly different. An X-ray photograph of the crystal would give me all I wanted in a single day.

It was tantalising, not having the stuff to hand. I could write and get some from Munich, but it would take a week, and a week was very long. Yet there seemed nothing else to do. I was beginning to write in my clumsy scientist's German – and then I remembered Lüthy, who had returned to Germany a year ago.

I cabled to him, asking if he would get a crystal and photograph it on his instrument. It would only take him a morning at the most, I thought, and we had become friendly enough for me to make the demand on him. Later in the afternoon I had his answer: 'I have obtained crystal will telegraph result to-morrow honoured to assist. Lüthy.' I smiled at the 'honoured to assist', which he could not possibly have left out, and sent off another cable: 'Predict symmetry and distances . . .'

Then I had twenty-four hours of waiting. Moved by some instinct to touch wood, I wanted to retract the last cable as soon as I had sent it. If – if I were wrong, no one else need know. But it had gone. And, nervous as I was, in a way I knew that I was right. Yet I slept very little that night; I could mock, with all the detached part of myself, at the tricks my body was playing, but it went on playing them. I had to leave my breakfast, and drank cup after cup of tea, and kept throwing away cigarettes I had just lighted. I watched myself do these things, but I could not stop them, in just the same way as one can watch one's own body being afraid.

The afternoon passed, and no telegram came. I persuaded myself there was scarcely time. I went out for an hour, in order to find it at my rooms when I returned. I went through all the antics and devices of waiting. I grew empty with anxiety as the evening drew on. I sat trying to read; the room was growing dark, but I did not wish to switch on the light, for fear of bringing home the passage of the hours.

At last the bell rang below. I met my landlady on the stairs, bringing in the telegram. I do not know whether she noticed that my hands were shaking as I opened it. It said: 'Felicitations on completely accurate prediction which am proud to confirm apologise for delay due to instrumental adjustments. Lüthy.' I was numbed for a moment; I could only see Lüthy bowing politely to the postal clerk as he sent off the telegram. I laughed, and I remember it had a queer sound.

Then I was carried beyond pleasure. I have tried to show something of the high moments that science gave to me; the night my father talked about the stars, Luard's lesson, Austin's opening lecture, the end of my first research. But this was different from any of them, different altogether, different in kind. It was further from myself. My own triumph and delight and success were there, but they seemed insignificant beside this tranquil ecstasy. It was as though I had looked for a truth outside myself, and finding it had become for a moment part of the truth I sought; as though all the world, the atoms and the stars, were wonderfully clear and close to me, and I to them, so that we were part of a lucidity more tremendous than any mystery.

I had never known that such a moment could exist. Some of its quality, perhaps, I had captured in the delight which came when I brought joy to Audrey, being myself content; or in the times among friends, when for some rare moment, maybe twice in my life, I had lost myself in a common purpose; but these moments had, as it were, the tone of the experience without the experience itself.

Since then I have never quite regained it. But one effect will stay with me as long as I live; once, when I was young, I used to sneer at the mystics who have described the experience of being at one with God and part of the unity of things. After that afternoon, I did not want to laugh again; for though I should have interpreted the experience differently, I thought I knew what they meant.

Part 2

Love and the Friends

Chapter 1

The uneasy freedom

I

For weeks after my discovery I was head over heels in work. But there was no strain now, and I went through it with content. I wrote three papers, entered into a long discussion by letter with a methodical American, who always began 'with reference to yours undated upon the structure of –', corresponded with Lüthy over a detail in his results, lectured to various societies in Cambridge and the Alembic Club in Oxford, visited several professors who had become interested in my work through Macdonald: it was an active, flattering, unthinking time. Then, as a climax, I was asked to read my papers to the Royal Society.

All my other work had passed into the obscurity of 'taken as read': and I half-wished that this had gone on happening, as I crossed Burlington Yard, feeling oddly nervous. A musty Victorian smell struck me when I pushed against the heavy doors and left the summer afternoon. Ever since, that smell, however it came, whatever my mood, has plunged me back into the moment of nervousness, excitement, pleasure, which I possessed as I stood in the hall of Burlington House and passed into the drawing-room. For this, you see, was my Mecca and my Westminster and my Rome; this was the greatest scientific meeting-place in the world, it was here I should come, when I was elected into the Society – I dared to hope within the next ten years. At least, in cold blood, among my friends, I should have said – 'I ought to be an F.R.S. at thirty-five': but now, walking into the room, I was so young and shy that my future had vanished utterly. I have never been as self-conscious as that before or since. As I went up to the table and asked for a cup of tea, I would have given any excuse to get away. To get away, to take the next bus to the Oval, to sit there in anonymity and give over the fight and the climb.

Then Austin came up and said resonantly: 'This work of yours has gone very well.'

'Yes,' I said.

'I always thought it would,' said Austin, 'from the first day you mentioned it to me. I could see it stretching out – in front of us –'

I felt better. I recognised some of the men in the room; one or two were very great names indeed: the room itself was full of memories of the great: there was Maxwell's portrait on the far wall, Faraday's near by: but now at my elbow was the reassuring fact of Austin's pomposity, as un-abashed here as in his drawing-room at home. The room seemed to shrink a little: I began to notice that the portraits had heavy gilt frames. There was a knot of very old men by one of the tea-urns: I began to wonder who they were. Macdonald came in, talking to another man I knew, and I felt the edge going from my nervousness. 'It was nice of the old men to come here for my paper,' I thought.

Soon the bell rang. The door into the lecture-room was opened, and the President passed through it. A few others, slowly, went after him. I turned to follow. The old men, having had their tea, went home.

But there was a respectable-sized audience, and as soon as I was on my feet I became something like myself; the first sentences faltered, and then I found myself talking almost naturally. I had decided long before that the best way to get the attention of a scientific meeting was to assume that everyone knew nothing outside his subject; I made a point of making it as explicit and easy as I could – rather, in fact, as though instead of addressing scientists I was confronted by their wives. This was the way of all the best scientific expositors, I found: I copied it, and it paid. Even this audience in the dim lecture-room roused itself from somnolence and gathered something of the dis-covery. Several men asked questions, and more than one added congratulations. The President himself was genially and noisily encouraging. As I relaxed in my chair and listened, without hearing the words, to the second paper on the list, I glowed with the comfort of having made a success. Macdonald and some more of my acquaintances told me so afterwards, as we went out; and the drawing-room became opulently friendly while we chatted just inside the door, with the President guffawing a few yards away.

I walked away down Piccadilly richly contented. The ecstasy of discovery had gone long since; it was only a moment, and even the next day it left no more trace than a dream. These visitations must come to a good many men, I thought; but they are so elusive that no one mentions them. Instead, we prefer the more concrete imaginings that we can hold on to in our minds; they are less rarefied, more comforting for common use; and, walking away from the Royal Society, I was enjoying the prospect of my ambition coming nearer. Soon, quite soon, five years or less, I should have my chance to lead a scientific attack. They were the desires I had told Audrey of, several years ago: they were crystallising, now. I should have my laboratory, my team of scientists, I could see some of the problems. The work would go brilliantly, I had no doubt of that, strolling on a rain-sweet evening while the warmth of applause still lingered. It would be strenuous getting there: but it need not be long. When I arrived, it would be more strenuous still; I wanted it so, I wanted everything which meant that I should have a part of science in my hands, and the power to bring it to understanding. I shall have it, I thought exultantly; the chances had gone my way, and this, that I wanted most of all, I should fight for and get.

2

A month later I was elected to a Fellowship in my College. Though it had been expected, the occasion did not lose its colour; and when the Fellows' butler brought the news and led me to the Chapel, as our custom was, I remember the streets of Cambridge looked unusually bright and airy. And our ceremony of admission seemed full of dignity, too, as the Master intoned in Latin and the candles flickered shadows that lost themselves high up in the roof. My first dinner at the High Table was very good, and the wine better than any I had tasted; and afterwards we sat round the fire in the Combination-room, and Merton and another man I scarcely knew presented bottles of port to drink my health, and I was told all sorts of customs that sound ludicrous now but were intimately pleasant to hear. Then we drank more port and I was shown the record of bets that Fellows had made since 1750.

At the beginning of the book I remember among a lot of local disputes that seemed oddly pathetic on the fusty pages, such as 'That Mr. – will occupy the living of Bourne before the coming Michaelmas,' and 'That Mr. – 's marriage will not bear fruit this year,' there was the entry: 'That the King of France will not be on his throne this day twelve-month.' It was a curious picture, those eighteenth-century clergymen, predecessors of mine, beginning dinner in the afternoon and then sitting round their wine for the night, suddenly hearing a rumble in the world outside. It must for the moment have troubled their security: but they made their bet and drank on, and wondered once more whether the next living would fall vacant soon.

I went to bed warmly happy and a little drunk. I gained a great deal of enjoyment in my first weeks as a Fellow. The solid and luxurious amenities had not come my way before, of course: the rooms which I was given were on a scale different from anything I had known; it was pleasant to sit at twilight and watch the light fade from the oak panels, and then walk to the window and see a mist drifting over the garden. I liked the affability of the High Table, and the wine. I caught myself wanting to bask in it all: in self-defence, ashamedly, I kept dwelling on the ambition that was a step nearer, now. I thought of running a scientific institute, how I should begin, get my men, help them to work; these were the first of the many plans I was afterwards to make. It was pleasant to indulge ambitions, still years away, while the present was full of well-being.

That first month was the most fallow time I had yet been through. It was like coming down into the valley after a moment on the peak. I cannot imagine any other time in my life when I should contentedly have gone in for long debates as to whether the doors of my rooms ought to be painted pastel-blue or grey-blue or dark-blue; yet at the time I spent hours on it, and it seemed natural enough.

I pleased myself by getting some fairly expensive pictures. For the first time I knew I had more than enough money for the next month's needs; it was a curious experience, being able to think whether there was anything I should like to buy. The Fellowship, together with its appurtenances, would bring me in nearly £400 a year; Macdonald kept on £200 of his grant; and so my income had doubled overnight, and I scarcely knew what to do with it. I remember strolling round Cambridge, feeling oddly as though I was acting a part when I bought a little Dufy for Audrey – as though this had only happened to me in a play, and that someone would come in and take the money away. To prevent myself touching wood, I ordered several pictures for my new rooms that I did not much like and which I was never able to use.

3

Then, quite unexpectedly, my mother died. One night, in the middle of dinner, I saw a porter come up, murmur to the Master, and hurry down towards me. He gave me a telegram: I was asked to go home at once, my mother was dangerously ill. I remember being surprised above every thing else; with surprise I saw myself ask the Master's permission to leave, walk quickly through the chattering rows of undergraduates in the Hall, get a car and drive away. It was all curiously mechanical; I do not remember what I thought about on the way home, or whether I thought at all.

My father took me into the sitting-room when I arrived. It was eighteen months since I had been home; during most of my Cambridge holidays I lived cheaply in London in order to be near Audrey; and suddenly it struck me how small the room was. Small and untidy and close-smelling. While my father was greeting me nervously, I could not help thinking that the room would go into a corner of my new dining-room. I had never seen it like this before.

'It's a stroke,' my father was saying. 'They fetched me home. I was at the office. And they told me it was a stroke.'

He looked very small and lost. An end of his moustache was drooping over his lip.

'Oh,' I said.

I added, unavailingly:

'I came as soon as I got word. How is she, now?'

'I don't think' – my father stopped – 'I don't think we shall have her long, Arthur. It seems strange. She was just like herself this morning. No one could have known –' He looked at me.

'I wonder if we shall ever be able to know these things,' he went on. His voice was distant. 'But perhaps it wouldn't be any better if we could.'

There was a silence.

'Can I see her?' I said.

'Of course,' he said, 'of course.' And then, 'She won't recognise you, Arthur. She hasn't recognised anyone.'

As I went upstairs, I noticed the carpet was worn through in patches. My mother's door, opposite the first landing, showed a glimmer of a light. I knocked and tip-toed in. There was one of the local nurses in the room, and a heavy sick-room smell. My mother was lying on her back, with eyes that stared unseeing at the ceiling; her mouth was twisted in what looked like a smile.

I went to the side of the bed, and called:

'Mother!' and, more loudly: 'Mother! I'm here.'

The nurse whispered to me: 'She can't hear you. She doesn't know you're there.'

I stayed by the bedside for a few moments, and went away.

In the early morning, while I was asleep, she died. They woke me, and I went down to her room: she looked no different from the night before.

My father was standing on the other side of the bed. A beam of sunlight came through the curtains and shone on his cheeks. I saw how unshaven he was.

I remained at home for the funeral and the high tea which an aunt of mine gave at the end of it. There were several relations there. I felt uncomfortable among the rush of memories they brought out. I had started among them, I had gone away, and they suspected me; they were shocked, I knew, because I was making no pretence at grief. I had felt almost nothing, and I could not bear to act my sadness. Why I could not dissimulate I did not know. It would have eased their minds – yet it was out of my power. All I could do was be polite, which made them think me more callous still, and watch my father, as he went from one to another dazedly answering their questions. I fretted at my impotence to help, as they forced sympathy upon him until he would look vaguely at me as though saying 'Oh, why are they here?'

The night of the funeral I contrived to get him away from them for a time. We left them looking over some of her photographs and knick-knacks, and went on one of the walks we used to take when I was a child. My father said nothing but kept at my side with his quick little steps. We turned up a lane that I remembered as smelling of limes: it was becoming a side-street now, with half-built council houses, and the grit of mortar in the air. Suddenly my father said:

'These people – they want your Aunt Bessie to come and keep house for me.'

'You won't have her?' I said.

'I'd rather go away to-night, and never come back.' He was sucking in his cheeks defiantly. 'If they pester me any more, I shall tell them so.'

We came to the end of the street, and turned out of the town. In front of us, across a field, I could see a man and a girl with arms crossed behind their backs, hands held at the waist.

'Arthur,' my father said, 'it wouldn't seem right if we never saw her again. I can't help thinking there must be something afterwards. I don't know what, but something. Not much like these people's heaven –' He waved behind us; I think he meant our relations. 'Not like this world, perhaps. Don't *you* think there's something, Arthur?'

He was appealing to me as though I were an authority. Imperceptibly, without my noticing it, he had come to ask me to settle his wonderings. The change had gone on through my young manhood; but now, when I fully realised it, it affected me to see the place I had grown to occupy in his mind. I hesitated. I half-wanted to say what I thought – 'There's nothing. As surely as I know anything, I know there's nothing ahead. Death is the end of all of us, for ever. And any hopes we have are just shams to keep ourselves from going out into the dark.' I said: 'We can't be definite, of course. But very likely there's something we can't pretend to know. Until it happens to us.' His face was eager, and I hurried on, trying to sound matter-of-fact: 'After all, life's the oddest thing in the world. It's so odd that any improbability connected with it seems perfectly reasonable. We *do* live: somehow or other the queer thing happens: and if we commit the improbability of living there is no particular reason why we shouldn't live for ever.'

'I'm glad you can say that,' he said. I felt uneasy.

'It makes it all seem not so much of a *jumble*. It can't be just a jumble. There must be some sort of a purpose behind us all. Though I don't expect I shall ever know what it is.'

'No one ever will,' I said.

'But if it's there –'

In my room that night, I retraced our talk. It was pathetic, and it hurt: it hurt that I should have had to give him the kind of escape which I despised: it hurt, and gave me a wry amusement, that he would be able to take refuge in his vague words and gentle speculations. Ah well, I thought, perhaps he'd be worse off without them. I leaned on the window-sill. The room was small and stuffy. Over the roofs beyond the little garden, I could see the lights of the town shining in the darkness; and, where the darkness fused into the starless sky, a signal light glowed red. Along that railway line, when I was a child, I had embodied all my journeys to come. I had looked out from this window and seen the lights of a train moving across the level blackness; and I had gained the double satisfaction of being snug in my room and going by that train to foreign lands.

It occurred to me that this was the last night I should spend in the room. My memory forced me to see a picture of myself ill, when I was fourteen or so, and my mother sitting by this bedside. I tried to shut out the picture, but I had been taken off my guard. In illness I had called for her, then: I told myself, with an emptiness inside me, that I had not spoken to her with the same affection until two nights ago, when I called 'Mother!' and she was unconscious.

We had been friendly, polite and kindly to each other; and I had thought, or pretended to think, that that was all. Now I knew it was not. Should I ever know how much more there was, or why I tried to conceal it?

I looked out of the window again, trying to take my mind back to lights in the distance: but I was feeling cold and empty. I had not often found barriers between myself and those to whom my heart turned. There was nothing I could do, now. There would never be anything I could do.

All through the years of research, there had been a half-thought in my mind: my father was getting old and might die before I was established. I should have to support my mother: it would cripple me. Now I had been given freedom from those ties. This was how freedom came.

Unavailingly I tried to comfort myself that she had got pleasure out of the success. I knew somehow that she spoke warmly of me when I was not there: I had a sort of self-protective consolation that she had been able to enjoy the news of my Fellowship. It must have seemed more of a triumph for her, to whom universities were strange and far-off, than it did to me. So I told myself, and I left the window; but it was a long time before I went to sleep.

4

Even to Audrey, I could not bring myself to confess that sudden pounce of regret. I suppose we all make conventions for ourselves of the sadnesses we may or may not admit; and at twenty-six, perhaps for reasons which went deeper than I wanted to know, I found it hard to recognise that my family was wrapped close round my heart. In the year before my mother died, I remember telling Audrey that my parents had never counted in my life. And I felt exaltedly detached and realistic. When young, many of us find it difficult to endure the softer facts of life: almost as difficult as the majority of people have always found the harder. It is a chastening thought which for years I had to force myself to keep in mind.

I met Audrey in London a few days after the funeral. I had gone back to Cambridge, and the walk with my father seemed a long time ago. It was weeks since I had seen Audrey: she had been on a visit to her aunt in Cornwall, and, busy with the arrangements that followed my Fellowship, I had been too occupied to go so far. It came as a delight, and yet with the intimacy of an old habit, to have her smile strike across at me and watch her hands as she poured out the tea.

'I'm sorry about your mother,' she said, after we had been comfortably quiet for a moment.

'It doesn't matter,' I said. 'You know, there was never anything between us.' She was looking at me intently.

'Nothing to matter,' I added.

'Still –' she began.

'By the way,' I said, 'we haven't celebrated the Fellowship yet. Let's do that to-night, shall we? I've even got a little money. Shall we? It'll be good to spend as much as we want. God knows we've gone without for long enough.'

'You'll be talking of settling down next,' she said.

'I can't believe I haven't got to think twice before giving you a decent dinner,' I said.

'We've got on pretty well,' Audrey replied, smiling.

We dined expensively at one of the fashionable restaurants. I have forgotten which it was; in my memory I keep thinking of it as Monseigneur's, but that is an odd delusion, for the place was not open at this time. But, though I cannot bring back to mind the room we sat in, I can remember Audrey very clearly: she was wearing a green dress that clung to her tightly, and her hair glinted like beaten copper, outside the circle of the table lamp.

We began to drink our wine. It set loose a spate of talk,

warming and exciting to us as we sat together. It was full of the associations that any lovers are bound to have: in that mood, a word would recall a person we'd known, a place we'd been to, an adventure of our own, and we could feel behind each other's words until the private jokes carried more of love than any declarations we could make. For when I told Audrey that I loved her, I was only saying what I could also say, in the same words, to any woman; but when I recalled how we had once spent a night in Nuneaton, that was something that was part of us both, a moment in our lives which would remain if we never saw each other after to-night.

At last we stopped talking. Audrey drank the last of the wine, and I watched the veins in her hand and lights from the next table shining jewel-red through the dregs at the bottom of her glass. She smiled, and a line faded from her forehead.

'I've a feeling,' she said, 'that you're going to get on in the world at a very great rate. From now on.'

I felt complacent, and a little ashamed. For three years ago we used to make our plans for the future – and Audrey's career was going to be brilliant as mine. And since then I had seen her try all manner of things, throw her quick mind into them, and then find they left her utterly cold: she had worked for the Labour Party in Surrey, but soon she came to me and said, 'Politics! They're just on the surface of things. What good are they?' She had toyed with the idea of doing some research for the League of Nations Union, and in a winter she laughed herself out of it. She did a little journalism for the progressive weeklies. Then that, like the rest, seemed to come to nothing, and during the last year she had been at home, talking with violent eagerness when she met me but never mentioning any career in front of her. I said:

'It's time things moved for me. And they ought to go on moving, with any luck. But I'm only one of us. What about you?'

'Too late,' she said.

'Nonsense,' I said. 'I ought to have made you do something before this. I should have done if I hadn't been struggling myself. And as it is I don't deserve much because I haven't. But there's still time.'

'I'm twenty-four, you know.'

'You can't waste all that energy.'

'I've wasted it pretty successfully up to now,' she said. 'Except I've managed to use some of it on you.'

'I've done all the taking,' I said. 'I'm beginning to see how much.'

She shrugged her shoulders.

'What is going to become of us?' she said, as though she did not expect an answer.

'I saw Mervyn the other day,' she added, after a pause. 'He got married last year. His wife's just had a child, he said.'

I remembered some of my old jealousies, and the evening, soon after we began, when she mocked at them as she told me of her first lover. I had never seen him, and I think this was their only meeting during our time together. My jealousy had vanished, so far as a pain in love can vanish, long ago.

'What is he doing?' I asked.

'He's an architect,' said Audrey. Her face was thoughtful. She gave a quick laugh that stopped suddenly.

'You wouldn't like to marry me?' she said. There was a sudden silence; before I could reply, she laughed again.

'But I wouldn't if you wanted to' – she was speaking very fast – 'because of your work. I mean, if anything went wrong, whether it was my fault or not, you'd always blame it on to me. You'd try not to let me see it, but there it would be. And I couldn't bear it. Think what you'd have been like during that last spell of yours if we'd been married!'

'You're making too much of it –'

She went on rapidly:

'It'd be as bad as marrying a man with a faith. It *would* be marrying a man with a faith. You're a religious, my dear. That's where you get your force. Perhaps not all, but some of it. And religion doesn't leave much room for anything else. You oughtn't to marry. Perhaps you ought to be a celibate.' Then she quietened, and smiled: 'I don't know. You're not so very celibate, after all.'

When we got to our room in a discreet little hotel in South Kensington, she lay quite still in my arms for a long while before we made love. Then she changed; she was trying to strain more out of love than it could give. Until I caught her mood, I was concerned, as I had so often been before, by the streak of desperateness that seemed to force its way out of her. And getting up early the next morning, for I had to return to Cambridge to give a lecture, I saw her face was still unrested as she slept. There was a shadow of the line between her eyes: at the corner of her mouth, where the paint had worn thin, her lips were pale and a tiny furrow ran on to her cheek. Uneasily I watched her; then I went quietly out of the room.

It was cold in the train, and the early sun shone frigidly on the flat fields. I had not had time for breakfast, my head was aching, the clatter of the train jangled on my nerves. I rubbed my cheek with the back of my hand: the bristles pricked and the skin felt hot. It was a pity the celebration should end like this, I thought. And persistently I wrestled with the question: Should I marry Audrey out of hand?

For I knew that in her protestations she was being, for once, less than honest with me – and perhaps with herself. She had spoken so quickly to shut out some other voice. I knew she would marry me if I asked her; and she would gain happiness out of it, and perhaps the content she had always missed.

I should like to pretend that this was vague to me and that I was entangled in uncertainties of what she wanted and what would be best for her. But I cannot excuse myself like that. As I looked out and saw 'Broxbourne' and an empty platform (and wondered, for a second, if ever a casual chance would take me there), I was certain that Audrey would, whatever she said, be glad if I married her at once.

And yet, all the time I was thinking of her, there kept running through my mind reasons why I should not marry yet. Reasons that did not go deep enough to calm me: and instead I had to chase them on the surface, not convinced by their very reasonableness. They were, of course, completely reasonable. While there was a chance I might have to keep my mother, marriage was out of the question. Now I had not to think of that, and for the first time I had enough money; but there was no sort of permanency or security about it. My Fellowship was certain for three years, probable for six; there were complications of College and University detail which made the future uncertain. Research is better paid in England than anywhere else, but inevitably one stays in suspense longer than in most careers.

But I knew perfectly well these were not the real reasons. They were worries, part of the risk that one would take a little less cheerfully because of them, but no more than that. I could not get away from the truth. These arguments of mine were a web I was weaving to defend myself from the facts. I did not want to marry Audrey. Why I did not want to marry her, I could not allow myself to know.

I tried to be honest, but it was not easy. I walked up and down my carriage irritably, trying to see her and myself clear of all the pretences that manufactured themselves. I was in love with her and she with me; I was grateful to her; she wanted to marry; her own desires left out, it would be the best thing for her – of that I was sure. I could marry without any grave risk. Yet I wanted to escape it. Those were the facts. But were they the facts? I thought. Did I love as much as a year or two ago? The question meant nothing to me: what could it mean? I was too young to know of passion dying. We had worn out some of our surprises to each other: many of our words, most of our ideas, we had heard by now. Yet this, if it took away the first shock of love, brought a delight of its own. I loved her. I had loved her for over three years, and I could scarcely think of a different state between us.

It was not that. Was it sheer selfishness, I thought distractedly, as I kept on my walk to-and-fro and the train swayed and rattled on. After all, I had very little to gain from marrying. I found the gaps between our meetings irksome but I had, as it were, acclimatised myself. And a week-end had an exuberance, an adventure, that I should lose altogether when we settled into a little house along Huntingdon Road. I could not be as selfish as that, I tried to think. It must be that the future was standing in the way. For all my hopes demanded that I should travel light, ready to take the risks. I ought to have my Institute working before I married. It was a more respectable hesitation than the others. I wanted to think it was true. I was as little altruistic as most men, I knew. But my selfishness, I thought, was on a different scale. Tiny bachelor freedoms, the amenities I must forgo – they were not the things for which I should deliberately hurt her. That might be another pretence, I thought, doubting myself, realising harshly again the complex dishonesty of one's own reasons. 'I don't know,' I cried. 'I don't know what's taken hold of me. I ought to marry her. I shall have to marry her soon.'

Chapter 2

Excuse for flight

I

During the week after my journey in that early morning, I was perplexed and a little angry. My mother's death had left me vulnerable, although at the time it was submerged beneath my cares for Audrey; and, coming when I was ready to be upset, the echo of Audrey's desire gave me no peace. I wrote her a long letter the morning I got back to Cambridge. I said nothing of our being married; it was clear enough that, when I could force myself out of my reluctance, I should have to act as though it was I to whom marriage was urgent. I remember thinking it was the first time I had considered any sort of simulation during our three years. I was worried and on edge. It began to seem inevitable that sooner or later the hesitations would recede, and I should go off, in a bad grace inside myself, to marry her. I went so far as to look at some houses on the Madingley Road.

Then – at the time I thought by accident – an idea, an off-shoot of my big research, threw itself upon me. It was so simple, so plain and straightforward, that I could not resist going into it. After a few days' work, I saw all sorts of prospects of which I had scarcely dreamed. Not only these structures I was unravelling at the moment, but others, quite complicated, right up to the simpler proteins, would give no very great difficulties.

A year before, these schemes I was devising would have seemed fantastic: now they were just a routine, so safe that I could let a first-year research student start on one of the organic structures. With a few months' hard work, I should have the outlines of a new subject, my own subject, my own branch of structural organic chemistry laid down sharp and clear. Whatever happened to me, there would be years of work in filling in the details. It was all beyond question. I was not even particularly excited. It all fell out so inevitably that it was difficult to remember I had started it. As I told Macdonald the news, I felt quite detached.

'It's a good line,' I said. 'Better than I hoped ... When I've got the outline done, there are years of work. Years of work for as many students as you can give me.' I had not yet told Macdonald of my ambition to run an Institute on my own. He thought slowly before he replied. When one knew him, it seemed odd that this ponderous-speaking man was making his mark as one of the most brilliant scientific publicists of the day.

'I suppose you're right,' he said at last.

'Yes.'

'You're a lucky man, Miles.'

I was a little chagrined.

'You've got a knack,' he went on, 'of getting on to things that open out – although you couldn't tell there was any opening when you started. It's a very lucky knack.'

He paused, and passed a hand over his square baldish forehead.

'It's a lucky knack. Or else it's a sort of flair. I've never been able to distinguish the two. Except by the pragmatic test, and that's obviously ridiculous.' I set myself to listen. He had a habit of going off on to argumentative monologues. But suddenly he stopped and his voice became brisk, as it often did when he was disposing of practical details which stood in the way of metabiological discussion.

'You'll go to Germany, of course. Next week.'

'What?' I said.

'You've got to get the main part of this finished. It's too important to risk a delay.'

'I can finish it here. In six months. Twelve, at the most.'

'Nonsense,' said Macdonald. 'Your first year as a Fellow – and Cambridge dinners – and your lighter amusements.' He had a knowing, elephantine sense of humour and, I sometimes suspected, a private life of his own. 'It would take you three years to finish it here. In Germany you'll do it in a term. There are no two ways about it. You can resign yourself to a little exile.' As he was talking, in his emphatic slow-spaced words, I found the resistance weakening. Half-surprised, I found I was willing to go away.

'I'd like to think it over,' I said. 'But – I suppose you'll make me go.'

'You'll go,' Macdonald said. 'And now to get back to the question of scientific flair. Is there such a quality, or do we just give the name to those who've had the luck? It's easy to say they've got flair after the event. I doubt if any-one has dared to prophesy a man has flair before he's shown it –'

2

I went to Germany. And I went in a hurry. I wanted to complete the work. I wanted to clear my head. It seemed, just as it has often seemed since, that by getting away I should give my difficulties a chance to adjust themselves. There was no reason in it: this faith in geography is a little pathetic, perhaps, but fairly common. So I sent a telegram to Lüthy, telling him that I was coming to Munich for three months (and got a cable in reply which began: 'It will give me much pleasure'), made my apologies to the College, spent a day instructing one of Macdonald's young men to carry on the routine work, danced, talked, and made love the night through with Audrey, and set off on my journey, tired, out of humour with myself and yet glad to be leaving, four days after Macdonald suggested it.

The parting with Audrey hurt. Since we met, we had never been separated for so long a time. And I knew that the separation was not inevitable, and she suspected it. I found myself concealing the truth, having to control the words. The spontaneity, that had lasted so long, was broken for the moment.

I remember her sitting on the bed in the early morning, swinging her legs. It was chilly, and she was half-wrapped in a dressing gown. In her eyes there was a look of bewildered pain.

'Things aren't too good,' she burst out. 'Why is it? What have we done?'

'It's my fault,' I said. I was standing by the mantelpiece.

'My temperament, more like,' she said. 'My passion for discontent. Queer how I chase it.'

'It's altogether my fault.' The lamp by the bed-head glowed on her skin. I noticed the hollow of her shoulder, left in shadow.

'Altogether,' I added. 'But — we must get everything straightened out when I come back.'

'It sounds easy. It isn't, though. It means, we've got to straighten out ourselves. And I've been trying to do that to myself for long enough.'

'We can do it,' I said.

She did not answer. 'Oh, don't let's talk,' she cried, after a moment. 'We've talked all night. We can say it all by letter. Don't let's talk.'

I tried to comfort her.

She came with me to Liverpool Street. Both of us had dark rings standing out on pale sleep-starved faces. As we kissed, I felt her mouth was dry.

All the way to Harwich, I carried that caress, and the picture of her after it: one short, quick wave and then she turned and did not look back. That was like her, I thought: and then so many other things like her came into my mind that I wanted to go back. To get the first train from Harwich, fly to her house, say: 'I can't go like this. Let's give up all this foolery. Let's marry as soon as we can.' I stood on Harwich station, undecided; it seemed a mere chance, over which I had no control, that sent me at last towards the boat.

I sat tired, heavy-headed, in the first hour out to sea. I remember being very rude to a fattish man with a north-country accent who tried to take my deck chair. Then slowly, as the ship moved on a sea that was like grey silk, a calm, a relief, mixed with my tiredness, and it seemed that this interval of watching the tranquil water would never end, that I should not have to worry any more. I was not thinking, I was soothed into a languid rest.

I settled down easily to work at Munich. There were no difficulties, I had all the ideas prepared, it was pleasant to see every hour of application eat its way into the mass of facts. I was in a mood for steady thinking along lines I already knew. It helped me to become quieter at heart again, as did my loneliness, which I resented and was soothed by at the same time. I got a kind of objective pleasure out of being with no one I knew, of having no one whose life was intertwined with mine; I could watch and enjoy, and I seemed to want nothing more. I was exhausted, and I think I slept longer hours than usual. I sat with charts and papers in front of me, working most of the mornings and afternoons. About four o'clock I used to leave off for the day. I found that five or six hours' semi-mathematical thinking was as much as I could do. I entertained myself by calling round at the university, talking to some acquaintances, very proud when I could produce sentences in German which were a little more than expressions of undoubted fact. Most evenings Lüthy politely suggested that we should go to some restaurant or other and drink beer. Occasionally we went to the Opera. Lüthy seemed to have nothing to do at night but take me out, and in my first weeks in Munich he never left me until after midnight.

Then one evening Lüthy, who had escorted me to a little café by the corner of the Ludwigstrasse, said, in the middle of some casual talk on education in England and Germany: 'Please. Will you allow me to talk to you?'

I had noticed that, through his indefatigable courtesy, he seemed a little troubled and preoccupied.

'Of course.'

He said, in his careful English:

'If I do not talk to someone, I do not know how I can go on. This last month –'

I had been in Munich for three weeks. I had been with him every day. I was beginning to be angry with myself.

'I cannot talk to my friends here. They would not understand. And there are other reasons which I shall show to you why I cannot tell them. But will you allow me? I ought not to ask you to listen; but you can be of help to me.'

'I want to hear,' I said. Lüthy ordered two more glasses of Hackenbrau, and began to talk quietly, feeling for his words, excusing himself when the English would not come:

'I will tell you of the beginning. It will take greater time, but it is better so.' He looked at me apologetically, and I nodded.

'It was two years ago. I was presenting my doctorate thesis and it was necessary for me to prepare translations of some papers in the Italian language. You will know the work of Antonelli? I do not know the Italian language. English – I only speak – as you know – one word and then another word, but I read easily. And French also. But Italian I do not know at all. It was thus necessary for me to obtain help. A friend told me to see a lady who work-ed at the Italian consulate. She was a German who had obtained a position in the consulate through skill at lan-guages. She kindly translated the papers of Antonelli. The afternoon I saw her for the first time – I knew she was to be to me as no one else had been. I did not wish to leave her; when I did, she seemed with me still. I loved her.' I had wondered where his preamble was leading to. But now I recognised the delight with which one invests every detail of a love affair. To Lüthy the consulate, the time at which they met, the papers they discussed – these were the vividest things.

'Soon we were much together,' Lüthy went on. 'We went to the operas, dances, cinemas, all such things. It was sum-mer. I do not think I can forget it. I can hear her words now. I can still hear how I asked if she allow – would allow me to call her "du". We were in the café in the Platz by the University, and we wished to go the cinema. She said I must not call her "du," I had known her only two weeks, it was too soon. We went from the café and walked many times in front of the cinema, I asking her to allow me, she still saying no.'

I could imagine Lüthy, polite and firm, arguing courte-ously as they walked under the lime-trees, and people watching their faces as they came beneath a lamp.

'I did not call her "du" that night. But in a few days we were living as though we were married. In all things. And I told her,' Lüthy smiled, 'it is strange that last week you would not allow me to call you "du".'

I laughed. Lüthy's eyes twinkled.

'So we have lived as though we were married. In all things. I wish I could tell you of her. She is tall and strong and – I think – beautiful. Though it would be strange if I did not think her beautiful. She lives in everything. Sport and politics and books – she lives in all things. And she is very gay with me. And I too with her. We laugh at little childish jokes. We are sometimes very childish together. I am not always as you see me,' he explained. He paused, and we drained our glasses and ordered more.

'We have been happy,' Lüthy went on. 'I never thought I could be so happy. She has been sometimes mother, sometimes friend, sometimes daughter. And each time I see her, it seems as though it was the first or second day.'

There were gaps between the words. But I felt the phrase sink into me.

'We did not marry,' he said. 'By marriage she must lose her position. And she has a good position. She will have a great career for a woman if she keeps her position. She is ambitious too. I have wished to marry. She too. We shall like children later. But with her position I could not marry her yet. Not until she has satisfied her ambitions. And until I am better situated myself. We are not paid like you in England, of course. I shall not have – what would it be in your money – four hundred pounds a year until another two years. Then I shall be thirty years old.'

I studied his head. His hair was a nondescript brown, his face long and thin. I had noticed with surprise the way in which women's eyes followed him as he came into a café. I thought of Charles Sheriff, who had the same gift.

'So altogether I am not a man to marry,' Lüthy said quickly. 'Most certainly not for a woman with her own position. A better position than mine. So we have not thought of marriage. We have been happy; and only our best friends know.' He paused, and looked across at me. His eyes were sad.

'A month ago,' he said, 'she was offered a position in the Italian Embassy in Berlin. It was a great position for her. You understand? It is an honour to be asked so when she is only twenty-two years old. I know that she wishes to take the position. But she does not wish to be far from me. And Berlin is far away. We can meet only a few times in the year.' He thought for a moment. 'I have not explained,' he said, 'that she must go if she can remain in the service. She must accept her promotion or she must leave. She is poor like me. She must go to Berlin, so that we are separated, or she must give up all and marry me. A month ago she must choose. I knew that anything I ask, she will do. And anything she asks, I will do. So I would not ask her to stay. She did not know what to do. At last she went to Berlin. Three weeks ago and three days. And I am sorry to have told you all these things, I am not so selfish when I am not miserable. But now, as I speak to you, I do not know how I can go on.'

I felt ashamed. I could not keep looking at him. I glanced through the heads at the tables round us; noisy cheerful heads: from another café nearby, hearty thwacking music came exuberantly out. It was a warm evening, and people were sitting in shirt-sleeves. The white buildings across the square were lit up by the moon.

'It's not easy for me to help,' I said at last. The remark sounded stupid.

'You have helped greatly already by your patience,' Lüthy replied. While he was speaking, his head was bent down over the table.

I had to say something: 'But may I tell you what I think?'

'Please.'

'I had something like this myself once.' As I said this, it seemed to awake my own troubles, solve them, make them remote and me warmly melancholy.

'Please.'

'It seems to me that you ought to ask her to come back. And marry you.'

'How can I?'

'If you did not, it will be because you are too proud to

ask her to sacrifice anything.' I heard myself speaking slowly to help him understand. If he had been English, I might have phrased it a little less pompously, I thought. 'I think it is a mistake to be proud in love. The greatest mistake. One ought to be able to humble oneself in love.'

Lüthy made me repeat the last phrase.

'Yes,' he said doubtfully. 'But of her? She has to give up so much –'

'She will be glad to give it up,' I said. 'I am sure she will be glad. She will love you more.'

'I think we cannot love each other more,' he said.

'But you are willing to lose her because you are so proud?' I felt myself getting indignant. 'You will lose her in time if you are away from each other. You are willing to do that?'

'Of course I am not willing,' he cried. 'But it is not so clear. Perhaps you are right, but it is not clear.'

'It is quite clear,' I said. 'If I could explain – oh! I wish I could talk German. But don't you see all these reasons and conflicts ought not to count by the side of the important things? If your love is right, you must be together; and if anything stops that, there is something wrong with your love.' Lüthy considered for a while, but I thought his face was not so stricken as when he was speaking of their parting.

'I must think,' he said.

Oddly light at heart, I drank some more beer. The night seemed pleasant, full of warmth and pleasant sadness and happiness to come. This café that I had never been in before was as familiar as the London of my student days; I was at home among this Munich crowd drinking and singing in the moonlight, and each of them, in that moment, had his loves and conflicts and aspirations, so like my own.

'Will you allow me to call you by your name? Without your title?' Lüthy was saying.

I smiled.

'Of course.'

'I must now thank you, Miles,' he said. 'You have helped me through this bad night. I must thank you for all things.'

4

Although I knew well enough that my irritation at Lüthy's indecision was inspired by my own, I found in cold blood that I was still not on good terms with myself. I sat in the sun by the lake, arguing it out. I realised ruefully how irritatingly trivial the best reasons are, when beneath them there is an obstinate desire. Or when, as with me, kicking pebbles into the water in my impatience, there was a medley of desire in opposite directions. My logic either seemed futile or else I could make as logical a case for the other side. At last I hounded myself to the finish; as soon as I got back to England, I should take Audrey somewhere on a holiday; and while we were living in love together marry her. There was still something in me which was uneasy, but when at last I announced my own future to myself in words, I was peaceful as I had not been for weeks.

I sent a telegram to Audrey. 'Back in six weeks lets go France immediately arrange future love.' I sighed with relief when I saw the clerk read over the printed capitals puzzled by the foreign words.

I went off and tried once more to persuade Lüthy to recall his young woman. He was more intimate with me now, and I was finding, as language grew less of a blanket, a sophistication and subtlety I had never suspected. I bullied him into what seemed more than ever the sensible, the only way. I was very much a preacher of decision, with my telegram off my mind. I passed over the thought that I had wavered for longer than Lüthy. With my trouble removed, Lüthy's confidences to hear, and work, which was going smoothly well, I enjoyed some of the most tranquil days of my life.

We talked a good deal of science. Lüthy was very much impressed by my new work. Often he criticised: 'That is a speculation,' he would say, 'you do not *know*.' Many of his objections were valuable to me later. In scientific things he had a scrupulous, academic, tidy mind. He had an immense grasp of detail. Problems on a large scale were out of his reach: he was amazed when I explained the scope of mine.

'I shall never think of things like that,' he said. 'It is marvellous. I shall never think – it is *wunderschön*.'

Those conversations on my work fitted into the peaceful days. Even my first meeting with Desmond did nothing to disturb them. I knew him by sight, for I had seen him several times at conferences: indeed I could scarcely have avoided it, as he had been vigorously making a name since the time Tremlin told me he was a rogue. He was a Professor and a F.R.S. by now. He arrived at Munich to look over the laboratory; Lüthy and I took him out for a drink.

'I'm trying to go round all the laboratories,' he said. 'We ought to get together now and then. All of us.' He had a round cheerfully unlined face, with a bald spot like a tonsure in the middle of thick black hair. His eyes were small and dark and shone with a merry opacity. He did everything quickly and untidily.

'I know of you,' he told me. 'Of course, I know of you. You've done this work on – on quinolines. I was very excited when I heard of it.'

He impressed me with his interest, though he had got my subject wrong. When I corrected him, he said quickly:

'Of course, that's what I meant. Quinolines would be ridiculous. Why should anyone do quinolines? But your work now –' Somehow, from the remark I had made, he was able to talk enthusiastically, his little eyes darting for a moment to Lüthy and back to me, each sentence packed with technical terms. I kept straining to follow, wondering what it was all about. But I felt a sort of humorous liking. I caught a puzzled smile from Lüthy. Desmond stopped at last, and drank a glass of beer. 'Wonderful work,' he said, 'wonderful work.' He smiled. 'We're doing some exciting things at Oxford.' He described them rapidly, unintelligibly, persuasively, rather as though they were samples he might get us to buy if he did not let us look at them too long. At the end he leaned back, wiped his forehead with a handkerchief, and said: 'It's nice to think of all this work going on in the Colleges.' He drank another glass of beer, and looked friendly and confiding. 'Doing science in the old Colleges. If I had the choice of the life I wanted, I couldn't choose better than that. I don't want anything better all my life.'

I was a little warmed with drinking.

'Perhaps,' I said. 'But don't you wish it were a bit more difficult? I mean, if science were harder to do, shouldn't we enjoy it even more?'

'I've often thought that,' said Desmond quickly. 'If –'

I went on: 'It's rather too easy. Anyone can get on if only they work hard enough. Industry oughtn't to be the only necessity –'

'Yes.' Desmond caught up my words. 'When I think of the dull dogs.' We felt very amiable, expansive and sympathetic. Reluctantly, he had to leave soon after, to travel to Vienna the next day.

After he had gone, Lüthy and I had another drink. Lüthy was looking bewildered.

'How much, he said, 'does Professor Desmond understand of what he is describing?'

'I thought very little,' I smiled.

'I also. Yet he has much reputation.' Lüthy was smiling too. 'Certainly he has a charm.'

'I suppose he has,' I said.

But I had scarcely given over indulging myself in those days of comfort when they were broken into, harmlessly at first, by a touch of anxiety. As soon as I arrived in Munich, I wrote to Audrey, and she replied, and in our usual way we had followed fast on each other's letters: since I went to Cambridge, we had got into the habit of writing often. A few days before my mind was settled, I wrote a long love-letter. I told her, I remember, that I was lonely, and it made me a little empty to sit in cafés at night and watch lovers glance at each other with a secret smile. She had not replied before I sent my telegram. I had not worried, and knew the telegram would bring one from her. But another week had passed, and I had heard nothing.

The first twist of worry I lulled by persuading myself that she was either with her aunt or on holiday with her father. Anyone who has waited for a letter from a lover will know the sort of comforting convolutions I went through. And anyone who has waited for a letter will know also how at each post the comfort utterly failed, and how I could feel my heart beating as I watched the post-man down the street until I saw there was nothing for me. Then I sank back, trying to calm myself by cogent reasons why she had not been able to write. Sometimes, before the post came, I argued myself into concluding that no letter was possible, and I went a walk, choosing my time to overlap with the post, as though I was indifferent to it. I always found myself returning soon after the post had been; and I walked up the street at a pace which I had consciously to control. As I opened the door, and caught in one moment the clean smell of the house and the sight of the little shiny black table where the servant used to put my letters, my throat was tight. I used to turn away, per-haps with a letter from Macdonald or Merton, telling myself that I had expected nothing else.

This went on for nearly a fortnight. Lüthy noticed that I was under strain.

'I expect you also find it difficult with your – with your Lady – away in England,' he said sympathetically. 'Diffi-cult in all things.'

'Yes,' I said. I did not tell him of the complications. His own depression lifted somewhat as he condoled with mine. Several nights he took me to one of the more dis-reputable haunts in Munich. It seemed to make him less gloomy, but I only felt more anxious, more troubled, as we sat by the edge of a tiny floor and watched sturdy fair-haired women roll their hips. They smiled mechanically at us, and I felt chilled. In that atmosphere of opulent, scented, gilt-mirrored sensuality, I was – absurd as it seemed – shy. Lüthy was amused, he laughed with some of the women, gave them his imitation of the Bavarian dia-lect, smiled with his shining white teeth. While he was carefree for a moment, I could not resist my shyness. I was homesick for the sort of love I knew; and when I thought of the love I knew, the worry took possession of me.

I wrote again. I pleaded, as neither she nor I had ever done. I did not know I could be so humble. As I wrote, I had a moment of relief. Then I had to go back to my waiting.

At last I heard from her. I had been at the university, trying to work away the time between posts. I came back to my rooms and found a telegram. Even as my hands unsteadily tore it open I had an impulse to burn it unread. It said: 'Must see you moment you return sorry Audrey.'

I tried to make what comfort I could out of it. But always at the back of the thoughts there was the sense of foreboding. Why had she not explained? What had happened? Why had she not written? I made pictures of how I would love her when I got back. I devised imaginary scenes in which I quarrelled with her and then gave her comfort. They helped while I kept them in mind; I believed, for occasional moments, in this future which was to be happy again.

I decided to return to England in a week. It made my visit a little shorter than I intended, but I told myself that the work was almost done. Lüthy was troubled when I said I must go.

'Let us meet,' he said, on my last night, 'when all things are good. We have been in difficulties all this time you have stayed. You have helped me so much. You are yourself in difficulties. It will not be always. Then we will meet once more.'

'Of course, we must meet again,' I said. 'I shall be sorry to leave you now.'

We were sitting in the café where he had told me his story a few weeks before. The great yellow clock face across the square shone from the white building. The wind was touching the leaves on the lime-trees, but it was warm where we sat. At the next table a man in a Tyrolese hat was talking about modern poetry.

'Aber wo ist die Kunst?' he kept asking. 'Wo ist die Kunst?'

Lüthy had a full glass in front of him, and he was looking downcast. I could see the moon reflected in a dark shop-window.

Suddenly I longed not to leave this place. I should have liked this moment, this neutral moment, to be played on by some trick of time and prolonged until I did not mind. I wanted to withdraw from the struggle, the disquiet, even the pleasures to come. I wanted to sit quietly and watch and not care. And I knew that, although I had been unhappy during much of my time in this town, my memory would let the strain fade away and give only the calm intervals: until, when I was tense with anxiety in the future, I should catch myself thinking 'Oh, if I could escape back to Munich and some of those placid evenings when I was young!' I can remember looking over the square, and the certainty with which I knew I should make a dimmed and pleasant memory of days when I had been torn with worry. Even now, though I ought to have been glad to get away, I did not want to leave.

I was escaping the doubts, going towards the certainty. Yet I did not want to leave.

'I shall be sorry to leave you now,' I repeated. 'But you understand how I must get back to England, how I'm aching to get back.'

Chapter 3

Homecoming

I

I arrived back at Harwich on a dull misty afternoon. All the last night I had lain wearily in the train, comforting and torturing myself by speculations: across the sea I could do nothing but stare at the slow waves that ran beneath the surface of the water. I was numb with fretting.

When I got on to the platform of Harwich station, I gained a moment's satisfaction from the familiar things — a cup of tea and the evening papers. I read for the first few miles; but soon I was gazing out at the heaths, where a light shone every now and then in the autumn mist. The evening to come was throbbing inside me again; she would meet me, where should we go, what should we say, what would the end of it be? And my eyes saw, without my knowing, the fields fade minute by minute into twilight. I was shaken out of imagining for a moment as we came to a station. I looked out along the platform, and saw the buffet lights glowing orange; it reminded me of Cambridge; I should like to have been at the end of the holiday, coming back for term, with nothing in store either excitement or dismay. Instead, the train started; I remember looking at my watch and, in my mind, seeing the hands move through another hour.

It was dusk outside now: the carriage lights came on, and my face was reflected in the dark-shining window. I was very pale and lined. I looked beyond the reflection, at black shapes of trees and an occasional light, until I thought I would glance at my watch again. We had left the station five minutes ago. It was a long time before the lights formed into patterns. When we came to the outer suburbs, I had waited so long that now time did not seem to matter. But at Liverpool Street I jumped from the train. My legs felt weak. For one sick moment I could not see Audrey. Then the crowd fell away, and she was coming towards me with her quick stride.

'Hallo,' she said, and kissed me. I clung to her. After a while she stepped back and put her hands on my shoulders.

'You're looking tired,' she said. Her own face was grave – but I could feel a difference in her.

'I've been travelling for thirty hours,' I said. 'Thinking about you and me – all that time. If you'd not been here!'

'You must have some food.' She took my arm.

'I want to talk,' I said.

'While you're eating.'

I realised I was faint with hunger. Audrey took charge of my luggage; I was only dizzily aware of what she did. She led me to the restaurant, ordered a whisky and some dinner. She was silent as I ate the soup: I noticed she was wearing a hat in a new fashion. She talked a little about a play she had seen the night before. I tried to say something about Munich. My voice sounded strained and breathless. I got through half a steak with difficulty, and, when I pushed it away, I found she was looking at me with steady shining eyes.

'I've got to tell you something, Arthur,' she said. 'I hate doing it.'

'Go on.'

'I'm going to get married.'

I felt nothing but empty amazement. 'Who to?'

'Charles,' she said. 'Charles Sheriff.'

'Why?'

'Oh, Arthur,' she replied. 'I happen to be in love with him.'

The words took hold of me, and left me nothing. I could see her across the table, gravely – I had not wanted to know her state, but now I was bound to confess it – gravely contented. Myself, I was speaking in a voice that seemed to be clamouring thinly far away:

'You can't be – after all our time together – after all this time we've loved – why in God's name didn't you write to me about it?'

'Do you think I wanted to write?' she said. 'Do you think it's been easy to tell you now?' she added.

'When was this?' I asked curtly, as though the facts were important.

'Does that matter?'

'When was this?'

She shrugged her shoulders. 'Oh, I've seen him once or twice a month for a fair time now. And, when you went away, I was lonely and – well, he took me about.'

'So it was when I was away?'

'Not altogether. We saw more of each other, though.'

'He made love to you?'

'Not technically,' she smiled. 'But he proposed to me a fortnight ago.'

'And you accepted him?'

'Yes.'

'If I'd asked you to marry me before I went,' I had to be certain, 'what would you have done?'

She paused. 'Married you, I think. To keep myself from falling in love with Charles. But I should have gone to him in the end, I'm afraid.'

I had worked myself up to indignation. 'He's been a friend of mine. For years. And now he takes you away behind my back. God, I should like to teach him –'

Audrey was smiling, a little sadly, a little mockingly.

'It's queer that even you have got to make a melodrama of it, isn't it? He can't help it. We can none of us help it' – there was a touch of the old desperation in her tone, but it was softened now – 'and if you want to teach him, I warn you, he's very much stronger than you are.'

Despite myself, I smiled; she seemed to lose her composure at the sight.

'Oh, don't do that,' she cried. 'What have I done to you? I never thought it would be quite as bad as this.'

We sat and looked at each other. The hurt pride and pretences had ceased to count; we were both bewildered, and I, sick with my own loss, felt an intrusion of concern for her.

'However can you live?' I asked. 'He hasn't any money –'

'His people may give him a little. He's just got a job at Southampton. Its worth two fifty.'

'And we used to wonder –'

'But we wondered because we didn't want to marry,' she said. 'Or we said we didn't. Now I do, it doesn't seem to count.'

I thought of my conflicts, when I had tried to persuade myself to marry her. I had been too obtuse to notice another love grow.

I tried to be matter-of-fact.

'I dare say it's not as important as we made out,' my voice sounded dulled. 'There are other things. Look, do you really love him, darling? I can understand in a way: he's a very attractive creature: but – oh! it seems ridiculous – will it last? I mean –'

'Nice of you,' she said quietly. 'I'll say it for you. He's not the man you are, Arthur. Not too many men are, you know. Lord, the world would be a pretty unrestful place if they were. Charles is immensely alive and amusing, but he's not your kind and he never will be. Don't think I've got any delusions as to that. But I want him. You must believe that, Arthur. I want him – as much as I wanted you four years ago. And I want to marry him.'

'Why?'

'Is it any good to try and explain these things?' she asked.

'It may be,' I said shortly. 'Isn't it possible this is just infatuation – the sort of thing one's body lets one in for?'

'It's possible.' She was rolling some bread into balls. 'But I don't think it's likely.' She looked up and I saw the cast flicker in her eyes. 'And can you separate these things, physical love and so on? I can't. Does one ever love just physically?'

'I don't know,' I muttered. 'I never have done yet.' I made my last throw. 'But why not try? Have an affair with him for a month' – I could feel my arms shaking, and a pulse throbbed – 'and see if you're tired by then.'

Very slowly she shook her head.

'It wouldn't make any difference. I don't want to try. And, oddly enough, I don't think Charles does.'

I was limp.

'You've made up your mind?' I asked.

'Yes.'

'Whatever I do or say, you'll marry him?'

'Yes.'

'When?'

'Quite soon.'

'When?'

She frowned. 'Next week,' she said.

'Oh!' A gibe flickered and faded, and left me more desolated. 'It seems a pity.'

2

We sat silent for a time. I kept turning round to look into the room, so that I could get away from Audrey's eyes; I looked back and saw her with her chin supported in her hands. I daresay people in the restaurant were curious about us, and one or two travellers must have got into their trains wondering vaguely about a young man and woman with lined faces, who had talked for an hour and then fallen into silence. I ordered coffee, and we drank it without speaking; and then I stood up to go.

'I may as well get the next train back,' I said.

'No. You're too tired.' Audrey stood up beside me. 'I'm living in Katharine's flat just now. I'm going to take you there and give you a drink. And there's a hotel just by. You can sleep there.'

I did not want to resist being taken care of. In the taxi, out of long habit, and because I was miserable and loved her, I put my arm round her, and she took my fingers in hers and held my hand to her breast. We stayed huddled together, like children in the dark, all the way to the flat, which was somewhere near Regent's Park. Once she sighed. I dared not speak.

She led me into the sitting-room she had borrowed. It was small, and I got an impression of white shiningness. She put me on a divan by the gas-fire, and mixed two drinks. I remember the taste of my first sip with a strange acuteness, and Audrey resting her glass on a little table, and the gas-fire roaring redly in front of us.

'This isn't too good a night,' she said.

'I don't want another like it,' I replied. I broke out: 'I shall see I don't get another like it.'

She shook her head: 'I think you will. I've got a chance of being happier than you. Although I'm good at making discontents for myself, and you're as cheerful as an intelligent person can possibly be. But I shall be the happier, I think. Because, you see, I'm not fighting any more. I'm not trying to be different from myself. As for you – you're not going to get much rest. You could no more drift happily along than you could give up living. You *couldn't* drift happily along.' She paused. 'Not even if you wanted to. And you may want to, some day.'

'I think I want to, now,' I whispered. 'I'd be content –'

'You wouldn't,' she smiled gravely. 'You wouldn't. Not for a week.'

'I don't think it's any use to argue,' I said. 'I don't think I can argue to-night.'

'I'm only talking because I don't want to cry.'

I had seen her cry very rarely: but now, as I heard a tremor in her voice, I looked up and saw her eyes were bright. Ashamedly, I knew I was on the verge of tears myself. I was lying on my arm, and I buried my head into a cushion, so as not to see her; if I had not been brought up in a convention of control, I should have wept, but the tears were tight behind my eyes. I felt Audrey move towards me and stroke my hair gently, saying:

'Darling, I can't bear much of this.'

'What will it be like when you're gone?' I broke out. 'Oh, my love, I'm all the things you know: as selfish as most men, more conceited than I've got a right to be. I've done all the taking during these last years. I'm not a good man to love.' I raised my head. 'I don't know why you ever loved me. You've put up with everything, and I don't know what you've got. That's all true' – she had drawn my head near to hers, and was stroking my cheek – 'and tonight is harder because it's true. But if you leave me, I shall never be a whole man again. I've always come to you; we know each other as well as two people can. If you go away, you'll take most part of me with you. And I'll never get it back.'

'Don't worry just now,' Audrey whispered in my ear. She was flushed, and her lips parted. As I heard her voice, my desolation became part of a desire I had not known, that sprang up as though from nowhere: I wanted her, for comfort, for love, with a seeking for oblivion I had never known before. We lay, our faces close together, and there was the moment of understanding between us; she shook herself, turned off the gas-fire and, without a word, opened a door and took my hand.

I awoke and saw her resting on her elbow, looking down at me. A strip of sunlight fell across her face; she was smiling, but a little wistfully. The night before came back to me, and with it a weight at my heart. I put my hand on her side, and she relaxed and lay down alongside me. Her hair was ruffled over the pillow.

'The last time,' she said quietly.

'Is there no way?' I asked, but I knew.

'You won't make it too difficult, now?' she said. There was not a question in her voice.

A little while after, she said:

'It's rather late. I think you ought to be getting up.'

My legs ached as I dressed. We talked in a friendly way of some of the places we had visited together and we exchanged a few of the private jokes that had accumulated in four years. She packed my bag, smoothed my tie, scolded me because I did not eat my breakfast.

She was pouring herself another cup of tea when I said:

'I must go. Or else I shall miss my train.'

She did not get up, and I made no move towards her.

'Good-bye, my dear,' she said. 'Thank you.'

'I've got to thank,' I said. 'I shall be grateful all my life. However it goes.'

Her face lit up. 'I love your saying that.'

'It's true.'

'Ah well,' she said. 'I'll hear from you some time?'

'Later,' I said. I went to the door. I wanted to say everything I was holding back. I turned; I almost cried out; I said: 'Good-bye.'

Chapter 4

No other suffering

I

I went through it all again, in the days after I left her. And as the loss grew upon me, it was bleaker than anything had been before. When she broke the news to me, she was there to excite, to soothe, to comfort; it had hurt as much as any parting could, and yet, in the desolating hopelessness of being alone, I found it was taking shape in my heart as the end of happiness, not the beginning of sorrow. The real sorrow, the sorrow we know nothing of second-hand because it is not dramatic, because there is no action nor painful pleasure in it, came to me a day or two after I had said good-bye. I was sitting reading in my rooms: the creeper on the other side of the court shone gold in a low sun: suddenly I realised I was alone, and I could do nothing to escape from loneliness. I was hungry, not for love, but to be with her. I should not be with her again. I must shut out the thought, the memory of her. When I felt that empty coldness, I knew no other suffering could be like this; it could not be relieved by letting oneself sink into it, it had to be dully lived through.

I could not bear it with any resignation. I was silent through night after night of dinner in hall. Angrily I resented having to take meals with other people. At this time of all times I resented casual conversation with men who were close enough to irritate, too far away to be a comfort. I saw that Merton and some of my acquaintances were surprised and rather hurt. At moments when the memory of Audrey was pressing less heavily, I felt guilty of putting them at a disadvantage: there were always malcontents who liked neither them nor their young protégés. Now I was presenting their critics with an ill-mannered young man who went off to Germany for months with scarcely a word, and who came back to utter nothing except an occasional dangerously radical opinion. Sometimes, unable to face a communal meal, I had dinner in my rooms in solitude.

I wrote to Audrey several times. While my mind was telling me the break was clean and there was no hope, I would write, pleading, asking her to meet me, trying to play on the past, doing anything I could to touch her. She wrote: 'We mustn't meet until everything's finished. It would only make it hard again. I often want to see you and talk, but you ought to understand.'

Once, before her marriage, I went to London to try to see her, but she was at home with her father. I could not bring myself to go again. I had a letter from Sheriff: 'I ought to feel,' he said, 'like the wicked friend in a melodrama. But I'm afraid I don't, Arthur; you must believe that when I fell in love with Audrey, only she counted at all. And it would have been the same if I or she had never known you. It was the fact of her being herself that meant everything. There was nothing important except that. There still isn't. I still feel that fact gives a rush to life that sweeps away all the little irritations. It's the highest compliment I can pay that I should write like this: if I didn't know you, I should try to disguise the happiness ...' He went on to ask whether I should like him to visit me. I had very little anger left against him, but I decided not, why I was not sure.

It was painful to look forward to the wedding; but when the day came, I was less worried than by some trifling things. I had a far sharper pang a week after, when a friend in London sent an invitation to 'bring your young woman to dine with my wife and me, and we'll go to a theatre and dinner. Just as we did last June.' I got some satisfaction out of choosing a wedding-present; at length I paid more than I could afford for a set of old Venetian glasses. Shame-facedly, as I bought them, I was hoping that they would recall an incident private between Audrey and myself; but I excused myself by thinking that they were very beautiful things.

After the wedding I was actively unhappy for a long time. I did some work, but I had to force myself to it, and I could not achieve much self-forgetfulness. At work or away from it, I longed only to escape from remembered joy. I tired myself out by twenty-mile walks, I went to a great many plays, I tried to work up some new intellectual interests, I argued a good deal about communism and read a certain amount of academic philosophy.

Of course, I did a certain amount of posturing to myself. Apart from the deeper hurt, my pride had been wounded, and I made silly little attempts to heal it. For a day or two I even started to persuade myself that I should never have lost Audrey if it had not been for my Science; that here was I, the brilliant young man, with my eyes on the search to which I was devoted, putting love in its proper place – and naturally she wanted a humbler and less divided lover. But it was all too ridiculous even as a fancy to console oneself. I could no more have stopped being engrossed in work than I could have kept out of love with Audrey in the first place. Made up as I was, with my urges, strivings and anxieties, I was inevitably led to some vocation which made demands of me; it need not have been science, some sort of art or politics would have done as well, but to dismiss them all as less clamant than passion is to build one's human beings in a vacuum. On the moment, passion counts infinitely more than anything in the course of one's life: but, if it drastically alters that course, it is only by – what shall I say? – a social accident. I loved Audrey with a completeness that made everything else I did seem pale and abstract; yet, looking back, I see clearly what I dimly realised at the time, that love altered my life far less than did science or anxiety about money. It is not so easy to confess the part that my fears over money played all through my young manhood. But to leave them out in one's search for the depths of the soul is – to show how little one knows of the depths of the soul. The desire for security (of which money can often be the symbol) decides much of the pattern of our lives; and it is only rarely that we can dismiss it altogether, and even then we are not rid of it for long. Later in my life I was able to laugh at security, for a while; but the laugh was not altogether convincing.

Literature has not had much to say, so far, on this unpicturesque side of life. Few figures in fiction have chafed against their nostalgia for security. Of the writers I know best, only Dostoevsky, who was not conventional in his understanding, has entered with compassion into the state I mean. And Dostoevsky happened to have led a harassed life. Most of the adventurers I know, if one could catch them in an unprofessional moment, would admit the truth of what I have been writing. In a sense, I myself have lived by my wits since I was eighteen; a failure in an examination, a bad start in research, a mistaken choice – and I should have been a schoolmaster all my life; and I shall be old before I forget it.

While I was posturing, and ratiocinating myself into honesty about my posturings, there was always a still more uncomfortable thought: that, whatever I had done, she would have left me. That really I counted very little; she had loved me once, and now she was in love with Sheriff. Even if I had married her six months ago, it would have been the same. Even if my life and I had been altered so much that I could spend all my days entertaining her, she would still have left me for him. In the bleak moments, I believed that. Sometimes it seemed untrue.

I remember sitting in my new rooms, where Audrey had never been, week-end after week-end. In the past, a weekend had meant Audrey; and, as I looked out on the provincially empty Cambridge streets of a Sunday morning, I felt a barrenness from which I could not get away. I kept to my rooms through those dreary days: I could not bear the sights which recalled, not the past itself, but what it had not been.

While I sat in my room, a book on the arm of my chair, my eyes gazing at the low fire, I began unconsciously to know the fickleness of pain's memory. I had sat in rooms where we had passed ecstatic days and not been made to feel a twinge of sadness. But in this new room of mine, where she had never been, I felt the love which had gone embody itself until it was painful merely to watch the fire.

145

Occasionally my regrets had, I think – or perhaps I hope – an unselfish side. I was also sorry for her, that we had parted. I like to think this pity came from the other side of self-comfort. We had fitted so well, I thought – and that was true. Making all the allowances for jealousy I could, I still was not able to believe that Sheriff would match her moods as well as I had done. After all, I had known him for seven years. I was very fond of him. When I met him again, I knew he would charm me once more. But all the depths and light and shade that were Audrey's – he could no more enter them than do my work. The secret understanding she and I had had; the algebra of humour that we had developed together; the errant strain in her which got its answer, though a weaker one, from me; it seemed incredible that she would find this again, and I was sorry for her. For I knew that, even if I suffered and she was happy, the loss of these things would cripple her the more.

2

On an impulse, during one of the black days, I went to see Hunt. I had sent him word when Audrey was married, and he replied, commiserating. Otherwise I had not heard from him for over a year. He was still in Manchester at the same school. One Saturday afternoon in late November, with another week-end stretching ahead, I had to confide in someone. Hunt came to my mind; I thought of his letter; he knew us all, and could understand; in our student days, it was Hunt to whom Sheriff and I went for advice, though we found each other more entertaining. In an hour, I was on Bletchley station, waiting for the express to Manchester. It was a slate-grey afternoon, and an east wind tore down the platform. There seemed no one else about, and I was bitterly cold. I remember eating a Banbury cake in the refreshment room: it was, I think, a particularly good one, and the room smelt of oil. I cursed myself for having set out on the journey, I was bad-tempered and miserable.

As the train went north, the evening grew dark with fog. Impatiently I tried to read the weeklies. It was nearly an hour behind time that I stepped on to the station at Manchester and saw Hunt, wearing a shapeless overcoat and looking cold. He came up quickly, with that irregular walk of his, and smiled. As we began to talk, rather stiffly and shyly, about the weather and the journey, I was thinking how his smile had drawn me to him years ago; and at the same time I was noting that his accent sounded more clipped, less cultivated, than I remembered.

'You won't be very comfortable. My lodgings aren't luxurious,' he was saying.

'Nonsense,' I said.

'They're different from your style of things,' he insisted. I was a little embarrassed.

While I went on talking I knew there was the wish, gnawing inside me, that I had not come; after this lapse of years, we could not meet either as friends or interested strangers; if there had been no break, I should not have been occupied by his awkwardness, his lack of ease, that irritated me now, because they destroyed a picture I had constructed in the past; if we had been strangers, I should have accepted them as an obvious part of a young schoolmaster who might have something to say. After a few minutes, as we sat in a tram-car that jingled and clattered through the fog along the road, there was silence between us. I had to force myself to speak. And yet a shop's lights, dim and aureoled in the grey swirl outside, stirred me with a remembrance of how we had gone along the Embankment on other foggy nights.

'Do you remember,' I said, 'how we went to meet Sheriff once? When he had that passion for the girl in the chorus at the Finsbury Empire?'

But my own memory had been more diffuse than that, made of many nights and not one, softened, more youthful than this I had allowed myself to bring to light.

Hunt smiled. 'Yes,' he said.

'We never saw her,' he added. 'I wonder if they ever met.'

'You didn't think so, at the time,' I said.

'I don't expect they did,' he replied. We were talking impersonally, as though we had nothing to do with those days and each other: although I had the chance to talk on about Sheriff, the words faded into silence, and I rubbed the window with my sleeve and stared out at a lamp which shone redly through the fog.

Hunt's lodgings were down a side-street, and when he unlocked the door I felt a dense smell that once I should scarcely have noticed because I knew it so well: it was the warm smell of small old houses, and for me it is associated for ever with my first rooms in London. My home, now I think of it, must also have smelt very much like that; but that was the background of all the sensuous moments of my childhood, and so I cannot separate it at all.

We were met in the tiny hall by Hunt's landlady, a youngish brown-faced woman, who reminded me oddly of a Bavarian peasant. Hunt said to her: 'Can we have supper now? Don't hurry if you're busy.'

His manner to her was quite natural and unaffected.

'It's all right,' she said curtly, and went away.

Then, as he showed me to a little bedroom, the constraints, which had gone altogether while he was speaking to the landlady, came back again:

'I'm afraid this is pretty poor,' he apologised. 'But –'

I became unnecessarily boisterous in trying to reassure him.

The meal went on in that style. Hunt was uneasy, asked whether I should like the food (which was the sort we had eaten together for years in London – steak and chips and beer and a heavy pudding) and whether I was not oppressed by his sitting-room. Yet he talked to his landlady, when she served us, without a trace of difficulty or affectation.

I was infected by his ease with her: and soon I joined in one of their conversations, and Hunt began to talk to me much more as he would have done in our London days.

We drank some beer, and smoothly, enjoyably, we sympathised over Sacco and Vanzetti. We were both glad to find we had preserved our indignations. At last the landlady cleared away, and we settled into our chairs by the fire, and she brought us a pot of tea.

'You used to like tea at night,' Hunt said, pouring out a cup. He had not asked me whether I wanted coffee, but there was the faintest defensive note in his voice still, I thought.

'I do,' I said. We were quiet, but the silence was becoming more comfortable, now. He broke it at length:

'I was sorry about this business of you and Audrey,' he said.

'It seemed – unnecessary,' I said.

He paused. I saw the firelight flickering on his furrowed cheeks. 'But inevitable, I suppose,' he said.

I started. 'No. It could have been stopped. I ought to have stopped it –'

He said: 'I don't think you could.'

'Of course I could.'

'I thought it wouldn't last.' His voice was uninflected, confident, and it was I who had become on edge.

'Since when?'

'Since the first time I saw you together. After you'd begun your affair.'

'Why?'

He leaned forward, and I saw a flame glint, reflected, from his eyes. 'It will only hurt if I tell you.'

'I've come to talk about this,' I said, 'whether it hurts or not.'

I added: 'It hurts more not to talk.'

'I know that,' said Hunt. 'I know that rather well.' His face was set into deep lines.

'Go on,' I said.

'You wanted different things,' he said. 'You and Audrey. Opposite things. And there had to be a break. I wonder it didn't come sooner –'

'We thought alike,' I broke in. 'We were closer than you have any idea. I tell you we thought alike.'

'But she wanted something different,' said Hunt.

'We were honest to each other.' I was angry. 'And she told me what she wanted.'

'She told you what she thought she wanted,' he said. 'But what she really wanted was – something quite different.'

'That's too easy,' I half-sneered. 'How do you know?'

'By watching you both. And by what's happened. You

see, I was interested in you two a great deal once. I knew you so well, and –' He paused. 'I had some other sort of reason for being interested in Audrey.'

I noticed his hesitation.

The gaps as he searched for words impressed themselves more strongly than they had ever done. 'It wasn't hard to see it coming. Oh, I know you were fond of each other. You were both very much in love, to begin with, perhaps. That kept you going. But she was unhappy in a way, right from the start. Isn't that true? Don't you feel that?' He asked the questions quietly, intensely, as though he must have my own admission of the hurting fact.

'It's not true,' I said angrily. 'She was discontented, often –'

'It was deeper. She was discontented because you were both trying something right off' – he paused – 'the ordinary human path. And not many of us can do that for long. You could, maybe; it was easier for you. But Audrey! She was giving up all the things that she was made for. Marriage and children and some sort of intimate life. Just to watch you work.'

'She wanted to do things as well as live with me –'

'But she couldn't,' Hunt said slowly. 'There was nothing there. Do you really believe she wanted to?'

'One part of her did,' I answered. 'With her mind she did –'

'Do you really believe she didn't want to marry you? Almost from the start? That she was longing for it, and you wouldn't see?'

Again I felt his insistence that I should share in my own abasement.

'I think you're right,' I said.

I broke out:

'But why Sheriff? And why like this? And why couldn't I have had the sense –?'

It annoyed me to see Hunt smile ironically.

'Is it very difficult? You wanted to live the sort of life that not many have ever managed. She would like to have believed it was possible for her.'

'I see what you mean,' I said.

'But look,' I went on, 'there's something wrong. This business of her coming back for shelter. Getting comfort in the way women have got comfort for long enough. That sounds all right: but, Lord, if she wanted that, she was better off as my mistress than Sheriff's wife. She's not marrying a nice respectable man in the city, you know, but Sheriff! Who won't be constant for five minutes. Who hasn't the money to give her the things that I could. Who hasn't any of the things you'd expect her to want.'

'Women like him, you know,' Hunt said, after a moment. 'But that isn't all.'

'What then?' I was getting impatient. Years ago, Hunt's mind seemed slow at times; and now I felt it slower still. I resented the deliberateness – and, I suppose, the effect he had on me.

'I think it's because Sheriff's very much like her. I mean he's always hankered after the securities. He made pictures of himself as a Selfless Scientist, or a Bohemian, or a Don Juan – but he's never made himself believe in them. He'd like to be a Professor, because it would impress himself. Perhaps he will be. But what he wants is a pleasant house standing back in its own grounds. In a pleasant suburb. And a wife. And a child or two. And those are the things he'd still want, don't you see, whatever adventures or absurdities he got himself into. He might have been any kind of adventurer, you know. But still he'd have come back to his suburban ideal.'

I remembered something Audrey had said, while we were on the way to see Sheriff and Miss Stanton-Browne.

'I think I'm right,' he said. 'Things you'd do without thinking are a strain on either of them.'

He paused. 'That must be true of Sheriff,' he was speaking very quietly and clearly. 'It was true of all his make-believe when I knew him. All his fantasies went the same way. He always wanted to persuade everyone he was an English gentleman, one of the solid middle class. I used to think it was the queerest wish I'd ever met – but there it was, and for a long time he persuaded us, you know. I fancy he sometimes persuaded himself.'

I was puzzled. I had found Sheriff out in a good many

extravaganzas; more than once, with his unashamed grin, he confessed that some new conquest of his had not been as complete as he had somehow let us think: that he didn't know her well: that in fact he had only met her once. But these other doubts had scarcely struck me.

'I didn't know,' I said. 'I still don't know –'

'I thought you must have guessed,' Hunt smiled. 'You remember he used to tell us he was at Radley –?'

'Yes.'

'Actually, it was a secondary school in Portsmouth. And his family – and the house in Chiswick they used to have – and the little place outside Arundel where they moved; actually they'd kept a boarding-house in Southsea since Sheriff was a child.'

I laughed, but I felt tight-drawn and uneasy. Hunt seemed contentedly pleased.

'How did you get to know?' I looked away from him, into the fire.

'Oh, we often used to catch him in little things. You remember. And one day something or other let me see into him. I forget what it was. Some boast he was making. And I started to check some of his stories. I'm not as busy as you,' he ended, smiling twistedly.

He was right, I knew; there was no sort of doubt: it leaped to the mind as being right.

'How did we stand him?' I asked. But before Hunt replied, I hurried on. 'Of course, we couldn't help standing him. That's all. If he were here now, I suppose we should find him just as stimulating. Just as charming. We couldn't help being friendly with Sheriff. And if either of us saw much of him now, I expect it would be just the same.

'He took Audrey in as well,' I added, thinking to myself.

'In a way, perhaps,' Hunt smiled. 'Yet I don't know. He'll flirt with other women, but all the while he'll believe in himself as the loving husband. Romance and domesticity rolled into one. He'll be faithless and in his heart believe in the conventions: you were faithful and didn't believe. He'll go on, adjusting the past to suit his wishes; you're a comparatively truthful man. And all the time, despite herself, Audrey will trust him more than she trusted you.'

'I'm sorry for her,' I said. 'The thought of what's ahead of her. It's distressing me.'

'It needn't,' Hunt replied. He added slowly, 'And of course, it isn't. At least, not much. What is distressing you is – that she's gone. That she won't come back. That she'll be happy. That she'll find out Sheriff's lies, and laugh at him and scold him – and not mind at all. That distresses you. Isn't that it?' He was insistent again. I did not reply. 'Isn't that so?' he said again.

He went on. 'And there are other things which distress you. Wishes, fears, that lie underneath all you did with Audrey. Just as there were wishes and fears underneath her taking Sheriff. Deeper than the other things. But when one tries to put them into words' – he smiled diffidently – 'they seem fantastic. Much more fantastic than Sheriff's story of his life. You'll be angry when I tell you that it seems to me – you're hurt because you've lost her; but you're hurt much more because, in a way, you wanted to lose her, and you're tormenting yourself with that.'

'That means nothing to me,' I said.

'All through the time you were loving her, you resented yourself for it. I felt it: I couldn't say how, but I'm certain it was there. Perhaps the same urge which sent you to science made you want to escape from your love; or perhaps there was something subtler than that. But there it was, mixed up with Audrey. It made you love her more, I think; and want to get rid of her, and feel it to the limit of pain when she went.

'But we know so little,' he broke out. 'I've got a feeling what I want to say, but the words, the ideas, aren't there. These causes, that count more than anything else – and they are as mysterious to us as your science to a pre-paleolithic man. We knew about the world outside us, which doesn't matter very much. But about ourselves – why, we're in the pre-paleolithic still.

'And yet we could know,' he added. 'We could know, maybe we shall. And, anyway, it seems the job of our time to try. Do you remember I once said something like this to you before? After a dance it was. Audrey was there. And Mona –'

The name puzzled me.

'Sheriff had cut me out,' said Hunt. 'When it was all over, I walked home with you. And I had the first glimmerings of what I ought to try to understand. It was all very crude and young, but it's led me on. It still seems to me, and more strongly than ever, that we're lost without that consciousness: we've got to find it; we've come at the time when it is most necessary; and you can throw everything else away, science and luxury and all our vicarious little triumphs, if only we get through to it.'

I found myself revolting, to my own shame: I was thinking how easy it is to renounce luxury when one is never likely to know it, and success, when the hope of it has gone. It is easy to renounce the world when one has already lost it. And yet, at the same time, I was impressed.

3

'If only we get through to it,' Hunt was saying.

'It won't help me,' I said. 'She's gone, and – you know how it is – I can't believe I shall forget it.'

'I know,' said Hunt. He smiled, as I had seen him before, with pain seeming to shine through. 'I know rather well.' He paused. 'I think perhaps you haven't so much to grumble at, after all.'

The tone caught me, and gave me the comfort of another's distress assuaging my own; I found myself turn with eagerness, with excitement, into Hunt's life.

'What has happened?' I asked. 'What has been happening to you?'

He sat quiet for a moment. 'You remember Mona?' he muttered.

The name struck me again, as it had done earlier in the evening; I went into the past and recaptured dimly a pale, pretty, silly face, blank to Hunt, lighting up to Sheriff, as we sat towards the dawn; the accent of Hunt's reference struck me afresh and, with a sudden pity, I felt his story.

'You mean,' I said, 'you're in love with her still.' He turned in his chair; the firelight threw a shadow over his cheek-bone, and I watched it deepen and lighten.

'I've been in love with her ever since,' he said. 'Over six years it is now.

'During that time,' he added, 'I've kissed her once. And I pretended it was a joke.'

'Do you see her?' I asked.

'Sometimes. When she's not too busy. Otherwise I write. Occasionally she writes back.'

I was embarrassed. He was being too frank about his humiliation. I said:

'Does she know how much you're in love?'

'She's not very intelligent,' Hunt said. 'But I think she's grasped that fact.'

'She wants someone else?'

'I don't know. Sometimes I think so. Sometimes not. Perhaps she doesn't know herself. But she doesn't want me.'

'She must, a little at least,' I said. 'Or else she'd have stopped it before this.'

'Oh, she likes having a man at her feet. Who wouldn't?' He looked at me; his face was pale, and there was a line between his eyes, which, with a moment's sadness, reminded me of Audrey.

I was full of a medley of distress, excitement, self-comfort and impotence to help: and above all I could not altogether understand. I had never known much of Hunt's relations with women. Now, as I heard the slow short sentences with which he revealed a passion so hopeless that it hurt to listen, instead of commiserating I was possessed by annoyance – annoyance that he, who understood much of other people's affairs, should be weak and unavailing in his own. I was beginning to realise that he knew something of human beings which made me seem resentfully ignorant; and all the more I wanted to reproach him for not acting. After all, I had made something of a job of my life; he, who had shown me some of the reasons for my stupidities (and had, I thought, left out my odd capacities), should have been able to do as well.

I burst out:

'Why didn't you break it off? Once and for all. It would be hard for a while, but anything would be better than this. Why don't you break it off?'

'Do you think that would be an easy thing to do?' Hunt smiled.

'Not easy,' I admitted. 'It'd be very hard. But – you must do something.'

'I should like to,' Hunt replied.

'Is it really so hopeless?' I fumbled on. 'I mean, she may come to you in the end. Have you tried –?'

'It is quite hopeless,' Hunt answered. 'Sometimes for a few minutes – or a few hours – I feel it isn't; I feel despite everything that she loves me. But in my mind I know for certain that I am almost nothing to her. When I am not there, I know she forgets me. When I am with her, she is a little flattered and a little contemptuous – and very bored.'

'She bored by you. Anyone as stupid as that, bored!'

'It makes it easier to bore her,' Hunt said. He looked tired.

I asked for a drink. I was getting beyond irritation, I wanted to get rid of the empty sorrow that was reflecting itself from him in me. I noticed he was only pouring out one glass. 'Why aren't you drinking?' I said.

'I used to drink a lot a year or two ago. To forget the school. The dullness of that place! You've no idea of it. And to forget –'

He gave me the glass.

'To forget I was in love. I managed to forget, sometimes.'

'And then?'

'Then,' he said deliberately, 'I decided I'd rather go through it than not feel at all.'

I drank, imagining the asceticism with which he was trying to preserve something of himself. Hunt's faith, his demands on my honesty, and then this thwarted life of his – they made a pattern which, as I drank on, sank into me with an insistence that went deeper than my thoughts. They were part of me, now; they had aroused something latent within me.

Then I came back to Hunt, my friend, to whom I owed such a debt of remembered warmth and tolerance and shared discovery; I looked at him, and remembered arguments in London bars, nights in our rooms, the long hopes and quick frets of our student days, all thronged to make up the picture of him when he was my older friend. Since we parted, I had gone some way to success, and he was left with nothing. But the picture stayed of him advising sometimes, talking not so much as I did, ironic and generous; and it blended with Hunt as he was now, unhappy, ineffective, yet compelling my respect as well as the shadow of affection.

'It's a long while since we talked,' I said.

Part 3

Track of Ambition

Chapter 1

Effect of a revolution

I

After my visit to Hunt, I found myself urgently wanting to work again. The world of people which we had talked about for a day and a night, the world of suffering and unconscious cause, attracted me and, at the same time, drove me away. I was unsettled now; love and my friends were showing new layers of reality; and I wished that I could forget them and lose myself in the structure of crystals and the ambitions that insistently revived.

I went back to work. I achieved some sort of calm. In a neutral state that was neither happiness nor unhappiness, I took up the problems left over from Munich and worked regularly at them. My hours were not as long as they had sometimes been; at night, when once I should have been in the laboratory, I stayed over the port in the combination-room, and gained a perverse satisfaction from the discussions that kept splitting our society. Those arguments were as much removed from my personal life as the structures of my crystals; and they gave me a more humorous repose. That winter, I remember, we were divided upon the question of painting the college arms over the front gate. There was a good deal of violent feeling, which gradually took on a religious flavour. The Catholics and High Anglicans were all for paint, the Nonconformists for the grey stone; the Broad Churchmen steered a judicious middle course. The unbelievers were, however, divided. The College antiquary used to make things more complicated by suggesting that we had no right to the arms at all. He was a pleasant, quick-tempered old man; and one night, he struck the table until the candles shook and smoked, and shouted that he was against our present arms, 'those parvenu Renaissance vulgarisms.' He went out angrily, and there was some grave shaking of heads.

So I kept away the more probing discontents. I was lucky that, outside my own work, I could not help having my interest caught by the discoveries of that year. I have written 'discoveries of that year' coldly – and yet it was one of the chief years in the history of science. We were living through the greatest of scientific revolutions. For the past two years only the mathematical physicists had known what was happening: the others of us heard rumours, read papers, were tempted to disbelieve. I remember talking half-sceptically to Lüthy that summer: 'It won't make much difference,' I said. 'It can't make much difference.' I read more papers, heard more discussions, but it was some time before I began to understand. I got interested, I argued with Macdonald. 'If it's right,' I remember I said one day, 'there's no knowing what it means. It must be the biggest thing. The biggest thing of all.' Macdonald was cautious: 'I'd like to wait a bit. It seems all right,' was the furthest he would go. Then, one night at a meeting of one of the Cambridge scientific clubs, a few of us got talking on the future of science. Most of the members had gone away; we were standing among a litter of coffee-cups and cigarette-ends, and someone was arguing in a high-pitched voice. Suddenly, I heard one of the greatest mathematical physicists say, with complete simplicity:

'Of course, the fundamental laws of physics and chemistry are laid down for ever. The details have got to be filled up: we don't know anything of the nucleus; but the fundamental laws are there. In a sense, physics and chemistry are finished sciences.'

It is two hundred years since Newton talked of our being in the search for knowledge like children who pick up pebbles on the beach. This man who spoke of 'finished sciences' was Newton's successor. As I heard his clipped, impersonal voice, saying what to him was an evident fact, I realised for the first time how far science had gone. We were not picking up pebbles from the beach any more; instead, we knew how many pebbles there were, how many we had picked up, how many we should be able to pick up. They had found the boundary to our knowledge; some things would remain unknown for ever; one of the results of this new representation of matter was to tell what we could not know as well as what we could. We were in sight of the end. It seemed incredible to me, brought up in the tradition of limitless searching, mystery beyond mystery, the agoraphobia of the infinite. I resented leaving it. I gazed at the speaker's opaque brown eyes, angry with him for the insight and the vision that made my own belief in a hazy, unending progress seem, even to myself – both tawdry and second-rate. I wanted him to be wrong. Yet I could see what he meant. *We were in sight of the end.* I comforted myself by thinking of all the biological sciences; there were hundreds of years' work before us there; but even there, soon the framework would be laid down, and we should be just filling in the details. The nucleus and life: those were the harder problems: in everything else, in the whole of chemistry and physics, *we were in sight of the end.* The framework was laid down; they had put the boundaries round the pebbles which we could pick up; and my colleagues and I were dutifully collecting them. How long before the nucleus was in the same state? A few years, fifty at most. And life? Not so much longer. *We were in sight of the end.* It struck me how impossible it would have been to say this a few years before. Before 1926 no one could have said it, unless he were a megalomaniac or knew no science. And now two years later the most detached scientific figure of our time announced it casually in the course of conversation. It had all happened under my eyes, almost without my knowing it. I had lived through the great, the final scientific revolution; and I had to be told about it.

I went away and read intensively for weeks. I had a mathematical friend, a young man at Trinity, who taught me enough technique to help me get the general drift of Dirac and Heisenberg. I got through most of the quantum mechanical papers in the spring, and though I was always being held up by lack of mathematics, I think I understood it better than many physicists at that time.

It is rather difficult to put the importance of his revolution into words. In fact, it is important because it cannot be put into words. However, it is something like this. Science starts with facts chosen from the external world. The relation between the choice, the chooser, the external world and the fact produced is a complicated one, and brings us before questions of relativity and epistemology: but one gets through in the end, unless one is spinning a metaphysical veil for the sake of the craftsmanship, to an agreement upon 'scientific facts'. You can call them 'pointer readings' as Eddington does, if you like. They are lines on a photographic plate, marks on a screen, all the 'pointer readings' which are the end of the skill, precautions, inventions, of the laboratory. They are the end of the manual process, the beginning of the scientific. For from these 'pointer readings,' these scientific facts, the process of scientific reasoning begins: and it comes back to them to prove itself right or wrong. For the scientific process is nothing more nor less than a hiatus between 'pointer readings': one takes some pointer readings, makes a mental construction from them in order to predict some more.

The pointer readings which have been predicted are then measured: and if the prediction turns out to be right, the mental construction is, for the moment, a good one. If it is wrong, another mental construction has to be tried. That is all. You take your choice where you put the word 'reality': you can find your total reality either in the pointer readings or in the mental construction or, if you have a taste for compromise, in a mixture of both.

The scientific revolution that began in 1925 was altogether a matter of mental construction. Before, a great many pointer readings had made it necessary for us to use the mental construction of atoms made like solar systems – the Atom with which Luard fired my imagination when I was a boy. These atoms, of course, were never objects in the sense that a pin is an object: they were – mental objects, transcendental objects, bridges between one pointer reading and another. And if we went from our pointer readings and constructed our atoms and made them obey certain rules, then we could prophesy a lot of other pointer readings. As mental constructions, our atoms worked fairly well. But not well enough. Too many pointer readings were left unexplained, and even such explanations as there were had about them a queer arbitrariness, a lack of neatness, which left most of us dissatisfied. For nearly all scientists feel, rather than think, that their mental constructions should have the sort of economy which produces an aesthetic response.

During the time between the end of the war and the beginning of the scientific revolution, there was none of this economy. The mental constructions were affairs of patches, expediency, makeshifts and hope.

Then almost simultaneously a few men began to think along different lines to the same end. The model atom was not good enough. So let us, they said, get rid of models altogether. Let us stop thinking of these transcendental objects as though they were ordinary objects we can see and feel. Instead of the transcendental objects, we will have mathematical expressions that will take their place. They will still be 'atoms'; but now we shall describe them in a definite mathematical way, instead of trying to make pictures with our senses in regions where the senses cannot enter. These new mental constructions are the most economical that can be made between pointer readings; the idea had an austerity that went home to a certain sort of mind at once. And it worked. It worked like no other idea in the history of science. As soon as the model atom was thrown away and the new mathematical constructions made, atomic science fell into order straight away. At the beginning, to perform the operations, one or two rather obscure mathematical techniques had to be unearthed. And then paper after paper came out in the German and English journals; anomalies ceased to be anomalies, with this new clue; facts which had puzzled us before now fitted in completely; everyone who could read the work at all was certain, as they had never before been certain of any conception in science, that this thing was right.

I reached that state of final conviction late in the spring. It was convincing beyond the quiver of a doubt: I had never felt anything like this contemplative intellectual certainty before. Then, with the whole system stretching in front of me, I had to decide what difference it would make to my own plans.

It was fairly easy to see how the new ideas would include a theory of crystals. I could imagine the sort of explanations which would soon clear up most of the problems I had worked on. Even as I was reading the early papers on quantum mechanics, the first suggestions on crystals and molecules were beginning to come out. I could see, in the near future, these new methods restating my own work – and making my ideas seem like the guesses of an erratically clever child.

And my ambitions, I thought, my plans to lead an attack on the structure of biological molecules – why, however successful I was, in the end my ideas and solutions would be jejune beside the answers which the mathematicians gave. For the first time, I became dissatisfied, not only with what I had done, but with what I should do in the years ahead. Any achievement in my power would pass; that was bearable so long as the final explanation lay in the unknown future. But now, to know that all my achievements were foredoomed to be taken over in a way I could realise myself – it took the zest from my planning. I wanted to change over, use the quantum mechanics myself. But it was not so easy as that.

I could taste the new explanations. But I could not devise them. I could see the way physics and chemistry were falling into shape but I could not help. At least not in the way I should have liked. For, as I have said, these new conceptions were brought about by a set of mathematical techniques, and to take part in them one needed a kind of training I had never had. I am, I think, a fair natural mathematician; if I had studied the subject as a youth, I should probably have done reasonably well – and certainly I should have been in at the kill. But actually I had only the perfunctory mathematics of a physicist and most of that was rusty after several years' disuse. I thought it over, hesitatingly. To fit myself for creative mathematical work would take three or four years at the least: I was getting on for twenty-seven: by the time I was ready many of the ideas I wanted to work out would already have been seized. It would be putting myself to school again, for a very uncertain end. If I were unlucky, I should lose all my advantages as a clever young man.

But I wanted to do it. I think, if I had been contented within myself, I might have done it. If my private life had been happy, if a rather different Audrey had been living with me, ready to trust me into foolhardiness, I think I might have taken the risk. But I was not sure enough in my heart to throw away, for an indefinite time, all my consolations: now that love had gone, I could not lose the creative work into which I let myself sink, the certain success that was coming my way, the ambition that had grown since I began research.

Self-trainings such as I contemplated must be very rare: I have only seen two in the whole of my experience in science: in one case the man was supported by a skilful, adoring, flattering wife; the other seemed to have no life outside science at all. For most men, certainly for one of my sort, it would be very hard. But as I write, I am wondering uneasily how honest I have been. It is so easy to blame it on to Audrey. Should I really have taken a different course, if she had been with me?

At any rate I could not bring myself to the change. I had to sit by and watch mathematicians using the technique I ought to possess, tackling the problems I should have liked to solve.

3

As soon as I had made up my mind, I felt relieved and got into action once more. I planned the next years of research more quickly than I had ever planned anything. I had the appetite for work that came of being away from it for a while. It was good to find things to be done.

With those half-dreams of quantum mathematics out of the way, I wasted no time considering the other alternatives. I had no doubt of my choice. It was my years'-old ambition, strengthened, it seemed, by the vanquished doubts. I did not even argue with myself. The plans made themselves. Exact science, now its fundamentals were laid down, had only two fields of adventure left. One was the search into the nucleus; for all sorts of reasons, because I lacked the training and the manipulative skill, that was impossible for me. The other was the vaguer extension outwards from chemical molecules to living things. Both these problems, the nucleus and biology, were included, must be included, in the scheme of the quantum laws. But they were included rather as California was included in Hamilton's dream of the United States: as something which must be, though how he could not imagine. As a vision of certainty, but not a fact in the present. And so, I thought, there are two scientific adventures which are now worth while. In them one can be almost original – almost as untrammelled as a discoverer ever was.

For me, as I have said, there was no choice. Everything was in favour of branching out on to the structure of biological molecules. For years I had played with the idea; my first big research took me very near it; it was interwoven with my ambition; the method I had developed at Munich brought me almost into touch with the simple protein molecules. If I went a little further, and chose molecules not because of the interest of their structure but because of their importance in life, it would be something like an extension of what I had already done. I had all the technique. I knew my way about. It would be just a difference of stress, of intention.

So my course was clear. I could make it lead to the Institute that I wanted, that I should get before long. I got to work with more zest than for months past. Once or twice, when I had been trying to force Audrey out of my mind, I pretended to myself an appetite for work that did not exist. But now I felt a calm interest that lasted through a year's research, never flaring up, never leaving me completely. In that time I disentangled the structure of a family of sterols. It was a good piece of work, and I got some satisfaction out of it. But all that year the hours away from work were arid. There were so many painful associations in Cambridge: most of my friends had gone away; my enthusiasm for academic conversation, always intermittent, had dwindled until I found undergraduates' discussion of life as tiresome as their seniors' discussion of the university; and gradually I, who had once loved company, became almost a recluse.

I took to refusing invitations. I suppose I cannot have dined out more than half-a-dozen times in the whole year. I entertained very little myself. And it was a new experience to go to the theatre alone, as I did one night in the summer, and find I had not a single acquaintance in the house. I remembered, too distinctly, how a year or two before Audrey and I went together on all the Saturday nights she was in Cambridge; some friends would cluster round in every interval, throwing about opinions bright and new and polished. At that time I had been impatient of discussing art with young men and women who proposed only to be spectators of it all their lives. I used to grumble to Audrey that I had not much use for the amateur in anything. Nor for jargon of any sort. But now, as I drank by myself and walked through crowds in which I did not know a single face, I would have welcomed back those discussions, jargon, pretentiousness, youthfulness and all.

It was very warm and the sky still glowing when I walked back that night. Lights shone behind open windows; girls, in the town for May Week, ran into houses along the road, leaving a laugh in my ears and their scent on the air; dance tunes beat out from gramophones. I was out of it, standing outside and watching, desolated because others seemed to be possessing happiness and I had no share. Even though I knew the tedium of those parties, the disappointment which they left; though I had been through them myself; even though the year of withdrawal, since Audrey left me, had brought achievement that I could not lose; yet still I was miserable, with the warm wind on my face, hearing voices call across the street. I wanted to go to a party, to sing, to laugh, to get drunk, in order not to face the cold of the loneliness outside.

Chapter 2

The first move

I

Later in the summer I was invited to go to a Readership at University College, London. They were just beginning their policy of concentrating the biological sciences there; and they wanted me on the strength of my biochemical crystallography. I was to continue my own work and have seven hundred a year and an assistant. The only explicit duties were to help the biological faculty when problems of crystalline structure came into their work.

I could have wished for nothing better: it was a step nearer, and flattering and useful in itself. I accepted the invitation the day it arrived. It was far too good to miss, and none of my friends was able to devise a reason against it. Macdonald said, with his slow surprising smile: 'You'll just be going in time to stop me getting jealous. When you begin to feel jealous of a young colleague, Miles – do as I do, and go in for philosophy.'

Though we had admired each other since our association began, there had always been a constraint between us; almost at once, after I left him, we passed into a friendship, comfortable, understanding, and that remark of his, it seemed to me, marked out the change.

For most of that summer I was brisk and busy with plans. By the middle of August, the laboratory was nearly ready to begin. I took Jepp, the brown-eyed, aphoristic mechanic, from King's; and I had engaged my assistant, a fair-haired, long-faced young man called Cranch, who had just finished a year's research at East London College. There were a good many applicants for the job, although the unemployed research worker was nothing like so common as he was to become a few years later. Some of them had more experience and credentials than Cranch, but he seemed to me very able, and with a fervour about him that marked him out different from the rest. I decided that he would have been a scientist in any circumstances; while the next best of them would have worked at any profession conscientiously, cleverly, and without a spark of passion.

I moved to London before the end of July in order to see the laboratory fitted up; I spent some time looking for a flat, and in the end took one in Lancaster Gate. Walking down from the Park on those summer nights, and coming to my bright unfamiliar rooms, I felt a blend of exhilaration and melancholy that brought back the London of my student days: in that mood I had walked so often, on nights when lamps merged in the blue dusk, nights when Hunt and Sheriff and I had wandered and talked while the sky seemed scarcely to darken before the dawn; and we were excited and alive, and did not stop to name the sadness that rested in the warm air. Or perhaps when I came back and was reminded of those nights, I put into them a melancholy that was not really theirs, that belonged to the heart which had felt those friendships and passions change, and which was touched because the nights alone remained.

But during that month when I was working hard to get the department equipped, before I went off to stay with Lüthy in Bavaria, I was glad to be in London. For months past I had been dulled; and now I could feel the dullness passing. I was restless. And after the seclusion I had made for myself, it was good to be restless again. I was in high spirits, a little moody, more fluctuating than I had been, but eager and full of zest. I was glad to shake off the last year.

2

I got back from Germany late in September, and things immediately began to go well for me. Cranch got on to something good in that first term; and this, with my own work steadily progressing, gave the department a good start.

Results poured out easily, and without much effort on my part. So that I had plenty of time to organise meetings, look after Cranch, talk over various fields of science with my colleagues, develop the plans for the future, entertain people who might be able to help in bringing them about. I was living, in fact, something like the life which is expected of a young scientist.

I was helped into this state by my friendship with Constantine. I had met him in my first year in Cambridge, without ever, I think, talking to him alone. I remembered a vague liking and curiosity. Since then he had taken some minor research studentship in London, and I frequently heard his name. All kinds of rumours collected round him.

He was, I heard, the most original, the wildest mind in England; but the two or three papers he had published were models of painstaking dullness. He was the best conversationalist of his day, someone said; on the other hand I learned that he sat through lunch parties without producing a word. He was extremely charming, many people told me; but others said meaningly that he would go further in science if his intellect were not held back by his personality.

At last we came together, after a meeting of the Chemical Society. He was a year or two my senior, a tall man with a mane of tawny hair and a flat, almost Mongolian face; but his voice was rich and pleasant and when he laughed he gave himself completely.

When we were first alone, he appeared sulkily silent. I was a little put out, but thought I could feel that, under his impassiveness, he was shy at a potential critic. I could imagine diffident people taking it for aloofness and going away wounded in their pride. I wanted to dissolve it. We walked down Piccadilly from Burlington House; I tried to talk about his work, I was giving him as many openings as I could, annoyed that I was humbling myself without success. At last we were passing the lavatories in the subway at the Circus, and I was reduced to saying:

'You know, if we had to describe this age, we might pick on ourselves walking through here. Scientists and sanitation. And sanitation's even more modern than ourselves.'

'No,' said Constantine. 'That's a curious error I've noticed before. Every civilisation until the middle ages had sanitation of a very reasonable order. The Cretans did it very well indeed. Perhaps you'd say they were exceptional because of the odd economic stability of the Ægean civilisation. And so they had time for sanitary luxuries. There's something in your case. I wouldn't deny it outright for a moment. But don't you think you can over-estimate the stability of the Ægean? And also there was sanitation everywhere else. Sumeria: I don't mean the Sumerian Second Period, of course. But the third was certainly as good as anything in Crete before what we might call the Cretan Renaissance.' Constantine's eyes were alight, he was talking as fluently as though we had been in conversation for hours, attributing to me opinions I should never have entertained about facts which I had never even heard. That was like him, though; very soon I found out that, with a tendency to magnify his listeners in every way, he assumed to himself that their knowledge was on the same scale as his own. He never realised what I did or did not know; but, as soon as he ceased to be shy with me and felt I was friendly, he behaved as though he was arguing with himself, with an awkward, humorous charm and his immense array of facts. There are more facts in the world to-day than there ever have been, of course; and Constantine, using all the opportunities of his age, must be on the way to knowing more facts than any man who has ever lived. But apart from its oddity I should not have been impressed by the learning, had there not been beneath it a mind of extraordinary subtlety and strength. On that first evening, while he was talking of Shi-Hwang-Ti and Sir John Harrington and went on from sanitation to economics and developed a theory of the economics of China under the T'ang and the reasons why machines were not invented there, I was certain I had never met anything like it before.

I think he would have made a profound impression on me in any circumstances, but it happened that he came just when I was most ready to be influenced. I was back in London, played on by memories of early youth and the ardour of my scientific passion; I was in sight of what I wanted, and yet at times something seemed missing from the fulfilment. The disturbance that Hunt represented had its moments of vividness, more acute now than in the first intimation. I was pursuing a smooth, determined course; but there were times (more often than I realised, perhaps) when entertaining people for the future's sake, I became interested in them for their own. Constantine made me contented with my progress, gave it at second-hand something of his eagerness and – it is a strange word to use about science – his humour. And I began to see something of his wide horizons. He sketched out great international teams, working on long-distance plans at the deep problems: it chimed with my more personal, narrower, more practicable scheme.

He recalled and concentrated all the ecstatic moments I had found in science. Here was a man of the greatest powers who spent his time doing rather dull experiments very accurately. He did not pretend that he would not like something more exciting; but that might come his way; meanwhile, he went happily on, doing his own work, reading everyone else's, fitting it all into a great cosmic scheme. His research was not as well-known as mine. He had not gone as far. He was content with it. He was willing to make sacrifices to go on with it. He lived in something like poverty. He was the secretary of one or two international editorial bodies, which did valuable, humble, completely unrewarded work.

I had met many other scientists who would have claimed to do what Constantine did, working with intelligent devotion, not caring over-much how knowledge was obtained as long as it duly came. But, in moments of doubt, I had never been satisfied with their intelligence or their devotion. To question either in Constantine's case, however, would have not been worldly-wise but merely absurd. I did not know a more remarkable mind; nor anyone who wanted so little for himself. He was, in fact, the personification of my boyish dreams. If at eighteen I could have pictured what I should choose to make of myself, Constantine would have been very near the ideal.

So he exorcised my doubts. I became friendly with him, felt happy and alive, finding work pleasant and the future full of adventure. We talked a great deal, and collaborated in an idea of his. I gained very much in learning, in entertainment, in companionship of a queer sort. I told him of my schemes for the Institute; he became immensely enthusiastic, suggested possibilities I had never thought of, made my own idea more desirable than I had ever felt it before.

Chapter 3

Appearance of content

I

Working comfortably and successfully, exhilarated by Constantine, with ambition not too far away, I consolidated a sort of content. The move to London had relieved most of my anxieties about money: and that helped almost as much as Constantine. I had a stable income from my job, now; the seven hundred a year they gave me was not much larger than my total at Cambridge, but it was assured. And I added to it occasionally by a little scientific journalism for the American monthlies.

I was now secure enough, and could afford to spend. I think one has had to be poor to appreciate how rich and many-sided a pleasure spending can be. At least, that is the excuse I used to give myself for my delight in buying luxuries. I am sometimes a little ashamed of that delight but it is with me still, and has been since I was a student and had a pound or two to spare.

The friends whom I made later on, who did not know me in my youth, seem often rather astonished by this trait. Constantine was living in poverty when I first met him; but he was, queerly enough, the son of a Devonshire squire and had been to Winchester and King's. He found it all quite incomprehensible. My exulting over the vulgarities of luxury! He used to shake his head and try to reconcile the facts; and so have others of my friends, puzzled by the naïveté of my delight, misled by the expertness of some of my tastes. For though they had been born into the amusements I adopted, my knowledge was often far the deeper. That, of course, if they knew my beginnings, should have been reasonable enough; coming with fresh eyes, excited, interested, I was bound to grasp more than they had casually acquired. It is a mistake, typical of the great comic tradition of getting something wrong and then exaggerating it, to make your parvenu not know his way about his new surroundings: it would be truer to make him know his way too well.

Once or twice I tried to explain myself to some of my friends. While I was talking I knew the explanation was embarrassing them more than the puzzle had done. It hurt them when I had to insist on the poverty of my childhood. Defensively, they wanted to believe I was exaggerating; and that both my old misfortunes and my new pleasures were over-coloured. They suggested that this gusto in luxury was an affectation.

I began to go abroad for most of my holidays now that I was in London. Travel was one of the luxuries I had promised myself; I can still remember the exhilaration of those first journeys, the swaying of trains across Europe, the flickering names of stations, arrival at a place which changed on a sudden from a label into smelling, visible reality. And all the excitements of the first night in the hotel, the pleasuring of finding it better than some Platonic ideal of a Worst Hotel which lurks darkly in my mind, the first walk in the morning round the town, and very often – for I was drawn to it – the sight of the blue calm sea shimmering in the sun. And there was another interest.

On one of those early holidays I took a woman in my arms for the first time since Audrey. I was in Taormina and it was Easter: I was standing on the terrace of the hotel, looking out to sea. The sides of Etna were shining like edges of a silver knife; the great white triangle gleamed under the moon, and below it shone the little yellow lights of the villages round the bay. Away in the open sea a steamer's lights were pricked on the dark water. I looked down over the terrace, down the cliff to the shore.

Then I heard someone sigh by my side.

'Have you ever seen anything like it?'

I turned round. I had not seen her before: she must have come to the hotel that night. In the cold light her eyes were very large.

'Never,' I said. 'Except perhaps last night.'

'Were you here last night?'

'Yes,' I said. 'You've just come?'

'Last night I was at Girghenti, looking at those temples. Oh! there's so much of the world. There's so much to see. And yet –'

We went inside and sat in the lounge. Everyone else had gone to bed. I looked at her: she was about my own age, I thought, and had dark hair brushed back from her forehead. Her face was pleasant but not striking. She wanted to talk about herself, and I was there to listen.

I sorted out her story as she told it me. It was not all quite true (how many of our stories, as we tell them to strangers to relieve our hearts, are true?) and yet beneath the pretences, some of which puzzled me and led me on, I could not help feeling something of herself. She was frank and eager and composed: below there was a disappointment that tore through everything she said.

She was not at all wealthy. She had some sort of job, though she was very vague on that. She was an American; she had saved up enough money for a tour in Europe. For a fairly lavish and extensive tour. But that she was having, and that was not all.

She was enjoying it but –

'I don't know people,' she broke out. 'I see places. Place after place, and they're all beautiful. More beautiful than you can believe. But somehow they don't hit me as they should. It might be different –'

She had been all round the Adriatic, Kotor, and Durazzo, and Dubrovnik, and Trieste, and Venice. To her, those names had been romance. When she came to them, everything else she had ever seen faded into a drab monochrome behind their loveliness; and yet, as she admired, she knew that she might as well be back in Iowa – she'd be happier there, for she would escape the mockery of being alone and feeling beauty's stab.

Most of this I gathered on that first night. She talked a great deal, and often broke into the most banal of clichés. Yet when at last I got to my room, I was oddly disturbed. I sat on my sofa, staring out of the French window; the air was cool now, and the moon low over the sea.

'Poor devil,' I thought, 'poor devil. It's a pity things aren't better arranged.'

I was interested in her, in a way which concerned myself very little. I wondered how much she gave a name to her discontent. Did she just ache for 'romance', not think of it as embodied in a lover? Was it just a blind drive? I thought it must be something like that; she would know a little, and for the rest be urged on, unconscious, unaware. Yet she was not altogether innocent, I would swear. I puzzled it out to myself, wondering where the truth lay.

At the same time, altogether aside from my interest in her, I was wishing that she was in the room and I could make love. I don't think I pretended to myself that it was because I was curious about her; the curiosity was genuine enough, but it scarcely came into this; my heart was not touched at all, and I did not try to make an artificial flutter. Nor did I want to argue that it would be good for her. I was just hungry for a caress after long monasticism, in which wave after wave of desire had drawn back from the memories of Audrey and the final pain.

We spent nearly a week together before she had to catch her boat from Palermo. She was a trifle happier when she left: at least, so I liked to believe. I was not her dream of romance actualised; for that, she would have done better to go into the town and find a young Sicilian, olive-skinned and glowing-eyed. But that she could not well have done; and I, at least, was interested and understood. ('You understand a little. In a way,' she said. 'Not altogether, of course. No man could.' She clung desperately to the last shred of mystery.) At any rate, my arms made it easier for her to face the moonlight.

I remember the night we parted. She was going by the late train, and we went for a last walk on the cliff. The theatre was like a gulf under us, the proscenium shining white and clear below. We turned our backs on it and the mountain cone far away, and looked across to the Calabrian coast. A green light shone solitary among the yellow clusters. We stood wondering what it could be. A ship was moving slowly through the straits. From its bows the water moved, shining like mercury.

Her hand tightened round my arm.

'That's what we are,' she said. Her voice was throbbing. 'You and I. We're ships that pass in the night. Ships that pass in the night.'

I wanted to smile. And yet I knew that, in all its banality, the phrase meant more to her than anything I could say; she had heard it so often that it wore a place within her. Not unhappily, she sighed.

'Ships that pass in the night,' she murmured.

There were one or two more affairs after that pattern.

I was not in the least in love. After a while I became anxious, half-afraid that I had lost the power to feel; I was driven to see Audrey again.

2

I had not met her since we parted, three years before. Sometimes on my holiday, when I was trying to find in someone else the calm and excitement she alone had given me, I weakened and wrote to her. At nights the past could still hurt. I got a painful consolation from writing: and perhaps, with the malice of love, a sort of revenge. I flaunted my success in front of her, let her see that I was travelling to the places we had once planned to visit, while she lived in domesticity in the suburbs of Southampton. I tried to write cheerfully, indifferently, but sometimes hints of how I longed to meet her would escape. These she ignored, though sometimes I thought, and hoped, her letters were as unsatisfied as my own.

Then, surprisingly, a postcard sent off on my way home through Tuscany one September brought me a reply in Paris. 'Let's meet,' it said. 'It won't help, but I'd like it. There are things to talk about. I'm coming to town to shop in the beginning of October. Will you be back?'

I asked her to have lunch at the Berkeley the day after I got back. On my way down the street, I kept telling myself that the old love had died, that it was better it had died, that this meeting ought to be got through and forgotten; but I could not stop my heart from thudding, and my throat was tight.

She was sitting in the hall when I arrived. She stood up and smiled.

'You're looking older,' she said.

I looked at her: I could have said the same. The line between her eyes was deep, now, and her skin seemed not so fine, and I thought the powder lay on it more carelessly, more lavishly. Perhaps she guessed what I was thinking. She Said:

'It's three years, you know. Life's going on.'

'Your fault,' I said. 'We could have met long ago.'

'Oh, well,' said Audrey. 'We'd better not quarrel now.'

We went in and began lunch. She told me of a play they had seen the night before; Sheriff was in London with her, they were going back to Southampton the next day in time for term. 'My husband,' she said once, as though I did not know him.

We were both expectant as we chatted, and yet comfortable. Something, I think it was a word on the menu card, set us in a rustle of reminiscence. Soon we were smiling at each other, warmed by remembered laughter. At last she leaned back, and said:

'How queer this is!'

'You mean –'

'You and I, here like this. Talking about the things we used to do. And not knowing what's happened to each other since.' Her mouth was twisted. 'I'm beginning to wonder what I've done.'

We sat quiet. I noticed my fingers tapping on the rim of a wine-glass. I said:

'Things aren't too good?'

'I got more than I expected,' she said. 'A good deal more.' She hesitated, and then went on very quickly: 'I didn't know Charles at all. When I married him, I mean. I knew he played the fool – but I thought I'd allowed for that. You told me one or two stories. But I thought you were jealous –'

'So I was,' I said.

'Most men are,' and I was hurt by her smile, proud, maternal, loving, withdrawn into a life I did not know.

'He's an attractive man,' I made myself say.

Her smile faded: she shrugged her shoulders.

'Yes. I felt that, you know. But the rest of him I had to find out. Rather slowly. And very painfully. Perhaps the most painful thing that's happened to me. And all very comic, which doesn't make it any easier.'

'Much harder,' I said.

'Oh – I suppose you know – but the lies he tells! The queer vulgar silly lies! I know most of us have got fantasy worlds that we'd prefer to our own. Even you, my dear, used to have your occasional fantasies. And you're a realist – for a man. Even I have. But most of us don't get mixed up all the time between our fantasies and what is actually happening.' She paused. 'Charles can never distinguish between them. If he wants a thing enough, he expects other people to believe it's happened. And oh! the silly things he wants!'

'I know some of them,' I said.

'He'd like to have been born in the upper middle-class,' she went on. 'You knew that? Why, God knows. He'd like to have gone to a respectable public school and had parents with a house in London and a place in Surrey. So he invented them for himself. And told me about them before we married. And I, poor fool, believed him. For months.'

'I did too,' I said. 'For years. Hunt suspected before I did.'

'I kept coming across odd little contradictions,' said Audrey. 'He'd forgotten the headmaster's name of his own prep. school. That worried me. Then I couldn't find his parents. He said they'd thrown him off for marrying me. But letters kept coming from Southsea. I used to wonder. One day I saw the signature. I read it all, but – well, I've never pretended to have the instincts of a gentleman. They were from his mother. It all came out after that. I didn't know whether to tell him that I'd found out. In the end I did.'

'What did he do?' I said.

'Looked like a small boy who'd just been discovered. Looked mischievous, and a bit shamefaced. And then' – her lips quivered – 'and then he laughed.'

'And you?'

'I couldn't help it – I laughed too.'

As she spoke, she began to laugh again; and I joined in, so that people at other tables looked sternly at us, while we shook with helpless laughter.

This clowning made too many things ridiculous; all we could do was shout with merriment.

Audrey was still laughing.

'He isn't even faithful,' she said.

'What does he want?'

'He can't resist looking like a lover,' Audrey chuckled, a little ruefully. 'You remember that girl we tracked down years ago? The English Miss – Miss Stanton-Browne, wasn't it? He still goes in for that sort of affair. He likes them young and respectable and virginal; I don't think he goes to bed with them. Or even wants to much. Why's that? I don't know. The more I see of people making love, the less I think I know about it. There are too many varieties for me. We were very young, my dear, when we used to talk about love and think we'd got it straight. And very naïve.'

'Charles's variety is beyond me,' I said. 'Ideal affairs with giggling girls – it's not in my line.'

'I'd almost rather he did go to bed with them. He has, with one or two older ones. But he gets tired of them.' Audrey said: 'With the others he doesn't; and I can't help having the feeling that there's something I can't give him. Am I stupider than the giggling girls?' she laughed to pretend she was not serious. 'Or have they got more soul? Or what is it?'

'Perhaps they haven't eyes,' I said, 'and you have. Charles must feel uncomfortable at times with you.'

She considered.

'I used to think that. But I doubt it. He doesn't really mind being found out, you know. In a way he rather likes it. No, I don't think it's that.'

She looked at me and said: 'Sometimes I wonder if he has lost interest in me. Because there isn't any mystery any more. Perhaps he's more interested in a woman when the mystery's still there; perhaps he wants to run away from me because it's gone. It's rather hard' – her face was set and lined now, and I felt despondent – 'if one can't make love without throwing everything away. Including love.' She threw her head back. 'Oh, well! I may not be right. And it doesn't matter much anyway. But it's a nuisance to spend most of my time alone; and when he's there he's only making silly little plans. You've no idea how good it is to talk intelligently for once.'

'If you flattered me on anything else I'd be more pleased,' I said. She smiled, affectionately, as though she had taken my hand. Then she said:

'We used to be quite intelligent together, didn't we?' She added quickly: 'Or am I making that up? Perhaps you weren't serious when we were talking? Was it just your way of making love?'

'Of course I was serious,' I said.

'I've missed that a lot. More than anything else of ours.'

'I've never talked to anyone else like that,' I said. It was true, perhaps, but I was thinking how love recalled differs to the lovers, how the illusion of unity breaks before our eyes. For me, the moments I remembered with aching delight were those when, with our minds at rest, we lay and murmured and saw, as one night at the sea, a star above the mist outside. For her, it seemed, the moments which returned most piercingly contained not love but words, were part of those nights when we sat talking, and the world stretched out marvellously clear, and the tea became cold and the saucers full of ash.

'I haven't talked for months. And I haven't laughed much, either. And that means more than you'd think. We used to laugh at the same things, you and I. Didn't we? Even when I was bad-tempered and you were tired. Our sense of humour chimed, didn't it?'

'You weren't bad-tempered,' I said. 'Difficult perhaps. Sometimes. And I ought to have helped.'

'But we laughed at the same things,' she insisted. 'However things were going. Don't you feel that?'

'Yes,' I said. 'But Charles — he's one of the most amusing men I've ever met.'

'Oh,' she frowned, 'I know he's good at entertainment. And parlour tricks. And all sorts of comedy. High, low and knock-about. But it's not my sense of humour, and I'm tired of it. It doesn't help. It doesn't give an edge to things, as yours used to do. Charles would have been a good film comedian; but I'm really not amused by comic Greek dances while I'm getting up.'

'He can talk, though. Very vividly and well –'

'Not to me,' said Audrey. 'Perhaps we don't fit that way. I like my humour dry. Charles's – splashes.'

We watched each other's eyes; a nerve was throbbing at my elbow.

'The worst of it is,' she said, 'I shall get used to it all soon. I shall get used to sitting down and not thinking. I shall become the sort of woman we used to jeer at. Comfortable and good with children, and without an idea in my head.'

'You're not made that way,' I said angrily.

She shook her head: 'I tell myself that, but I wouldn't bet on it.'

'You've got to take yourself in hand.'

'One can't in these things.'

I broke out: 'That wretched fatalism of yours –'

Audrey smiled: 'I remember how you used to curse me for it. A long while ago.'

'If I had the chance, I'd curse you out of it now.'

'You're the only man who could,' she said. She looked at me with her mouth pulled into a smile; her pupils were very large. 'If anyone could shake me out, it's you.'

'You mean –'

'If you wanted, you could keep me awake.'

I hesitated, fumbling for neutral-sounding words:

'That wouldn't be so easy.'

'You mean you might be upset. But you wouldn't fall in love with me again. Do you think so?'

'I should resent it if I did,' I said. 'And perhaps you'd resent it if I didn't.'

She laughed.

I said: 'I've never contrived to fall in love with anyone else.'

'You will. And it sounds mean, but when you do – I shall be jealous.'

She added: 'I must go and meet Charles soon. When can

I see you next? If you're going to help me, you'll have to come down to Southampton. And stay a week-end now and then. That would give us a chance to talk.'

'I'll come very soon,' I said.

3

I did not go. For a time I played with the idea, imagined myself making love to her, in secret or in the open, speculated as to whether I could risk a scandal. But now I was only half in love: and I was out of love enough to know that the fancies could never happen. If I went back to her, I was not risking a scandal; I should merely be walking with my eyes open into jealous pain. For there would be no scandal: and that was too great a risk. She would not leave Sheriff. She was, I knew, still in love with him; sometimes despising herself for it, trying to escape, longing for some flavours out of the past, nevertheless she was captured in love. Whatever Sheriff did, however inconsequently he behaved, would only strengthen her love, I told myself; I knew too well, having learned through my own heart and hers. And also into my experience had come, not so directly but close enough to feel, the evidence of Hunt's passion.

Everything she had said, every tone in her moods, everything I had painfully gathered about the way love goes, told me the truth; that she would go on loving Sheriff regardless of herself and me, wherever it led her, until in the end she was healed by time itself. If I came back into her life, it would amuse her, but not take away her essential discontent nor the love that was deeper than unhappiness; she would sleep with me, and I should get some flickers of the old ecstasy; but it would not matter to her, and I was still enough in love to be hurt. I could imagine the pain when at last, after making love behind the curtains, something happened, as it must, to make her choose between staying with Sheriff and living with me. She would smile with regret for me, love for him, and say, 'I can't come. You knew all along, didn't you?' I had to keep away, I knew. There was a bleak pleasure in being able to do it.

Sometimes still, and for long afterwards, a quiver would come from the past; I was lonely and often hungered for love; but now, after my meeting with Audrey, it was for love generalised that I longed, not so much the love of Audrey. Because she had represented love for me, she came back to my mind, but without that quality which had once belonged to her alone, which had made her more real than love.

In some way this change had forced itself over me at our meeting; now, when I recalled her words, I remembered how many, which would once have hurt, had passed away as though instead of talking of her life with another lover she had been describing a new taste in clothes. As I listened, I had been hurt once or twice: but then in a way I could scarcely believe, although when I remembered them they hurt again. With amazement, shamefacedly, I had to admit that the mention of 'home' and 'husband', the breath of her present discontented settled life, went to my heart as nothing else she said. I tried to excuse myself by thinking that it was because Audrey, the Audrey whom I had loved, was being tamed into domesticity which she could never fit. But I was not hurt because of that. I was angry, not because she had taken to the conventions, but because I wanted them for myself. I was an emotional vagabond, with no ties except my work. But when I heard Audrey talk of 'home,' I wanted, more urgently than I could believe, all the trivialities, the worries and discomforts, the trifling joys, the trifling sorrows, that made up this intimacy of the commonplace from which I had escaped.

Often I remembered how Audrey and I used to jeer at it. 'Fine you'd look, putting my slippers on and sitting by the fire,' I would say. Now, when I walked by myself through autumn nights, and saw the street lamps shine under trees, I found my words of years ago tasting wryly on my lips; and, as I went past houses standing back from the road, and watched the windows glowing red, inhospitably warm through the darkness, I begrudged Audrey, coveted for myself, all the things which had once brought us together in mocking laughter.

One night, Constantine and I were walking through Kensington, talking science. For a long time now I had had no one to confide in. Hunt was too far away; and so I had listened to a good many stories, and told none of my own. Breaking through Constantine's ideas, some picture, some scent of the past made me suddenly empty. I began to talk of Audrey and myself. Recently I had found that Constantine, in an eccentric theoretical-seeming way, made love to a surprising variety of women. Perhaps that encouraged me to think he might help.

He looked a little shy and awkward as he listened, but in a moment he was as eloquent as ever: 'I've wondered sometimes if it helps in human relationships to make a systematic representation of all the possible forms of the three-body problem. In most unstable or metastable personal relations there are three people, of course: so we could easily give a formal description of all the systems which commonly occur. In fact, I did it once, a year or two ago. You start with the rather improbable case that all the three people are attracted equally and to the same extent. That case can be neglected, I think, though I can't see why it doesn't happen now and then. The other limiting case isn't very likely but might happen: the three people are repelled symmetrically and equally. We can work out a representation for that. Between the two there are all the other varieties ... including yours, of course ...'

He was sympathetic, even interested; but irritably I was thinking how he and I saw people with different eyes, how the human beings round him were shapes in an abstraction. A clever, wonderfully intricate, beautifully coloured abstraction of an ideal world – that was his vision of things, and it was so alien to mine that he might have been speaking in a language I did not understand.

I felt ill-done by, and at the same time amused. I turned the conversation back to science, and Constantine became incredibly ingenious about the composition of the atmosphere just before the time that life emerged.

By an ironical accident it was Constantine who set me free of the past, who brought about the crisis of my ambition, who was the cause of the most exciting time I had yet lived through.

Chapter 4

Success of a friend

I

I remember distinctly how Constantine first told me his news. I was giving a dinner party at my flat; someone had just told a story, and among the laughter Constantine hurried in. He looked more unkempt than ever, and very tired.

'Oh,' he muttered, awkwardly, 'I didn't know –'

His face set in sullen lines. He was restless with excitement; and I knew he felt helpless, neglected, among strangers. He turned to go, but I persuaded him to sit down to wine with us, and he stayed silent as the claret passed round. It was a queer sight. Anxious as I was to be left alone with him, I could not help being amused. My guests were two respectably emancipated professors and their wives; both the women tried to make conversation with Constantine, but he looked down at the table, a strand of hair hanging over his eyes, his flannel jacket grimy in the middle of their evening dress. They all became uneasy, and their voices grew a little louder; I wondered if they knew his reputation, if they knew that he was everything they tolerated in theory, and revolted from in practice – with his eccentric loves and politics and intellectual absorption. Whatever they knew, they were suspicious of his silence; I could see them taking it as a sign that he was too uninterested to talk, too disdainful to notice them as people. They would never have believed the truth, that he was simply too shy to speak. For him, atmospheres were either hostile or friendly; he could hardly say a word until he was soothed by habit or deliberate effort on the company's part. These people at my dinner table were to him

189

mysterious figures, possibly clever, probably disapproving; they were symbols of a world from which, in Bohemia, in women, in science, in the intricate abstractions of his mind, he happily escaped.

I had never felt so utter a lack of sympathy come suddenly into a party. Nor so many instinctive insecurities going wildly astray. If the rest had known what he was feeling, everyone would have been charmed. It was interesting to watch; but I was glad when my guests went, earlier than they had intended. Constantine had started to talk before I was back in the room:

'The most exciting thing is beginning to happen. I don't expect you'll believe it, but still –' he gave his quick pleasant laugh – 'it does look as though there is a method for making proteins just waiting to be used. Properly making them, synthesising them, I mean: it sounds fantastic, and the method's more fantastic than you can possibly believe. Not because it is complicated, but because it's easy. You see –' and he talked, with the eloquence and learning that still fascinated me, over a mass of facts and ideas, sometimes inventing objections for me that I should never have had the knowledge to raise. At last I got the outline clear. I had one or two questions of my own. He dealt with them. There were a great many complexities on the way to the conception; but, when reached, it was very beautiful, very simple.

'And it works? How strong is the evidence?' I asked.

'I should think it was pretty strong if anyone else had done it, but – you know – as it's my own I can't quite persuade myself it's true.' He was a little fine-drawn, but very cheerful. 'But I can't manage to get up a real argument against it except the Principle of Personal Fallibility. And there's not much use having a principle that one can't believe in. I expect I'm wrong, of course, but I should like to be convinced of it. I thought you'd see all the difficulties I couldn't.'

'This is tremendous,' I said. 'Lord, it's one of the biggest things.'

'If it's right' said Constantine.

'It sounds right,' I said. 'Oh, it's right.'

I was certain from the start. Perhaps because I was trying to keep my jealousy in check. While he had been explaining, I could feel the desire, the ungenerous, undetached desire, to find a flaw. My critical mind was sharper in edge than if I had read of this as the discovery of some unknown young man. I wanted to disprove him. I wished I was sharing in the discovery, I wanted to take a part.

'Where are the results?' I asked. 'Can I see them?'

'Everything's at the lab,' he said. 'I've been living there for the last fortnight. Literally living there, and sleeping beside the apparatus.' He laughed. 'It hasn't given me much extra time, but it's kept people away.'

'Let's go now,' I said.

His room at King's was more untidy than any laboratory I had ever seen. Before he could find his note-books, we had to clear his desk of layers of bills and letters; 'God!' said Constantine, as we turned over sheaf after sheaf. 'God! I never can find things when I want them.'

At last he saw them. 'I knew they were there all the time,' he said triumphantly; and for hours he explained while I read through figures and notes in his big childish handwriting. He was inexhaustible, full of facts and speculations, so much that I was both convinced and tired. He was happy, exuberantly at home, overflowing with a sort of scientific wit. He made a good many of his involved jokes that night; and I remember getting a surreptitious glance at a mirror which was hanging irrelevantly behind his desk, and seeing his face lined with laughter. Very pale, grey rings under his eyes, and his face strained but utterly at peace: so I remember him.

It was bright dawn as we went out of the College. Before I left him we strolled down to the river; the water was running fast, and there was a clean cold smell in the air.

'I expect I shall think of thousands of reasons why I can't be right,' Constantine was saying, 'as soon as I wake up. I always *have* been able to think of too many arguments against my own ideas. Sometimes I've wondered if I could be more useful by going in for a dialectical process in public: I mean, publishing the argument for one of my ideas, and then publishing the argument against it.

Instead' – he grinned – 'of waiting for someone else to do it for me. As they would have done if ever I'd put out anything interesting. The dialectical process might have been of more use. It couldn't very well have been much less. I've done astonishingly little, you know. When I look back, I can't quite believe the little that I've done.' He was laughing. 'If there aren't any holes in this, it might make up for some of those sins of omission. But something's bound to be wrong.'

2

Nothing was wrong. There was more in Constantine's discovery than he had dared to hope; and when it was announced, a couple of months after he broke into my dinner party, it immediately made his name. Constantine was the talk of all the scientific circles I mixed in. Many times I had his eccentricities, his universal knowledge, his Bohemianism, related to me. I got practised in listening with interest to stories which I knew to be untrue.

During the year after his discovery, I saw Constantine dragged out of obscurity, lionised by hostesses, promised a special Professorship by the Senate. It made little difference to him; he began to talk more freely among strangers, I thought, and occasionally he appeared in a new and almost modish suit. But that was more likely due to the influence of a new mistress than to success.

Of course, I was often jealous. That flicker of ungenerous discomfort which came as he first told me the news was not the last time I felt sick at heart because of my friend's triumphs. Sometimes I repressed it for long periods. I got some reflected glory as an intimate of his; I felt the gratification of having tipped an outsider; and also, there was a trace of genuine friendly pleasure. In the reaction from these moods I would tell myself that, in his unself-seekingness, more complete than anyone I had ever met, he was the last man in the world of whom one could be jealous; but I contrived it all the same.

It was the first time anyone with whom I had grown up scientifically, so to speak, had left me far behind. There were several men about my own age who had gone much further than I, but they were in different subjects; among the branches of molecular physics, one or two Englishmen were as successful at twenty-nine as I was, but no one had outdistanced me until Constantine reached fame. Actually, he was a little older, but we had been contemporaries in research at Cambridge; in fact his College refused him a Fellowship in the same term that mine elected me. Since then, in our companionship in London, it had always seemed certain that I was destined for achievement and he to be admired by his friends. Everything helped to make me feel a shock of envy, which, ashamed of it as I was, lasted for some time.

To myself, I was amazed at the convolutions that jealousy can take, just as when Audrey fell in love with Sheriff I could scarcely believe the sinuous windings of that other jealousy. Never, to anyone else, would I admit that Constantine had been lucky. But instead I found myself attacking his taste in women. I remember suggesting to Macdonald, who had become a friend of his, that his new mistress would have gone to anyone who was on the spot and blind enough to take her. We both laughed more fervently than the remark deserved. Quite often at dinner parties, talking of Constantine's greatness, I would lay a little too much stress on his incapacities, make him out a little more indrawn than he really was.

3

Constantine was proposed for the Royal Society in the year after his discovery, and I was with him the afternoon that the result came through. He was more distracted than I had ever seen him; several times he started a conversation and then let the words fade away, staring at the papers on his desk. I found it difficult to say anything. I was not sure enough of the details of the election to know how good a chance he stood; there were odd facts about his candidature that I did not understand. He had been put up by Fane of Manchester, whom I knew slightly in his Cambridge days; I was equally uneasy as to why Constantine's own professor did not sponsor him and why Fane did. For he was a man of acute and tortuous cleverness, already a little disappointing, not quite living up to the impression he made on everyone who met him. Constantine had come and stolen some of his thunder: and he was nominating Constantine. It might be chivalry, but I was uneasy.

And also I heard from Macdonald that Constantine was to be treated as one of the border-line candidates, who, instead of being picked by the sub-committee in their own subject, were discussed by the Council as a whole. I could not decide whether it added to the probabilities for him or against. We had talked about it this afternoon, when it became less of a strain to give up seeming indifferent.

'The physicists won't like me because I'm a renegade from physics,' said Constantine, with his smile of humorous humility. 'And the chemists won't like me because I am a physicist. And the biologists won't like me because I do biology. And the mathematicians won't know about me because I don't do mathematics. So I really don't see what I stand to gain by coming up before the whole lot of them.'

Not long afterwards he said:

'It's curious I should be so concerned about this affair.' He was genuinely, naïvely, surprised. 'It's quite unreasonable of me. I shan't be any the worse if I'm not an F.R.S. to-morrow, and there are all manner of stupid men who are F.R.S.s and some of the best scientists we know who aren't. It won't make any difference to my job or my research, and in the end all the good I get out of it is the pleasure of being recognised by people none of whom know enough about my work to have the right to express an opinion. It's hard to find a reason why I'm worried. But I am, you know.'

I did know; and I had to press back a smile at his words, so characteristic of him in his belief that actions are governed by reason, in his unrealism, in his preposterous honesty.

I turned him off on to the practical advantages which might come with his election. I led him to talk about our plans for the new Institute of Biophysics, my dream which he had adopted; if he were elected on the strength of last year's work, it would be an impetus against all the parsimony and hangings back; his voice would count far more with all kinds of officials, scientific and otherwise. To the outside world, Constantine in the Royal Society at thirty-two, ten years or more before the ordinary respectable scientist arrives there, would be an altogether more formidable and impressive creature than Constantine as a disreputable young man reputed to be gifted with one notable discovery to his credit.

Although I coveted the opportunities that lay in his reach, I was half content to teach him to make the most of them; and the afternoon slowly passed in his laboratory as I kept instilling into him: 'If this comes off, there are things you must do at once. Talk to the President and the D.S.I.R. and the Rockefeller people. Tell them *this* and *this* –'

'It's a pity it all has to be so complicated,' he grumbled. 'A few years ago I used to think human considerations didn't come into science. Perhaps' – he grinned ruefully – 'that's why some people dislike me still. I admit human considerations do come in, now. I can't help admitting it. But how much easier it would be if they didn't.'

Once, in a pause in his sentences, I heard a clock ticking. I schemed for a glance at my watch, hiding my wrist below the desk. It was nearly four. There was at least half an hour to wait.

I found a lump of Plasticine and played with it, pressing it into an elaborately curved shape and pricking it with pins. Constantine noticed it after a time, while he was talking.

'I may want that for models,' he said with a shamefaced brusqueness, and took it away.

'I didn't know ...' I said lamely. We looked away from one another. There was a long gap of silence. I felt a pulse throbbing faintly in my neck.

At last the telephone bell rang. I wanted to answer it myself; irritably, almost angrily, I saw Constantine lift the receiver, and heard him say 'Hallo,' his voice curiously muted. In the seconds while he was listening, I gazed over his head at the window. It was nearly sunset and thin red strips of cloud ran horizontally across the sky.

'Thank you,' said Constantine. He turned to me. 'They've elected me,' he said.

He sat down, lines of fatigue in his face, but his eyes shining. As I congratulated him, I could feel the calm delight which flowed from him. It was a moment; to a singularly happy man, it was a moment different in quality from the other ecstasies he knew, more personal than his scientific moments. For it was the recognition of himself as a scientist, as an inheritor of Newton and Faraday: and that was perhaps the thing he most wanted for himself. I began to talk very fast, warmed by his pleasure. But once more I wished it was happening to me. When we had decided that Constantine must be the most disreputable F.R.S. since Humphry Davy, he came conscientiously to elaborate plans for the Institute; I was not as cordial or as interested as I had been half an hour before.

That night I gave a party to celebrate, and Constantine sat on the floor in the middle of the room, with women all round him. As a rule he would have talked at his best and most involved, unaware that they were not understanding one idea in ten; he basked in their admiration and his words became a sort of sexual plumage. But to-night he was unusually silent and roused himself only with an effort. I knew that the aftermath was on him. He was sick with that depression, that sense of clear-sighted futility, which comes to us all with the achievement of what we have greatly desired. He would suffer from it less than most men, I thought; but even for him it was strong enough to spoil an evening.

I broke up the party early, and walked back with Constantine to his flat. A high wind swept against us, and the sky was black. Breathlessly, against the wind, we made our plans for the future. Now at last they came equally from both of us and brought us peace. For he forgot the disappointment that all triumphs are lost as soon as gained, and I the residue of my jealousy, while we realised in imagination a campaign that would require us both.

Chapter 5

The institute is talked about

I

Soon after Constantine's election, the Royal Society appointed a Committee to report on the desirability of a National Institute for Biophysical Research.

Macdonald sent me a note on Thursday evening, after the Council meeting. I remember the anxious thrill with which I read the names of the five Committee members; for they held part of my future in their hands.

Austin (London), Chairman. In Macdonald's big, neat handwriting there was a comment: *The President wouldn't sit on the Committee, because of that other affair of his. So your old chief, Austin, is to run it.*

I wondered why. Except that Austin was the sort of man who got himself on to Committees. Rather in the same way as he had just become a knight. The Institute's work was not his subject at all; but he had force, I knew, and an obtrusive personality – so here he was. What it meant to me, I could not decide. He had liked me well enough once, when I was in his laboratory. On the whole, I was not dissatisfied.

Fane (Manchester). I knew much less of him, I had only met him at symposia. He was about forty, and looked remarkably like Cardinal Newman as a young man. I was interested in him, and would have liked to know him; but I was not pleased that he was on this Committee. His sponsoring of Constantine began to worry me again; I wondered, though it seemed too subtle, if there could be a connection.

Desmond (Oxford). He was still progressing in the scientific world. I smiled as I thought of him, irrepressible, effervescent, contriving to be cynical in action and sentimental in his heart. There was a resentment between him and Fane, I knew: which might be a good thing.

Pritt (Cambridge). I knew nothing of him at all. He had gone to a Chair in Cambridge just after my time. Before that he had a long tenure of a professorship in one of the Welsh Colleges.

Constantine (London). He could not have been left out, but it was reassuring to see the name.

They have been given power to co-opt, Macdonald wrote. *That is meant for you. You couldn't be on the Committee, but in effect you'll be able to do as much as though you were a full member. There is no doubt in anyone's mind, of course, that you've got to have the Directorship of the Institute when it's formed. See that the Committee does its job without any more stupidities than are really necessary.*

That was like Macdonald. Uncompromising because in affairs like this he refused to let himself see more than the one, the obvious, the desired course. I wished he had been worse. So far as I could see, the Institute would be formed, substantially as I wanted it, within a few months: and it was for me to get myself the Directorship. About that I had no sort of doubt; it was the job I had wanted since I became mature, it was the job I should do well. It was the chance to reach my own ambitions, both the personal ones and those outside myself. In a few years the Institute would clear up the problems Constantine and I had first explored; I should be doing it, vicariously and with my own mind; and I should be well placed for the esteem and comfort that I needed. That was all. As soon as I read Macdonald's note, I knew my position with complete simplicity.

2

I was co-opted on to the Committee at their first meeting, as Austin wrote in a pompous letter, 'with all the privileges of expressing views of a full member, excluding the power to vote.'

I was looking forward to the struggle. I went to my first meeting keyed-up to play my hand. Before we sat down, Austin welcomed me, standing in the middle of the room and shaking his watch-chain.

'I am speaking for us all, I know, when I say how delighted I am that Dr. Miles is going to be with us in future – even if it's only in a non-elective capacity.' He laughed. 'I have known our friend Miles longer than any of you, of course. He started under me, *not* so very long ago, and the work we managed to do then has had its own modest share in making the project we're to discuss into a practical proposition.'

The same Austin, I thought; that 'we', that patriarchal assumption of responsibility for everything that went on round him, reminded me of early days when I began to find him out. But now, if he projected himself enough into my success to feel it was his own, it would be all I wanted.

We arranged ourselves round the table; and as, by a trick of habit, we sat in the same order through our months of meetings, it has become etched into my memory, probably as a composite picture of all the meetings rather than the first. But it is the first to which I fix it. I can see Austin leaning back and breathing hard, his face redder than his lips, and his paunch obtruding his businessman's waistcoat and watch-chain. There were papers in front of him, but he never wrote. On his right Fane sat, half turned in his chair so that his shoulder pointed towards us, often a smile on his subtle ecclesiastical face. Desmond, on Austin's left, was so much a contrast to Fane that the thought amuses me still; his bright dark eyes flickering like a lizard's, catching ideas, half-understanding them, throwing them out again. The supreme commercial traveller, the salesman of science, I thought again, as I had at Munich: glib with staccato phrases, unaffectedly the ordinary man, his round affable face looking like a Buffalo second in command, a lieutenant Elk. Next to him was Constantine, either abstracted or eloquent, usually not quite at ease. He appeared in an almost new flannel suit, but only seemed more out of place by the side of everyone else's office-like respectability. I was on his left, at the end

199

of the table, and between Fane and me Pritt had his place. I could not remember seeing him before; he was a not unhandsome man in an impassive way, with a high conical head from which dark hair was thinning and an out-thrust chin. His eyes, when I caught them for the first time, were opaque and dull.

That was the Committee as I still see it. Its first discussion, which lasted most of the meeting, was about the place where it should meet.

'I take it,' said Austin, 'we shall meet at regular intervals until we have thrashed out a report. And I take it that London, either here in Burlington House or in my rooms at the College, is the obvious meeting place.'

'I wonder,' Desmond put in, his eyes darting round us, 'whether we mightn't perhaps do better. London's a long way for some of us – particularly Professor Fane.'

Fane smiled.

'Oh, perhaps Professor Fane will say he doesn't mind leaving Manchester,' said Desmond cheerfully. 'That's reasonable enough: but ought we to bring him quite as far? We could put you up at Oxford, you know. As often as you like to come. I could put two men up in B.N.C. – and the other Colleges' – he waved his hands, and seemed to indicate Colleges pressing hospitality on scientific committees.

'It would be inconvenient to many of us,' said Austin, 'to have meetings out of London. And it would upset the centre of gravity of the Committee.'

'I should like to remind Sir George,' said Pritt, in a high, harsh voice, 'that we're not paid travelling expenses. If we have all the meetings in London, it will come unfair on those of us who live out of town. I should like to support Professor Desmond's suggestion that we have them in Oxford – and Cambridge. And in London in vacations.

I was learning. Austin's attitude, of course, I expected. He could not imagine a meeting taking place anywhere but round himself. But he was not a mean man with money, and the question of expense would never have struck him. Pritt's sounded like sheer peasant meanness; he was laughing with the jocularity of a man who does not intend to be done. And Desmond – he liked to think of entertaining us in Oxford, and he liked to think of saving money; he liked to look round us, reflect Constantine's Bohemian indifference, Pritt's peasant caution, all at the same time.

Fane said, 'If we took a distribution of our geography, we should reach a centre somewhere round Banbury. Would that satisfy Desmond and Pritt?'

Desmond at once responded to the satirical smile: 'While we're about it,' he said, 'we might have a good time every week-end at the seaside. Go round the coast, starting at Eastbourne and going west. Like Labour Party Conferences.'

'We're not as rich as Trade Union Leaders,' said Pritt. The rest of us were beginning to smile. Constantine was working out something; he spoke for the first time:

'Our average income must actually be a good deal greater than the Trade Union Chairmen or Secretaries,' he announced. 'Even if none of us had any private means, which is improbable statistically and which I believe isn't true.' With his born indifference to money, he might have expected the others to disclose their incomes: but, knowing that most of them would be shocked, I headed him off:

'Where do these Committees usually meet?' I asked. It was a relic from College meetings, the question of an irrelevant precedent. But it pleased Austin.

'The first I ever sat on,' he said loudly, 'was in old Kelvin's day. He died a year or two later, but, of course, he didn't expect us to go to Glasgow; he came to London himself, without any argument. I consider our friend Pritt has got this out of *proportion.*'

'Perhaps,' said Fane, 'we could get out of this impasse by what I might call an equipollent compromise. If we met in rotation three times in London, once in Oxford, once in Cambridge, and once in Manchester, that would represent us with equity enough to satisfy Desmond and Pritt: and, in addition, be quite remarkably inconvenient.'

'Only twice in London,' said Pritt. 'Miles is co-opted. He can't count for this.'

'As Chairman I should rule that Miles did count for this purpose,' Austin enunciated, 'if we adopted any such unworkable plan.'

Desmond broke in, 'Of course, we've got to have an arrangement which will work. It's easier if we meet at the same place. And at the same time. Like lectures. And bridge-parties. And any sort of whoopee.' He was enjoying himself. His sentences finished a little breathlessly, I noticed, and he looked round for an answering smile. The supreme commercial traveller, I thought again: and I recalled a public house where I went as a youth, and the travellers gathered round the fire. They would have welcomed Desmond as a man and a brother.

Fane smiled. His eyes were cold grey.

'I suppose you're thinking of Uncle Toby?'

Desmond laughed as heartily as if he had understood. Constantine's face suddenly broke into wrinkles of laughter. Pritt looked at him with distaste.

'We're wasting time,' said Pritt.

'We're considering a suggestion from our Oxford and Cambridge colleagues,' said Fane.

'The sense of the meeting is, I feel,' said Austin, 'that we meet in *London*.'

3

Ridiculous as it was, that first meeting taught me something. I had more insight into Desmond now; that flickering mental mirror of his showed as much of itself about a meeting-place as if he had been telling me the story of his life (not that it would be difficult to persuade him to tell the story of his life). The danger was, I told myself, that one forgot how that flickering mirror, that immediate salesman-like response, went hand in hand with an intuitive cunning; that men of Desmond's sort sometimes had the unconscious craft of a coquette; and that Desmond, who had very little mental machinery, against Constantine, who had the best I knew, would always win in a worldly battle of wits. It would be chastening to one's intellectual pride, if one set much store by the usefulness of intellect. But at the moment I could not see any personal motive for Desmond; and if he had none, he would merely go with the majority.

Pritt, on the other hand, might be a nuisance. Rudely, stubbornly, he would resist anything new or disturbing or adventurous. I was afraid, for I had seen it happen before, that ultimately the others would take him for a strong sound man.

Whether that happened or not he might cause trouble. For, as he was bound to, he resented Constantine, who was almost the negative of himself; and Constantine, as well as reacting sullenly from hostility, had the profoundest contempt for Pritt's work. 'Sound?' he said to me, when we discussed the Committee just after the names came out. 'Sound? They call Pritt sound because he has never done anything wrong. I should like someone to tell when he's done anything right.' Which was uncharitable, for Constantine. I wondered what Fane thought of Pritt; what Fane would say, if one could get him to talk in confidence. But I could decide nothing of Fane yet; after our next meeting I was enlightened a little, puzzled a little more.

We discussed whether we approved the principle of establishing an Institute. Later on, Austin said, we could consider whether the present time was opportune; for the moment we ought to consider whether we gave our sanction to an Institute at all.

'For my part,' said Austin, 'I am in favour of Institutes of this nature. With safeguards. Such obvious safeguards as attaching them, both formally and in fact, to some University. We must see that an Institute doesn't become a research factory, doesn't lose altogether the atmosphere and *contrast* of a University.'

'That's exactly what we do want to lose,' Constantine burst out, throwing back his hair. 'It's exactly that which will keep our scientific organisation medieval, even when our individual science is years beyond its present level. Why should we pay all this lip-service to Universities? What are Universities in their present form, after all? Accidental agglomerations for the study of Christian theology with Latin and Greek appended. And they didn't even do that well. And in their later days, they called what they had been doing humanism – which meant that it was cluttered up with superstitions and religion and morals and social barriers, and that they lived monastically while they were doing it – and added on a little science as patronisingly as they dared. Why don't we cast off all that – tradition of unreal thoughts? We've got a problem here, a definite problem, which it's the job of our Institute to solve, just that and nothing else. Why don't we work out just the best possible Institute to solve that problem? And if we find that it ought to be done among adult people instead of monastic young men, then let's have it among adult people and forget the rest. We're starting a new thing, after all, and why don't we work it out from the start?'

Fane spoke over his shoulder, smiling:

'I'm afraid I've not Mr. Constantine's faith in *a priori* thought. If a thing's been done before, we may not get the best: but we know how to avoid the worst.'

'That's what you mean by tradition?' said Constantine quickly.

Fane nodded. 'There might be more pretentious definitions.'

'We ought to admit, though, that there is an end to tradition. Where you're dealing with something quite new, qualitatively new, different from anything we've had before, I know we usually pretend it isn't new, and smuggle it under the wing of our tradition. Like science in the University. But it's an inept and frightened and inefficient way of doing things.' Constantine's head was flung back, and his eyes were looking, not at Fane or any of us, but into the distance.

'Somehow we rub along,' said Desmond. 'Patch up the system here and there. If you'd call it a system. We put Institutes into Universities, and call them University labs. It seems to work. Just like us in this country. Things seem to work.'

'Our friend Desmond is right,' Austin boomed. 'That is the way we introduce our changes, unobtrusively, discreetly – why, *anonymously* almost. And we don't mind what they're called so long as they justify themselves. I suppose Constantine wants to have an Institute with teams of workers on to each problem. Important problems, and teams of men with different functions . . .'

'Of course,' said Constantine. 'It's going to be the only way in the science of twenty years ahead.'

'... Well,' Austin smoothed his waistcoat, 'that'll happen of its own accord if you give it time. When I was a young man your age, I thought myself lucky to have one assistant; and in your laboratory you'll have nine or ten men, I expect, by the summer, ready to be made into a team if you want. That's how things happen, without any of us realising it.' He paused. 'But we seem to have got through as much work in my young days as you do now.'

'Perhaps I've not made myself clear,' Constantine protested. 'I want this Institute to have teams on a very different foundation. It ought to have teams got together for definite purposes – say, for example, the reproductive vitamin – work it out in all its possible lines, all the workers having a share in deciding the programme to be followed. It may take years, you would want biochemists, a zoologist or two, an organic chemist, a crystallographer and so on – then send them away and start another problem. Research ought to be consciously organised now; surely we have had enough of individuals muddling through?'

'I'm not sure we have,' Fane said, his voice lower, colder than Constantine's. 'I'm inclined to think we want more individuals in research, not less.'

There was a strange note in his voice, I thought, a brittle intenseness.

'I don't think much of an Institute made up of teams,' said Pritt. 'It would be like a crank school. We don't want a crank Institute,' he laughed.

'Sooner than an Institute on those lines,' Fane said, and I caught the note again, 'I'd rather have no Institute at all.'

Constantine, with a surprised interest, utterly genuine, leaned forward: 'But doesn't solving the problem count incomparably more to you than the details of how it's to be done?'

I was thinking, 'Save me from my friends.' Fane's cheeks had a faint flush.

'I don't believe very much in these teams of yours for solving problems,' he said, 'and even if I did, I think I'd prefer a few things in life were left to the individual man.'

'Faraday didn't work in teams,' Desmond commented brightly. 'Or Willard Gibbs. Or Maxwell. Hermits, all of them.'

For a moment he was, I think, imagining himself a stern misanthropic scientist, secluded from the world.

'We're getting away from the point,' said Austin very loudly. 'We were discussing the general question of establishing an Institute in principle. I suppose Constantine would be for establishing an Institute, whatever form was finally decided on by *us*?'

'I'm for any rather than none,' Constantine replied. 'Obviously, because any Institute will do a certain amount of work that needs to be done. The kind I want would do more in a shorter time, that's all.'

'What about you, Fane?' Austin asked.

'I'd rather have none than the mechanised pattern,' Fane said quietly. 'Definitely, I'd rather have none.'

4

After that meeting, I felt it was time I took a hand myself. Things were going badly; opposition right at the start was something I had never considered. Even discounting all I could for the reaction to Constantine's crusading, there was left a core of resentment which showed itself more and more. Resentment on Pritt's part to aggressive, successful, extravagant youth, both in Constantine and, more dimly, in myself; on Fane's part, resentment, as deep, perhaps more dangerous, but to what I was not sure. To youth, perhaps: to success he had just missed: I did not know; perhaps to the passionate faith which breathed in Constantine, which, if he had not lacked it absolutely, could have carried Fane so far. Perhaps he did not know himself. But he looked like being against every plan of ours. Of ours – it was a little unlucky I was allied so closely with Constantine. Without the presence of his greater success, his less amenability, they might have accepted me with more grace.

But, though annoyed, I was not in the least depressed: I

had to go through it by myself, I decided. Constantine would be worried and self-reproachful if I told him of the need for any sort of diplomacy; and probably become, through nervousness, more inept on Committee. Take away his spontaneity, and you took away his only personal weapon. No, I had to make my own plans and keep my own secret; and, if it came out right, give myself the pleasure of telling him about it at the end.

The next Thursday I found that Desmond was giving a paper to the Chemical Society. I listened through a long and petulant discussion in which he looked like a badgered small boy, his eyes flying about for help and sympathy. As the meeting thinned, I made my way to his side.

'Why are chemical societies always more quarrelsome than physical ones?' I whispered. He looked round and beamed.

'I've always wondered,' he said.

'Come and have a drink. You'll have time before your last train,' I said. By the time we were outside he had recovered his normal buoyancy.

'A queer, fierce, quarrelsome crowd they are,' I said. 'Why is chemistry the most conservative of sciences?'

'Because it's got no mathematical basis,' he said promptly. When he was not reflecting one's own ideas, his seemed to come at random. I tried to work it out.

'You mean,' I said, 'that there's nothing to test the new ideas by? And the old ones have all the force of tradition behind them. Back to Kolbé, as it were.'

'Any science without mathematics is bound to be conservative.' He was trotting with short steps beside me as we went down the road towards my flat. 'Physics is just the opposite. New ideas get a hearing. I'm a physicist by temperament myself, you know. Only I didn't have a mathematical training.'

I thought how often I had heard that regret, a little pathetic, a little absurd! On a more elaborate scale, I had even uttered it myself. It is the scientific equivalent of the regret of the clever uneducated man – 'If only I had had a proper education!'

'You *think* like a physicist.' I said.

Desmond replied brightly:

'After all, Faraday had no mathematics.' For a moment he was the great scientist, working not with formulæ but with a deep intuitive understanding of the reality which lies behind them. 'None at all. He got on pretty well.'

'But the Chemical Society wouldn't have approved of him.'

We were in the lift of the flat, and Desmond laughed all the way up. He settled comfortably into one of the chairs, and I gave him some whiskey; he glanced round the room, which was looking light and cool.

'Sometimes, Miles, one gets tired of these dull dogs. Chemistry and dons. I've often thought I should like a flat in town, rather like this.'

He drank some whiskey.

'One gets tired of Oxford, you know. The Parks Road and High Tables. One longs to move about in a big town again. Your life must be very pleasant,' he said. 'Coming back here from the lab. when you want. Coming back into the world. I've often thought I should like to do that.'

He became, as he spoke, the bon vivant and scientist, making the best of two worlds. I filled his glass again, and he said amiably: 'Happy days.'

'That's rather like the business we had on the Committee the other day,' I smiled. 'You remember: whether the Institute should be attached to a University or not.'

'Oh, Constantine's new model.' His eyes were very bright. 'That's a remarkable man, Miles.'

'A very remarkable man,' I said. 'But what are you going to do about his scheme?'

'People would be against it –'

'I should be against it myself on the whole.'

'I think I should, although –'

'It would be impossible even if one thought it worth while.'

'With you,' Desmond said. 'With you all the way.'

'But are you,' I asked, 'going to let the whole scheme slide just because of one idea that won't work? Are you going to let Fane stop the Institute altogether just because no one likes Constantine's model? You see: you're the only man who can carry the Institute through now. I mean, you could get an Institute established as an attachment to a University. If you made it London you'd carry old Austin, probably you'd *have* to make it London to carry Austin. It would be better at Oxford with you to keep it moving; but, with Oxford physics as it is, you'd never get it there, do you think? All the influence of Cambridge and London would be against you, wouldn't it? As well as Fane.'

'I suppose it would,' Desmond said unwillingly.

'It would be a lot easier for you to come to London when the Institute is started than to bring the Institute to you,' I said. 'Anyway, as it seems to me, you're the only person who can bring the Institute off in any shape whatever; and the only way to bring it off, I'm afraid, is to send it to London. It would strengthen your hand, of course.'

'Of course,' said Desmond, happy again.

'Austin would support you, naturally. Poor Constantine would too, and not mind in the least because it isn't his scheme. As he said, he's for any scheme rather than none. Then the others — well, they don't matter, and you've won.'

'Fane' — Desmond's eyes clouded — 'can go on watching cricket and trying to prevent anyone doing anything at all. We can say Scram to Fane.'

'You can,' I said. 'And it won't be only the Committee who will thank you.'

We drank a good deal of whiskey. He told me several dirty stories, breathlessly, with immense vivacity. He told anecdotes about German professors with German dialogue. He became merrily drunk very quickly, and synthesised his exploits as a raconteur by telling a dirty story about a German professor with dialogue in German and American. I drove him to the station, and he just caught his train.

'Why don't you come to Oxford?' he said out of the carriage window. 'Permanently. New blood. Liven up the Colleges. The old Colleges. It's what they want, the old Colleges.' I noticed he usually talked about Oxford as 'the Colleges'; and now he was beginning to call them 'old' and get slightly maudlin.

'You come to London, and liven up everything, Institutes and all,' I said.

As the train moved away he waved his hand vigorously, erratically.

I had it clearer now. I could rely on Constantine, of course; Desmond and Fane would be on opposite sides, probably Desmond on mine, though he was too fluid to be certain of. But, if Desmond found some other project he wanted for himself, Fane would be for us, I thought; and anyway, Fane would probably not be in bitter opposition, which was a real gain. For a determined enemy could upset a majority of vague friends.

So it looked like two against two, in the end. It would depend on Austin; I got myself invited to dinner. It was a long time since I had been there, I reflected, as I walked along the road in Kensington; and a long time since I met Audrey there, eight years ago. But the memory was all in my head, and did not strike home, nor did it when Lady Austin said at dinner:

'You knew that Audrey Tennant got married two or three years ago? She was a friend of yours at College, wasn't she, Dr. Miles?'

'Yes, I knew her quite well,' I said.

I added: 'Her husband's a friend of mine, too. He was in my year.'

'Really?' said Lady Austin. 'Audrey's a charming girl, I always thought.'

'Very charming,' I said. 'And clever.'

'We've not seen her for some time. I suppose you haven't?'

'Not for a year or so, I think.'

Not since we met and she asked me to relieve her dullness and I dare not; and before that, not since she told me of her marriage, and for pity took me the last time as a lover. Not since then. Again the memories did not hurt, did not go below the thoughts in which I framed them.

'I wonder when we shall have the pleasure of celebrating your marriage, Dr. Miles,' she said. She had always liked me, even in the days when I sometimes tried out of conscience to educate elderly ladies in post-war politics and post-Edwardian literature. I found, meeting her again after some years, that I could listen to Lady Austin, and like her. I remembered talking to Audrey about her years before; and our youthful verdict, definite and drastic. It was impossible to laugh with that old fervour, made up of malice, indignation that the world does not act logically, snobbery on both our parts, on mine lower class consciousness, which filled Audrey and me, as we retold the story of the visiting cards in Australia. Now, I had come down from those heights of disapproval; and I found I liked Lady Austin.

'My marriage,' I said. 'Not for a long time yet, I think.'

'These young men haven't time to work and marry nowadays,' Austin guffawed. 'We used to help ourselves to both, in my young days.'

'But Dr. Miles has plenty of time in front of him,' said Lady Austin, liking me for it.

'Yes, we shall see him settling down all right.' Austin said cheerfully. He cut up an apple. They had strong views on diet, I remembered, as I watched the table-light flash in reflections off his knife. 'He'll settle down soon. Though I must say, Miles' – he was chewing with Gladstonian thoroughness, with twentieth-century belief in vitamins – 'most of your generation are a wretchedly weak-kneed lot. They've no backbone, and no blood, nothing they believe in, and nothing they want to do.'

'And when they're not like that,' he enunciated, 'they're wild, *long-haired*. Like that man Constantine. He's very clever, he's got sincerity that you can't help feeling, but he doesn't know when to *stop*. And he's too long-haired to learn sense. He'll never realise you can't do everything at once.'

'I expect you want to talk business with Dr. Miles?' Lady Austin asked, shining with tact as she rose.

'Just a little talk, perhaps, about my Committee. For a few minutes,' said Austin.

He spoke more vociferously when his wife had gone.

'Why does Constantine want research teams and nothing but research teams?' He paused.

'Because that's the way the Bolsheviks are trying to organise their science.' He answered his own question. 'Long-haired nonsense. It will get in the way of his proper work, if he doesn't take care.'

'But do you think,' I asked, 'that you need take that side of him very seriously? Even on the Committee? He's very much more accommodating than his theories, don't you think?'

'He's a likeable man in himself.'

'Wouldn't you go further, though? About the Institute, for instance. Theoretically, he would like an isolated Institute somewhere near Birmingham – organised in enormous teams. But in practice he'd be perfectly contented with an Institute that was exactly on the style of a University department. Don't you think so? From the way you handled him last time, I thought you did. If it came to the point, he'd vote for an Institute attached to any adequate University. That is, provided you can guarantee it would be somewhere near a man of broad scientific outlook. You wouldn't persuade Constantine to let it go to Fane.'

Austin nodded heavily.

'If you want to put the Institute at Fane's place, Constantine would stick out for isolation. But several Universities he'd approve of, this University – your College, which is really a University of its own. I'm sure he would. Anyone would.'

'Ah!' said Austin. 'Ah!'

I sipped my port. 'Professor,' I said. 'Are you going to get this Institute formed or not? Or are you going to let those others stop it?'

Austin coughed.

'I've been thinking over the whole question ever since that discussion at the last meeting,' he announced, 'thinking it over quite impartially and trying to get the plan into relation with science as a whole. If there were any serious danger of these detached institutes springing up all over the country – like *petrol pumps* – I should consider it our duty not to set the precedent. But, as we've been saying just now, there is no danger of that. These innovations aren't really innovations, and they will fit into the normal University framework. I have satisfied myself of that; and therefore I am definitely in favour of the establishment of the Institute.'

'In that case,' I said, 'the Institute will be established.'

Austin smiled. 'I shall do my best. There may be a certain amount of opposition. In a committee like this some members never take the *long view*. But' – he guffawed – 'I shall be a little surprised if we don't secure the Institute.'

'As to the minor questions of principle,' he went on, 'where the Institute ought to be attached, and so on, they will have to be thrashed out by the Committee. It would be a mistake to think they are so minor after all. The stimulus the Institute gets from its environment may determine its future irretrievably, one way or the other.'

'Would you consider the responsibility of having it under you? That is, attach it to King's – with you as general supervisor. We should have to placate the biologists by giving you one of their Professors as a sleeping partner. As it's going to be a biophysical institute, we couldn't avoid that. I've not seen much of these things, of course,' I said, 'but that would seem to me an ideal arrangement. It would save the Institute at the start. But probably it's unfair to call on your time in that way –'

'I've a great deal on my hands.' Austin leaned back in his chair. 'But I still hold to my belief that if it is one's duty to take on another responsibility, time can always be found. However much you dislike it, you can always get a little extra work into the day. If I were convinced I ought to supervise the Institute, I couldn't persuade myself out of it just because I was occupied enough already!' He laughed good-humouredly at his own sense of duty.

'There wouldn't be a tremendous amount of formal work, if you decided it was a possible scheme,' I said. 'The Institute would have its own head – I suppose – for the direction of research and the internal administration. He'd be responsible to you, of course, and you'd be the connection between the Institute and the outside world. You would take it like that? Or have I got your intentions wrong?'

'That's exactly right,' said Austin. 'It's a very reasonable plan.'

'Any intelligent scientific opinion would rather have that arrangement than any other. It's not my idea, of course, it's just the general feeling. Whether all the Committee would share it, I don't know.'

'You're too much impressed by Committees,' Austin replied. 'When you've served on as many as I have, you won't treat them so respectfully.'

'There couldn't be anything more fitting than your supervising the Institute,' I said reflectively. 'When one thinks of the work that has led to it. The work in your laboratory years ago; you can trace back all this new stuff to that. Constantine's and mine, and those Americans. You're responsible for us all, whether you like it or not. You're responsible for the Institute, whether you take it over or not.

'Whatever you do,' I said, 'it's your Institute.'

Chapter 6

Party in action

I

Austin began the next meeting:

'I have no doubt everyone has been giving the deepest consideration to the arguments we heard last time. I have gone into them myself very seriously. I would like to know if all of you are of the same opinion as you were then. If so, whether one of you would propose a motion to the effect that we approve the principle of an Institute, provided it is under the general control of a University. Most of us would feel that desirable in any case ...

Desmond proposed it, no one said anything more, and it was passed at once. I was coming to appreciate Austin's rough and ready methods in the Chair.

'Now we ought to discuss,' said Austin complacently, 'the general scope of the work that the Institute will do. Until we have a general idea of its aims and possibilities we cannot go much further with the business. Our friends Miles and Constantine are the experts on the *details* of this kind of work at present, so if the Committee approves I will ask them to give us an outline.'

I gave them some of my schemes, as definitely as I could, finding points as I went on to meet each of their interests; '– *this* will connect with Professor Desmond's work,' I said, 'we should want the physics of cataphoresis done in full, of course – in this other problem, the physics would have to converge on the biochemistry, and Professor Pritt's method would have to be used, intensively.'

It was delicate going; perhaps it is fair to say that my main outlines were sound enough, and in fact were actually used with success.

Constantine followed, magnificently. He flung his head back and gave us plans, not only for this Institute, but for a series of others, physical, biochemical, genetic, mathematical; so that every problem in our Institute was supplemented by all the others. He developed something like the course of science for twenty years; and all of us, except perhaps Pritt, realised that, though it was extravagant, it was also prophetic; along with his knowledge, which might have been comic, there was a vision which lit it up, which was not given to any of the rest of us. His suggestions for the immediate work of the Institute, when he returned to it, were completely practical and clear; one could almost see Desmond catching at them as they came, gratified that after the wide stretch of future science he had got something he could understand.

Constantine spoke for nearly half an hour. He stopped all of a sudden, for no particular reason, and said shyly: 'I'm afraid I've been talking too much.'

'Not at all,' said Austin pontifically. 'Not at all. We've all found it very stimulating, I'm sure. Even' – he guffawed – 'when it had nothing in particular to do with our Institute.'

Constantine smiled, but he was troubled, I could see. He wished that people could understand how every word he said was directly relevant. They never could understand. Even when they admired him, he often felt they could not see those mental paths of his, a little complex perhaps, and yet so clear.

Austin got up to close the meeting.

'We have made some progress,' he said as we walked out. 'What I call *genuine* progress. But I shall have to tell Constantine to keep to the point another time.'

2

Then, for meeting after meeting, we settled down to the long struggle of attrition which was to decide where the Institute should be attached. I listened to those arguments, often funny in themselves, which mattered so much to me. I had to listen most of the time in silence. Often it was interesting, I could hear the signs of hidden motives; sometimes it was tedious; and was always a strain.

The position as I saw it was fairly simple; but one has to remember that none of the others, not even Fane, had a clear idea of it; and that throughout the Committee's life, even at the end, no two of the five members knew each other well.

Austin was for London. Simply, sturdily, and all the time. 'Having regard to the interests of the Institute, and of science as a whole.' He said that frequently. Loudly, pontifically, cheerfully, he explained why it should go to London. Quite often he let it be seen that he took it as his own right.

Desmond, now that the Institute was safely launched, wanted it for Oxford. I had expected it, of course. It was too bright a toy for his eyes to miss. He looked at me a little shamefacedly, when first he suggested it in committee; but he soon forgot anything he might have said in the past. Amiably and loquaciously he unfolded Oxford's advantages to us, almost as though he had them on the table. 'You see,' he used to say, 'we can give you everything. Professors to advise. Students to recruit. All the traditions of the Colleges.' Then he would look round at us all. 'And, what's more, you can give us something. The old Colleges want this kind of thing. It would brace the Colleges up. It would make them zip.'

Pritt wanted it for Cambridge. Stubbornly, because if it went elsewhere, it would belong to someone else.

Fane's attitude was not so direct. Once he would have liked it for Manchester, but he was getting used, almost expecting, almost forcing himself to be passed over. He seemed to be working for a balance of power – or rather a balance of fame. He wanted the stature of those who were coming not to transcend his own. And so he had manoeuvred about Constantine and the Institute, because he knew that Constantine with an Institute under his control would in ten years be one of the greatest scientific figures in the world. That was why he had got Constantine installed as a research professor, which would give him nothing like the scope. Then, with Constantine installed in his Chair, Fane could come forward, as he did on the Committee:

'But surely a Biophysical Institute in London is either superfluous – or unwise? Professor Constantine is starting a school; in two or three years we shall see how it's going. We all expect it will do remarkable things. In that case, it would be wasteful to have another biophysical laboratory in London. If the improbability happens, and it doesn't do so well, then I put it to the Committee that it would be injudicious to invest all our biophysical interests in the same place.'

Austin was silenced for a moment. Constantine bewilderedly hurt, by this cleverness that seemed deliberately misguided.

It was for this that Fane had hurried on the Committee's formation; if there must be an Institute he would keep it out of the most able hands. Constantine was to be isolated in London; Desmond, who moved him to a jealous contempt, must not be allowed near it, or else he would boost it after a fashion, and gain still more a success of influence. Thus Fane was left discussing an Institute whose creation he resented, of whose destination he was only negatively sure. As he opposed London and Oxford on committee, I could feel the sterility behind his wit; he did not even know where he wanted it to go. In the end, I fancied, he would support Pritt and Cambridge; because he only despised Pritt, and on the other hand Pritt would not relent in obstinacy.

It was clear how the decision would resolve itself, I thought as I listened impatiently to those hot afternoons being talked away. Austin and Constantine would be firm for London, Fane would be forced to second Pritt; and then, because Fane was on the other side, Desmond, the most flexible of the five, would join Austin and Constantine. If so, I had got halfway with my plans: if not, then there was no hope. So I went on listening, intervening in private now and then.

3

For weeks they bandied reasons across the room.

Austin argued: London is the obvious place for any Department which is mainly financed by the Government. An innovation such as the Institute would fit more naturally into London than into an older University. A Department having some connection with the outside world could be assimilated more easily into London than into a small University town. The technical staff would live more comfortably in London than as townsmen in Oxford or Cambridge. There was infinite room for laboratory expansion in London, as opposed to the congestion in Oxford and Cambridge; and, in fact, quarters could be found for the Institute in some of the London Colleges (notably his own) without building at all. There was a serious danger of centralising research too much in Cambridge: research gained by healthy competition between Universities.

Pritt argued: That Cambridge was the best University for science. Since all research was being taken there, the Institute should also go. There were less diversions in Cambridge than London. There would be less trouble with discipline, and men would work harder.

Desmond argued: That he agreed with Austin about the danger of centralising in Cambridge and with Pritt about the disadvantages of London. So everything pointed to Oxford. As for lack of space for building, the Colleges had found room for everything for six hundred years (I remember he was moved by this thought). Oxford would be a very friendly compromise.

Fane argued: That Desmond's friendly compromise would be friendly to whom? That the disadvantages of centralising in Cambridge might suggest the establishment of the Institute at Norwich. (He got sharper-tongued as the meetings went on.) That the only valid arguments against Cambridge had been given by Pritt. But as Pritt did not completely represent Cambridge, these were not serious. The Institute in Cambridge would attract benefactions as it grew up. This would never happen in London. In Cambridge it would get the best material start in life. ('Where did you send your son, Austin?' he asked.)

Constantine did not argue much. His chief exploit was to waste at least three meetings. It was done in all innocence. He took up Austin's point about buildings: 'Professor

Austin has suggested that if we take the Institute to London, we shall not need any buildings,' Constantine began. 'Though, as I have said before, I'm for London, I can't admit that argument in its favour. Surely the Institute must have a new building wherever it goes; a building conceived for the purposes of the Institute and nothing else. We've got to begin scientific architecture in this country some time, and we shan't have a better chance than this . . .'

He described the features that a modern laboratory should have. He made comparisons between Pasadena and the Physicochemical Institute at Leningrad, and provoked a violent and wandering controversy. For the Committee was more at home with irrelevant concrete facts than with relevant abstractions; and because buildings lasted longer and were easier to see than individual lives, they loomed larger in their minds. I thought, as I heard them get heated, how often at Cambridge I had found 'the College,' when said with the maximum of passion, meant simply the College buildings.

The Committee leapt to discuss buildings, as though it were once again on familiar ground. Austin, not unnaturally, was annoyed with Constantine's approach; but arguing about, for, and against buildings was a thing he had done all his life, and he was ready for this. Soon the accustomed words began to be exchanged: 'Estimates.' 'Economy on main structure: expenditure inside.' 'Economy on main structure is false economy.' 'Suggestions by an architect.' 'Architect must be first class.'

'We must have teak benches,' Desmond observed. 'We *must* have teak benches.'

I saw the decision, the essential decision about place, moving further away; the sun was shining outside; an eddy of wind would come sometimes, and, throwing aside tobacco smoke and the smell of chairs, bring a breath from the park. I gave up listening often, and scribbled on sheets of paper. One afternoon, I remember, when the discussion of buildings was at its height, I entertained myself by classifying these five at the table into categories, as many as I could think of. According to Jung, Desmond, Austin and

Fane would be extraverts, Pritt and Constantine introverts (a noble introvert, Constantine, I smiled). According to Kretschmer, Desmond and probably Austin would be cyclothyme and pyknic; Constantine schizothyme and leptosome; the other two nondescript: but it never seemed to me a good dichotomy, it does not even divide, let alone divide well.

One afternoon, when there was no Royal Society meeting after ours, I walked with Austin towards his house.

'Things are going rather slowly, don't you think?' I suggested.

'They're not as fast as I'd hoped,' Austin said. 'By no means as fast. There's a good deal of *obstinacy* on the Committee. It's surprising, from men of scientific education, when the proper course is utterly obvious.'

'The plan of yours –'

'Take the Institute to London; I can find it space in King's. It is very difficult, Miles, when these Committees won't see plain sense.'

'I know you've tried everything,' I said, 'but I wonder if you'd mind me talking informally with one or two members of the Committee. Saying more or less what you've just said. But I can speak more freely than you, as I'm not really on the Committee.' I smiled. 'And being an irresponsible young man.'

'With one more of them for London,' I added, 'the thing is settled. And it seems to me just possible that one or two minds could be changed – if they knew exactly what you felt.'

'You won't take my name in vain, I hope,' he said loudly, and the echo amused me. 'But I know you're reasonable about these matters. You're not one of those *long-haired* young men.'

'It won't do any harm,' I said. 'And it might save it.'

4

I travelled back from Oxford to London the morning of our next meeting. I was not surprised to see Desmond, but he was to see me.

'What are you doing here?' he said, cheerfully. 'Come clean.'

'Talking to one of your Clubs last night,' I said. 'But I only came because I wanted to see you. I called on you last night, but you weren't in.' If he had been in I should not have called; for I wanted to leave no time before the meeting for his fluid personality to re-collect itself.

'I nearly invited myself over earlier in the week,' I added gravely.

He looked rather hunted.

'What have I been doing?' he said.

'It's the Committee,' I said.

He relaxed into relief, and became a man of affairs, tossing off business as he travelled. He lit a pipe.

'Let's have it,' he said.

'You know this impasse you've reached.' I leaned forward. 'About where the Institute shall be. It's all mixed up with building complications –'

'Fane,' said Desmond quickly, 'never goes into his own labs. I ask you, how does he know how to build someone else's?'

'Yes,' I said. That was a piece of luck for me. 'Anyway, if you put the building on one side –'

'We ought to have done.' Desmond nodded his head. 'We certainly ought.'

'We come back to the old position about the place. You for Oxford; Austin and Constantine for London, of course; Fane and Pritt for Cambridge. That's how things have stuck. Since May it must be.' I paused and gazed at him. He shrugged his shoulders.

'Committees,' he said, 'Committees, Miles. One's helpless. One does one's best.'

'Well,' I said, 'things won't stick much more.'

'What?'

'Austin and Constantine won't keep together much longer. They'll probably give to-day. This building question: Austin wanting London so that building's unnecessary, and Constantine insisting. It's split them. I talked to Austin last week-end. He was very tired of it then. He said he was prepared to let it go –'

'Oh,' said Desmond.

'To Cambridge,' I said.

'Fane,' I remarked, 'will be pleased, and he deserves to be.'
Desmond looked unhappy.

'What does Austin think?' he asked.

'He's very angry. Very angry. There'll be trouble later
on. He says if everyone wants to see every piece of scientific research in this country being done in Cambridge he
can't stop it by himself.'

'You know, Miles,' Desmond began quickly, 'nothing
would have pleased me better than see it go to London.
I've got the greatest respect for London. There was only
one thing held me back. You know what that was –'

I murmured.

'Duty. My duty to the Colleges. That was all,' he said. 'It
doesn't seem right that because I've done my duty the Institute goes to Cambridge. Just to please Fane.'

'Of course,' I said, 'there's no guarantee Austin'll give
in. He may hold out. I expect he was rather jaded last
week. Constantine may hold out, too. It's likely as not
to be a false alarm. But I thought you should know.'

'I've seen it coming,' said Desmond. 'I've seen it for
weeks. You can't see Fane and Pritt giving way, can you?'

I could not.

'Fane's not man enough,' Desmond said, 'and Pritt –
Pritt's too dumb. They'll stick out and the others will give.
That's what we're frightened of, Miles. That's what we're
frightened of, you and I.'

By now, he had appropriated the suggestion for himself.
'That's what you've got to be frightened of. Believe me,'
he said.

He brightened up. He chewed his pipe, shone bright eyes
at me: 'I'll make them show. There's not a chance for the
Colleges, now. I've faced up to that long ago. So my next
duty is to the next best place, Miles. I'll tell Constantine to
propose London this afternoon, and second it myself. I
don't think Austin will cross over then. That'll settle it.'

'That'll settle *them*,' he added.

'It would be generous of you. And strong,' I said.

'Sometimes,' said Desmond, 'one has to be, you know.'

I watched Fane's face as Constantine proposed, right at the beginning of the meeting, that the Committee recommend the Institute be attached to the University of London. He was smiling, and Constantine, as usual when going through a formal act, was ill at ease. Fane, still smiling, said that he continued to oppose. Pritt nodded his head. Then Desmond said, his tone a little raised:

'I should like to withdraw the suggestion I've been making at these meetings. Off and on. The suggestion of Oxford. I feel it's time to consider the wider issue. I should like to support the suggestion of London.'

'You're supporting the actual motion?' said Austin very loudly. 'So that we can have a decisive vote?'

Desmond looked abashed. He stared defiantly at Fane, then took his eyes away.

'Yes,' he said in a clear metallic voice.

'Then with my own vote London has it,' Austin announced. 'And I must say it's a surprisingly quick and welcome end to this part of our labours. I am personally very gratified that the Committee has seen fit to make this recommendation; and I am quite sure, gentlemen, that it is the wise and right one.'

Fane's mouth had been pulled to one side. His hard eyes were fixed on Desmond.

'I need hardly say,' said Fane, 'how much pleasure the Chairman's assurance gives to — may I term ourselves? — the less ebullient members of the Committee. Perhaps it would act as a symbol of my pleasure if I now formally move the recommendation of the University of London.'

It was courteously done, and I found myself closer to him than any of the others, wishing that he and I were on the same side.

Pritt sullenly voted against.

I was beginning to let myself hope, as Constantine and I walked away that afternoon. It had gone my way so far, and I had lost nothing, and gained a good deal. Constantine began to talk fervently about a day-old idea of his that would occupy the Institute for a year. I was thinking, I had taken some risks (but one shies from the thought of a risk that has only just gone); the luck had been with me; in a month I ought to be safe.

Suddenly I felt tired and rather depressed, and we turned into a café and had tea.

Chapter 7

Towards ambition

I

The Committee now began to draw up its first report, and simultaneously set about considering its second. It was a tedious, time-wasting business, and I resented it the more now that I was grudging the minutes, let alone the hours. Both hope and tension were drawing to an edge; for at occasional meetings Austin would smile knowingly and ask me to withdraw. They were considering what Austin called 'the Executive Personnel'; by which he meant the Director of the Institute, the Assistant Director (one of these two had to be a physicist, the other a biologist), and a head of the chemical staff. I heard most of their deliberations direct from Constantine, by heavy allusions from Austin, as-a-hint-from-one-man-to-another-though-I-am-pledged-to-secrecy from Desmond.

They were a long time starting. They fenced with general principles about the Directorship: did they want a man already of senior position and a F.R.S.? or alternatively did they want a young man who had been in at the birth of the new subject? If he were not the first, as Fane pointed out, he could scarcely have the necessary standing; but Constantine replied, with surprising acidity, if he were not the second he would have none of the necessary knowledge. They offered it to Constantine, as they were bound to, and he immediately declined. Without considering me, he would still have declined; he had just taken the Research Chair with no administrative ties, and that was the height of his desires. Then they voted on the principle, and by three to two decided to appoint rather for promise than for standing.

'It's yours,' said Constantine. 'I've got a scheme we might carry out together as soon as you're installed. We could get the apparatus beforehand so as not to waste time.'

'I shall soon be taking off my hat to you,' said Desmond.

'It will give me a great deal of satisfaction,' said Austin, 'to see this Institute attached to my own College and directed by one of my own students.'

Austin, in fact, went about saying it. At a dinner he met several of my present seniors at University College; the next morning I was asked to go and see the Principal.

'Well,' he said, 'I hear you'll be leaving us soon.'

I murmured.

'On the best authority,' he said. 'The Chairman of a certain Committee.'

'There is a chance,' I admitted. 'I couldn't tell you about it before.'

'Naturally,' he said.

'I couldn't tell you anything. But –'

'We shall be sorry to lose you,' he said. 'But it will be a big thing for us, your getting this. A very big thing.'

I got used to evading congratulations and curiosity during the rest of that day. I found myself a little shaken. I went and instructed Jepp over some experiments I wanted doing. During the commotion of the last months my new assistant had struck a useful line of his own, and I had made him keep to it; so that now, when by accident there came the sudden flash of an idea, I had to leave the experiments to Jepp. I was too busy and tired myself for long routines; and he was doing them very well. By luck, by sheer luck, I seemed to have struck one of the bigger things of my life. It was an odd reward for restlessness, I thought; but often, exacerbated by anxieties, I would try to put them aside in thinking of it, by giving Jepp orders, by looking over his results.

Then a newspaper got hold of the Institute. The Committee's first report was just out, and one of the London dailies appeared with a front-page article, why I still do not know. I can still feel in my nerves the shock with which I saw the headlines: SCIENCE OF LIFE IN LONDON they ran.

A CURE FOR CANCER! Great Institute for Great Work, say Professors.

Someone had interviewed Austin, which was natural enough, and had gone on to Desmond, which struck me as curious. He had been in particularly good form, and I imagined the journalist's glee at finding at last a scientist who would entertain any woolly suggestion and would chat about anything from psychic research to the synthesis of life. The cure of cancer in the headlines had been due to him, I guessed. On being asked whether the Institute's work would give a cure, he could not possibly resist saying something like: 'Wonderful things are happening every day'.

But the sentence which concerned me was at the foot of the column:

'It is understood that the directorship of the Institute will shortly be offered to a brilliant young scientist at present working in a London laboratory, whose name is well-known to readers of monthly magazines.'

That was a definite description to a number of people. To anyone who knew a little of the Institute's history, it could only mean me.

I was disturbed. I did not see what harm it could do now, but I wished it had not happened. I wished, too, that an article of mine had not recently come out in *Nash's*. Usually I had confined them to America, but this offer I could not resist: and I hadn't expected the article to be printed so soon. I wondered how the papers had got to know. Had Desmond talked? or – I tried to think of any acquaintance of mine who could be a channel. No one seemed likely.

Yet, during the next days, the thought often pricked suddenly through my comfortable anticipations. I went through the puzzled, suspicious, slightly worried questioning again. I was sleeping badly, waking frequently throughout the night; and then the thought had me at its mercy, with the other, the worse, the inevitable, behind it: 'What if it should not happen? What if it should not happen?'

That was the fear which had been latent all this time. I had not dared to face it. Least of all dare I face it now. For my boats were burnt, I told myself, hanging on to the phrase for comfort, in those dawns when I lay and felt my skin was moist. My boats were burnt. Too many people knew. I was no longer in obscurity. If it should not happen –

I stared at the window, grey in the darkness. I could hear my heart beating.

2

The next meeting dealt with some trivial matter of equipment; I was on edge to hear, to feel, if there were any difference in their attitude since the newspapers came out. But even to my hyperæsthesia there was nothing suspicious; Austin was particularly jovial, and Desmond went out of his way to monopolise me as we walked down Piccadilly. This immediate reassurance soothed me as nothing else could; the anxieties were lulled for hours together, and I slipped into a worn but contented mood. For almost the first time, I had flashes of triumph. The future was secure, certain, comfortable, full of achievement. 'I'll take the rest of the summer off,' I thought. 'Bask by the sea and not think for weeks. I'll go where I know no one, to the Adriatic perhaps, and *rest*.' The word itself was calming. 'And then I'll come back and make this Institute go as no one else could.'

With confidence flowing back, I made some arrangements for an unusual week-end; Hunt and Sheriff were coming to stay with me. I had invited Hunt many times, and at last he accepted. Sheriff had invited himself. I had not seen him since he married Audrey. His letter had come during the week, and I decided to have him along with Hunt rather than seem to put him off. Actually, I was interested, a little excited, to see the two of them together again.

Sheriff came first; there was his quick step outside, and he walked across the room with his comic rolling gait.

'Hallo,' he said, a trifle breathlessly.

'Hallo, Charles,' I said. 'It's years since I saw you.'

He was much older-looking, I thought: or rather he did not look older so much as like himself five years before, permanently worried and short of sleep. His cheeks were not so full, and the colour on them had gone patchy. There were lines on his forehead and round his eyes, and an eyelid twitched, I noticed. He was not as well dressed as I remembered. But as he sat down, he smiled; and then his eyes had all the old gaiety, the sparkle, the irresponsibility.

'This is a very pleasant flat,' he said. 'Though I am not so impressed as I ought to be. Southampton can provide decent houses; and that's about all it can provide. It's not a good town, Southampton. It's not a place for a young man of spirit.'

I smiled. He was still a little nervous.

'How is Audrey?' I asked.

He hesitated.

'Well,' he said. 'Very well.'

He burst out: 'Arthur, she's going to have a child.'

It was strange to hear.

'When?'

'Six months,' Sheriff smiled, himself again. 'Think, Arthur, a child. Or possibly two.'

'A queer creature it will be,' I said.

'Me as father,' he laughed. 'God, what a start in life that child will have!'

'I suppose,' I said, finding a satisfaction, a consolation in the words, 'money will be a difficulty?' Too many regrets had come alive, but I felt sympathetic. The regrets were almost impersonal, as of things gone by. To him, buffooning vivaciously in front of me, I felt more friendly than I had done since our intimacy.

'You're right, Arthur.' He looked harassed, though he was still smiling. 'You're right as you always used to be. On this occasion, rather platitudinously so, perhaps. I get £300, and I'm in debt, as you'd expect. I don't see how the situation will be improved by the child, do you?'

I recalled some of his gasconades about wealthy relatives eager to shower money on him, so that he would be a man of leisure at thirty if he cared, not that he would have cared in those days; he wanted to work for work's sake; but perhaps he would accept some of the money. I had believed those stories once, growing slowly, so slowly, incredulous, when he seemed always even poorer than Hunt or me. Incidentally, in theory he must still owe me fifty pounds or so.

'It's a nuisance,' I said.

'Not only that. The things that matter happen in the heart. But money would help. I could have more heart then.' He shrugged his shoulders. 'Think what I could do,' he smiled, 'if I had more heart.'

We went to meet Hunt, and saw him pale-faced, stooping a little, but his head still above the crowds that swarmed from the northern train. His face lit up as he saw us; he and Sheriff went through a patter of reminiscent greeting as we drove off. We called at the flat and then walked out for dinner. The air was warm; and away from the lights across the park, the sky shone densely purple.

'Do you realise,' said Sheriff, 'that it's eight years since we had a meal together? *Eight* years. When I think of all the people I have had meals with in that time: put end to end, they'd stretch from here to Southampton.

'What a pity,' he remarked, 'that it can't be done.'

Hunt smiled. 'My line would stretch about between those lamp-posts.'

Sheriff turned on him. 'Why don't you know people? Oh, I expect you still find out about their souls. But I mean – know them socially. Go to dinner. And dances. There must be hundreds of women in Manchester who'd like to dance with you.'

'It would bring me out of myself, I suppose you mean,' Hunt laughed, uneasily.

'I do,' said Sheriff. 'It's a pity I've not been about these last few years. I'd have made you enjoy things. Things on the surface, if you like. But the things we enjoy *are* on the surface. When you appreciate them, you will also grasp that the fact of living itself counts more than the minor annoyances associated with it. Among the minor annoyances being' – he grinned – 'the depths of the soul.'

We went to a restaurant in Jermyn Street, and sat by the open window on the first floor looking down on to the road. Hunt reverted to words which for Sheriff had already gone into the past. It was characteristic of them, I thought.

'If that's what you mean by minor annoyances,' said Hunt – Sheriff looked puzzled and then remembered – 'I do prefer them –'

'That's what's wrong with you,' said Sheriff quickly.

'– to your fact of living itself. Whatever that may mean. It's too religious for me' – Hunt was slowly thinking it out – 'too much a phrase that stands for an emotion and nothing else. Like – God –'

'Or,' I broke in, 'like any other phrase that strikes a chime in your mind and hypnotises you into thinking that it's an idea.'

'Talking of which,' said Sheriff, 'you could do with some enjoyment of the fact of living yourself, Arthur. You're becoming a great man; and you're forgetting you used to enjoy things. When did you dance last?'

'At Christmas, I think. Abroad.'

'You see. Do you play cricket now?'

'Not for a long time.'

'I don't know why, but you used to enjoy it. Love?'

'In off moments.'

'In off moments! That's not what I call love.'

I did not remark that it would be truer for me to say that it was not what I called love.

I had ordered a good dinner; Sheriff drank a fine hock with the fish.

'I expect you eat and drink well,' he said, 'I'll give you that. But, after all, they're the pleasures of someone who's past enjoying anything else.' He screwed up his mobile face, and his eyes stared at me, large, seriously mocking. 'Arthur! There's *time*,' he whispered.

'For what?'

'To take yourself in hand. If you say to yourself every day "I will be more human, I *will* be more human," it would make all the difference. Just keep that thought in front of you, and when the temptation comes – push it aside. Concentrate on being more human. Don't be put off. It may cost effort. It may mean sacrifice and discipline. But if you try hard enough you'll win through.'

His manner amused me still. Hunt was smiling.

'I've got confidence in you. Even now,' said Sheriff. As dinner went on, Sheriff drank enough to excite him, and I also was a little drunk. It was a strange meeting. Sheriff was fooling more consciously nowadays, a flaunt of cheerfulness against the worry, the emptiness that sometimes showed through. In the past he had played some soulful parts among his others, but now he was half-resigned to a picture of himself nearer but still not quite the truth. Now he tried to be, to himself as to us, the man of gaiety who took life as it came, made love and laughed. For almost all the time, he carried it off with spirit; by his side Hunt's slowness became irritating, his quietness dull, and I found my own remarks addressed themselves to Sheriff.

Later in the evening, a young woman came in by herself and sat at the window opposite to us. I saw Sheriff's eyes several times watching her with a steady cordial stare, his red lips a little parted.

'That woman's attractive,' he said. 'God, she's attractive.'

She took out a cigarette, and her hands fluttered about from lap to table. Sheriff had left his chair on the instant, and was striking a match in front of her.

'May I?' we heard him saying. 'But of course I may.'

He sat down by her and I could see his mouth smiling, talking very fast, his eyes laughing into hers. I heard her long delighted 'No' of protest, his words still quicker, her laugh in which he joined. Soon he was walking out of the room with her.

'Think of the time you'd have had,' said Hunt, 'if you'd been like that.'

'By the way,' Hunt went on, 'you remember – Mona, I told you of her once?'

'Of course,' I answered.

'She got married at the beginning of the year.' Hunt's mouth twisted. 'To a bank clerk in her native town.'

There was nothing to say. So this was the end, for Hunt. Ten years of unrequited love, for a woman who as stupid, graceless, whose prettiness, so he told me, had gone with the years. A woman who was nothing except that he loved her. She had given him nothing, now she was gone and it was over.

'They met the Sheriffs not very long ago. She wrote and told me,' Hunt added. Then I knew it was not over even yet. He was still tied enough to bring in the fact that he had news of her, just for the sake of telling it, to secure a moment's familiarity at a distance.

'When Sheriff met her,' Hunt said evenly, 'I expect he slapped her bottom and kissed her outside the door. If he noticed her enough.'

I let it pass in silence.

Sheriff himself came back a moment later, and smiled at us a little ruefully.

'She's got a husband,' he filled his glass again, 'and he'll be at home to-night and to-morrow. Damn him. I wonder what he's like. Something wrong, or she wouldn't be wanting love so badly.'

'Are you sure?' said Hunt.

'I'm right, nine times out of ten,' Sheriff said, 'and the tenth – I get my face smacked. Ah well! She'd been at Bedford College and has intellectual pretensions. Big ones. They would have been rather a bore. But' – he smiled over his glass – 'I got her address. I'm rather like a dog hiding bones. It's pleasant to feel there are some in reserve.'

'I hope you enjoy them in the end,' Hunt said.

'Do you suppose,' Sheriff asked, 'I kiss their hands?'

I wondered; for I knew he was not a passionate man.

The night was still warm, and we were heated with wine. Sheriff and I finished the last bottle.

'When I remember us three drinking together,' Sheriff's eyes were bright and his face flushed, 'years ago – I take it hard that Hunt has drunk one glass of wine.'

'Sorry.' Hunt smiled.

'When I remember how we used to drink and talk – and God, how chaste we were, how – how – portentously chaste!'

'Of all the lights on our system!' He laughed. 'We knew about sex, we talked about sex, and we didn't do anything about sex until we were twenty-two and more. But I'm a normal man, not what you'd call inhibited. I've every reason to suppose that Arthur also is comparatively normal. And I know nothing to the contrary against Hunt. Except that he has given up the drink. Which may be a sign of worse.'

'Perhaps,' said Hunt. 'I wasn't chaste in those days, though. Nor for a long time before.'

Sheriff's mouth opened in surprise.

'Didn't you know?' asked Hunt.

'I sometimes wondered,' I said. 'But I wasn't sure either way.'

Even now, it was hard to reconcile with Mona, with his shyness of women.

'Oh, it's true enough,' he said, piercing my doubts with one of those flashes which belied his slowness. 'I'm not a schoolboy, I've got beyond sexual pride.' He glanced at Sheriff. 'If ever I had much, it wouldn't have lasted the time I've had.'

'You see,' he added, 'I paid for my nights, such as they were. I have never had a woman without paying. But I started long before I knew you two. When I was about eighteen. And it went on for years. It still does, sometimes, not often now. Perhaps it has prevented my getting anything more satisfying. Such as I wanted.'

His voice was casual-sounding:

'I used to fancy it was because I'd got used to sex without love, I found it so difficult to imagine love and sex together for myself. When I fell in love, I couldn't make love; I didn't know how to ask; the thought repelled me. It sounds silly, but it got in my way.'

'You mean you divided women into two compartments. Those who would and those who wouldn't. The second compartment corresponding to the middle classes and above,' Sheriff said rapidly. 'What a superb Victorian you must be!'

'You can call it that,' Hunt said. 'But I haven't arrived at this state deliberately; and it's kept me from some of the better things.'

'I'm sorry.' Sheriff was distressed. 'I must be drunk.'

'It doesn't matter.' Hunt smiled unexpectedly, charmingly. 'It is all rather comic. I used to laugh at it myself.

But it's a relief to talk. And when I'm talking to Arthur, I know he won't let me get away with the easy explanation. The one I've just given you. That, because I began with prostitutes, it spoiled love for me. Like all attempts people make to explain their own twists – it's facile and it lets one keep a shred of self-respect. I mean, I could console myself: if I hadn't been unlucky enough to fall in with prostitutes first, it all might be different. One feels encouraged and ill-used. All self-explanations are on those lines. And they're all wrong. So is mine.'

I had been thinking, if this self-justification comforted him, he ought to be left with it; and if his insight, used on himself, was incomparably less penetrating than into other people, in that respect he was in good company. I was glad, though, when he swept the excuse away. He might be less happy, but it was more fitting that he should see with clear eyes. If Hunt deceived himself, I knew no one who could be trusted to be honest.

'What do you think is the reason, then?' I asked.

'Oh, some sort of timidity which must have come so early that I don't know why. It has been there all my life: and come out in other ways as well as this. I've not had the things I wanted, I've almost kept myself from having them.' He smiled. 'In a sense I've taken to the sordid and obscure for its own sake.'

Though my own interpretation would have been a little different, it was a brave attempt, I thought. Braver than most of us would do about ourselves.

'If I hadn't been made like this, I should have done more,' said Hunt, 'a lot more, perhaps. But I don't think I regret it. Is it possible to regret one's own experience?'

I said: 'You mean, if anything had been left out of your make-up, and what's happened to you, you would not be yourself now –'

'And that's unthinkable,' Hunt said, 'because, for everyone, not to be oneself would be the greatest calamity of all. To oneself, you see, one is the purpose of the universe. Even if one has a nostalgia for the sordid.'

'It does one good to hear you.' Sheriff turned down an empty glass. 'To hear Hunt confess he is occupied with the drama of his own personality. I used to think I was alone in that. Before I took to enjoying things.

'Why won't you let me persuade you to enjoy things?' he pleaded to Hunt. 'I did some work yesterday, have had a good dinner to-night, shall get off with a pretty girl to-morrow. At least, I hope so. Don't you think it's enough? If you'd drunk glass for glass with me, you'd think it was more than enough.'

Hunt shook his head. 'Not even you can make it convincing. Not even for yourself.'

Sheriff waved his hand. 'In that case I shall sulk. I shall sulk for the remainder of the evening.'

He looked round the room. 'This restaurant appears to be empty. I think I'll change my mind. I shall not sulk.' He looked at us with bright eyes.

'I propose to sing,' he said.

3

Hunt left late on Sunday afternoon, and Sheriff and I returned to the flat. He had become subdued as soon as we were left alone, and I could feel there was something he wanted to ask. I thought it most likely that he was going to borrow money. Instead, he burst out suddenly:

'You're moving to the Institute soon?'

'I suppose so,' I said. 'Nothing's settled,' I added quickly, with a thrust of timorousness, an impulse to touch wood.

'It's fine,' he said absently.

'How much will they pay?' he asked. 'It's fine.'

'A thousand or so. More later.' I remembered that these words would go to Audrey. 'A good deal more,' I said.

'Who are you going to give the other jobs to?' he said lightly. 'What are *they* worth?'

I was amused.

'There'll be a biologist at £700 or £800. Probably Tremlin. You remember. He was a lecturer at King's in our time. A rather dull man. And a chemist at £600. I don't know who that'll be.'

He grinned, half impudently, half shamefacedly. He had come for this, waited all the week-end.

'You know, I think I should fill that job very gracefully.

With a good deal of character, and a certain amount of industry. And think, Arthur, think how I should brighten up
the place.'

I smiled.

'Look,' he went on. 'I should be the centre of the Institute's social life. Thanks to me, you'd be known as the
most humane director in the world. Laugh while you
work. Genius and jollity. No one else could do that for
you.'

'No one could.'

'Have you read my last papers?' he said. His face was
strained. Being an unsuccessful adventurer was none too
easy, and one's own merriment must go dark at times.

'One,' I said. 'It was good. Much better than anything
else of yours I've seen.'

'The latest is better,' he said. 'Much better.

'I'm not very good with money,' he added. I laughed. He
had spent some time the day before trying to persuade me
to join in a fantastic scheme for minor chemical industries. It was quite impracticable and mildly dishonest.

'But I'm not like that at science. I don't pretend I'm inspired or fanatical about it. But I'm quite competent, and
I should be reasonably hard-working. I may not be sound
in the head, but I *am* good with my hands.'

'Yes,' I said. I was thinking: he was right in a sense. We
could get a good many young chemists who were better
scientists, who had more insight and imagination. But, for
the purposes of the Institute, those qualities were not as
valuable as others that I ordinarily despised. We wanted a
chemist who could turn out beautiful crystals, not one with
an intuition into molecular structure. And Sheriff had the
most delicate manual imagination that I had ever seen. I
still remembered envying him in our student days for the
precision, the rapidity, the elegance, of his experiments.

'Would you like the job?' I asked. 'I might manage it for
you.'

'And how much,' I thought, 'am I led by Sheriff's experimental skill? How much by all the intertwined desires – to
show my indifference to the injury he had once done me,
to demonstrate my own success, to display my power in

front of Audrey, to have her remember me in every material fact in her life?'

'I would be incredibly grateful,' he said eagerly. 'Really grateful. Even I should be.'

'You mustn't be too certain,' I said. 'There's a committee to persuade. Most of them approve of me – but they might be difficult.'

'Who are they?' he asked.

I gave him the names one by one. Fane, he commented, knew and liked him, but when I said 'Pritt' he looked doleful.

'God,' he said, 'just my luck. Is that the man who's just gone to Cambridge? A boor with a face like a harassed army officer?'

'Yes.'

He swore.

'What's the matter?' I asked.

'He was at the last B.A. meeting – at Leeds. I happened to be there.' Sheriff's face was almost comically dejected. 'And – I flirted with his wife.' I could not help breaking into laughter; Sheriff began to smile.

'She's very nice,' he said. 'Quite young and more than average pretty, in a soft sort of way. How men like Pritt get wives as charming as that I've never gathered. They had a ball at Leeds, you know, scientists showing how gay they can be. She was easily the most attractive woman there. Ah' – his mouth drooped again – 'she wasn't worth this, though.'

'It needn't matter,' I said. 'He's always in the minority on the Committee. He'll oppose you, of course. On what grounds I don't know. Probably he'll say that the women on the staff would dislike you. But as a rule Fane is his only supporter. And if Fane approves of you, you ought to get it.'

'Splendid,' said Sheriff, cheerful again. 'If this comes off, do you know, Arthur, I shall have to change. I shall begin to steady down.'

A little later he said:

'Oughtn't we to do something about Hunt?'

'We ought,' I replied. 'But I don't know –'

'Anything would be better than the way he's going,' said Sheriff. He was intent and eager.

'Perhaps,' I said, 'but he's not actively unhappy.'

'Are you prepared to see him,' Sheriff asked quickly, 'just fade out?'

'He's got resources inside himself.'

'Why doesn't he use them? What can one do with internal resources? Why doesn't he – write?'

'I've hinted at it once or twice,' I said. Sheriff was in one of his gusts of exchanged personality:

'If I were Hunt, I couldn't stand it for a week.'

'He's very different, you know.'

'You ought to have done more than hint about writing. You ought to have told him to,' Sheriff said.

'*I* did last night,' he added. I smiled:

'When did you get this passionate concern for someone else's life?'

Sheriff grinned: 'When I was thinking of ways of making you take a hand in my own.

'I want that job,' he said. 'If you get it for me, I shall be safe. For the first time.' He paused. 'And you can't imagine how I want to be safe,' he said.

4

I mentioned Sheriff's name privately to Austin and Desmond on the following Thursday, and they were both favourable and treated it more as my responsibility than theirs. I wrote encouragingly to Sheriff; and I added that luck had played into our hands, for I had been able to couple support of him with some exciting news of my own.

I had been presented with a discovery. The idea, which arrived when I was fatigued, thinking of nothing, during the talk on buildings, had come off; Jepp had shown me the result when I arrived at the laboratory on Monday morning; I spent three days checking, collating, thinking, in my room almost all the time. It came out right. I was elated. It was nothing very wonderful in itself, I was amazed no one had thought of it before; but it was something everyone could understand, it was neat, and for me it could not be more opportune. For a discovery of some importance just before the appointment would leave the Committee no doubt, even if they had been less friendly. So on Thursday morning I wrote a six-line note to *Nature*, and had a promise that it would be published in a fortnight; in the afternoon, I mentioned it casually after the meeting.

'I congratulate you,' said Austin. 'This is a very *significant* advance. It shows how much that early work of ours has led to.'

Desmond smiled confidentially, and pressed my hand. 'It's good, old boy, it's good.'

Pritt was unexpectedly affable, and Constantine smiled with delight:

'This is exactly what we wanted,' he said. 'It leads us to all the problems we're really obliged to do. The important thing is to recognise the three varieties of problems in front of us: those we can't do, those we can and needn't, those we can and must. Well, this work of yours' – he had already assimilated it, made it quite familiar in his scientific cosmos – 'is at the back of the categorical imperatives. You see, of course –'

Austin was laughing. Since the decision in favour of London he had come to smile tolerantly at Constantine. Once I heard him say: 'He's a wonderful fellow. In spite of his long hair.'

I was sorry Fane had left the meeting early.

So now I had to wait until the first week in August, three weeks ahead, before the next meeting of the Committee and the definite appointment. I was over the worst of the anxiety now, though my nights were broken and I still had the sickness of worry as I tossed drowsing in the dawn. But the days were almost contented, often happy. I spent most of them at Lord's and the Oval. In the evenings, quietened by the days in the sun, I walked slowly round the parks, at last permitting myself to make plans for my own Institute.

They were plans of the fairly distant future, most of them. The next year or two did not require planning. The Institute would start along lines already laid down. I had four ideas, of which three would certainly work;

Constantine had ten, of which I could count on five. The main research of the first year war already settled.

My plans went a long way beyond that. I had to create the Institute so that it did the best work and attracted the best men, and that was going to take years. I could perhaps have decided to concentrate on one great problem, running the Institute like a team on Constantine's model. But to do that successfully required a very great scientist at the head, and I knew I was no Constantine. For me, it seemed clear, the obvious thing was to direct my own lines of research; and, as my second string, try to obtain young men on the chance that now and then I should happen on a genius. Having once got research going, men coming in, the others would follow by that curious process of imitation which has filled every institution from the Academy to the Cavendish.

And so I had to draw young men, and, having got them, see that they were not wasted. That, I thought, was where I ought to be useful; for, from all the laboratories I knew, the number of men thrown away by negligence, by incompetence, by sheer ignorance of the fact that there are differences between young men, would be enough to stock a reasonable scientific society in South America.

As far as I knew, I had not seen anyone with the promise of greatness fall into obscurity. That is, I thought almost always a man as gifted as Constantine would come through, whatever the luck; and in fact Constantine's own early career was a record of complete discouragement. But scientists of calibre just a little below the genius were being lost every day. The Austins, the Fanes, the Desmonds – I could replace them, I knew, by men who had gone frustrated into industry or teaching, and I should gain by the transaction. And as for the lesser figures, those who never get to the top, it seemed to be a matter of sheer chance who stays and who goes.

Of course, there are bound to be men who start research without any kind of aptitude at all. It is right that they should be sent to some other job as soon as the mistake appears: with a little personal intelligence, the mistake might often be discovered before they begin. There must

242

be a certain amount of trial and error, however, and one cannot expect a career in science or anything else to be adjusted with immaculate precision. But there is altogether too little trial and too much error. Luck must play a big part; but that does not seem a good reason for letting it decide altogether.

I realised this acutely as I called on my memory and took an inventory of names I had once known, names which I had last remembered in the journals, of whom I knew nothing now. I compared some of them with their contemporaries in research, and wondered: 'Why ever did he fail and *he* get on?'

That was the question I worked at on those long July nights, watching lights hazy in the blue mist, lying on my sofa with the room shadowed by a single lamp. What could be done? And how was I going to do it? First of all, I thought, I've got to distinguish between a new subject and one already mapped. To be useful in physics now, a man requires one of two sorts of technique very highly developed. Either one must be a mathematician, able to do certain operations whose shape is already known; or else one must be an accomplished experimenter, not in the old amateur sense but in a manner more like minor engineering. One of those two tricks is essential nowadays for fundamental work. Both Constantine and I started our science in physics, and both of us were without either the highly developed mathematical or experimental skill; and so there was no place for us, and we turned naturally to a less developed subject.

In any science less complete than physics, the more general mind still has its uses, though every day the chances grow less. For some time it will be such minds as Constantine's which make the great generalisations in the less exact sciences, and in my Institute I had got, as a major task, to nurse that sort of mind.

My job was to take care of young men with the 'general' scientific mind, who would usually have a little mathematics and adequate experimental skill. If they were good at either, so much the better; but for my purposes, for a subject in its youth, I would cherish a Constantine if he couldn't divide and was incapable of boiling water in a test tube. But Constantine's was not the only sort of general mind I wanted; a mistake like that, expecting everyone to think according to one pattern, is responsible for much of the wastage that I had condemned. For there are exactly as many ways of approaching the scientific world as there are individuals in science; it is only because the results are expressed in the same language, are subject to the same control, that science seems to be more uniform than, say, original literature. In effect, in the end, it *is* more uniform; but if we could follow the process of a scientific thought through many minds, as it actually happens and not as it is conventionally expressed after the event, we should see every conceivable variety of mental texture.

These varieties seemed to me to fall into two main types. Perhaps this was a shape I imposed for myself and corresponds to nothing real; but they are types observed often enough before in human affairs and I still believe that they are not entirely artificial. Applying them to scientific thinking, I should call the first the problem-solving type; minds which choose out of all the world round them a certain piece of experience and drive through it to an explanation. The probing, analytical, pragmatic minds, which at their best can reach the heights of Rutherford and Darwin, at their ordinary level work the way of Austin's or Desmond's. In every-day affairs it is probably the commoner type of mind, and so the performances of its highest exponents seem familiar and easy to most of us, they are of the same nature as our own: which means that we under-estimate them unduly, on the principle that what is not mysterious cannot be profoundly admirable.

The second type, the abstracting mind, of which Constantine is an example, gets perhaps more than its share of admiration, just because it is difficult for most of us to argue with, speaking as it does a different mental language from our own. These minds do not drive through a portion of experience; they wait for experience to make itself into shapes in their minds, they assimilate, correlate, find resemblances in different things, differences in similar things. At their best, in Faraday, Einstein, or in my generation Constantine, they are the great generalisers; at their worst they are infantilely fantastic and removed from all reality.

I needed both sorts to make my new subject advance. There were plenty of problems for the first kind to thrust themselves through; but above all, perhaps, we needed abstract generalisations such as Constantine's. The peculiarity of these minds, it seemed to me, is that they are only good when they are very good; an indifferent Constantine, generalising at many removes from reality, is far more nuisance than use. On the other hand, a couple of real Constantines would lay the framework of the subject ready for the problem-solvers; and within ten or twenty years I ought to have secured them. The danger was that they might get lost on the way. For the chances are against the Constantines from the time they begin research until they have reached a senior position; after that they may get more than their share of the praise. But at the beginning of their research, they are treated like everyone else, which looks just, which is ludicrously unjust; they are set a small definite disconnected problem to show how good they are. Naturally, the problem-solving mind races through this, gets an answer, draws a line neatly underneath it, and asks for more. The Constantines are left unhappy, wondering if this is the adventure of the mind for which they prayed, often incomparably less good at their little problem than a crude tough mind of the other sort. It is as though every young writer, to prove his fitness for serious literature, had to write a detective story; a good many would carry it off, but we should lose some great writers on the way. It would look equitable – 'treat them all alike,' as I once heard Austin say.

The difficulty would be, I decided, in finding early work for the Constantines to practise on. To select them, to separate newcomers to the Institute into problem-solvers and conceptualisers, would be fairly easy: no one ought to be in charge of the personal side of research if he could not trust himself to do it. But what to do with your conceptualisers when you had them was not so obvious. One could help; one would expect less in the way of finished work, more in ingenious abstraction. In this new subject there were one or two Constantine ideas which a potential Constantine would tackle more readily than a clear-cut problem. On the whole, though, the problem-solvers would come through more easily – unless I weighted the scales myself.

That is, if I thought I had discovered a Constantine, I should back my judgment and see that he had an easier start. The problem-solvers could be trusted to go through the difficult problems; my young Constantine would have the simpler ones, gain confidence, and have enough time to show what his abstracting power was like. If it did not turn out first-rate, he had been lucky; if it did, I had gained the man I wanted.

Unfair? It was fairer than blind chance. Liable to personal motives over which I had no control? So is every choice in the world: and more than most men, I should be on my guard. Giving them too easy a time, too sheltered from the lessons of experience? I saw no reason why life should be a moral gymnasium; adversity brings out the meaner qualities in almost all men; I had had a fairly hard time, and I should keep others from it if I could.

And so I should foster my Constantines; with any luck at all, I should find one or two before the subject was too old to need them. I thought, a trifle amused, that after I had brought one along with all the foresight I could command, he would probably leave me and do his great work somewhere else. That was a risk; it might happen, just as it may whenever one depends upon someone other than oneself; perhaps on the whole I should gain from defection rather than lose. For, unless I became deadened through habit, I should know something of these young men's desires; the faith, the ambition, the need for the ordinary human securities, which make a three-fold blend guiding any man's creative work.

It would take some skill to do it. But it could be done. It would need a good deal of handling.

The night before the final meeting I went to soothe myself at a cinema, as I had done frequently in the last few days: and as I came out I felt the thought streaming

246

through the residue of worry. 'It is going to be exciting, it will be worth all the struggle, because for the first time I shall be used to the full!'

Chapter 8

End of a journey

I

I had been asked to attend the beginning of the final meeting, to help discuss some small matter of Constantine's. It was assumed that I should then withdraw for the last time. As I turned out of Piccadilly I was slightly nervous with the luxurious nervousness that one knows is soon to be substituted by delight; I should listen for a few minutes, I thought, go away for the afternoon, and hear the news at tea-time.

The moment I got inside the room I knew it was all wrong. Someone stopped speaking as I entered. I made some remark to Desmond, who was nearest to me. There was an instant of silence before he replied, in a forced staccato. I felt empty. Constantine was sitting alone, pale and miserable.

Austin coughed. 'This is extremely unfortunate, Miles.'

'I'm afraid I don't know –' I said.

'This latest work of yours,' Austin was heavily troubled, 'someone has told Pritt it won't hold water.'

I turned angrily on Pritt: 'Who?'

Pritt said:

'Archer. I was in his place yesterday. He's doing the same work. He said your stuff couldn't be right' – Pritt smiled – 'you must have forgotten something rather elementary. Either that or your results are different from his. Under the same conditions –'

I thought feverishly, trying to hope, inventing reasons, rejecting them. I tried to keep anything but mild concern from my face.

'This is rather sad,' I said. 'If it's true.'

248

'Can it be true?' asked Austin loudly.

'I'm not certain,' I said. 'I'll look into it later to-day.'

I saw Desmond catch Pritts eye.

'It won't take long,' I added.

I sat through the first piece of business. It was one of the hardest things I had ever done. Constantine was speaking in a dulled voice. I could feel, I could not help but feel, the doubts, the pleasure, the regret, that came between the others and me: I knew what had been said, what would be said when I was gone. I longed to go, either to know the worst or prove myself right. In an hour or two I could look up the results, come back and say, very quietly: 'Professor Pritt's friend is wrong.' I stayed there, with my face as impassive as I could make it, keeping my hands from wandering.

Constantine stopped short. After they had voted, I got up and asked permission to withdraw. There was no friendly resonance in Austin's 'Yes.'

I took a taxi to the laboratory, went to my room, pulled out the records of the experiments, my notes, Jepp's films. I made false starts looking through the books. Thoughts kept branching jaggedly from one another, leading me on with trembling fingers. I spread out the films with quick, uncertain movements. I had to wipe my forehead to stop drops of sweat spoiling the films. Once I thought all was well. That's right – and then that – and, thank God, it all comes out perfectly. I knew I could not have made a mistake.

Then, quite suddenly, quite definitely, I realised I was working on a fact given me by Jepp. Which was wrong. Which he could not know was wrong, because there was a small technical point involved. Which I had looked over twenty times, but passed because of his assurance. Which if I had inspected it with a moment's care would have shouted itself as wrong. Upon that flaw, the whole structure rested.

I felt sick and giddy. But through despair a coolness of mind returned. I was able to work the whole thing out, how the mistake arose, how I had been led astray; on the other hand, I drew out the real inference from the experiments.

I even wrote down an account of it. It was a queer exercise. For I knew I was broken, and I could not realise it.

Constantine burst into the room a few minutes afterwards.

'Who have you appointed?' I asked.

'We are meeting again at five,' he said.

He looked at me, appealingly.

'What about this –?'

'I was wrong,' I said. 'Quite wrong.'

'Oh God,' he sighed.

I explained it to him, showed him the description I had just written. Disconsolate on my account as he was, he still became interested in the new possibilities. 'You see that must mean –' he said. Then he remembered:

'Oh, why *couldn't* you be careful?' he cried. He looked helpless, strangely forlorn.

'Perhaps I can persuade them still,' he added. 'After all, one's allowed a mistake or two –'

'Not in circumstances like this,' I said.

'I must go back,' he said. He wanted to stay.

2

They appointed Tremlin. After Constantine returned to the meeting, I walked the streets until the time we had arranged for dinner. Slowly my numbness passed. I began to feel what had happened to me. All the time I was hoping, though there was no hope.

Constantine told me how the meeting went. He was dejected; we ate rapidly at dinner to hinder a conversation that was hurting both of us. For me, I could not tell whether it was more painful to hear the details of my rejection, or leave them unknown to be guessed at in moments of reproach. I stopped him brusquely in one part of the story; at another I pressed him to tell all. I did not know what I wanted. More than anything I thought I wanted to escape. So that I was never sure of all that happened.

Constantine went back, I gathered, with my news; he had to tell them that Pritt's friend was right, but he made the best show he could of explaining it away. It was a mistake, but a natural and venial mistake. He gave a lavish and complicated description, which was the best way of defending me. He did everything he could; it was a task he loathed, for which he had no gifts, but he did as well as anyone could have done. Finally, he proposed that they should give me the Directorship. 'This triviality,' he said, 'has not affected the position, which is simply that we have the best man we could hope for.' I fancy he was more eloquent than that.

Fane suavely intervened. He had always had doubts, he said, about the prudence of appointing as Director so young and – if he might suggest – so unpedestrian a man. (I could imagine that double-edged sneer.) Now, of course, it was quite impossible. It would cripple the Institute at its inception to appoint a Director whose work had an element of – airiness.

Desmond thought Fane was right, said how sorry he was for everyone, but felt how lucky it was that this came out before they appointed me. Though he himself had always thought they would be wise to make a safer choice. He told them an anecdote of how I had talked lightly at Munich of research being easy. He looked earnestly at the committee. 'That's not the right spirit,' he said. 'I felt it then. I did'nt like it. And I must say I feel justified by results.'

That casual remark which I could dimly remember, thrown off when Desmond and I were drinking cheerfully together, seemed to incense them. More, perhaps, than anything else I had said or done.

Pritt said that I might be able to talk, but I couldn't get down to good hard spade work. That a man who couldn't do honest spade work himself would simply turn out flashy stuff at the Institute that everyone would laugh at. That I was not a scientist at all; spent my time having holidays on bathing beaches; that I was unbalanced on other things besides science, and should alienate all the future benefactors of the Institute; that I was a charlatan, and the sooner I was got rid of the better.

(Even from Pritt those remarks hurt, hurt too much to hear in full, and I cut Constantine short.)

Constantine said angrily that for Pritt to give an opinion

on my character and habits was an impertinence. He lost his temper, and Austin and Desmond tried to soothe him down.

Austin disapproved of the tone of Pritt's remarks, but was disappointed in me, felt that my future was not as certain to be brilliant as he once hoped, and had to withdraw the support he tentatively thought of giving. Austin was angry with me, of course, for his own sake; it was a rebuff to himself, he would no longer have a young man of his in charge, his patriarchate was shattered. And also he was genuinely fond of me, which made him more indignant still; I had disturbed his arrangements, hurt his scientific conventions, repudiated his affections all in one blow.

Constantine had no support, and my name was rejected. Pritt then proposed Tremlin – 'a sound man who won't let us down,' and he was elected after a perfunctory discussion, Constantine and Austin not voting.

'That's all,' Constantine said to me at the end of dinner, 'that's all.'

'It seems enough,' I said.

Constantine was frowning. He was puzzled as well as distressed.

'Does it make any real difference?' he said. 'Oh, I know it's disgusting, I know how you feel. But in practice, now, what difference does it make?'

I had a savage amusement at this practicalness.

He persisted: 'You'll still be able to do your research. Your present job –'

'It isn't much to the point,' I said. 'But, as a matter of fact, they think I'm going. It wouldn't be so easy to stay on –'

It would be impossible, I thought.

Constantine burst in:

'But we can soon settle that. They'll give you the assistant directorship at the Institute. It was mentioned – this evening.'

'Very gracious of them,' I said. 'A good assistant to Tremlin I should make.'

Constantine was hurt.

'Of course, it's annoying, but that job would keep you

here and let you do your work in comfort. We could still get on to those ideas –'

'In comfort?' I said tiredly. I could not explain. I searched round for an excuse. 'I want money –'

Constantine smiled eagerly:

'You'd get about as much as assistant director as you do now, and if you want more – well, I can let you have any amount. What can I do with £1,200 a year? You can borrow £300, £400 a year for as long as you like.'

'Thanks,' I said. 'I'm grateful.' I tried to mean it.

'You see,' said Constantine, 'this affair won't be serious at all. It can't affect you in any way except make you angry, and that's only temporary. You won't be angry for very long. In a couple of years you'll have all the new ideas carried through, and everything will be completely unaffected as though this had never happened.'

He was talking fast, in protection from my bitterness. I tried to respond to him, but it was too difficult. He insisted:

'And so everything will adjust itself?'

'No doubt,' I said. 'Oh yes, Leo. Only it's been rather – sudden.'

Then Desmond came up to us; and I felt both maddened and relieved.

'I've just seen you,' he said affably. 'I've been eating alone.'

Constantine muttered something, looked embarrassed, and, after staying a moment whilst Desmond chatted, said that he must go. We watched him leave. Desmond gave me a glance, half-cheerful, half-furtive.

'I'll have to run away soon,' he said. 'But let's get down a drink or two first.'

We walked out to one of the bars near by, and stood in the middle of a crowd so noisy that Desmond's voice became a tone more strident:

'Wonderful days,' he shouted over his glass.

He saw my face set harshly. He said:

'I'm sorry I couldn't do anything for you this afternoon, Miles. Believe me, I would have done anything I could. But it was no use. You'd dropped too big a brick, you know.'

'Yes,' I said.

'Of course I should have overlooked it for myself. We're all human. I've dropped bricks myself. But the others wouldn't. You can't blame them altogether. They have to think of their duty to the Institute.'

'They've done their duty,' I said. 'With their present choice.'

'Tremlin?' Desmond laughed confidentially. 'Oh, Tremlin's a dull dog. Most of them are dull dogs. But it doesn't matter. We can't have everything we want. We rub along somehow.' He looked at the clock. 'I must run for my train. These drinks are on me.' He gave me some money and rushed off. I remember that he did not give me quite enough.

The night was a long one. For hours I sat in my rooms trying to read. New forms of my humiliation kept rousing themselves. I should have to write to Sheriff; there was not much chance for him now; he and Audrey would talk of my disgrace together. I went to the desk to write the letter. I could not get beyond the first words, and I looked at them so long that they grew faint and I wondered if the light was failing. At last I left it. There were the notes of a new paper on the desk. It had been designed to give the Institute a good send off.

I slept in exhausted snatches, waking each time, it seemed, to an emptier world. When finally I woke up late none of the pain had gone; it was not an imaginary misery that vanished in the morning. With a sick nervousness, I rustled through the newspapers as soon as I was out of bed, but they were merciful. There were neat little paragraphs in one or two: 'Biophysical Institute Director appointed – Honour for young scientist. Yesterday the Executive Committee of the Institute for Biophysical Research elected a brilliant young scientist, Dr. R. P. Tremlin, to be the Institute's first Director. Dr. Tremlin, who is now a Senior Lecturer at Birmingham University, has had a most distinguished career at Cambridge and London ... he is thirty-seven years of age.'

That was all, and I had a touch of relief. I ate a heavy breakfast. Then I did not know what to do. I wanted to avoid everyone I knew: on the other hand, I told myself anxiously, I ought to make some plans. I sat while the tea went cold, a medley of fears and anger and indecisions, pretending to myself that I was thinking.

At last I telephoned Macdonald's London flat, found he was there and called on him. He had the scientific world at his finger-tips, and was one of the shrewdest men I knew; it was good to see his square intelligent head again.

'Well,' he said, 'this is a nasty mess.

'I heard of it last night,' he added. 'All sorts of twittering there was. They all enjoyed seeing a man come down. You'd better tell me the story.'

I told him everything, a little resentful because I had to excoriate myself again. His small steady eyes were alert; at the end he said:

'No one seems to come out of this with any particular credit. Except perhaps Constantine – and if I'd been there I should have made a better fight. I should have tried to persuade them to adjourn. It was incredibly stupid of them not to have you, of course. And it was incredibly stupid of you to take the slightest risk just at this point. It's a pity when we do get men in science of something like adequate intelligence, they go and get mixed up in scandals. You don't deserve much sympathy.'

I asked sharply: 'Apart from the moral – what am I to do?'

'That's quite clear.' Macdonald lit his pipe. 'You've got to rehabilitate yourself. Which will take a longish time. You've got to accept the assistant directorship if they offer it to you – which I think they will. You've got to work absolutely steadily, without another suspicion of a mistake. You've got to let yourself be patronised and regretted over. You've got to get out of the limelight. Then in three or four years you'll be back where you were; though it will be held up against you, one way and another, for longer than that. It will delay your getting into the Royal, of course. That can't be helped. You'll have a lean time for a while; but you're young enough to get over it.'

'This isn't nice to hear,' I said.

'Did you want me to say something nice to hear?' he asked.

'I'm afraid I did,' I said.

'That wouldn't help,' Macdonald said.

'No,' I said. But I suspected him of enjoying the truth he told. He would have prevented my disaster if he could; he was sorry, he would help me in the future; he was a sincere, a capable, and active friend. Yet my suspicion was there and I made no effort to be rid of it. He was deriving some satisfaction from the wreck, and it was not altogether with dismay that he sketched so crisply, so truthfully, the humiliating path of my next few years. I thanked him, and left. Later on I recognised that the note I caught in Macdonald's voice is to some extent true of all of us.

When I listened to Macdonald, however, I was incapable of feeling more than angry disappointment. I heard satisfaction in a friend's voice; that was all, that was more than enough. I had to find a friend who would be sorry. Years before I might have gone to Hunt, but not now; there was too much to explain, too many complications to pass his slow mind before I reached his sympathy. Another man might have gone to a woman, but that I never could have done, not even if Audrey and I had been still together.

I could think of no one. I had several intimates and a great many friends. Some, like Constantine, would not understand how badly I was hit; some did not know this side of my life; many, I felt despairingly, would have something of Macdonald's satisfaction. At last I turned to old Hulme, whom I had venerated in my student days. I had seen him fairly often since I returned to London. He was an Emeritus Professor and old now, but he was working calmly on. I went to his house after lunch. He was asleep but got up and welcomed me with his gentle courtesy.

'I think I know why you've come,' he said. 'This mishap of yours at the Institute.'

'Yes,' I said. The story was going round already. 'How did you know?'

'I saw the appointment in *The Times*. I could not understand it. And so I went to see Austin this morning.' He sat half-sideways in his armchair. There was a small fire burning in the grate.

'I needn't tell you, then. That will be a relief.'

'I'm sorry.' Hulme looked at me. His face was minutely lined, but the eyes were clear and alert as I first remembered them. 'I'm more than sorry. I had something like this on a smaller scale when I was younger than you. I couldn't forget it for a long while. And I felt it was unfair that this should happen to me. I expect you feel like that, too, don't you? Haven't you asked yourself – "Why should this have happened to *me*?" '

'I think I have,' I answered.

'And I expect you feel as I did, that you're being unjustly treated? I mean, not by fate, by human beings. You must feel they should have appointed you.'

I murmured an assent.

'Naturally you do, and so did I. My case was a little different, but I felt the same. But, Miles' – he smiled – 'I think maybe we were wrong, I in my youth, you now. I mean, this Committee of yours, those electors of mine, may be right judged by the wider interests of science. I know your Committee were not acting in the wider interests of science; I'm not altogether blind, even yet, you know. I don't think my electors were. But it is possible they do better than they know, perhaps. Because, you see, we both committed a crime against the truth. A crime in good faith, admittedly, honest, simply a mistake. Your mistake, if I may say so, was even stupider than mine. But there we were; we issued false statements. Now if false statements are to be allowed, if they are not to be discouraged by every means we have, science will lose its one virtue, truth. The only ethical principle which has made science possible is that the truth shall be told all the time. If we do not penalise false statements in error, we open up the way, don't you see, for false statements by intention. And of course a false statement of fact, made deliberately, is the most serious crime a scientist can commit. There are such, we both know, but they're few. As competition gets keener, possibly they will become more common. Unless that is stopped, science will lose a great deal. And so it seems to me that false statements, whatever the circumstances, must be punished as severely as is possible. From the wide point of view, from the justice of science as a whole, it is right that I should have been treated badly, and that you should now. It is expedient that you should suffer for the common good,' he said.

His smile was kind. We talked on for a time. I was not indignant with him, as I had been with Macdonald; but he added something to my ache. He had talked with delicacy, as he always did; I fancy that he exaggerated his own misfortune to ease mine; but if this was the best I could hope for, from an old man who liked me, who was of singular tolerance, what treatment could I expect from the rest? A problem in scientific ethics, for my older friends, with perhaps 'It's a pity: a very promising man,' thrown in; on the other side the sneers of Pritt and his companions.

When I left Hulme, I was in a worse state than the night before. I should not have believed that I could feel persecuted; yet I was impelled to avoid glances in the street, behind each voice there seemed a hiss of gossip. Macdonald and Hulme – all my more eminent friends would take this attitude, interestedly commenting; perhaps Constantine alone would defend me with passion, and he was too abstracted to count. Wherever I went, at the University Club, at my restaurant, I should meet acquaintances who knew the story; I imagined their curiosity, their inquisitive sympathy. I could not face it. I could bear no longer the presence of people I knew. I must get away, I thought. Leave it all, and get away where each word does not suggest other words behind my back. Get away, and calm myself, and think. Get my future clear. Leave them all to enjoy my downfall, and escape.

The thought of action stiffened me a little. I bought tickets, went to my flat, packed, drove to Newhaven for the night boat. It was mistily calm on the water, and I got an hour or two's sleep.

As soon as the car was disembarked I set off. My plans for a long holiday to celebrate the Directorship had been almost completed. I had everything ready for travel, and a route across Europe. Now it seemed as good as any other, and I followed it. I drove into the sun of that fresh August morning; for a while I was exhilarated, I was getting away. Then habit took control.

I remember very little of the long drive. The first night I spent at some village in Lorraine. Through those four hundred miles there were names which must have aroused me, old history and new; associations of the war must have gone through my mind, moments superseding the thread of my disaster; but all I now recall is winding through desolate hill roads in the dark, a sombre hotel where I slept, worn-out.

Of the second night I have a clearer memory. I got up soon after dawn, ran through the Black Forest and the Bavarian highlands, over the Scharnitz and into the Tyrol. Nothing of that stays except what I have seen at other times. But late that night I was drinking outside a café in Sterzing and a woman came and sat herself at the table.

'You are staying here?' she asked, in German.

'Only for a night,' I answered.

'You are unhappy? Lonely?' she said. Her hair was lighter than her brown and shining skin. I remember, too, strong, square fingers resting on the table.

'A little,' I said.

'It is not good to be unhappy,' she said. Oddly, that statement of general principle returns to me often; and I hear it in its cadence of that night, with the rustle of dry leaves across the deserted square. 'It is not good to be unhappy.'

I liked her in the half-light from the café. I think that two nights before I might have gone with her, excited by the aphrodisiac of sorrow. But I had driven eight hundred miles in two days and had very little sleep for a week. So that, on the spot, I never considered it.

The next day I went through the Dolomites, over the Tre

Croci, down to the Friulian plain. As I went over the baked road to Monfalcone, through fatigue, through bitterness, that permeated a small and private joke; for here the Italian armies ran from Caporetto – and I thought of Mr. Hemingway, and how much better any of his heroes would have done on the night before. After that, I had a glow of pleasure at the sight of Trieste in the evening, as the first lights came out along the water front. It is one of the loveliest towns, I thought. Then, for the last hundred miles, I was too tired, too shaken, to know anything but physical misery and the aching necessity of seeing the road in front. The climb over Istria in the growing darkness was only a torment; and then, after Susak, an hour's drive, rocking over the rough road to a little town on the Slovenian coast, where, just before midnight, I finished my journey.

4

I slept until the next afternoon. I woke and ate, talked in a mixture of languages to the owner of the hotel, walked by the sea until sunset, then ate and slept again. Absurd as it seemed, I was the better for my flight. I had broken down to myself, and it had released me. When I woke next morning, I was worried and angry, but I could begin to think.

I lay on a rock and threw stones into the blue, the transparent water. It was very hot; protected by years of sunburn, I was nevertheless blistered on the shoulder. Through the water I could see fine, regular shells. I tried to drop a stone on to one of them. And all the time, as an undercurrent, I was thinking –

I ought to get out of science. –

There is nothing for me, now. Not for years. Macdonald was right (I resented him for being right). With patience and penitence and effort –

Why should I be patient and penitent?

Why should the drab and jealous men, the peasants, get me in the end? Make me have a respectable success – after working respectably enough, dully enough. I should be tamed as everyone else was tamed.

Either I got out of science or else I had to be patient and conform. There was no other way.

I thought –

If I get out, what can I do?

I cannot afford gestures. Money and leisure I must have. I want them for themselves – and for the freedom which I have won, the freedom of which they are a sign. If I had been wealthy in my youth, perhaps I could afford to take up poverty now. As it is, I am bound by the prizes I have won. I must have the time and money to get the simple pleasures, the oldest, the simplest, the expensive pleasures – such as sitting in the sun by the sea.

As I am doing now. If I give up science, can I come here?

What can I do?

I am able and versatile enough.

What can I do?

Industry? Scientific industry? Underpaid and no leisure. No successful don would leave academic science for industry. Until they have academic leisure, or are fabulously well paid to compensate them. Scientific industry is the refuge of the not-quite-successful enough (which is why industrial thousands are wasted on research). And also I should be utterly unsatisfied with work that was only work. That narrowed the choice.

I am thirty. Too old for anything I cannot step into straight away.

Teaching? Not academic teaching, which is instructing people in unimportant subjects by a method in which one does not believe. But real teaching, getting into people, feeling with them. I might enjoy it – but I should run into another catastrophe. For I was too dangerous a heretic to be allowed power in the most conventional of human activities. And too heretical in my heresy: for my views on the human soul are offensive to a public-school headmaster; but they are also offensive to an orthodox Freudian, though not in precisely the same way.

Scientific journalism? Could I write more articles and live on them? It was too big a risk. The bottom was falling out of the American market. And, of course, a successful

261

scientist makes more from scientific articles than a professional journalist.

It is a bad time to be unattached. Perhaps the world will never recover from this collapse (it was the August of 1931).

Whatever I do, there will be some unpleasant years. In science the unpleasant years will be safe. In anything else I shall have as bad a time without the safety.

I am a little in debt.

Yet to think of going back. Watching the dullards gloat. Working under Tremlin. Having every day a reminder of the old dreams.

It occurred to me that I had forgotten my devotion to science.

It occurred to me I had no devotion to science.

5

I took it, I remember, very much as a matter of course. My thoughts had been running on, something as I have written, though they were like any other thoughts, more random, more shot with chance associations than seems profitable to write.

I have tried to give an impression of the general drift of my thinking; and, in the middle of it, that sudden realisation. It was afternoon, and the wind was getting up from the sea. I am not devoted to science, I thought. And I have not been for years, and I have kept it from myself till now.

Uncomfortably, I felt how much easier if the realisation had come before my disaster. I suspected myself; one can throw up a faith in petulance, and find good reasons for it afterwards. But I became almost certain it was not that. There were so many signs going back so far, if I had let myself see, if it had been convenient to see. The impression Hunt had made on me in my youth; the night I had listened to him in Manchester; they had led to that human interest of mine, that had grown into a passion, that was – I saw it clearly now – a rival to my science. Had been since its first days. Further back, perhaps, than I knew. As far back as I could remember, those passions had been competing: and for a long time, the human one, which called on all my mind but went far deeper, had been winning in the dark. My disaster had brought it home a little sooner, that was all; in the Committee itself, when all my scientific plans seemed secured, my absorbing interest had been the human conflict, the motives and the difference between those motives and their conscious shape. But it was not a faith, I thought, this human exploration. It was a substitute for a faith. Perhaps it had grown up to supply the loss of my faith, the only one I ever held. Because I am a man of eager interests, I had thrown myself into human beings – to escape the chill when my scientific devotion ended.

That might be. It seemed not to matter very much. Of the end of my devotion, though, there was no doubt: and it was an event in my life. It was queer that it should come on an afternoon by the Adriatic, I remember thinking; I was very much interested, not at all disturbed, and for a while the future faded from my thoughts.

I wondered that I had kept the doubts away so long. They might have come as clearly as now, before the mistake, the disaster – and then it struck me how maybe they had helped to bring the mistake about. I could make excuses, tiredness, strain, sheer chance; but despite them all, if I had been intent as I was once, I wondered if it would have happened. Why did one make mistakes? How much purpose was there? It is half-amusing, half-distressing, that we shall never know, I thought.

Why had I ever been devoted to science? And why had the devotion faded? I remembered arguments with Hunt and Audrey, years ago. Intuitively, it seemed, they had been wiser than I, though all the logic was on my side then. What had I told Audrey were the reasons why men did science? I should still say much the same, except that nowadays I should allow more for accident; many men become scientists because it happens to be convenient and they may as well do it as anything else. But the real urgent drives remain: there seemed to be three kinds. Three kinds of reason to give to oneself, that is. One can do science because one believes that practically and effectively it benefits the world. A great many scientists have had this as their chief conscious reason: for me it never was and at thirty it seemed more foolish than ten years before. Because if I wanted directly to benefit the world, I should, as I once told Audrey, have done something quite different. By this time (1931), I felt that more strongly still.

One can do science because it represents the truth. That, or something like it, was the reason I had given in the past. So far as I had a conscious justification, it would always have been this. Yet it was not good enough, I thought, watching a red-sailed boat running between an island and the shore. Science was true in its own field; it was perfect within its restrictions. One selected one's data – set one's puzzle for oneself, as it were – and in the end solved the puzzle by showing how they fitted other data of the same kind. We know enough of the process now to see the quality of the results it can give us; we know, too, those sides of experience it can never touch. However much longer science is done, since it sets its own limits before it can begin, those limits must remain. It is rather as though one was avidly interested in all the countryside between this town and the next: one goes to science for an answer, and is given a road between the two. To think of this as the truth, to think of 'the truth' at all as a unique ideal, seemed to me mentally naïve to a degree.

Just as to think that science within its restrictions is not truthful is to be ignorant of the meaning of words. Constantine, I know, would agree with both these statements. But where we should differ is over the value to be given to this particular, restricted, scientific truth. I should hold that now its nature is established, now we know the way in which our minds determine its restrictions, its value lies only in application; a scientific fact now does not enlighten us on the nature of all facts; its meaning we know before we find it out; it is important only that it gives us a new unit in our control of the outside world. In the days I argued with him, Constantine, however, would give scientific facts a value over and above their use – an almost mystical value, not as truth so much as knowledge. As though, somehow, if we knew enough we should have a revelation.

One can also do science because one enjoys it. Naturally anyone who believes wholeheartedly, either in its use or its truth, will at the same time enjoy it. Constantine, for example, gains more simple hedonistic enjoyment from research than most men from their chosen pleasures; and though he is the most devoted scientist I know, there are many men to whom enjoyment comes as a consequence of faith. But I think it is also possible to enjoy science without believing overmuch in its use, or having any views upon the value of its truths. Many people like unravelling puzzles. Scientific puzzles are very good ones, with reasonable prizes. So that either without examining the functions of science, being indifferent to them or taking them for granted, a number of men go in for research as they would for law; living by it, obeying its rules, and thoroughly enjoying the problem-solving process. That is a perfectly valid pleasure; among them you can find some of the most effective of scientists. They no doubt get their moments of ecstasy, as I did once in my youth, when I saw a scientific truth disclose itself in my mind; these ecstasies do not depend upon a belief in scientific values, any more than a religious ecstasy depends on a belief in God.

Perhaps this last reason, simple, uncritical enjoyment, is the commonest of all, I thought. Well, it was a reason good enough, I had to admit. But I did not want to admit it; because, for me, I should always need faith in the results before I could enjoy. Human intricacies I might enjoy for their own sake. But not scientific problems, unless they were important to me for something richer than themselves.

'There's nothing in it for me,' I thought.

'The wonder isn't that I'm not devoted now; it is that I persuaded myself of it for so long.'

'I shall never get the devotion back,' I thought.

6

I walked along the shore, among the sharp grey rocks. My future was affected by this realisation, I thought. Or it ought to be affected; I ought to leave science. I ought not to go back.

But the earlier questions returned. What could I do? How was I going to live? I could not escape from those arguments of mine. If I left science, at the best I was taking an immense risk; at the worst, I was throwing away all I had gained. Yet I ought to leave.

However, I was not so distressed or troubled now. I was getting my world straight at last. For a day or two I stayed by that calm sea, and sometimes, though I have never been there again, I am homesick for it now. I thought out my future more carefully there than I had done before; I seemed able to think, after the nervous strain, with a keen lucidity; science, my own plans, the European crisis in which my later life would be involved, all fell into order in my mind. Despite the anxiety which I could not lose, I had a sort of intellectual contentment.

I wondered once if this is how priests felt, when their only obstacle to success in the Church is a troublesome disbelief in God.

If I go back, I thought, I shall have to do all Macdonald said, rebuild my position, work fiercely at science – without any delight in it. I shall have to take the assistant directorship: I shall have to placate them so that they give it to me. I shall have to renounce Sheriff, perhaps, to show how penitent I am. That will be the unpleasantest thing, I thought dishonestly; and then corrected myself, that will be the thing I shall like least when I have to write the news to Sheriff, knowing that Audrey would hear. There will be all manner of humiliations. I shall have no pride left. If I go back, I thought, I shall be working fiercely at science: and all the time I shall prepare the way for leaving it. For if I go back at all, I must not let myself relax. I must not find it too comfortable to leave, when I am established again. I shall be tempted, I know. For soon, incredible as it seems, I shall have fought my way into a sort of peace.

Slowly the thoughts grew less urgent. Distress lessened to an ache I nearly forgot, anxiety became lost in the plans it made. My body became full of a lazy well-being, as I lay in the sun by the sea.

Part 4

Away from the Stars

Chapter 1

The new beginning

I

I went back. I called on Austin and tried to persuade him how penitent I was, how sorry I was that I had failed him, how resolved to make amends. He was mollified in the end:

'It's a pity,' he said. 'It's a pity. But – you are taking this in a good spirit.'

I was still, anomalously, a co-opted member of the Committee. I offered to resign but Austin would not hear of it.

'We don't want any more *trouble*,' he kept saying, 'we don't want any more trouble.'

So I had to attend the Committee's meetings in September. I had already told Constantine I was going to be amenable. He alone knew the secret of my flight; I called on him the day I got back, and I remember the surprise, the friendly, the overwhelmingly relieved smile with which he greeted me. It touched me that he tried to talk only on my immediate concerns; when he was tempted to break off into a cosmic sweep, he said awkwardly: 'But I don't want to make you listen to something that – that isn't important just now.'

The meetings, however, were hours of exacerbation. Tremlin was there as a full member now; his manner, always constrained, fluctuated from jocular to formally polite. I was still sensitive to every whisper: I could not help thinking that each private conversation was about me, smiling at my fall, threatening my future. For the Assistant Director had not yet been appointed. The hiss in every whisper – and this Committee had many subdued dialogues – was for me the sibilant at the end of my name.

269

I had some reason to be nervous; if I were not appointed I should be seeking a job; and the formation of a National government was not a very good sign for a young man without secure means of support. Perhaps University College could be induced to resurrect my position; but not having been appointed to two posts is scarcely a strong recommendation for an act of grace.

It was then I sacrificed Sheriff. He had no chance, with my influence gone; there was another man I liked in the running, for whom Constantine's support, withdrawn from Sheriff, might secure the job. But perhaps I should have done it in any case, to propitiate the Committee; it remains one of the things of which I am ashamed. Constantine in my place would have fought loyally, not realising that it was useless, barely realising that it would only harm himself. On the other hand, I knew how they would each vote, and how Pritt had made Sheriff's name a danger to its proposer. With my eyes open, I let them know that it would be better if Sheriff's claims were not considered.

Austin and Desmond were pleased, and Pritt not so hostile, after the withdrawal. It was something of an open apology – an apology, as it were, for all the reckless, arrogant gestures of my youth. They received it with considerable gratification. I was becoming tamed, they felt; as always, the respectabilities were winning in the end.

They elected me to the Assistant Directorship at the next meeting. Tremlin spoke strongly in my favour, Constantine told me; no one took the trouble to bring up another name, though Pritt declined to vote. I was relieved; I could live much as I had been living; I had secured safety and a breathing space. But now I had it, it seemed tawdry enough, for all I had given away.

Constantine was in high spirits:

'You'll be here, that's the important thing,' he said. 'We can go ahead, now. Just as though everything had gone perfectly.'

I settled down to the plans I had conceived by the seashore. There were three years of work ahead, at least: by that time I should have regained my position; by that time I should be ready to leave science. More strongly, now I had come back, I wanted to leave science only when I had retaken my success; if I left just after a reverse, there would always be a suspicion in my mind. I should not be able to say an unfavourable thing about a scientist for fear that I was merely being jealous of what I might have been. It occurred to me that this process might be carried too far; if, when we decried an occupation, we had to prove our lack of jealousy by excelling at it – well, one would spend a good many years becoming an Archbishop.

I got to it. I had two students under me at the Institute, and by late autumn we were all working hard. Tremlin gave me a free hand, and asked for advice and ideas with self-conscious gentlemanliness. Actually, though, he tried to ease an awkward position, and I was grateful to him. He has had his reward by now; for the Institute's fame, which quickly became considerable, owed something to my work during those years.

Concentrating on work which had to be done, which I did not enjoy, I led a solitary life. I was something in the mood that came after Audrey left me. I worked savagely: some ideas succeeded, but the light had gone out. At the best, I got a grim satisfaction from work completed. It was a step nearer. That was all. Even Constantine's ideas sometimes palled, but for two years I kept steadily at work, and, judged by results, with success.

In the middle of that period I fell in love again. It happened slowly, not like the quick thrust of my first love: but I should still have remembered the first sight of Ruth, even if I had never met her again. Constantine was becoming actively busy now, getting together groups of the left-wing intelligentsia for all kinds of collective disapproval. One night he took me along to a flat in Bloomsbury; it was a meeting of about thirty people, some of whom I knew, and the names of most of the rest; we were to discuss the founding of an anti-war movement. Several men talked with knowledge and intelligence about the consequences of another European war. Another gave us good reasons for it happening. Constantine described how science was subsidised by national governments in order to be under control for military purposes.

Then suddenly a clear, warm voice inquired:

'But what is the *use* of all this?'

I chuckled, and turned to see who it was. I saw a profile very fine cut, with a nose a trifle irregular, and a twist to the lips; her hair was darkish, carefully waved, and she was well dressed, so far as I could see.

'What is the use?' she went on. 'We all know this, we're all for peace, I imagine. Why don't we accept the horrors and get on?'

There was a hint of laughter in her voice, but she was in earnest.

'What are you going to do?' she asked. 'Most of you have got reputations. When the war's on top of us, what are you going to do – except martyr yourselves?'

Constantine answered, smiling with cheerful humility.

'That is exactly the purpose of this movement, to find out and get to work. You ought to help. We –'

'If so, we shouldn't start on it like a college debating society,' she interrupted him. 'Like children. That's our disadvantage. We're children. Clever children. We can't handle things until we grow up –'

I was attracted from the start; and intently listened to those last words. There was an undermeaning, I fancied, from her own life. Perhaps it had crept out unawares: I should like to know.

I saw her several times during the next few months. We discovered some friends in common, and I found out something about her. She was called Ruth Elton, was two or three years younger than I, had plenty of money, and spent her time organising a curious sort of intellectuals' circulating library.

'I must do something,' she said to me. 'I shall do something better soon. When I've got the trick of running things.'

There was an emptiness in her life, as I had felt that first night. Love had treated her badly; or she had made love difficult for herself. I could not tell for certain; she was in London only rarely, I seldom got her alone. I did not want to explore her life deeply, in case I was too much attracted myself. For I could dine, chat, satisfy some of my interest and still not be lost.

But Ruth became fond of me; and when she did, I could begin to fall in love. I had been too badly wounded by Audrey to love anyone spontaneously.

When I got to know Ruth, when she showed herself fond of me, I saw how much she wanted love. There had been an unhappy love affair, I knew, where she had given her heart, but not her body. She had been much in love, passionately, despite her holding back. After he left her there had, I fancied, been one or two attempts to get 'experience'.

Ruth's 'experience', I felt sure, could not have helped her much. I suspected it had not gone far. I could not imagine her plunging into amorous adventure. She was too fastidious, had too many checks, I thought. When I first kissed her, I knew for certain.

3

After that, I hesitated a little. I was in love by now, and was coming to know her well enough to trace some of the associations behind her words. I knew how proud she was that I was doing effective work. 'Science' to her meant something impersonal, lofty and massive. Often I talked astronomy with her, and once I described the beginnings of my scientific passion as a child. Her eyes shone:

'It's pure poetry and it *works*,' she said. 'It's poetry in action. It's – everything.'

Sooner or later, I thought, I should have to break the news. It would make no difference ultimately, but she would be troubled. Her keenness once established on a track was hard to move. She liked to talk about my work, which she did very well; she came several times to the Institute, and sat about while I was working, and had an efficient scheme for collecting all my notes, and having them filed with a neat office routine. She took down the readings of a long experiment, quickly, competently, cheerfully.

Ah well, it had to be tackled. I took her to the theatre one night, and we went back to my flat. She sat in the arm-chair opposite mine, looking young and happily flushed; she got an endearing pleasure out of being taken out; even when she was scorning a play directly, scathingly, as she so often did, she was glad to be there.

I switched off the main light, and we were left with the lamp by the fireplace.

'Ruth,' I said, 'I wonder if you would like to get married?'

'I think I should,' she said. 'Oh! of course I should.'

'You're being rash,' I said.

'If I am,' she laughed.

'Nonsense,' she added. 'Why is it rash?'

She was laughing, mockingly; she made a habit of laughing at my deliberations. This time, however, she did not laugh my next words away.

'You know what you're marrying?'

'I've got a rough idea,' she said.

'That's not quite enough, but still – I've got no money, you know.'

'What does that matter?' she asked. 'With mine.'

'I've not even got riotous health,' I said. 'I'm older than I ought to be at thirty-one.'

'Perhaps I could change all that,' she replied.

'Too much work for too long,' I said. 'And too many worries. They won't get less just yet. But there you are – if you want a poor man with doubtful health on your hands, here is one.'

I smiled across at her.

'You mustn't think,' I said, 'that I've even got a certain future to promise you. I may have, but it's a gamble.'

She frowned:

'But your science? Everyone says –'

'I'm going to leave science in a year or two.'

She laughed: 'Is this a joke?'

'I mean it,' I said.

'But I don't understand,' she said. There were puzzled lines on her face, changing it from contentment. 'Has this happened all of a sudden? It's ridiculous. Oh, why?'

'That would be a longish story,' I said. 'And you'd still disapprove at the end of it. But let me tell you two things. That after I've done a job I've set myself, I shall count every hour at the Institute as an hour taken off my life. And that when I leave science I've not finished living, you know: I think there's a chance I may do other things better. The things we've talked about as jokes. Remember?'

Then I said:

'Anyway, I'm afraid my mind's made up. On most things you will find me easy enough to manage, if you have me. On this you won't. I shan't have a scientific job in – two years at the most. If you marry me, you'll only get the bare minimum of a man. Without position or money or a job –'

'What have you got?' she was smiling.

I wondered to myself how I should have proceeded if I had doubted her answer. I had been, as we all like to do, enjoying the proof of her love; that was all, I knew.

'I'm in love with you, which is something. Though you ought to have done better for yourself.'

'What else?'

'A few miscellaneous tricks,' I said. 'Miscellaneous experience – no, you ought to be compiling this catalogue.'

She smiled:

'An odd sense of humour –the best listener I ever knew – oh, and you're grown up. Which most of us aren't.'

I said:

'These aren't flattering enough. Can't you think of anything else?'

'Nothing else,' she laughed. 'How they would help you to live if you gave up science, I don't know. It's a good job you're going to have a wealthy wife.'

'If you weren't wealthy, I shouldn't have a wife,' I said. 'I should have made love to you. But marry you, how could I? In your list you missed out expensive tastes.'

'I missed out courage, and all the things I admire you

275

for,' she said. I saw her lips were trembling. I went over and kissed her. I could not yet allow myself to make love. She ought to have been my own age in love: but as it happened, she was not.

Her eyes were wet and she closed them. She said:

'Most of all I missed out honesty. Are there many men more honest than you?'

'There are any number,' I said, 'who think they are.'

'But they're too stupid to know what honesty means,' she said quickly.

I sat on the arm of her chair with her fingers in mine.

'If you are going to be fool enough to marry me,' I said, 'it may as well be soon.'

'Any time,' she said.

Then she looked up.

'But you won't leave science,' she said, 'until you've thought it over with me?'

Chapter 2

Risks in attendance

I

We were married within six months. We went to see Ruth's mother, a gently satirical old lady who had a villa at Menton. There were no difficulties of any sort; we arranged to be married at the end of the term, and spend Christmas in Spain. In November I resigned from the Institute.

Ruth was still upset about my leaving science. At times she thought it was a whim of mine. How else could a man leave the most fascinating of work, at which he happened to be good? I can still see her clear profile as she complained: 'But it's all so – so temperamental. Are you sure you just don't want a rest?' But when at last she saw that, whatever the causes, they were too deep to remedy, she was resolved. She had the money, if I wanted to leave the Institute, why not at once? I thought: I had done enough; in two years I had opened my scientific career again; I wanted no more; it was time to go now. There were a few pieces of work I should like to finish, but I could do them away from laboratories. It would not be a clean break, I saw; I doubt if it could have been. For ten years I had been living among science and scientists; I had many friends left in it, and their interests could not help rousing mine; I had a curiosity, which was enhanced the nearer I came to leaving, in the problems on which I had worked myself. I should still want to know the answers. I should not be able to keep myself from reading the journals. Over matters where I had some special knowledge I had not published, I might still want to intervene. I explained this to Ruth just after I resigned; she was gratified, and thought it was a sign that I should soon go back. It struck me as an ironical joke that when I was in the full rush of scientific enthusiasm, I fell in love with Audrey who could not understand it; and that when I had exhausted the passion for research, I loved Ruth who wanted to keep me at it.

And so I resigned in the middle of the term. Tremlin was primly disturbed, very polite and awkwardly courteous; he was genuinely sorry I was going, for both our sakes. He even persuaded me to wait over a week-end before I sent in the final resignation. I remember him, looking quizzically, anxiously, through his spectacles: 'You'll forgive me saying so, Miles, but you're always a little impatient.'

I had to see Austin, who was so obviously disappointed that he recovered himself by giving some heavy advice. Macdonald received the news in his unmoved, practical way, and at once arranged a dinner party for me to meet people who would be useful in the new future. Desmond dropped in at the Institute, told me he had often thought of giving up science himself, and said that he must go and choose the wedding present. I should like to have seen his choice.

Then there was Constantine. I shirked telling him until the last, and he was upset. In some way he felt it was his fault:

'If I had done better,' he said, 'you wouldn't be doing this. I ought to have known what you wanted. You got tired of these problems – I've got something new on the last one –' He described it for a moment, and then broke off, suddenly.

'We ought to have worked out some of the new ideas, we could have done it,' he said. 'They would have interested you. As it is, this is a disaster. I wish I could –'

'If anyone could have kept me,' I said, 'it's you.'

Hair dishevelled, eyes on his desk, he looked disconsolate.

'I'm guilty of a lot,' he said. 'I don't know why I'm not better at these – these personal things.'

2

Ruth and I were in Malaga before Christmas.

Our honeymoon was very difficult for us both. Knowing

her shrinkings and conflicts, I had feared it might be so; but nothing I imagined came within reach of the aching, the desolating fact. Morning after morning I walked in the early sunshine, the sea brilliant beyond the rocks, and the scent of lavender and wild thyme in the air; I was here with the woman I loved, and all I knew was the frustration that tormented her. 'Why am I not a better lover?' I reproached myself. It would be difficult for anyone, I thought; but why had she not loved someone who took his pleasures more casually than I? So that, if all this must be, her lover would not take it so bitterly to heart. Why had love thrown us two together? she to whom disappointment must come, who felt it with enhanced distress, and I, who could not shield myself from the twisting of her nerves.

Why had I fallen in love with her, I complained to myself one morning (for these walks were all the solitude I had, and in the rest of the day I was trying to keep a control, a cheerfulness that I never felt). Just as the sun was getting hot, it struck me: *perhaps so that this should happen.* Had I always shied a little from Audrey because of her greater worldliness, her utter realism? Had I waited all this time to restore a youth's pride? To find an odd exception, a woman who was as shrinking as, in my heart, I once had been?

Maybe: but even if it was true, the reflection did not lessen the present misery. I told myself that I was exaggerating too much what most people diminish; I was forgetting this unfulfilment passed, just as others pretended that it never happened.

Yet, if I had not been over-sensitised, I think we should have quarrelled. For Ruth argued fiercely in those early days, partly out of resentment of me, which was inevitable enough, and partly to redeem her self-respect. Since a career, as well as love, is a man's responsibility, she attacked my plans for the future more bitterly than during our engagement.

'Scientific work,' she said one afternoon as we were walking over the hills, 'has a value of its own, whether you're liking it or not. It's – there. It's permanent. It's

279

work which is always going to last. It's real creation.'

'If one feels like that when one's doing it, certainly,' I said.

'The great scientists *must* feel like that.'

'Probably they do,' I said. 'If one does anything better than the rest of the world, it's bound to seem important.'

'That's rather cheap,' she said.

'Ruth,' I said, 'I should say the same about myself.'

She paused; for always during that time she was trying to check the hurting things she said.

'Would you have been a great scientist?' she asked.

'No,' I replied. We had reached the top of the hill, and were sitting down, watching the long roll on the sea shimmering in the sunlight. 'Not ever.'

'How good would you have been?' She could not keep herself from trying to hurt now.

'A very good second-rater,' I answered. 'And so able at other things that most people would have taken me for better. You'd have been a professor's wife, and all that: you wouldn't have been anywhere near a scientific genius.

'Until Constantine came to dinner,' I added, 'and he'd tried to make love to you.' She smiled more contentedly.

'Why couldn't you have been as good as that?' she said.

I said: 'Because I'm not made that way.'

'But I've heard you called a very gifted man.'

'So's Constantine,' I said, 'and his special ability goes to his work, and mine never has – yet.'

Her face was set.

'It may all be a mistake, such a childish mistake you're making.'

'Perhaps,' I said, 'but I'm afraid I must go on making it.'

3

In a while I knew that ultimately we should make something of it, with a joy that laughed at, though it did not remove, the scars. Thyme and lavender began to smell fragrantly now in the dry sunlight; we began to make expeditions over that full-toned, that lunar country, where neither of us had been before.

The tone of our first meetings came back sometimes as we talked. And yet often there was the aftermath, the continuance of strain; her remarks in that mood mattered more than I admitted, because they struck directly at my maturer dreams. She knew that side of me very well; even in the happy later days she has found it difficult to share; for much of that early time, she did not want to share it. She tested my resolve more severely than insecurity or the fear of poverty or failure. For she knew where I doubted, where I was cowardly, where I was bragging to myself. If I survived her lack of faith, I survived my own. And there were moments in those sunny, lonely days when I came near giving in.

I was sketching out a book on the state of Europe in the next twenty years, which was afterwards published as *The Gadarene Swine* and had a fair success. Ruth read the first chapter as I wrote it.

'It's good, I think,' she said. 'But – will it help?'

'It may,' I said, 'influence two people profoundly, and make ten others slightly dubious.'

'Is that good enough for you? Aren't there enough men with social consciences doing the same?'

'It isn't good enough,' I said. 'I may do better, and, as you know, it's smallish by the side of other things I want to do.'

'It relieves your conscience,' she said, 'even if it does no good. That's really why you do it.'

'Well, yes,' I admitted. We were sitting in the garden, drinking tea. 'It relieves my conscience – and also my fears.'

'You see,' I added, 'you and I are in a different position from your father and mother, say. They hadn't the certainty, more or less, that civilisation was going to crash in their lifetime. We have.'

There was another obstacle between us – a father who had died when she was a girl, whose wisdom still had something of childhood's infallibility. He had been a lawyer, idealistic and liberal. She spent some time trying to combine his views with mine, giving him a foresight I thought improbable, making believe that we should have agreed at heart.

Ruth's keen mind fought against all these shadows. On the whole, it won. She might even have liked me to enter politics actively. But my deepest interest she continued to distrust.

'We've got to behave as though your father and his friends were right,' I said. 'We've got to hold by humanism and social democracy. But there's a difference; we've got to hold by their faith and throw away their views on human beings. They were ineffectual because their human beings were ideal; we may be ineffectual, but our human beings must at least be real. We want a liberal culture: but it has got to be based on human beings driven by their fears and desires, human beings who are cruel and cowardly and irrational, with just a streak of aspiration – human beings like you and me.'

Ruth looked at me. 'You're so certain over these things,' she said. 'You haven't any *doubts* about people.'

'I have,' I said. 'A good many. But I'm sometimes right.'

'I know,' she admitted. 'You're often right. A sort of illuminated guess-work, it seems to me. I know it's a passion with you. But what does it amount to?'

She stared at me: 'Except an elaborate sort of suspiciousness,' she said.

'I've heard that before,' I replied. 'How I take all the good things out of people, and leave them – well, more unpleasant than they are. And drain all the strength out of emotions, because I won't take them at their face value. Well, do I?' I asked.

'You don't leave much,' she said. 'You may be right: but often I feel you're missing something out. And any way, what is the good of it?'

She resented it, to some extent because it had displaced my science, but more, I think, for the most obvious of reasons.

'I could make excuses for myself,' I said. 'But I won't. I do it because I can't help it. And on the whole, I've enjoyed people the more. I like a great many, you know. Far more than you, for instance. There's only one man I really dis-

like, I think. A man called Pritt. And that's mainly because he hits a blind spot of mine. I just can't imagine
what it's like to be him. Some day I may be able to. But
the rest I can imagine enough to like. I may be wrong. Often or always. But at least I think I'm trying on the right
lines. I'm not so egomaniac that I begin by giving all the
weight to the emotion people produce in me. That's the
way one creates qualities like saintliness, or arrogance, or
effectiveness or all the rest. Saintliness isn't a quality that
the man himself feels: it's a quality you wrap round him
when you watch. I'm interested in him; both what he
thinks he is, and what he is in fact. The wrappings other
people made for him, the labels they have taken over from
convention – they seem to me about as useful as the Greek
labels for the world, earth, air, fire, and water, which were
obtained in just the same child's egocentric way. But when
I try to take away those wrappings, you all feel cheated,
and think I am taking something from the man himself.

'I shall never persuade you,' I said. 'For instance, it'll be
a long time before I get you to disentangle your picture of
me from the man I am. You've given me all sorts of qualities; you've thought of me as a courageous, determined,
self-made man, who's ploughed his way ahead. Don't you
see those are qualities you are investing me with, utterly
different from the way I or any other man thinks of himself, more different still from the man I really am?'

'Don't you feel,' said Ruth, 'that you go out of your way
to overstress one part of yourself? Just to suit your ideas?'

4

Gradually the strain grew weaker. We left Spain at the
end of January and took a house on the river at Rich-
mond; and when we had furnished and decorated, and
done a good many trifling things together, we settled down
into a tired content. One night, misty outside so that
through the windows we could only see the reflections of
our lights, we sat together on the sofa, and Ruth put her
hand on mine and whispered:

'It's been worth it all. Now.'

Now we had come through, and there was something safe in life at last. I was left too spent, too contented, to want anything else for a time. I wrote a little; but I was not in the solitary emotionless state which is the best for starting a new venture. On the other hand, the habit of work was too strong to break. I read a good deal, both books that were to be useful in the future and the scientific journals. I remember Constantine's great paper, which I had seen in the making, came out that spring. After a time, I began to work steadily on the political book and made some more ambitious schemes. But it all seemed trivial against the slow happiness which had come.

I am almost in the state, I thought, when I could go to the office and do a meaningless day's work, without resenting it. I should almost like a dull routine by way of background to happiness. After all the accidents of my life, Audrey, the rise and fall and rise of my career, the agonising honeymoon, it was like coming safely home. If I had been doing science now, I should have gone to it in content; done it competently, without excitement, enjoyed it for the pleasure it gave Ruth. I began almost to wish I was still doing science. It would please her and it could not take away from the present peace. Never have I felt less like adventure: for what was there to go in search of? When I had this?

And Ruth? She was happier even than I was; proudly happy, delighted to entertain and show how shiningly successful the marriage was. This was love as she had imagined it ought to be. In her fondness for me, I could feel a humility growing; it came strangely from her; she was humble for no other reason than that I had brought her this happiness.

By every sort of action she tried to withdraw the words she had spoken during that month's trial. We never referred to her doubts now: she gave parties for all sorts of people who might help in the plans she had adopted. Patiently, tactfully, she watched me, saying nothing of my future, intimating she was with me whatever I did.

So I basked. But there were stirrings. Time was going by, this was a breathing space, soon I must be busy. I found myself wishing that my career was certain; by this time I should have arrived; I ought to be distinguished, not starting afresh with the odds against me. In science, even with my disaster, I should have been important in three or four years. As it was, I might do nothing.

She had given me happiness, stolen some of my confidence. For echoes of her doubts rang with me still. It would hurt to fail now. 'I ought to have started this alone,' I thought sometimes, 'made sure of some success before I married. But if I had, I should have missed this real, this concrete happiness.'

I felt an obscure satisfaction that I had not irrevocably parted with science. I could go back if I wanted. There would be no devotion or passion now – those had gone for ever – but I had the certainty of an achievement that would win the praise of others and of Ruth. And perhaps in myself I still sometimes thought it worth doing, for a faith is lingeringly slow to die. Often I revolted from the thought, and worked intensely on my new plans. One night I walked by the river, thought of this quandary, and laughed. There was a warm wind blowing, and the water was flecked by rain. 'Ah well,' I thought, 'I've broken one career, repaired it and left it half finished. I've started another in which I may not succeed. But if I do succeed I shall have the deepest triumph outside of love, and yet all sanity says, 'Go back to science and live the life you've begun.' I may do either: but whichever way I go, I shall have some satisfaction and some regrets. Life has never been unmixed for me; it never will. All I ask is that I keep honest with myself until I die. I hope I may take risks still, live as strenuously as I have done; but if I fall into security, let me not conceal it from myself. Whatever I do, risk or cowardice, my own way or the others', I want to know what is in my heart; if I come through to success, may I be honest enough to recognise the jealousy at what might have been.'

Chapter 3

They discuss a change

I

By an accident, it was through Ruth that the decision came. At least she unknowingly arranged the setting; I cannot believe but that sooner or later I should have gone the same way. However, if it had not been for the thrust of Ruth's happiness I should not have seen Sheriff and Audrey that Easter; and if it had not been for that meeting, the choice would have come later, and in a different form.

Ruth became curious over my past. It was a sign, I thought, how much she was released. For when she first loved me, I was more an escape than a person; someone to clutch on to for love, not a man with friends, old passions, and all the ordinary human trappings. It was only now, when she was free, not needing to assert herself by guiding my life, that she was able to enter it.

She wanted to meet Audrey. Once she had the desire, Ruth wasted no time, and invited Audrey and Sheriff to spend a week-end with us, at Easter. Audrey accepted. I remember seeing her big jagged hand on the envelope at breakfast, the first time for years. Thinking it would be wiser to enlarge the party, I suggested we should also have Hunt.

Audrey and Sheriff arrived on the Friday afternoon, and over tea Ruth talked about their son, now two years old.

'Education must seem even more difficult, when you've got to think of it,' said Ruth, 'than when you're just appalled by it from the outside.'

Audrey shrugged her shoulders: 'We've all scrambled through. Somehow.'

'But it must be worse,' Ruth insisted, 'when you're watching someone of your own. Through all the chances and stupidities.'

'Yes,' said Audrey. 'Yes.'

'Where *shall* you send him?' Ruth asked. 'One of the new schools, I suppose? Have you thought of Dartington?'

'We can't afford it,' said Audrey casually, in the brusque way that I expected, that made Ruth embarrassed.

'I don't know whether we should if we could,' Audrey explained. 'But – there just won't be the money.'

Sheriff shifted in his chair. 'I don't know about that. There are years and years. I expect I shall pull something off.'

I saw Audrey smile to herself.

'Of course,' said Ruth, catching Sheriff's eye. 'In five or six years you may have a Professorship.'

He brushed a hand over his head. I noticed that he was beginning to go bald.

'Or other things,' he responded, smiling eagerly at Ruth. 'There are all sorts of possibilities we've never even tried. Simply because we let the stupid people make money. Why, there's money in small chemical industries. One could make a small chemical industry go.'

Ruth, liking him at once, was still a little dubious: 'I should have thought the I.C.I. –' she began.

Sheriff burst out: 'The I.C.I.'s just a – a blind elephant. Galumphing about, knocking things over just because it's heavy. A small firm with intelligence could run between it's legs. And trip it in the end.'

Audrey smiled at me while they were talking. It was different from our last meeting. I felt suddenly that she was happy, happy in a way that could not be shaken, for all the trappings had gone long ago. On the surface there were worries. Money would always worry her. Her dress was not new this afternoon; her hair had not been recently waved. She was jealous of our luxury, and jealous of Ruth for giving it me. That, perhaps, was a reason why Ruth talked of expensive educations; for Ruth was envious a little of the past, but more, I thought, of Audrey being unassailable, with nothing to lose, and still happy through the discontent. Sheriff's affairs hurt her a little, but by now she knew that he would always come back. Even now, while he was talking to Ruth, his whole heart going out to engross her attention, Audrey was watching with a smile, a little annoyed, but fundamentally undisturbed. She herself, I reflected, may have other lovers. Probably she has; she was passionate herself, and she liked giving comfort to another. But that made no difference. She knew what her life was, and accepted it.

It was strange to watch the three of them. Sheriff, leaning forward, his large eyes alight, telling Ruth a story with all the animation he possessed; the sunshine streamed down on him, and he looked a good deal older, with the cheeks pale below his eyes and only reddening on the sides of his face. There was strain and anxiety etched there, for me who remembered him years before; but the gaiety was left, even if he did not always convince himself about his schemes. I remembered what Hunt said that night in Manchester. Charles would be satisfied if he could settle down in middle age with Audrey, in a comfortable house, on a comfortable income. I was amused, as one is when time brings home another of its mockeries; when we are shown how a beauty we adored, an adventurer who lifted up our hearts, have passed into the background of drab and prudent things.

Ruth was in high spirits, bantering back to Sheriff. Her pale profile stood like a miniature, carved and perfect, as she listened and then broke into laughter; I was a little jealous. But, at least, there would be nothing of the awkwardness I feared, when for a moment soon after Audrey came in, she and I and Sheriff had drifted back into a common memory. Ruth had looked hurt then; she was ready to resent Audrey's abrupt manner; it was better that she should be warmed by Sheriff's flattery.

Audrey lay back in her chair, her legs crossed, the sunlight gleaming from her hair. I wondered: how would it have been if we were still together? If we had married? I remembered her strivings, her moods, her desperateness, when we were lovers. They were her protest against the marriage which was bound to overtake her. But it had to be with a man whom she loved as completely as she loved Sheriff; whom she had loved without an illusion, and yet altogether. She could never have loved me like that; she was never tied to me through stupidities and deceits and lack of understanding; and I could never have brought her to this peace. So I thought, as I saw her listening to the others' talk. I had a trace of regret, slight enough to vanish as I laughed at one of Sheriff's jokes.

2

I had explained to Ruth something of Hunt, and she thought hard about choosing a woman to make up the party for dinner on that Friday night. At last we decided to have no one else. Whoever we had, she would make him ill at ease, the others would not know her well, and it would prevent our talking freely. In the summer we would have him down alone, we thought, and surround him with young women whom he might like.

As it was, he was awkward with Ruth until we got talking round the table, and Audrey, who liked him, went to the trouble of bringing him into the conversation. I was relieved, and the party suddenly seemed intimate, as I heard Hunt speak, saw Sheriff hold his glass up to the candlelight, listened to Audrey's laugh, glanced across to Ruth and smiled. It was warm that Easter, and we were dining with the windows open: so that below the reflection of the candles, I could see a beam of light undulating with the river's swell.

'So you've left science, Arthur?' Hunt asked, a little later.

'Yes,' I said. I did not want to talk of it, until it was all beyond doubt.

'I thought you would,' he said. 'Long ago. You remember.'

I did. But I was thinking that his old arguments would seem rather childish, now.

'At least,' I said, 'I've no scientific job.'

'Once I thought you might throw it up,' said Audrey. 'But when you got on so fast, I didn't think you'd move.'

'With no question of what I wanted to do?' I said.

'Not much,' she said. 'Don't we all shake down and tolerate the thing which comes easiest?'

Hunt smiled. 'Not always.'

Ruth broke in: 'But don't you think he should have left science?' It was asked defensively, neutrally, as though to assure me she was only interested in their opinions, not in the question itself.

Sheriff smiled: 'I think it was a mistake,' he said. 'We all get tired of it at times. We want all the things that science doesn't give us. The human things. But when you've got them, they seem so flimsy! And you're glad to get back to something calm and certain, with the rails laid down.'

Audrey saw the smile on my lips and returned it. But Sheriff was feeling convinced: 'I've thought about lots of other jobs,' he said. 'Why, I even talked about chemical industries this afternoon. But I've never changed. And, Lord knows, I'm not an oversteady man.'

'That's why you don't change,' Hunt put in, astonishingly quickly for him. Sheriff did not notice.

'I've never changed,' he went on. 'And I don't suppose I ever shall. I should like some more money. I should like a Chair some time. I should like to do better work. But as it is, I don't think the work useless and I often enjoy doing it.'

'So you're content with your science?' Ruth looked at Sheriff.

'I am,' Sheriff was talking to her, then looked round for our eyes.

'It's permanent and fixed. It's going on for ever. It's a sort of immortality. We stray away, do the things which are private and die with us. Make love and dance and laugh. And then we come and contribute our piece to immortality.'

Then his face moved quickly into a comic twist: 'Mind you,' he said, 'my share in immortality is only a little one. In science, I mean. I've not had Arthur's luck. And I've not got Arthur's gifts. I'm a sort of rather slack lance-corporal. While Arthur could have gone as far as he wanted. He was just getting to the top, getting *back* to the top –'

he grinned at me, 'with interesting work and men and money and success. Lord, what I'd give for the chance! And Arthur throws it away.'

Audrey joined in: 'It surprised me. When you were just arriving.' She was looking at me. 'Because after all you're an ambitious man. And you've got the trick of plunging into anything you're doing. Or' – she smiled – 'you used to have.'

Ruth said, 'I thought it surprising. Until I knew the reasons –'

'Of course it *wasn't* surprising,' Hunt broke in with his transfiguring smile. 'Of course it wasn't surprising. That trick of plunging into anything is deceptive, you know.' He looked at Audrey. 'Charles has got it so much that he plunges into every moment. And each is different from the last. To-night he is the convinced believing scientist. To-morrow he'll believe with equal sincerity that all that matters is to be the natural animal man. Which means that he sticks to what he's doing, for none of the plunges takes him far enough away. But sticks to it without much concentration, if I may guess, Charles?'

'You may,' said Sheriff a little sullenly.

'But Arthur's plunges,' Hunt went on, 'last a good deal longer. They're almost the complete successful life plunges. This new one may be. If it goes the way I think, I believe it will. But the scientific plunge couldn't last, because, you see, Arthur never lets himself quite go. There's always a piece of him detached and wondering "Now why am I doing this?" He plunges and asks. Most people only plunge or only ask. But if you plunge and ask and can't answer the question – well, the plunge ends. It's just that piece of Arthur that I knew about in a vague way years ago; it's prevented him believing anything; but the ability to plunge has made him know what it's like to believe something. He's been able to go into things – up to a point. The detached part has got in his way so far. But to me – and I'm a completely unsuccessful man,' he smiled at Ruth, 'so complete that there's no envy left – it's the most important part, because if ever he gets the plunge and the detachment going in the same direction, you'll have an unusual combination. Wth luck he'll do that. And I take it he thinks it's worth the risk. But it won't be in world affairs,' he smiled.

'I like being flattered to my face,' I said, 'almost as much as knowing I'm being flattered behind my back, but hasn't this gone on long enough?'

'Hunt's right,' said Audrey. 'You are like that, you always were.'

Ruth asked quickly, more of the other two than Audrey:

'What was he like as a youth? I've often wondered.' She looked at me. 'But I just can't imagine.'

Sheriff made an odd grimace:

'He was thinner and wilder and oh! – he used to say silly things and be angry when you argued with him. And sometimes he got drunk and talked about experience. Altogether he was an entertaining youth; but you wouldn't have thought he'd have turned out so grave.'

'Nonsense,' said Audrey. 'He was graver, often. I remember being surprised when I found he was high spirited.

'The chief difference,' she said, 'is that he's quieter now.'

Hunt said: 'He's had a pretty strenuous life, you know. Imagine him with that taken off. He's gained something by it.'

'And lost something,' said Sheriff.

'What?' asked Ruth.

'Human frailty,' said Sheriff.

'No,' said Audrey. 'Illusions.'

'No,' said Hunt. 'Certainty.'

'Well,' Ruth said, 'there's something left.'

A moment afterwards she took Audrey out, and we sat drinking claret. The other two were talking, and once or twice asked me questions; but I put them off, drank my wine, and went over to the window. The red lamp of a boat was flickering slowly away, down to the sea.

Thesefour were the people I had cared for most, I thought. Ruth I had loved and helped. The other three, when they had filled me with love and friendship, I had done nothing but inspire the same in them; now, when I could understand and try to help, I had no feeling but a slight ache from the past.

I laughed.

'What's happening?' said Sheriff at the table. I turned away from the window.

'I just thought of a joke,' I said.

3

The week-end passed pleasantly. We were all for one reason or another bent on being considerate and warm. Ruth went for a long walk with Audrey; Hunt and I played tennis, and Sheriff, always good company at a party, was in his most enlivening form. We made them stay till Tuesday, and were sorry to say good-bye to Hunt, the first to go.

'I like that man,' said Audrey. 'I always did. I wish I had fallen in love with him, almost.'

'It would have been good for him,' I said.

'He's quite charming,' Ruth said. 'And I don't usually believe in these things, but he does suggest — odd reserves to draw on. But —'

'He'll teach in the same school all his life,' said Sheriff.

'Yes,' Audrey smiled.

Those thoughts of the first night had remained; I wanted to atone a little, to add a little to their progress.

'I wish we could find something,' I said. 'It may be possible some time. It's difficult, though; his qualities are such flagrantly unsuccessful ones. Yours aren't, Charles, on the other hand. Do you mind if I prod you into being a successful scientist?'

'If I keep a tight hand on myself,' Sheriff smiled.

'Shall we go away and talk about it?' I suggested. 'It's mainly technical,' I explained to Ruth and Audrey.

'I should like to listen,' Ruth said.

'I'd better,' said Audrey.

To fasten Sheriff down to work one wanted an audience, I thought.

'Well,' I said. 'You've never done anything on a big enough scale. You've always done your research from hand to mouth, as it were. Picking up a little problem, 'doing it – very competently and skilfully – and then going on to another little problem quite unconnected.'

'That's true,' said Sheriff, 'that's perfectly true.'

'It's the way most people potter along,' I said, 'but it's not good enough for you. It's not the way to do research – or write books – or do anything else, as far as that goes. There's no conception behind it.'

'I never could think,' Sheriff said. 'I'm an intelligent man except for that: but I just can't think. Not continuously, I mean. I expect I haven't got the character. You see,' he explained to Ruth, 'I never played cricket.

'It makes a difference,' he added.

I smiled: 'If you want to make a success of science you've got to acquire a conception or two. There's just got to be an idea behind the skill.'

His mood flickered, changed. 'I'd give a lot to be successful,' he said. 'I've been bright long enough. I'm tired of not having any money. I shan't be good for much if I muddle on any longer. But how' – he asked – 'am I going to get these conceptions?'

I paused.

'You see, I've a good many ideas that I shall never carry out, now,' I said. 'Some of them promising. Several I can guarantee. And a couple I'd actually begun before I left, and know they are bound to work. The obvious thing is for you to take over my loose ends – we'll choose the best, later – and settle down to a real field of work. You'll have made a reputation before you're forty.'

'Splendid,' Sheriff cried. He added, as a casual afterthought: 'I suppose you won't want the ideas yourself, some time?'

'No,' I said. 'There will be plenty more if ever I want them.'

'Do you think this really might come off?' Audrey asked.

'Why not?' I asked.

Sheriff was fighting his impetuous longing to cheer, take the ideas, begin work to-morrow.

'It's not much in my line,' he said. 'I don't know much physics. I'm just a simple ignorant chemist, remember.'

'My dear Charles,' I said, 'the amount of physics required in most of these problems is completely negligible. For the crystallographic part you'll have to get someone to help you. Who's that lad at Southampton – Hensman? – he'd be perfectly adequate. You'll do the chemistry and work out the general scheme. You couldn't have anything simpler. It needs at least four years' consistent work, that's all.'

'I think it's a superb idea,' said Ruth. 'You two will stay over to-night, won't you? And then they can have the afternoon working at it,' she said briskly to Audrey.

'Four years to Arthur means eight to Charles,' Audrey said.

'You wait!' Sheriff burst out. 'I'll do it in less than four. It's time I got on the map. I might have arrived long ago' – he chuckled – 'if only someone had given me a chance.' He looked at me: 'What about you, Arthur, apart from being Fairy Godmother? What do you get out of this?'

'I shall be interested to see the ideas carried out,' I said. 'It's irritating to have them lying useless. And once, you remember, I couldn't find you a niche. This may make up –'

Ruth looked puzzled.

'I tried to get Charles the chemical job at the Institute,' I explained to her. 'But the Committee wouldn't have it.' None of them knew the true story, but I could not forget it. 'So this will give a sort of vicarious revenge,' I said. 'But that isn't the real reason.'

'What are you going to tell us?' Audrey asked.

'You remember Friday night, how I laughed to myself?' I said to Sheriff.

'An irritating habit,' he said.

'Well, this is the result,' I said.

4

The four of us went to the theatre and on to a night club for supper. I asked Audrey to dance, and as we marked time on the crowded floor I mentioned that during the whole week-end we had not had a word alone.

295

'Make your face as blank as you can,' Audrey replied. 'And look over my shoulder.'

'Your wife's looking at us anxiously,' she said.

'Its by intention I've not talked to you,' I admitted.

'Yes,' she said. 'There's no point in worrying her.'

We danced on, our faces set and bored; instead of smiling her hand pressed my shoulder.

'Where have you learned this technique?' I said.

'Charles is very jealous, too,' she said.

'That's rather comic.'

'Wouldn't you expect it, though?'

'I should expect anyone to be.'

'I don't want compliments from a man who was in love with me – after I left him. For longer than he thinks. And anyway we shan't have another chance to talk,' she said. 'So don't waste time. How's it going?'

'Very well,' I said.

'I thought so. It looks like it when you're near each other,' she said. 'Strange, I shouldn't have thought it.'

'What?'

'You'd marry a woman like Ruth. She's very nice; too nice for you, my child. But I thought it would be a different kind.'

'Someone more like yourself?' I mocked gently.

'Someone with more vices, and a lot more careless. Who liked you in bed and didn't respect you so much.'

'Instead of which?'

'Ruth is certain you're a great man. Erratic but wonderful. Arthur,' she pressed my shoulder, 'I should never have thought that. Even if the rest of the world told me so.'

'Why not?'

'Oh, you're clever and I liked talking to you more than anyone I ever knew. Even in our time, you were obviously going to do things. But I shall always think of you –' and casually, shamelessly, she whispered a reminiscence that made me suppress a chuckle in my throat. 'After that I couldn't have you a great dignified figure.'

'It oughtn't to make it impossible.'

'It does,' she said.

We passed in silence by Charles and Ruth, who were

dancing well together, Ruth glancing at us as we passed.

'How about you?' I said.

'Oh, I've got Charles. Who before long will try to make love to your wife. She won't let him, but she'll be very pleased,' said Audrey.

'It would be a little hard if he took my wife – as well.'

'He did you a good turn taking me away,' she said. 'You're much better off as you are. With me you'd have been happy at thirty and very unhappy at forty. If you hadn't left me before.'

'I don't think I should,' I said.

'No,' Audrey said. 'I'm afraid you wouldn't. But I'm not a wife for an active man. I gave over being serious too soon.'

Again we were quiet, passing Ruth and Charles.

'But if I asked you to come back,' she said, 'I wonder what you'd do.'

'I don't know,' I said, trying to match her naturalness. 'It's just as well that you won't.'

'Perhaps it is,' she said.

'What are you really going to do?' I asked. We were talking without pretence.

'I'm fixed,' she said, 'with Charles. There was a time I thought of leaving him. I never shall now. I'm fixed.'

'I thought you were,' I said, remembering the first sight of her in the afternoon three days before.

'That's not to say if I met you for the first time now, I should mind flirting,' she said. 'Though I tend to go in for large and stupid men.'

'What about Charles?'

'Charles gets furious. And is faithful for a short time himself. We've got used to each other.' She went on suddenly: 'Arthur, I'm grateful for this idea of yours about him. You'll see he brings it off? He'll be lazy and make excuses and tell you he's doing it while he's really trying to make money at bridge. You know all that! But you will stand over him?'

'Yes,' I said.

'Because he's got an itch to make a name, you know. He'll get worse without it. And as I'm fixed to him, it would be pretty intolerable for me, him growing middle-aged and disappointed.'

'I'll see he has a respectable career,' I said.

'You and I have had an odd time,' said Audrey. 'But this is the way it was bound to go.'

5

When they had gone, Ruth was affectionate all day. We had tea in the garden, talking lightly, finding pleasure in being alone. We were in the state which comes when, after a successful party, you say good-bye to the last of them with relief, turn to each other and sigh with happiness.

'They're very pleasant people,' Ruth said, finishing her tea. She lay back in her deck chair.

'I think they are,' I said, 'though I can't judge, of course.'

'You mean one's friends —'

'One's first friends always seem bigger than they really are. Even if one found out they were of no quality at all, they would still matter a good deal, I think.'

'I liked Sheriff very much,' said Ruth.

'I liked Audrey too,' she added. 'I think I can understand why you were in love with her once.'

'She was much more attractive at twenty,' I said. It was half true, it was pleasant to enhance the past, to get a mild revenge on old humiliations. 'She's gone off rather quickly.'

Ruth nodded. Then quickly: 'Yet there's something still most women haven't got.' She was determined to be generous. I was fond of these resolutions of hers. She added:

'I wonder if she's altogether good for Sheriff.'

I looked surprised.

'I mean,' said Ruth, 'he might have gone further with a wife who wasn't so — casual.'

Ruth would like to take Sheriff's career in hand, I thought with some amusement.

'He'd be difficult for any woman.'

'Are you sure?' Ruth said.

'He's got none of the steadier virtues,' I said. 'He hasn't

even many of the careerist virtues. He's not honest. And on the other hand he isn't dishonest in any thought-out systematic way.'

Ruth frowned: 'I can't help thinking you're misjudging him.'

'Most people would think so, at sight.' I smiled. 'Apart from the essential, impalpable things, like charm and life,' I said, 'there's precious little to be said for him, however. Some residue of generosity mixed up with the frauds. He paid for meals, sometimes, when he hadn't much money and I had none at all. And he threw himself into a lot of my successes and schemes, and was never discouraging through meanness. Things like that. That's about all.'

'What is there on the other side?'

'I've known him for nearly fifteen years,' I said. 'During that time he's told innumerable lies – most of them quite pointless. He's borrowed money as often as I'd lend it, and never paid a shilling back. He's cheated me at least twice over debts we had in common. He took away my girl. I've no doubt he'll try to seduce my wife.'

'Yet,' Ruth smiled, 'you're inconveniencing yourself to establish him in a career.'

'Why not?' I said.

'He may be all you say. He must be, I'm sorry,' said Ruth. 'But for all that I want to see you set him going. He might improve with the chance.'

I was amused: it seemed to me improbable.

'At least, I should like to make him comfortable,' I said.

Chapter 4

Another climb

I

During the next few months I spent some of my leisure managing Sheriff's career; it had become an interest of Ruth's as well as mine, and often we made plans, impatient we should have to wait so long for the results. However, I got him safely started on a good problem, and Ruth had him to dinner with Austin and Constantine. He made an immediate impression. I had to listen, smiling a little wryly to myself, while Austin said it was a pleasure to meet a young scientist enthusiastic over his work in these days when they were getting too temperamental to stand the grind. Austin had concluded that my defection was due not to lack of ability, which he scouted, nor to lack of inclination, which he would not understand, but simply to laziness. At the time I was writing eight hours a day, which is equivalent to a day's work in science of about fourteen hours.

Sheriff looked respectfully at Austin, and said:

'Don't you think, sir, the enthusiasm ought to last – even when the work's going wrong? I've had about ten years' research now; nothing much has come of it. But I've enjoyed every minute.

'Exactly,' Austin boomed. 'That's exactly how a young man should feel.'

Constantine also found the atmosphere sympathetic; he embarked on one of his complicated, ingenious discourses, ostensibly to provoke me, in reality to capture Ruth's attention. Though as a rule she would have asked a devastatingly practical: 'What's the use? Where are you getting to?' she knew his vanities by now, and produced murmurs of approval, seconded by Sheriff. I could see Constantine putting them both into the rare class of those who could follow his ideas; when Austin left, the other two stayed in great amity, one talking, the other listening, until the small hours.

We shall bring it off, I thought, and sometimes I was uneasy, for I could not see my own future as clearly. *The Gadarene Swine* was finished, and as a piece of political invective I knew it to be fairly good, but quite a number of young men could have done it as well, and several considerably better. Ruth was playing her part, though I felt she still hoped that from directing Sheriff I should be lured into active science again. She tried to conceal her wishes, however, and spoke as though she was wholeheartedly concerned in the present, entertaining very skilfully and with some effect. On the whole, if I failed, I should deserve to, I thought; but that did not ease the doubtful moments.

Taking charge of Sheriff, on the other hand, seemed simplicity itself. He was working surprisingly hard; his colleague, young Hensman, came to see me and exuded competence and energy. In three months they produced a paper which was interesting on its face value and full of potentialities, some of which I had foreseen, some quite new. Sheriff brought it for me to look over before his professor communicated it to the Royal Society. Ruth stayed to hear my enthusiasm and then left us alone in the study.

'This is admirable, Charles,' I finished.

'I always said I could work,' he smiled. 'Given something to aim at.'

It was the beginning of July. 'What are you going to do now?' I said.

He hesitated. 'I don't know.'

'Why not?'

'I've been too busy.'

I laughed. 'You'd better confess. What nonsense are you planning?'

'As a matter of fact,' he looked slightly ashamed, 'I've been thinking it would be a good idea if I tramped round

Ireland for a few weeks. I should come back fresher, you see. And get down to it twice as hard.'

'Instead of which,' I said, 'you'll work continuously up to the end of August. You'll then have three weeks' holiday and work through to Christmas, when you'll take a fortnight off. That's all. You're a perfectly healthy man —'

'I'm not a machine,' he grumbled.

'I'm studying your needs,' I said.

He caught my amusement. 'I'm not used to this,' he said. 'But — I suppose it's in a good cause. If it were for anyone else's sake I wouldn't do it.'

'The more you can get done now, the better,' I said. 'As soon as you're started, people will warn you about publishing too much. Don't believe them. There are two kinds of advice: one which is designed to help the person who receives it, the other the person who gives it. You'll have a good deal of the second kind. Publish as much as you conceivably can: if you doubt it —'

'I don't,' said Sheriff, cheerfully.

'Look up the rate of publication of the really successful scientists in their young days. I don't mean the great scientists: I mean the successful ones. That's your category, Charles. Publish a great deal, some in collaboration, some by yourself. If it's all by yourself, the jealous men will say you're impossible to work with; and if it's all in collaboration, they'll say you're no good on your own.'

Sheriff was laughing. 'I sometimes forget,' he said, 'that you used to be bitter at times.'

'I'm not in the least bitter,' I said. 'It's the practical truth. It's equally the practical truth, no doubt, in any profession whatever.'

'I admit,' I added, 'that the practical truth can sometimes convey the wrong impression.'

'But how much better than the whole truth,' said Sheriff. 'If only because it's shorter.'

'One other thing,' I said. 'Not too many jokes. At least not your sort of joke. Much less mine. Make as many scientific jokes as you like. But jokes with an edge to them are the most dangerous form of amusement in any society. I learned that to my cost once —' I remembered how I had joked to Desmond at Munich. 'It's much better to behave everywhere as though you were talking to a gathering of Elks: drink your pint of beer, laugh heartily at underclothes, smoke your pipe, and be a man's man.'

'That's easy,' said Sheriff.

'Oh, and for God's sake don't make love to Professors' wives. You had better rule out all scientists' wives for safety. If you don't, I give you up. There'd be no chance of manœuvring you anywhere. To be attractive to women on your scale and in your way – if they realised it, that's the one thing you could never be forgiven.'

'How you think I shall have time for affairs of the heart,' Sheriff chuckled ruefully, 'I just don't know. Eight hours a day for forty-six weeks in the year: it's not my sort of life. But I promise, Arthur, not a scientist's wife. Not one. Not even a woman scientist.'

I went back to his paper: 'There's one side-line here,' I said, 'that's shouting to be done. Someone else will be in on it if you're not quick. And you'll have finished it by Christmas. You see –'

2

The months passed quickly. I was very busy and beginning to attract a little notice; life with Ruth maintained a rhythm of content. With pleasure and self-satisfaction we watched Sheriff's progress: a paper read at the September Meeting of the Faraday Society, another in the Proceedings of the Royal Society in November, a third finished by Christmas, and ready for publication in the spring. Nearly all of it was good; there were no blunders of commission, though, rather too often for my taste, he missed an inference at two removes.

I was gratified one day when I met Desmond, the thermometer of scientific gossip, and heard him begin cheerfully:

'Young Sheriff's doing some sound work these days. You knew him, didn't you, Miles?'

'He was at King's, London, with me,' I said.

'Oh, yes. Didn't we try to run him for a job at the

Institute? And the others wouldn't have him. It looks as though they were wrong. As they were about other things we know.' He smiled meaningfully. 'Still, Fane won't be on many more Committees. It's a pity you're not in the thick of it now, old boy.'

He was right about Fane, who was dropping out of favour in high places, so I heard from Macdonald; Desmond himself was becoming much more of a power. It amused me; and I learned partially to understand the emergence into history of characters who seem, at the distance of a hundred years, to have been only a name and an office. Desmond might, with almost equal ease, have arrived in some mysterious way upon the Directory and had knowing talks with General Buonaparte; or have been in any Cabinet in any English Government. No one would ever know why. Unless one knew Desmond and his colleagues intimately, his place in scientific affairs was just as incomprehensible.

As I left him that afternoon, elated with his news of Sheriff, it struck me there was some resemblance between the two of them; Desmond, on a coarser, respectabilised level, had some of Sheriff's qualities, something of the same quick response, the same outpouringness. Like Sheriff, he had the endearing property that when he did anyone a bad turn he bore no resentment afterwards.

With my own career moving, if almost imperceptibly, and this vicarious one of Sheriff's going well, I lived with that expectant happiness which is among the most sustaining of moods. The only serious intrusion that winter came the day I received a parcel from Hunt.

It was the manuscript of the novel I had often hinted he should write. I read all morning, and finished it. In the afternoon I asked Ruth to read it, without telling her the author's name. She gave it me before dinner.

'What do you think of it?' I said.

'It's atrocious. I can't think how a book can be as bad.'

I nodded. I thought much the same. It was a strangely negative book. The writing was neither good nor bad. There was no plot; I had scarcely expected one. It was very dull; I was prepared to suffer that for the deeper qualities. But – there was nothing else. I had expected some glimmer of his personal insight to show, however bad the rest was. A glimmer would have redeemed the book for me, since I read novels for that more than anything else. But I had read with sympathy and hope, and I could find nothing there.

'Who's it by?' asked Ruth.

'Hunt,' I said.

'I'll swear,' I burst out, 'that he's got more understanding than most of the people who have ever written books.'

'It doesn't show,' Ruth said.

'He's got none of the literary tricks,' I complained.

'Worse than that,' Ruth answered. 'There's no sign that he could express anything, even if he had. In any way. I should think one could be a hopelessly bad writer, and still get something across.'

'I'm afraid you're right,' I said.

'It's as though something was holding it back.'

It hurt very much. In the midst of hope and movement and achievement, this came. It could not be escaped. Hunt had meant a good deal in my life; probably my human curiosity would have grown without any help, but so far as anyone else was responsible, Hunt was. His seriousness, his tolerance, his suspicion of himself, above all his passionate humble desire to understand – they had left their mark on me. For me he exemplified the spirit in which to approach human beings; and that was not too small a debt to owe.

I had paid nothing of it back. Now, it seemed, I should never have the chance. For, in the only ways in which he might be helped with satisfaction to himself, I could do nothing unless he provided the material. His book deprived me of any hope of that.

He would remain all his life without any fulfilment, I thought that night, sitting at my desk long after Ruth had gone to bed. I cried out angrily, Why? But in fact I knew the answer. 'Something seemed to hold him back,' Ruth had said. She was right: it was himself. Just as in love he was so made that he could only love where any satisfaction was denied; and could only bring himself to take satisfaction where his heart was cold: just in that way, it seemed to me, he had to live his life so that no fruition came. He was driven to tasks he could not perform, just as he could only love a woman who was indifferent; when it seemed that he might escape, through work in his student days, through writing now, some restraint, imposed by himself beyond his will, intervened to preserve the pattern of self-abasement that underlay his life.

Of so much I was sure; but the reasons for it, why it should come to Hunt's life more than another's, were mysterious mockeries. I only knew that our explanations are so crude as to be worse than wrong; the words we use are labels for our ignorance, and by talking of masochism, instead of coming near understanding, we merely become confused. For masochism is used equally of a laceration of the soul, like Hunt's, and an appetite of the body. The two traits are utterly different and need have no connection. They do not often occur in the same person: one is often present without the other. Hunt, whose self-torment in the mind was beyond doubt, had less than the normal interest in sexual pain, and I have met others, excited by sexual pain, to whom any mental torment is foreign, and whose lives are happy and successful.

I opened the manuscript, saw the words standing out clear under my lamp, read a page or two, which seemed more lifeless than before. Why are lives crippled in themselves? I could not help thinking. Are not the chances of heedless pain enough that many who feel it most deeply are compelled to search it for themselves?

It is a grim, an almost cosmic joke, I thought. There is only one consolation, and that is a poor one when you see a friend's life pain-ridden. It is just that the higher aberrations demand their price. Sometimes, as with Hunt, too big a price. It would be pleasant to have a Dostoevski who was a cheerful lover and competent with his money; but it is likely that profound, heart-torn insight goes hand in hand with unconscious drives which can only wreck a life; for all the strange, complex, spiritual lucidity of Newman's mind there was, perhaps, the inevitable price of chastity venerated like a timid girl; the selfless courage of E. A.

Wilson was linked with a faith of rigid narrowness and harsh asceticism.

And yet, and yet, from near to the man himself, one might have wished he could give up anything to gain a year's serenity. If Hunt's life had been wilder and more anguished, and he too had written great books, I wonder if I should have wished he could become a Sheriff?

I was tired and wretched, looking down at the desk, away from the pile of manuscript. In Hunt's case there was no choice. There would never be any compensation for the distress within himself. He would live in my mind, in one or two friends', until we died; there was nothing else. There was nothing I could do.

3

We had Hunt down for the week-end, and, though I softened it to meaninglessness, he was too sensitive not to gather my opinion. He made one or two of his illuminating personal remarks. He was, as always, quiet and pleasant.

When he went away, by a transference natural enough, I began to work on Sheriff's career more energetically than ever. I sent him ideas and comments regularly, and in March, just before we went away, he came to London for a symposium and again brought Audrey to stay with us.

Sheriff was effervescing with high spirits. He came back from the meeting, and burst out:

'They were interested. They asked questions. They asked my opinion, they nodded their bald heads. Ha! I'm getting it across to the dull grey men.' It was towards midnight, and we were drinking tea. Sheriff sat down, took his cup and laughed at us.

'Did you tell them what was coming next?' I asked.

'I was fine,' said Sheriff. 'I looked modest, said I didn't want to commit myself prematurely, but thought I could safely say that certain possibilities were obvious. They nodded their heads again, very wisely this time.'

I laughed. 'Was Constantine there?'

'Of course. He got up as soon as I said that and pointed out how important one of the possibilities was. In enormous detail, and no one followed him. He told them how important it was I had got on to this possibility; actually it had never occurred to me. Or you either, I think.'

'Very likely,' I said. 'But it's all to the good.'

'Yes,' said Sheriff. 'I'm enjoying this. Everyone ought to have some job that's worth while. So that they can enjoy the process of work. I'm glad I have.' I saw Audrey's eyes shining; even now, she found the thought of Sheriff working consistently rather funny, when it took the combined forces of both of us and his collaborator to prevent him taking every other month off to 'freshen himself up.'

'Oh,' Sheriff chuckled. 'Old Austin introduced me to his wife. I had another success.'

'Old ladies always like him,' Audrey remarked.

'I scored considerably,' said Sheriff, 'by making sympathetic noises about Russia. She told me she'd just read the only book on the subject that really did seem to her to be *unprejudiced*. Funny how all these old ladies read everything about Russia, by the way. I asked her what it was called. She thought the title could have been improved – it was *Away from the Red Devils*'.

'What did you do?' said Ruth.

'Promised to read it, of course. Said I had never found a book on Russia yet which struck me as absolutely unprejudiced. She agreed she hadn't, till this one. We got on very well indeed. And Austin approved of me considerably.'

Ruth looked a little shocked:

'Is this really necessary?'

'It helps,' I said. 'If you're fighting for a place like Charles. It doesn't matter if you're as good as Constantine. You are above rules then.'

'I almost wish I had known what it is to fight,' said Ruth, 'when it mattered.'

'I can tell you.' Sheriff's eyes were smiling at her, determined to take away her frown, but I thought for a moment his face had an unusual strength. 'I'm not a desperately ambitious man, Ruth. But to get myself comfortable and of some use in the world – why, I'd deny things I really believe, let alone Russia, which I don't care about either way. There are only a few things I wouldn't do –'

'What wouldn't you?' Ruth said.

'Oh, I wouldn't take Arthur's name in vain, say. And other sacred things –' he came back to laughter. Audrey broke in, said she was tired, and they left Sheriff with me to devise the summer's work. We made another pot of tea, and I sketched out on paper a line of work that looked a little laborious, but which was certain to produce two or three good papers within a year.

'It will consolidate you,' I said.

'Yes,' said Sheriff, with an intonation that showed he was not altogether convinced.

'What's the matter?' I asked.

'Look, Arthur,' he was a little hesitant, 'doesn't this idea of Constantine's alter things a bit?' He explained it rapidly. 'I mean, if it came off, it would be better than this scheme of yours, wouldn't it?'

'Very much,' I said.

'I should have got somewhere.'

'Yes,' I said.

'And it would only take six months or less, not a year,' he said.

The gain in labour counted, I thought; but more, he had followed instructions obediently for a year, and now he had a chance to assert himself. Most men would have been forced to it earlier.

'As impartially as I can,' I said, 'I think you ought to take the longer one. That's certain, you see. Constantine's isn't. It's very likely all right. His ideas usually are. But he has so many that one's bound to go wrong some time. And I've got a prejudice against this one. I tried something very like it once, starting slightly differently, coming into the same line. It looked hopeful, and then there were snags, and I gave it up. It might easily have come out with a few more months' work – but I didn't think it worth while going on. So I'm definitely against Constantine's. It might waste six months; and that would be a disaster, with everything going well.'

'Yes,' said Sheriff. 'But it *might* work.' He sat looking dejected; I remember hearing the scrape of his spoon on the bottom of the cup as needlessly, continuously, he went on stirring. Suddenly his face lit up. He smiled quickly.

'All right,' he said. 'I'll go the virtuous way. And train my character.'

4

I talked for a few minutes alone with Audrey before she left.

'Charles ought to arrive sooner than I thought,' I said.

'Is that true?' she said. 'He seems optimistic. But then he almost always was.'

'He's done immensely well,' I said.

'And what about you?'

'I've done well, too. But Charles really has done wonders,' I answered.

'He can do most things, you know. If only he's made to.' She was smiling, her eyes full of disillusioned pride.

'My dear, that's just it. Look, I'm not going to pretend. He's still got to be watched,' I said. 'You've got to do it. I'm too far away. You see, there are two problems. One of mine which is perfectly safe and rather tedious, and one of Constantine's which is short and spectacular and may possibly not work. Charles, of course, wants to do the second. Well, he can't afford to take the risk. So I've made him promise to do mine. But I'm a little uneasy –'

'Of course,' Audrey smiled.

'It seems to me your job.'

'Yes,' she said. 'I'll see he does your problem.'

She looked tired, humorously tolerant – and suddenly, I thought, rather old.

'It won't be too long before you've got him to his niche?' she asked.

'A year or two, with any luck,' I answered.

'I shall be relieved,' she said.

Chapter 5

From the stars

I

Several times in the early summer I wrote to Sheriff, asking him how the work was progressing. His replies were cheerful, but I was worried that he gave me no details. When, in answer to some specific questions, I received a postcard: 'Going splendidly. No time to write,' I became suspicious. I persuaded Ruth to send a letter to Audrey so that I could add a line. In Audrey's reply she said: 'Tell Arthur everything is all right. I talked to Hensman yesterday. Charles's present work was suggested by Arthur, and he has decided Constantine's idea was too speculative.'

Ruth looked interested.

'I thought Sheriff might be spoiling all our plans,' I said. 'But I was being unfair.'

Satisfied, I went back to my own work. I was getting busier and busier; and in June I had a minor success, which was very sweet. I found increasingly that I was enjoying the days, however busy I became. Once or twice I felt a little guilty that I had not been to Southampton to keep Sheriff going, but I had my hands full of work. Altogether I was out of touch with scientific news. I saw Constantine only once; it must have been from him I heard that a subsidiary Chair at Leeds would be vacant in the autumn. I remember thinking idly that if it had been a year or two later Sheriff might have got it.

It was a wet and dismal summer in England, and Ruth and I went abroad in July. My study was transported en bloc to a villa outside Portofino, where I worked on a terrace which hung over the sea. The first morning I felt again that lift of the heart, that sense of exhilarating peace, as I saw the sun gleaming on the water.

Ruth smiled: 'Ah, darling, you should have spent your school holidays at Menton.'

'And you should have lived in my town,' I retorted.

The weeks went by. I was finishing a book; Ruth was busy getting together a conference of modern educators for the autumn. We had neither of us ever felt better. Our only social act was to walk into the village at night, talk bad Italian to the people outside the little inn, and dance under the plane trees.

One morning after the maid had thrown open the shutters of our bedroom, and I was blinking in the brilliant light, Ruth gave me a letter. 'Whose handwriting is it?' she asked.

I stared at some queer unformed characters.

'Constantine's,' I said. 'I wonder why –'

'This is a splendid piece of work of Sheriff's,' he wrote, 'on that idea of mine about his sterols. He has put in for the job at Leeds. Austin and I are supporting him strongly. It's worth £800 and would give him time for research, which he ought to have . . .'

I was puzzled, a little by Constantine's concern for Sheriff's income, much more by the way I had been deceived. Why had Audrey reassured me? I still could not understand. It was a triumph, a real and independent triumph; he would deserve this job and ought to get it; Audreys troubles should be over, and Sheriff comfortable for life. And, more than anything else, I was extremely angry. I told Ruth.

'He's got there, anyway,' she said. 'And quicker. He ought to have told you, of course. I can't think why he didn't,' she smiled. 'Still, he's an engaging creature.'

'It's sheer buffoonery,' I said, more disturbed than I should have been, pricked in my own pride – and also vaguely uneasy. I was curiously upset, too much on edge to work. I went down to the village and sent a cable to Sheriff, saying I had had a letter from Constantine. Irritably I waited for a reply. There was no telegram, a letter would take two days. Two days passed, three, four, five. I spent my time watching for the post. Ruth became infected by my anxiety.

'You're letting this get on your nerves,' she said.

'Of course I am,' I said. 'And it looks as though I'm right.'

At the end of the week, a letter came for me, addressed in Audrey's handwriting. I was too much concerned to explain to Ruth. Audrey wrote:

'I've been trying to persuade Charles to write, but he won't. I only found your telegram by accident. He keeps saying he does not want to write to you until he has been appointed to the Leeds job. He'll have justified himself then, he says. He doesn't know I'm sending this; but I'm too ashamed not to answer you. As you know, I don't make excuses often, but I don't think he's himself now. This work must have been a strain and he's very moody and irritable.

'Isn't it splendid, though? I never thought he'd do anything as good on his own. I'm sorry I misled you over that; but it wasn't my fault. He had told Hensman that this idea was yours, so as to put me off if I enquired, I fancy. Charles doesn't leave these little personal things to chance, I ought to have known. He keeps saying that you'd have been hurt, because he wasn't doing your problem; and that his only justification for doing the other was to make a success of it.

'What a success, though. It's more in your line than his. Constantine came down last week to talk science. He's a darling. One night we all got a little drunk to celebrate, and Constantine held my hand absent-mindedly for a long time, and made a very eloquent speech to say that he didn't often come to a party in order to talk to his hostess. You would have got some sardonic amusement in watching Charles being absurdly jealous on the one hand, and not wanting to annoy Constantine for the sake of his career on the other. The career won. Some day I must meet Constantine again.

'I'm sending you one of Charles's reprints, which have just arrived. You won't let him know that I've written ...'

Quickly I read the reprint. He had sent the news of his

313

discovery as a letter to the *Journal of Chemical Physics* in America; as I was reading, this struck me as strange, for although the American journals are very rapid, an Englishman ordinarily sends exciting work to *Nature*. I read it through twice. It was neat, crisp and logical; the facts marched to one solution; it was an important solution, and Constantine had foreseen it.

I had a flash of pleasure. After all, Sheriff had become a good scientist; I ought to expect oddities in his behaviour: this was first-rate work, and he had more than justified himself.

Then I read it again. It converged, as I had told Sheriff, on an old abandoned research of mine. I began to have stirrings of memory. I went into the room where Ruth had arranged my books. There, in one forlorn corner, were the notebooks of results. In a little while I found the one I wanted. I took it out into the sunshine, mentioned to Ruth that there were one or two side-lines from Sheriff's work that might be interesting, and went by myself to the end of the terrace.

There I compared Sheriff's results and my own. There should have been a stage where they agreed; they were wildly different. It happened to be the stage where I had given up just because the results fell into no sort of order. If Sheriff had found the same results at that stage, as he should, he too could have progressed no further. There was no solution there, not yet, nor perhaps for many years. Sheriff's results, however, were not the same; they had simplified themselves down to just those facts which led to a solution of spectacular clarity.

It was a mistake. I knew my facts were right; my assistant and I had been over them many times, hoping they would sift themselves out. It was a convenient mistake. Without it Sheriff would have wasted months of work. I thought for a moment. I pictured again the way these experiments were done: Sheriff in his room watching the movement of a thread of mercury in a pressure gauge, scrutinising a grey film with black spots against a background of light, seeing an illuminated circle swing across a scale. He must have done all these. It would be impossible to make the same mistake by accident. It was a deliberate mistake. When I said it to myself, I had no doubts at all. It was a deliberate mistake. He had committed the major scientific crime (I could still hear Hulme's voice trickling gently, firmly on).

Sheriff had given some false facts, suppressed some true ones. When I realised it, I was not particularly surprised. I could imagine his quick, ingenious, harassed mind thinking it over. For various reasons, he had chosen this problem; it would not take so much work, it would be more exciting, it might secure his niche straight away (for the Leeds job must have been in his mind quite early). To him, it looked as certain as mine. But I must not know, half because he was a little ashamed, half because I might interfere. So Hensman, who was not collaborating on this work, and Audrey, must, for safety's sake, also be deceived. All this he would do quite cheerfully. The problem began well. He felt he had a success of his own: Leeds was as good as his.

Then he came to that stage where every result seemed to contradict the last, where there was no clear road ahead, where there seemed no road ahead at all. There he must have hesitated. On the one hand he had lost months, there would be no position for years, he would have to come to me and confess; on the other his mind flitted round the chance of a fraud.

There was a risk, but he might secure all the success still. I scarcely think the ethics of scientific deceit troubled him; but the risk must have done. For if he were found out, he was ruined. He might keep on as a minor lecturer, but there would be nothing ahead.

What was the risk? The chance that anyone would do these experiments again for some time was very small. Given a few months he would have gained his position; and he could not be deposed from that even if there were whispers. Also, once in a Chair, how plausibly he could explain it away! He would do that more gracefully than anyone. There was myself, but he did not know how much I had done on the problem; he did not know that I had damning results. And, for fear of what I might know, he had actually taken all precautions against my hearing the news until the Leeds position was secured. After that, I supposed, he would have come up humorously, apologetically, and told me it was one of his little pranks.

There was only one mistake, I thought. He could not have foreseen that Constantine might let me know. That was too remote a chance. But he certainly ought to have told Audrey the whole story. She would have kept it secret and lied to me, angrily, protectively. As it was, probably a little jealous of her opinion of me, he had tried to keep his success in her eyes. He must have resented her disillusioned love: and he chose this time to put the illusion back. Successfully, so far as Audrey went, for she had been utterly deceived, so much deceived that unknowingly she had given me the whole story.

At lunch I told Ruth I was worried by one or two points in the letter. Afterwards I sat out on the terrace, considering what I should do. It was straightforward. Here was a published scientific communication; I knew it contained a mistake in fact; the motives behind it were irrelevant. In my hands I had the material to correct that mistake; unless I did so, and at once, I was an accessory after the fact.

I should have to write a letter to the journal in which it appeared, I thought. It would be a little less conspicuous than in *Nature*. I began to draft it through the hot afternoon. It was a long time since I had composed a scientific article; I found it strangely difficult to handle the clumsy conventional heavy prose. I wrote that some time ago I had worked on a problem similar to that described by Sheriff. Some of the experiments were common to the two problems; my results for those experiments did not agree with Sheriff's. I had not published mine because as yet they were without any interpretation; if one substituted them for Sheriff's in his paper, the solution he gave was obviously untenable. The letter was quite short, and I made it carefully neutral in tone.

I typed it out after tea. When I read it through, I felt suddenly chilled.

Knowing all it meant for Sheriff and Audrey (some-times one of them occurred in my thoughts, sometimes the other), I was doing this. Why? I asked myself. Was there anything more than scientific conscience? Was I hurrying to take my revenge at last for the time when Sheriff broke up my life by taking Audrey from me? Was there some undercurrent of resentment, long hidden, that was forcing itself through this best of all excuses?

I did not know. There was too much of my life entwined in this act: love, and friendship, and my own forsaken ca-reer, that – I knew for certain, now – I had tried to build again in Sheriff's, in case I should be drawn again to science and also as a sort of an amend. From this medley I was feeling anger, sorrow, and, beyond doubt, a harsh gladness as I wrote my letter. How they arose I could not tell; but, I thought, this is the mood in which most self-righteous acts are done. I could soften it by thinking what would I do if I had seen Sheriff's letter and not known the man; that is the way in which self-righteous acts are made more righteous still. In fact, I thought, if it had been by a stranger, I should not have studied the letter carefully enough to find the flaw. But, as it was by a friend, I was able to ruin him and be gratified.

I was quiet at tea-time, and told Ruth that I was still un-decided about some details of Sheriff's work. Soon I left her, and walked down to the shore.

I shall not send the letter, I was thinking. Let him win his gamble. Let him cheat his way to the respectable suc-cess he wants. He will delight in it, and become a figure in the scientific world; and give broadcast talks and views on immortality; all of which he will love. And Audrey will be there, amused but rather proud. Oh, let him have it.

For me, if I do not send the letter, what then? There was only one answer; I was breaking irrevocably from science. This was the end, for me. Ever since I left professionally, I had been keeping a retreat open in my mind; supervising Sheriff had meant to myself that I could go back at any time. If I did not write I should be depriving myself of the loophole. I should have proved, once for all, how little science mattered to me.

There were no ways between. I could have held my hand until he was elected, and then threatened that either he must correct the mistake, or I would; but that was a compromise in action and not in mind. No, he should have his triumph to the full. Audrey should not know, she had seen so many disillusions, I would spare her this. Ruth should not know, though it would be hard when she saw in Sheriff's success what I might have done.

I stayed by the shore for a long time, in my hands the letter I should never send. The sun was setting, and suddenly, in the diffusely glowing sky, I saw the evening star, just as I had that night I walked with my father as a child. It was twenty years and more ago, I thought, that night when my scientific passion first broke hot upon me; and, through curiosity, satisfaction, ecstasy, strenuous work, a career, disaster, recovery, partial severance, I had come to this. The passion was over now. I lit a match and put it to the corner of the letter; the flame was steady in the still air, golden and smoky edged. The passion was over. I had repudiated it, and I should never feel it again.

And so after the years of struggle the personal things had won, I thought. Perhaps they were always bound to win. With one of memory's materialisations, I recalled the time my father and I had finished making our telescope; and how, to allay his disappointment, I had pretended to see wonders which were not there. Perhaps that was my first denial of science, right at the birth of my enthusiasm; and whether I had known much of myself or little now, I should still have saved Sheriff by the same instinctive drive. Ah well! I had acted at last; and now I was alone, having set myself apart from the final collective faith.

With a nostalgia for the past, I gazed at the evening star again. Whatever one has done, whatever one has lived through, has its claim on the heart from which it will never be cast off. The failures and successes, the scheming and comradeship, the hopes and aspirations, I never should forget. Yet I was free of a cloud that for so long had come between me and the future; I was liberated from all the faiths and superstitions, and at last there was only the honesty I should try to keep with myself. There was an exhilaration in the bleakness, a cold exhilaration as though after long waiting one had thrown open the window of a heated room and breathed the cold air outside. I was eager for the life that lay ahead.

I ceased to look at the stars shining over the sea. With a deep content, I walked towards the house, whose lights were streaming through the tranquil twilight.

C. P. Snow

C. P. Snow has firmly established his reputation as a novelist with his ambitious sequence of books, *Strangers and Brothers*. Altogether the sequence forms an impressive study of both the great public issues and the private problems of our age.

STRANGERS AND BROTHERS
(To be retitled GEORGE PASSANT)
The story of George Passant, a Midland solicitor's clerk.
(1925–33)

TIME OF HOPE
Lewis Eliot's early life, in the Midlands and at the bar.
(1914–33)

THE CONSCIENCE OF THE RICH
The story of Charles March, scion of an Anglo-Jewish banking family. (1927–36)

THE LIGHT AND THE DARK
The story of Roy Calvert, a brilliant Cambridge linguist.
(1935–43)

THE MASTERS
The struggle for the mastership of a Cambridge college.
(1937)

THE NEW MEN
The story of Martin Eliot, Lewis's brother, and the exploitation of atomic fission. (1939–46)

HOMECOMINGS
The middle life of Lewis Eliot and his second marriage.
(1938–51)

THE AFFAIR
A miscarriage of justice in a Cambridge college. (1953–4)

CORRIDORS OF POWER
The ninth novel in the series, a study of the settings of English political power, is now available at your booksellers.

THE SLEEP OF REASON
Eliot's return to his home town and his part in a sinister murder. (1963–4)

NOT FOR SALE IN THE U.S.A.